Praise for Emma Curtis

'An excellent read! So original and clever that I was
completely absorbed . . . Gripping, tense and twisty
with an unexpected ending. Phenomenal.'
Claire Douglas

'A compelling, twisty read that kept me turning
the pages late into the night.'
Kerry Fisher

'A dark, gripping page-turner.'
Sarah Vaughan

'It's so good that I had to put everything
on hold just to finish it.'
Nuala Ellwood

'*When I Find You* is a winner . . . I absolutely
raced to the end.'
T. A. Cotterell

'A tense and utterly engrossing story.'
Tammy Cohen

'A dark page-turning debut of friendship,
deceit and lies.'
Woman & Home

'Kept me up the entire night.'
Cari Rosen

Also by Emma Curtis

ONE LITTLE MISTAKE
WHEN I FIND YOU

and published by Black Swan

The Night You Left

Emma Curtis

BLACK SWAN

TRANSWORLD PUBLISHERS
61–63 Uxbridge Road, London W5 5SA
www.penguin.co.uk

Transworld is part of the Penguin Random House group of companies
whose addresses can be found at global.penguinrandomhouse.com

First published in Great Britain in 2019 by Black Swan
an imprint of Transworld Publishers

A CIP catalogue record for this book
is available from the British Library.

ISBN
9781784164010

Typeset in 11/14 pt Sabon by Jouve (UK), Milton Keynes
Printed and bound in Great Britain by Clays Ltd, Elcograf S.p.A.

Penguin Random House is committed to a sustainable future for
our business, our readers and our planet. This book is made from
Forest Stewardship Council® certified paper.

1 3 5 7 9 10 8 6 4 2

This book is dedicated to
Hedi Radford.
A very dear friend.

He would not stay for me, and who can wonder?
He would not stay for me to stand and gaze.
I shook his hand, and tore my heart in sunder,
And went with half my life about my ways.

A. E. Housman, 1859–1936

PART 1

GRACE

Saturday, 14 April 2018 ~ Day Zero

HE DIDN'T TAKE THE DOG.

I check my phone to make sure I haven't turned the sound off by mistake and missed a message, but there are no notifications. Nick said he wouldn't be long, he just needed to clear his head, but he left before nine and it's gone eleven. I knew something was amiss when I came down to find Toffee shut in the kitchen.

I peer up and down the street from my position in the large bay window. Beside me, his front paws on the windowsill, Toffee yawns widely and gives a gruff little yelp. The stillness of suburbia is usually a comfort, but tonight the windows in the houses opposite give me back nothing but blank stares, as if they don't want to get involved. I shiver and turn away, swiping my thumb over the In-Step app to check Nick's stats. His numbers aren't rising. He isn't moving.

I sometimes wonder if I'm the only one who does this; who watches the numbers change, imagining where the members of my small group are, what they're up to,

3

who's with who. It wouldn't occur to Nick, but the others, well, maybe.

I crouch and stroke Toffee's head, then pull him against me until he gets fed up and wriggles out of my arms, his nails catching at my dressing gown. I added Nick to the app recently because he's been moaning about his sedentary job. Since then he's taken over Toffee's early Sunday morning walks, leaving me to linger in the warmth of our bed. I doubt that's going to happen tomorrow; he'll want to sleep in after this. I smile to myself. Unless I kick him out.

My smile vanishes. This isn't funny. I can't sit around fidgeting any longer; I run upstairs and put my clothes back on and let myself out into the night.

The sky is clear and there's a thin crescent moon rising above the Common. The street lights cast a soft orange glow over the pavements and colour the leaf buds on the trees. I follow the route Nick is most likely to have taken, avoiding the Common, both because it's scary after dark, and because without the dog he will have had no reason to go there. When I reach the parade I'm surprised at how many people are out and about; a late worker on his way home from the station; someone coming out of the minimart; a couple walking their dog. When I get to the pub, I pick Toffee up, push open the door and do a quick circuit, then leave once I've established Nick's not there. There's no way I'm asking the landlady if she's seen my boyfriend. That would be embarrassing.

Fiancé, I think, with a jolt. He's my fiancé now. After

4

seven years together, seven years of Nick helping me raise my daughter, today he asked me to marry him and I said yes. That's why this is so weird. With Lottie at a sleepover we should have been spending a romantic evening together; instead I'm all worked up, pounding the streets in search of him, dragging a reluctant dog along with me, trying not to think the unthinkable: that he's with someone else.

A cool breeze lifts my hair and sends a small piece of litter scuttling into the doorway of the estate agent's. A young couple leave the burger restaurant, crossing the road towards the bus stop. Behind me someone pushes open the door and I jump out of my skin. A man comes out, telling a story over his shoulder to the woman following him. She laughs and lights a cigarette.

Sirens wail in the distance and I wait, watching the main road that flanks the Common as the blue lights flash. He's had an accident. I imagine a hit-and-run, Nick's body flying, his head smashing into the kerb. I hold my breath as two police cars speed by, but they don't stop.

Toffee strains at his lead, wanting to get back to his nice warm bed. I walk away from the parade into the residential streets and soon find myself at the end of Camomile Avenue where Anna Foreman lives. The lights in her cottage are out. I linger in the shadows for a few minutes, crouched beside Toffee, my hand on his head to keep him from getting anxious. I watch her door then walk away, angry at myself. My suspicions are laughable; awakened by such a tiny thing. Nick wouldn't. He's the most loyal person I've ever met.

I type out a message. *Where are you? I'm getting worried.* Two minutes later I still haven't had a reply. My phone is hot in my hand.

He might be back when I get home. Oh God, I hope so. And if he's not, then he will be some time during the night. I imagine waking up to find his warm body beside mine, the excuses he'll make. Then normality; downstairs to let Toffee out into the garden, coffee on to brew, and the familiar slow routine of a Sunday morning. That's normal. That's what will happen. All this is just a wrinkle. It'll smooth itself out.

The house is silent, Nick's keys aren't in the dish, and his coat isn't hanging from its hook; their absence as tangible as the objects themselves would have been. I unwind my scarf, remove my coat and hang them up. In the kitchen, I check In-Step again, as Toffee yawns and settles back down in his bed. Nick hasn't moved.

In desperation, I call our local A & E, but they've had no one in who matches Nick's description. An odd mixture of relief and disappointment churns through me.

Should I call the police? If I do, it makes it real. If I don't, I may regret it. But they'll think I'm pathetic. They probably get calls like this all the time: some clingy woman can't sleep because her boyfriend hasn't come in. I lay my phone down in front of me and switch on the television, scrolling through Netflix until I find something to take my mind off the time. It's past two o'clock when I finally can't stand it any more and crack.

The voice on the other end of the line is a woman's; her tone is sympathetic but professional. I answer her questions and feel her lose interest.

'I'll get a message to Control, but he doesn't sound as though he's at risk.'

'But he hasn't come home.'

She sighs. 'Come into the station in the morning if he hasn't returned.'

I'm a cliché, a needy girlfriend. She thinks I'm an idiot, a time-waster; either I've forgotten he's told me he'd be staying out, or he's playing away.

I shut Toffee in the kitchen, then sit on the bottom stair and watch the door until I grow cold, then I give up and go to bed. I drift off, waking at regular intervals, reaching for my phone, checking for messages.

Birds are singing, the morning light is a pale shimmer at the edges of the curtains. I open my eyes, forgetting, then touch the emptiness beside me, the smooth, cold pillow, the cool sheet. He hasn't come home.

GRACE

Thursday, 12 April 2018 ✎ *Two Days Earlier*

'GOD DAMN IT. WE'RE OUT OF MILK.' I CLOSE THE FRIDGE and cast around for my keys. 'I'll nip out to the shops. Can you finish the peeling?'

'Don't worry, I'll go.'

'But you've only just got in.'

Nick scoops up the dog, averting his face as Toffee tries desperately to lick him. 'No problem. I need to get some more steps in. You want to go out too, don't you, boy? Yes you do!'

I laugh. 'Put him down, you'll get hairs all over your suit.'

He leaves, Toffee beating him to the door, wild with excitement, I go back to the potatoes and Lottie makes a start on her homework. Not that she appears to be tackling it with much enthusiasm. A maths book is open page-side down on the table while my ten-year-old daughter's fingers fly across her phone, her head bent, fine brown hair falling forward.

'Who're you talking to?' I ask.

No response.

'Lottie.' I pause. 'I've decided to get a tattoo.' No reply. 'On my forehead?'

'Oh, Mum. Shh.'

'I thought you were doing your homework.'

'I'm having a break.'

'Your life is a series of breaks.'

'Ha ha.'

I cut myself a triangle of Cheddar to nibble. The mince is simmering in the oven, the sun is dropping, and I feel chilled and content. I reach for my phone, as bad as my daughter, and tap the In-Step app. Six thousand seven hundred and thirty-four steps today. Two hundred and ten calories burned. Almost four kilometres walked. Not as much as I'd like to have achieved, but not bad; better than Cassie or Mara. My avatar on the app is a dog; Nick's is a bird.

I watch Nick's numbers rising; two thousand four hundred and fifty-four, fifty-five, fifty-six. I help myself to another wedge of cheese. He stops, and I wrinkle my nose, imagining him waiting while Toffee has a pee, then they're off again.

I forget for a bit, and get on with the supper, then pick my phone up a few minutes later. Anna Foreman, one of the new school mums and a recent addition to the group, is on the move too. I don't know her well, but Cassie added her, to make her feel welcome. Her avatar is a cup of tea.

I keep half an eye on their stats, sipping my wine, occasionally glancing at the garden. We're halfway through April and my flower beds are already full of colour, grape hyacinths mingling with yellow-green euphorbia. The foxgloves are showing hints of new growth in the depths of their thick leaves. I love foxgloves. There's a flurry of activity around Nick's newly refilled bird feeder. Two goldfinches and a couple of tits fly in and out, while beneath them a pair of ring-necked doves peck the grass for fallen seed. Having been brought up in a gardenless flat, I don't have a clue about birds, apart from the obvious. Nick tells me who's who.

I glance at the app. Both Nick and Anna are still walking, although Nick must be nearly at the shops, even if he did loop through the Common. When his numbers stop rising, I imagine him at the till, handing over the milk, tapping his card. Anna isn't moving any more either. A minute passes, and another. The oven beeps and I open it, take out the mince and give it a stir. It's stuffed with this week's leftover veg, everything tinged orange by the sweet potato. Five minutes later, when I check again, their numbers are still in stasis. I find that I'm holding my breath. Then Anna moves and a second or so later Nick moves too.

I put the phone down slowly. Probably a coincidence. I look out of the window, follow the arc of a goldfinch as it flies between the holly tree and the feeder. And I feel odd, weighted down and queasy, with a strange sense of urgency and a low-level hum in my brain.

TAISIE

July 2000

TAISIE BRUSHED HER HAIR WHILE ROSA CHECKED HERSELF
out in the long mirror attached to the inside of her wardrobe door. Taisie had the biggest bedroom, after her mum
and dad's, because she was the oldest, but she still regret-
ted not picking Alex's when she had the chance, because
it was under the roof and not on the same floor as anyone else's. Unfortunately, when they moved here Taisie
was only eight and hadn't known any better and Alex
was four, so their mother chose for him. When she was
thirteen, she'd tried to persuade Alex to swap, even brib-
ing him, but the little bastard wouldn't budge. She loved
him, really. Well, kind of. She wasn't a fan of small boys.

Rosa was her best friend, although sometimes she
wondered why. She was so self-obsessed; always bringing the conversation round to herself. They could be
talking about the weather, and next thing you knew,
they were back to Rosa again. Rosa was off to California next week. Taisie was going to Devon, like they did
every year, to visit family friends. This year was different

because the Ritchies were coming, which meant Nick would be there. Taisie put the brush down and wove her fingers through her hair, draping a few strands across her forehead, to look more mysterious. She rummaged through her earring box for the black onyx pair she'd got for her birthday and put them on.

'What do you think?' Rosa asked, tugging at the hem of the dress.

'You look gorgeous. The colour really suits you.'

It was Taisie's, but she didn't mind lending it, because Rosa didn't look half as good in it as she did.

Rosa came over and squeezed on to the chair beside Taisie and started to do her make-up.

'Got your eye on anyone in particular?' Taisie asked.

'Nah. They're all idiots. What about you?'

She smiled. 'I have my plans.'

Rosa dabbed spots of foundation over her face before blending it in with her fingers. 'They all fancy you.'

'Don't be silly. You're much prettier than me.'

'Aw. Thanks. What about Nick?'

'Nick?' she said innocently.

At the barbecue at her house last weekend, he had kissed her. She hadn't told anyone even though she wanted to, and she was sure Rosa didn't see anything. Taisie wasn't altogether sure how she felt about it yet, because she and Nick had been friends since they were two. And what if no one else thought he was fit? They'd had a lot of the punch, but even so, it felt like he was really into her. Nick was sixteen, the oldest in their year group, with his birthday on the third of September, and that gave him a certain kudos.

'Yes, Nick,' Rosa said. 'Is there anything going on there? You were very cosy at the barbecue.'

'We're just friends.'

Taisie didn't want to tell her yet. For one thing she hadn't seen Nick since; not to speak to anyway. She'd passed him in the corridor at school and had spotted him in the distance in the playground. But he was always surrounded by his friends.

'Don't you fancy him?' Rosa leaned forward with her mascara wand and combed it through her lashes, opening her eyes wide.

Taisie shrugged. Rosa was angling, but she didn't trust her. What was hers was Rosa's. That was how her friend's mind worked.

'So maybe he doesn't see you that way,' Rosa said. She picked a tiny blob of mascara from the end of one eyelash and wiped it on a cotton bud.

'Actually,' Taisie said, because she wasn't letting her get away with that. 'He's been after me for ages, but I keep saying no because he's, like, part of the family. I only have to snap my fingers, though, and he'll come running.' She demonstrated, laughing.

'Alana's into him,' Rosa said.

'Alana?' Taisie felt a twinge of concern, but she managed to sound off-hand. 'She doesn't have a hope in hell.'

Rosa leaned back and gave her an odd look, her eyebrows raised. 'You like him,' she teased.

Taisie shoved her so hard that she fell off the chair. But she was secretly pleased.

* * *

Nick rang the doorbell dead on seven o'clock. Taisie and Rosa ignored it, waiting in her bedroom until Alex got off his bum and sloped out of the sitting room to let him in. Then they sauntered downstairs.

Her mother appeared and told Rosa she looked stunning. Then she remembered Taisie. 'You look lovely too, darling.' She went outside to speak to Nick's dad, who was waiting for them in his car.

Their school was only a bus ride and a short walk away, but Tim insisted on getting them there in style. He drove a sports car, so she wasn't arguing. He used to be in a rock band, like donkey's years ago. They made one album apparently, though Taisie had never listened to it. It was only on vinyl.

Nick was wearing ripped jeans and a T-shirt and looked really good. He wasn't exactly the best dresser normally, which was surprising because his dad always looked so cool. Maybe Tim had given him a few tips. Once she was his girlfriend, the first thing Taisie was going to do was go through his wardrobe. She glanced at Rosa. She was giggling and batting her eyelashes. Perhaps she should have been clearer. Nick was hers.

Alex went back to his TV programme, but Rory and Izzy came running out of the sitting room and stopped dead, looking up at her and Rosa and back at Nick. Izzy's eyes filled with envy. Taisie gave her a shove. Her sister was thirteen and desperate to be going to parties.

'You look wicked,' Rory said.

Nick high-fived him. 'Thanks, dude. You look pretty cool in those pyjamas.'

Rory glanced down, smoothing his hands over the

14

picture of Thomas the Tank Engine. 'I got them for my birthday. I'm eight now.'

'Well, lucky you.'

Izzy was still staring.

'You look like a frog,' Taisie said.

She snapped out of it and stuck out her tongue.

Nick caught Taisie's eye and smiled, his cheeks colouring, and she felt her heart give a little skip. 'Are you ready?'

'You'll be the belle of the ball,' her father called after them. 'Knock 'em dead!'

She stuck out her tongue. 'Embarrassing.'

They linked arms as they left the house. Tim had his window down and his forearm resting on the frame, and he was drumming the door lightly with his fingertips. His smile took in both girls as they teetered down the front path in their high heels. He winked.

'Well, look at you,' he said.

She grinned, unsure whether he was teasing. You could never tell with Tim Ritchie. He took the piss a lot.

Nick scowled at his father and slid into the front. Taisie sat behind him. The car smelled of leather and Tim had Pulp playing on the CD player. There wasn't much legroom, but she and Rosa opened their windows and rested their elbows on the frames, like Tim, and smirked at each other. Taisie glanced at Nick's profile and fantasized about him kissing her again. It was amazing how much had changed. She didn't see him as a kid any more; but as someone with potential. Despite the angry crop of spots at the corners of his jaw, his dad's aura of cool was beginning to rub off on him.

GRACE

Thursday, 12 April 2018

LOTTIE IS LAYING THE TABLE WHEN NICK GETS BACK. I'm standing beside the hob with a glass of wine in my hand, waiting for the potatoes to cook through so that I can mash them. The door thuds, his keys clatter in the lopsided blue-and-red dish that Lottie made in Year 3. He comes in and passes me the shopping bag, stopping to ruffle Lottie's hair.

She pushes his hand away. 'Nick! I'm not three years old.'

Once upon a time I tried to get her to call him Dad or even Daddy Nick, but she wasn't having it. My ex, Douglas, is Dad, for better or for worse.

I prod a potato with a fork, then switch off the heat and drain the water out of the pan. Nick rests his hands on my waist and plants a kiss on the back of my neck.

'Oh God,' Lottie groans. 'Please don't do that in front of me. It's gross.'

'Dangerous too,' I say, as steam billows into my

16

face. 'Do you know how many accidents happen in the kitchen?'

'Nope. Do you?'

'No. But I'm sure there's a scary statistic. So, did you bump into anyone?'

'What do you mean?'

'Just wondering. You were longer than I expected.'

He takes the potato masher out of my hand. 'Here, let me do that. No, I didn't see anyone we knew. I walked further than I meant to. It's gorgeous out there this evening. It feels like summer's come early.'

Lottie pours three glasses of water and lays the table. I notice how careful she is to make it just so, knives with their blades facing in, forks exactly parallel. I don't know if that's because she's naturally like Douglas, or because he's made her like that.

'Friday tomorrow,' I say.

'Thank God. Have we got anything on this weekend?'

'No. Nothing. But Lottie's out on Saturday night. We could do something.'

She and half her class are going to be at a sleepover at Hannah's. It means a bonus evening all to ourselves, but the pay-off will be a tired and grumpy child on Sunday. I don't envy Cassie and Evan Morgan. They did the same last year – gluttons for punishment.

The conversation rumbles on, a backdrop to the choreography of a normal mid-week evening. I barely notice it at first, but after a while I realize I'm doing most of the talking. If Nick does speak, it's mainly to Lottie.

17

Nick takes a beer out of the fridge. I steam the greens. Lottie complains about her history teacher who is 'a nut-job', a sadist and a loser who enjoys tormenting his pupils.

'You should feel sorry for him,' Nick says. 'Imagine what his home life must be like, to have turned him into such a monster. Maybe teaching is the last thing he wants to do, maybe he thought he would be a rock star.'

He could be describing his father. I dart him a look. He sounds overly jocular, like a teacher trying to buck up his class at a rainy sports day.

'Maybe his wife's run away,' Lottie says.

Nick laughs. 'Looking on the bright side. Well, let's hope not, poor chap.'

'You'll never leave Nick, will you, Mum?'

'No, of course not,' I say. 'He's stuck with me, poor man.'

I glance at Nick, meaning to share a smile, but he's not looking at me. A shadow crosses his face.

'Everything OK?' I ask.

'Yeah. Fine. Supper smells good.'

The timer pings again and I take the mince out of the oven. Nick dishes up generous heaps of buttery mashed potato and Lottie carries the plates to the table.

This is my family, my little boat.

Later, I'm reading my novel waiting for Nick to come to bed. When half an hour goes by and he doesn't appear, I pad downstairs and find him sitting at the kitchen table staring blankly at his phone.

'Are you coming up?'

18

I wrap my arms around his shoulders. I can't shake off a sense that there is something he's not telling me. I worry that he's found out about my past, but there's no way he could have done. Not after all this time. He turns and wraps his arms around my hips, presses his head against my abdomen and briefly kisses my stomach, and I breathe a silent sigh of relief. I stroke his hair and he looks up.

'I love you,' I say.

'I know you do.'

'Then come to bed.'

He smiles and closes his laptop, then takes my hand and we go upstairs. I watch him undress with that familiar feeling in the pit of my stomach that is part familiarity, part excitement. After those awful, confusing years with Douglas, I feel so lucky to have met him.

'Fuck!'

'Nick?' I mumble, pushing myself up on my elbow and fumbling in the darkness for the light switch.

Nick is crouched in a corner of the room, with his arms crossed over his face, shrinking back against the wall as though he's being attacked. I dash over to him, but he lashes out when I try to help. I lurch back, landing on my bottom.

'Nick, it's OK. It's not real.'

When was the last time he had one of these episodes? Not for at least three years. They're brought on by stress and change.

He lets his hands drop to his knees and goes still. When I hold him, I feel shudders ripple through his body.

19

'It's OK. Everything's OK.'

'Did I hurt you?'

'No. I'm fine. Come on, back to bed.'

He gently prises my arms away, pushes himself up off the floor and crawls under the duvet, rolls over and falls asleep.

Why now? I spoon into him; feet, calves, knees, thighs, stomach and breasts; the length of his body against mine, my head pressed into the gap between his shoulder blades, my hand cupped round his hip. Then I can sleep.

The next day I get in with Lottie to find Nick already home. He says he needs to concentrate on a presentation and goes up to his study. I follow him, feeling anxious because he hasn't kissed either of us hello. When I open the door he's sitting hunched over his computer, one elbow on his desk, his head supported by his hand. The room is tiny, one of those half-landing ones. It feels as though it's floating over the surrounding gardens. He has it because he's the birdwatcher and nature lover. Mine is at the top of the house and looks down on the street.

'Hey.'

He swivels his chair round, and I walk in. I stroke his hair, but he takes my wrist and pulls my hand down to his chest.

'Do you want to talk about last night?' I ask.

'Last night?' His brow creases.

'Your nightmare.'

'Oh, that. It's just a bit of work stress. Sorry, Grace,

20

but I've got to get this done. It's for Monday and I'd rather get the prep over with now than spoil the rest of the weekend. I'll be all yours tomorrow.'

I keep hold of his wrist, lingering, until he pulls away and turns back to his screen. I wait a moment, before quietly closing the door behind me.

Nick can't bear people worrying about him.

TAISIE

July 2000

SHE STARED FIXEDLY OUT OF THE WINDOW AS THE countryside swept by, trying to tune out her siblings. She had been looking forward to spending time with Nick on holiday, sort of scared but excited, and now she couldn't think of anything worse. She couldn't rid herself of the image of Nick kissing and fumbling in the shadows with, of all people, Rosa. And she wasn't the only one who had seen; so had all her friends.

Her father kept glancing at her in the mirror. He did it every bloody five minutes. Honestly, what had it got to do with him? But at least he knew she existed. Her mother was oblivious. She wouldn't notice if her eldest daughter was dying, let alone at a crisis point in her life.

Why had she boasted to Rosa like that? *Snap my fingers and he'll come running.* God. She felt sick to her stomach. She had never felt anything like this before. She didn't think she would ever get over the humiliation. All she could do was stalk off with her head held high, but she had been followed by Rosa, who ran after her insisting that it wasn't what she thought.

'And anyway,' Rosa had said. 'You told me you weren't into him.'

No doubt she had relayed the whole thing to everyone by now. They would all be laughing behind her back.

'Are you looking forward to seeing Pansy and Freya?' Izzy asked.

Taisie dragged her gaze from the window. 'You've asked me that, like a million times.'

'Sorry.'

'You're not to be a pain and follow us around.'

Izzy scowled. 'I don't see why you have to keep them all to yourself.'

'Because we're fifteen and we need to be able to talk about things that you're too young to hear.'

'But that's not fair. I'm not a child.'

'Yes you are.'

Izzy went puce. 'I am not!'

'Whatever.'

She did actually feel sorry for Izzy. Her sister was past the point where she wanted to play with their little brothers, but she wasn't mature enough to hang out with Taisie and the Moody twins. She could always tag along after Nick. That would serve him right.

The thought of him dragged her all over again into that dark, hot well where her feelings were churning. She would never, ever forgive Nick Ritchie; not for as long as she lived.

She released a long sigh. Her father glanced at her – *again* – and she shot him a filthy look. His eyes smiled but she wasn't interested. Her mother reached between the front seats and took Izzy's outstretched hand.

'All right back there?' she said.

Why was it always Izzy who got the sympathy? When they got in last night, after dropping Rosa and Nick home, her mum had yawned and gone up to bed. It wasn't that Taisie wanted to confide in her, or anything, but she could at least have noticed that she was unhappy. It had taken a huge effort not to cry, but Taisie was sure it showed. Her eyes stung so they must have been red.

The drive home had been totally weird. Nick got into the front even though it was Taisie's car, leaving her to sit in the back with Rosa. Rosa was all sweet and caring, telling her how much she was going to miss Taisie while she was away, and how she was her best friend. And she kept looking at Taisie worriedly, and oh God, it was so false and put on. Nick talked to her mum, banging on about films he rated. He looked at her only once, in the rear-view mirror; a questioning look, wanting to know if they were all right. Well, they weren't.

Rory leaned forward and put his sticky hands around her head, blindfolding her.

'Get off!'

He laughed and let her go.

'What *is* the matter, Taisie?' her dad said. 'For Christ's sake, cheer up. You've had a face like thunder all morning.'

'I bet Taisie kissed a boy,' Alex teased. 'And he ran away.'

'Fuck off, you moron.'

24

'That's enough!' her mother said and slapped her on the leg.

It stung, but Taisie welcomed it. It interrupted her misery, shot it through with energy. She sighed loudly then turned back to the window, put her earphones in and blocked the lot of them. She was not going to let Nick get away with this.

GRACE

Saturday, 14 April 2018 ❧ Day Zero

THE WIND CATCHES AT MY HAIR, FLICKING A STRAND across my face where it sticks to my lips. I pull it away and twist it behind my ear. Nick, Lottie and Toffee are running towards me. Toffee is well ahead, but he keeps turning to check they are behind him.

Nick bends double with a stitch and Lottie imitates him.

'Old man,' she says. 'Sort yourself out.'

'I've been thinking,' I say. 'I might ask Anna Foreman to dinner.' I watch his reaction carefully.

He's about to throw a stick, but he stops, arm mid-arc. 'Anna Foreman?'

'Yes, you know. Kai's mum. Perhaps you haven't met her. She's new and I feel guilty because I haven't made much effort. I owe her for that time she picked Lottie up when I had to work late. I'm thinking of maybe asking Cassie and Evan. And Susanna and Peter? I'll have to dredge up an extra man from somewhere. Unless you think that doesn't matter.'

He walks ahead of me, flings the stick and shades his eyes with his hand, watching the dog sprint gleefully into the bracken. 'To be honest, I'm not in the mood for a dinner party.'

'It wouldn't need to be anything formal. Just a casual kitchen supper. I don't much like dinner parties either.'

He waits for me. 'Let's not. I can't face it.'

'OK. We can do it any time. Perhaps it was a bad idea. She can come to a barbecue in the summer, when there're lots of people round. It'll be easier.'

When I get nervous I tend to placate. I understand that I'm safe with Nick, that this is leftover insecurity from a chaotic childhood but sometimes it's hard to control. It used to irritate Douglas, but he gave me good reason to feel jealous and insecure. Nick has never done that.

'Don't plan me into anything, Grace.'

'Well, of course I won't if you don't want me to. Is there something wrong?'

He doesn't answer for a moment, but he walks faster, striding through the long grass. I keep up, tucking my arm through his. He wraps his hand around mine.

'Sorry. It's office politics. Things aren't great at the moment.'

'I thought you loved it there.'

'I did, but I'm not sure that I like the way the company is heading. It's only money, Grace, stress and money and greed. It's beginning to feel meaningless, a way of pedalling through life. There's got to be more.'

'You can do what you like,' I tell him. 'Don't stay if you hate it.'

He pulls me round and hugs me. 'Even if it means I take a pay cut?'

'I don't care how much you earn. I just want you to be happy.'

Toffee barks, exhorting us to come on; there are sticks to be thrown, birds to be chased, smells to investigate. Lottie runs up and joins our hug and Nick breaks into a smile of pleasure. It's family that makes him happy. It's the three of us.

Toffee scampers up and I pat his flank. 'Yes, you can join in too, you old softy.'

He spins round and drops his chin into my hand, looking up at me with those forlorn eyes; the eyes Lottie and I couldn't resist when we found him at the dogs' home. His character is needy and touching on obsequious, but Lottie and I think that's because he worries that as we took him from the home, we have the power to take him back.

'Nick said we can go to the cafe,' Lottie says.

I glance at him, and he shrugs. 'I said you'd have to ask your mother.'

She smirks. 'Which means he agrees.'

Nick laughs. 'I wouldn't mind.'

He slips his arm around my waist and we turn back along the footpath, Toffee taking the lead while Lottie roots in the undergrowth for sticks to throw for him.

It's a glorious spring afternoon and Wimbledon Common is busy. The shrieks of children bounce across the open spaces; there's birdsong and laughter and the occasional whistle for an errant dog. My mind is miles away when Nick suddenly speaks.

'Will you marry me?'

I'm so surprised I hit him, not hard, just my palm against his chest. He grabs my hand and holds it there. I look up into his face. His smile is so wide, it makes my mouth stretch too.

'Are you sure?'

'Of course I am. I love you and I want to spend the rest of my life with you.'

He is shot through with adrenaline; I can see it in his eyes. I ignore the tiny voice warning me that such a huge swing of the pendulum, from withdrawn to an almost manic excitement, is odd, especially in the light of his behaviour over the last couple of days. I ignore the voice because this is what I desperately want.

He smiles and strokes my hair away from my face. 'Do I get an answer?' He looks so hopeful it brings a lump to my throat.

I lean over and kiss him. 'Yes. Yes I will. Shall we tell Lottie?'

He blinks and looks away, shielding his eyes so that he can see her. 'Can we wait until tomorrow? I want to buy you a ring first. I want that to be how we tell her. Can't you picture her face?'

He turns and smiles winningly, and I melt. I can absolutely picture it. I'll hold out my hand, let the gems twinkle in the sunlight, and she will spot it and squeal, and throw herself at both of us.

I put my arms around his big shoulders and kiss him. He looks down and something in his expression makes my heart ache. He looks haunted.

'Grace, I want—'

But he doesn't have a chance to tell me what he wants, because Lottie shouts from the gate to the cafe where she's tying Toffee up. We yell back that we're coming, and sprint, holding hands. Toffee lifts his paws in the air and scrabbles at my jeans, caught up in our excitement.

I watch Nick, my big, handsome bloke, being mercilessly teased by Lottie and I think how lucky I am. I love his integrity, his everyday courage, his way of looking at the world. He doesn't anticipate problems like I do, he deals with them as they arrive. Faced with turbulence he becomes preternaturally calm; he prioritizes, fixes, solves. He makes me feel safe.

Then a cloud floats across the sun and I shiver. My childhood taught me that the ground can collapse beneath me without warning. It happened to me twice. I gaze at Nick's face, and he smiles back, his eyebrows raised in query. I shrug with a grin and turn away.

Everything is fine. We are getting married. I'm happy.

Even if I don't deserve to be.

It's only the next morning, after everything's fallen apart, that I remember this moment, and the odd intonation in his voice. He wanted to tell me something.

NICK

July 2000

GOD, WHAT A BUNCH OF STUCK-UP COWS. TAISIE, WHO he's always thought of as his closest friend, and the twins, Pansy and Freya, make him feel like a second-class citizen. What is he even doing here? They arrived at about seven on Saturday evening because his dad had stuff to do earlier. They sat in traffic all along the motorway and he had to listen to his parents arguing. Jesus. Two weeks of this. His mum said it would be a fantastic opportunity for him to meet new people, get some country air and stay in a lovely house, but he's not brain-dead. This is about his father getting two weeks of some rich guy's undivided attention. Money, money, money.

The house itself isn't so bad. A sprawling grey stone pile that looks like a film set, cheered up by some sort of climber, leaves fluttering in the breeze. There's a big arched door at the front that no one uses much. You step into a hall that is pitch dark after the sunshine, and that leads to a rabbit warren of rooms. There's a library, Angus's study – out of bounds – drawing room, kitchen, a snug

31

with a narrow set of servants' stairs leading off it and, best of all, a games room with a snooker table, dart-board, table football and a cupboard full of board games, packs of cards and puzzles. Upstairs there are so many bedrooms he doesn't think he's counted them all, and three tired-looking bathrooms with yellowed enamel baths and worn-out carpets. It's all quite grotty, but that's OK. It means you can put your feet up on the sofa and slob around without anyone yelling at you. Outside there's an unheated swimming pool – for a millionaire, Angus is seriously tight-fisted – a tennis court and wood-lands that lead to a river where they can kayak. There's a housekeeper – Mrs Burrows – who he likes. She's nice and doesn't mind them raiding the biscuit tin.

Taisie had said it was fun down there, that her fam-ily had been visiting the Moodys every year since she was a baby. Her mum went to university with Lorna Moody. It's Lorna's house and the furniture has belonged to generations of her family and can't be changed. It's sacred or something. They actually live in Kensing-ton, but also own a chalet in Switzerland and a villa in Anguilla.

Taisie said they could camp in the woods if they wanted. She even said the twins were great; friendly and cool. A bit of dramatic licence there. Cool, yeah, but not in a good way. More like cool as ice. And friendly – if you can call looking him up and down before cracking an excuse for a smile, friendly.

Things he does not want:

He doesn't want to be here. He doesn't want to be forced to bear witness to his father's attempts to hard-sell

32

his latest venture. He wants to be back in London, preferably under Westway, on his skateboard.

He doesn't want to watch his mum struggling. She and Jess Wells have always been close, but Lorna Moody has known Jess from before babies, and they keep going down Memory Lane and talking about people his mum hasn't met and the fun they had at university. Taisie's mum is a different person here. Yesterday afternoon he heard them all talking, then Jess said to Nick's mum, 'Cora, you look tired. Why don't you put your feet up and read a book? We won't mind.'

Not subtle.

He doesn't want to be sneered at and talked down to by Taisie and her precious mates. He doesn't know what's got into her, but she's changed overnight. He doesn't even know if it's something he's done, or if she's got PMT or what. You're not friends with someone since nursery and then go off on one for no reason. He supposes getting off with Rosa after he and Taisie had kissed only the weekend before wasn't a great idea, but Rosa cornered him and stuck her tongue down his throat.

He draws a deep breath and lets it go; no matter what, Taisie is his oldest friend and upsetting her is a big deal. He's used to her – she's the only girl he is used to – and the last thing he wants is to lose her friendship. Yeah, she has flashes of temper and can be unreasonable, but she makes up for it by being his friend and by being fun. At least she used to. Maybe that's it. She's changed and expects him to change with her and is cross because he won't play her games. Should he have kissed her? She's gorgeous but he finds it uncomfortable to think about her in that way. He still feels weird about their drunken kiss at the barbecue. It felt incestuous, although of course it wasn't. Whatever. They know each other too well.

If it *is* about that, then there's not a lot he can do. She'll come round eventually.

GRACE

Monday, 16 April 2018

'IS NICK BACK?' LOTTIE SAYS SLEEPILY AS I OPEN HER curtains.

I am barely awake myself, still groggy from the sleeping pill I took at two in the morning. Sunday was an awful day. A trip to the police station elicited nothing but a confusing set of statistics and a request to wait. Nick has been classed as *absent*. He won't be officially missing until Thursday. Picking Lottie up from Cassie's house, I couldn't face saying anything. Cassie looked utterly exhausted, her house was in chaos and she was practically throwing children and sleeping bags at their parents. Explaining to Lottie why Nick wasn't there was impossible. I thought about telling her that he'd gone to visit his grandmother who hasn't been well for a while, but in the end I couldn't sustain the lie. Lottie asks too many questions.

'No. Not yet.'

She pulls the duvet over her head. I sit down and wait

with my hand on the curve of her shoulder until she peeps out. I feel like getting under the covers with her.

'When's he coming home?'

'I don't know, darling. But soon, I hope.'

'Doesn't he love us any more?'

I pull her into my arms. 'Of course he does. He loves us both very much. I know he'll be missing you a lot.'

She starts to cry, and I stroke her hair. Children don't like uncertainty; they want to know what's going to happen and when, and most of all, they want to know who's in charge. I don't have the answer to the first two questions, but the answer to the last has to be me, I am in charge, and I'm not going to let her down by spiralling into panic myself.

I chuck in a wash, fold away the dry clothes and cram Nick's shirts into the ironing basket. We have a utility room; a source of amazement to me. In the tiny kitchen of the flat I shared with my mother, the washing machine was next to the fridge and the clothes horse was a constant feature, something pushed out of the way, bumped into, tipped over. When I moved into Gran's council house, there was a bigger kitchen with a wooden clothes airer above the sink. The room was always dark because our clothes would block the light from the small window. She took me in after my school finally recognized that there was a reason I smelled unwashed, stole other kids' snacks and was unable to concentrate, and she gave me a home, too, when Mum died. For all her grumpiness and complaints, I miss her. She could be very funny. Gran's jaw would have dropped if she'd seen where I ended up. Banker's wife. That was not supposed to be my destiny.

Lottie's eyes follow me as she eats her toast. I try to look unworried, but she's ten, not five, and she knows what the implications are of Nick popping out and not coming back.

'Will you call the school if he comes home?' she asks, as she stacks her plate into the dishwasher.

'I don't think that's a good idea, Lottie. In fact . . .' I pause. 'Look, darling. I think it would be best if you didn't say anything yet.'

She picks up my phone, glances at it and puts it down. 'We could use code. You could ask them to get a message to me. You could say that my grandfather has pulled through his operation.'

She's excited, imagining it happening, the drama of it.

'Sorry, I don't want people to know about this. Not yet at least. Not until we have more information. I don't want people gossiping, when he might be back any minute.'

She looks at me, then nods her head.

'Go on, up you go. Clean your teeth. Hannah'll be here soon.'

I vacuum round upstairs and give the kitchen floor a sweep, then call Phillipa Travers, the office administrator at Nick's work.

'Phillipa, I am so sorry, I meant to call you, but it's been one of those mornings and it went out of my head. Nick's ill.'

'We've been worried,' Phillipa says. 'He was supposed to be in a meeting this morning.'

'Oh God. He did tell me that. This is my fault, but he was up all night vomiting and he went back to sleep, and then I had to get Lottie ready for school and walk the dog.'

'Poor thing,' Phillipa says. 'Can I talk to him?'

I grimace. 'He's asleep and I'd rather not disturb him. I'm sure he'll be in tomorrow, but I'll pass on the message once he wakes up.'

I don't care that I lied; I'm a good liar and I'll lie for Nick. In his world you don't wobble, because the moment you do, you're perceived as weak. Nick would do anything rather than demonstrate frailty, physical or mental. And after all, this might all go away. Mum vanished for an entire week once, then walked in the door like nothing had happened. Nick will have some excuse. I go still. Do I really believe that? What excuse could possibly cover this apart from some terrible accident? I don't want to think about it. He'll come home.

Methodically I start to gather my things – my keys, sunglasses, notebook and digital recorder, tape measure and pencil – and line them up on the counter. These days I work for a property developer carrying out inventories, sorting out contracts, finding tenants, overseeing refurbishments. Rupert, my boss, gives me free rein but has high standards, as do his clients. The properties I manage are upmarket homes in the smarter boroughs and the tenants tend to be foreign, of high net worth and equally high expectations. If I'm doing an inventory I'm generous about it; these houses rent for thousands of pounds a week, so it doesn't pay to be nit-picking. If the client is bringing their own furniture, I see to its installation. I make sure the fridge is stocked with basics before they arrive and that there are fresh flowers in the reception rooms. Attention to detail and a welcoming atmosphere make a lasting impression.

When I've got everything together, the worry comes surging back in and I collapse heavily on to a chair. I'm tired to my bones and it's making me nauseous. I've been picking at food indiscriminately since Lottie went to school. Biscuits, an apple, cheese. Half a flapjack. A chunk or three of chocolate. Two cups of coffee and one mug of strong tea. My stomach is protesting.

I've got to get on. I tidy myself up. Straighten my top. One step at a time.

Outside, Mrs Jeffers, the woman who has lived in the house next door for forty-five years, stops to chat. It's the last thing I want.

'How are you two lovely people?' she says, cradling her bulky shopping bag to her chest. 'You must come round for supper soon.'

Diane has lived on her own in that vast house since her husband died nine years ago. She has a daughter, two sons and half a dozen grandchildren who visit from time to time, but she's lonely. I sometimes have a coffee with her in the mornings. Nick will stop by and change a light bulb or clear the stretch of guttering overhung by one of our trees. In return, she keeps our spare key in case one of us gets locked out and keeps an eye on the house when we're on holiday. She has two cats who torment Toffee.

'We will,' I say, smiling gaily and feeling utterly desperate. 'Perhaps next week.' I put on my helmet and swing my leg over the motorbike. I zip around on my beloved red Vespa. It saves a lot of hassle.

Home feels echoey and strange when I get back. I call out for Nick and my voice sounds tentative, almost embarrassed. I stand at the bottom of the stairs, listening, my blood rushing. But there is no sign of him. I wander into the kitchen and drop my bag on the side, and see his jumper folded over the back of the sofa, where it's been since Saturday afternoon. I have nothing, not a clue as to why this has happened. I sit down, put my phone in front of me and push my fingers through my hair, leaning into my hands. All I have is an app, a friend, a coincidence. I tap In-Step and it lights up my screen. I tap Group. Anna has done fifteen hundred odd, I've done two thousand – well under my target, but steps are not exactly a priority right now; Nick is at zero. He isn't moving, or he has switched off his phone. I call him, and my call is redirected to voicemail, where I leave another message.

'Nick, please tell me what's going on. I'm freaking out here.'

TAISIE

July 2000

TAISIE SHOVED HER HANDS INTO HER POCKETS AND her shoulders drooped. How was she going to get through this? She had never fallen out with Nick before, and it made her feel lonely. If he had apologized she would have forgiven him, but he was so arrogant. Pansy and Freya were great, but once she was back in London she would be at a loose end. Rosa wouldn't be back from California for another week – not that she would call her anyway, after what she had done – and she wouldn't be able to hang out with Nick either. It was all spoilt between them now. He had spoilt it.

She knew what she was going to do. It took a day to figure it out, but it was the perfect thing. Nick didn't much like being alone – growing up, he was always in their house – so they would pretend he wasn't there. The others took some persuading, but when Taisie told Pansy and Freya what a two-timing bastard he was, they were on her side. The boys could be bribed. Izzy required more work.

'What's he done?' she asked. 'I thought you liked him.'

'I might have done once, but that was before he decided to treat me like shit.'

She frowned. 'Nick's not like that.'

'So you like him better than me?'

'No. But it's not fair. We're supposed to look after each other, not leave someone out. Mum won't let you do it.'

'Oh, but that's the fun of it, Izzy,' Taisie groaned. 'When the adults are around, we behave normally. Like nothing's happened. You can act, can't you?' She heard a note of desperation in her voice and pulled it back. 'It's just that he hurt me a lot, and he needs to know that you don't treat girls like that. You don't ask someone out then get off with their friend.'

'Did he really ask you to go out with him?'

Her scepticism was irritating. 'Are you saying I'm lying?'

It suddenly felt overwhelmingly important that she got all of them onside. He had made her feel small and insignificant, like her mum always did. She was neither of those things; she just wanted to be respected.

Izzy scrutinized her. 'But you told me you didn't even want him in the first place.'

'That's irrelevant. Grow up.'

Izzy mulled it over, her tongue caught between her teeth, her eyes all frowny and worried. Then she took a deep breath, as if she was about to dive into the sea. Taisie loved her little sister, but she was like a nun, or a headmistress, all high principles and over-developed conscience. She nearly died when she was a baby and it made her some kind of saint or something. It was so annoying.

'How long for?' Izzy asked.

Taisie smiled. 'Until I decide to stop.'

'Tell us about Tom Gale,' Taisie said. 'Is he hot in real life?'

They were in the garden lying on rugs and sunloungers after a morning spent messing about on the river. She ached from kayaking and had been sunbathing. Freya and Pansy lay beside her, their whispers making her drowsy. The twins were petite and pretty, not identical but very alike. They had freckles and great figures, thin enough to have a gap between their thighs. Taisie was closest to Pansy, but they came as a pair.

Her brothers were expertly manoeuvring a football around the apple trees, while Nick sat a little way off, reading a book. She wished she knew what he was thinking.

'Tom?' Tim brushed grass off his bony feet. 'He's a great kid.' He smiled. 'Maybe you'll get to meet him one day.'

'Has Nick met him?' Pansy asked.

Hearing his name, Nick turned his head.

'Yeah, Tom's been round to the house,' Nick said laconically, as if it was nothing.

'Wow,' she said. 'You're so lucky.'

Taisie frowned at her, and Pansy caught her eye, mouthed, 'Sorry', then rolled over and dropped her head into her folded arms. Taisie sat up, leaning back to feel the sun on her face. She was wearing a bikini and she felt Nick's eyes on her, but when she looked, his head was in his book. Tim, though – he had seen. Taisie wrapped her arms around her knees and pulled them close.

Tim was a cross between David Beckham and Hugh Grant. He was old, like forty-five or something, but he was totally gorgeous. Even the twins were impressed and envied Taisie's easy relationship with him. She had known him for years, but it was the first time he'd treated her like an adult. The best thing was, Nick was jealous of his dad. It was blatantly obvious. When Tim made any sort of fuss of Taisie or the twins, he went beetroot. Nick made her feel all cringy and angry, but his dad confused her. Often, the only way of getting through that was to be rude to him. Sarcasm helped too.

'Who's Tom Gale?' Lorna asked.

'Mum, you know who he is,' Freya said. 'He was on *Parkinson* last week.'

Lorna shrugged. 'I don't remember. But I'm sure he's wonderful.'

'He is,' Taisie said, deciding to give Tim the benefit of her support. 'He's a real artist, not someone who's going to come and go in a flash. He's got this great single out now. I've got it on my MP3 player. We can listen to it later if you like.'

Tim stretched, and his T-shirt rose, showing his hips above the waistband of his shorts and the arrow of hair below his navel.

'Loving your midriff, Tim,' she said, raising her eyebrows. 'Kind of you to share it with us.'

He laughed. 'Yeah, I know, I'm not sixteen any more. I should keep it under wraps in case I shock the kids.'

His lightly mocking tone sent a dart of adrenaline through her body. Disturbed, she started plucking daisies and dropping them on to Pansy's back, until Pansy

44

flicked her thigh irritably. Taisie turned to Nick. He was looking down, but she could tell he was scowling. Then he lifted his head, raked his fringe out of the way with his fingers and held her gaze with eyes that were hot with anger. She was the one who blinked first.

GRACE

Monday, 16 April 2018

WHEN I WORKED FOR A HOMELESS CHARITY YEARS ago, there were all sorts of reasons why people left their families but what they mostly boiled down to were money, sex, addiction or emotional problems. As far as I know, money and addiction aren't issues for either of us; so that leaves sex and emotional problems. Could I be wrong about Nick? Could he be having an affair? I feel as though I'm tumbling.

He wouldn't; he loves me. I bite down on my lip and think back to the last dinner party, the last drinks, the last casual meeting while walking the dog, trying to picture Nick with the women we know. Most of the people we see are happily married. What about work? I realize I haven't the slightest idea, but Nick was back early from his staff Christmas drinks, so I doubt there's anything going on there. And anyway, I'd know. There would be signs. No way would Nick smile at me the way he does, that big beaming smile that embraces me. No way would he tease me and Lottie, joking that he's at the mercy of our whims. No way would he have proposed. I press my fingers hard against my eyes. This is all wrong. Nick hasn't run away from me; he's out there, hurt and unable to get home.

I take a sheet of paper and a pen and start to put down figures and tot up Nick's day. We had compared our steps after Wimbledon. He had somehow managed to do five hundred more than me, and we couldn't work out how that had happened. Nick had done almost four thousand, me more like three thousand five hundred. After lunch we'd taken Lottie to buy Hannah's birthday present, adding another two and a half thousand or thereabouts. On Saturday night Nick stopped moving at eight thousand five hundred and forty-three steps, so that means he managed between one thousand nine hundred and two thousand two hundred steps. I open my laptop, type our postcode into the search engine and click enter. I pull up the map and mark a radius around our house.

So now I have a fairly good idea of how far he walked before he stopped. I visualize the routes that I know he takes, to shops, to the station, to friends' houses. Toffee whines at my feet, as anxious as me.

I clip on his lead and leave the house, striding north, phone in hand, tapping the screen to check the app every few seconds, dog-legging through wide, tree-lined streets. We are conservation here, red-brick, detached double-fronted Victorian villas, far enough from central London to have been built with a generous gap between them. Nine hundred steps brings me to the edge of the Common where I let Toffee off his lead. He scampers around, racing up to other dogs, but he doesn't stray out of earshot. One thousand three hundred more steps take me to the far side, where I linger by the bus stop, looking across at the minimart, the gift shop, the estate agent's and the Costa. It's full of women chatting over their lattes, prams beside them. I imagine Nick crossing the road at a stroll, with no particular aim. Or was he hurrying; needing to be somewhere, to talk to someone? Was it a woman, or a man? Did he owe something? Loyalty or money? Love or sex?

I cross at the lights and walk to the Queen's Arms, bracing myself. Even though I'm now incredibly scared it still feels a little embarrassing to be in a pub asking if they've seen my man.

I show the barkeeper a picture of Nick on my phone, and to my surprise and relief she nods.

'He came in on Saturday night, but he didn't stay long. He had one drink and left.'

'Did he talk to anybody?'

'Not so's I'd notice.' She starts to wipe down the bar.

'How did he seem?'

'All right, I suppose, maybe a bit dejected. He sat over there.' She indicates a table in the corner. 'No one joined him.'

All I can think of is that word. Dejected. 'Do you remember what he drank?'

'Whisky. A double with ice.'

'Really?' Nick has never been interested in spirits – a tot of brandy in a hot chocolate on a winter evening, but that's all.

From there I check the shops that would still have

48

been open. The manager at the minimart wasn't in on Saturday night, but says that if Nick did come in it'll be on their CCTV. He takes my number and says he'll check when he has a chance. He gives me a pitying look as I leave, like he thinks I'm deluding myself. I can imagine what he's thinking: the boyfriend's done a bunk. It's tough, but people do that shit.

In the off-licence, the owner says good afternoon, hands on the counter, leaning forward. He knows me.

'Didn't see him,' he replies to my enquiry. 'Are you sure he came in? Didn't go to the competition?' He tips his chin in the general direction of his rival, the minimart.

I blush. 'Maybe.'

He smiles and shrugs. 'Use us or lose us.'

I leave quickly and hesitate at the kerb, not knowing whether to keep walking. He could have gone off in any direction. He could have got into someone's car and been driven away – someone he thought was a friend but who meant to harm him. Christ, I think, it must be money. What if he's hiding a huge debt, or found himself in a situation he could see no way out of. Except one.

One thousand five hundred steps take me to the station. He either caught a train, or he walked further.

I walk east, past the school to the streets of smaller workers' cottages beyond it. These are painted in pastel shades, though some of the newer arrivals have gone for a Farrow and Ball palette. In estate-agent speak the area is called the Garden Triangle because all the streets are named after flowers and shrubs: Primrose, Forsythia, Larkspur, Clover, Camomile. Anna Foreman's house is in Camomile Avenue. Maybe she did see him on

Thursday evening. She might have recognized Toffee tied up outside the minimart and gone up to pet him. Everyone likes my dog – he's a great one for offering a paw – then Nick came out and she introduced herself. Maybe she saw something.

Anna's house is pale pink with cracked tessellated tiles leading to an olive-green front door. Down this street the residents are amicably competitive about their tiny front gardens. There's a rose showing signs of bursting into leaf, clambering up the wall. In June it will dance with white blooms tinged with yellow.

She doesn't answer my knock. I try a couple more times and wait. I phone her landline and hear it echoing through the house. Her mobile rings out as well. I'm typing out a text, asking her if she wants to come round for a coffee, when she opens the door. She's wearing painter's overalls and her hair is tied back and partly covered by a scarf.

'Grace,' she says. 'Hi.'

'Are you busy? I thought I might pop in for a cuppa. I'm at a loose end.'

Anna's surprise shows in the way her eyes narrow, and I realize how odd this looks. We're not on dropping-in-unannounced terms, not like I am with Cassie and the others. I first met her at a coffee morning organized by Susanna to introduce her to the neighbourhood. I didn't warm to her then, and, to my shame, I've avoided getting to know her in case I can't shake her off. There's something not quite right, a slyness about her. Her throat and cheeks are flushed pink, but if I've caught her at a bad time, I can't help that.

What if it wasn't the first time they'd met? Jealousy flickers into life. I haven't felt this way since Douglas, as though a seam of it is running through my body, lighting up, a lurid green. What if she and he . . . I grit my teeth. I will kill her if it's true.

She grimaces. 'Sorry. Any other time, but I'm getting behind on orders.'

'Oh, well. That's fine, I just wanted to ask you something.'

I'm the one going red now. Her eyes are on my face, her eyebrows raised.

'What?'

'Did you happen to bump into Nick on Thursday evening?'

'Nick? Is that your bloke?' She frowns. 'I've never met him.' She tucks a loose strand of hair up under the edge of the scarf. 'Why?'

I study her face, trying to gauge if she's telling the truth. She looks back steadily.

'Sorry. I don't know why I thought—'

Her face softens. 'Tell me.'

'He's . . .' A tear squeezes out of my eye. I wipe it away. 'Sorry, I haven't had much sleep. He's gone.'

Her fingers move to her ear, twisting one of the pretty diamond studs. 'Look, my house is a shit-tip, so don't come in, but let's go for a walk.'

'What about your work?' I say, sniffing.

'It can wait.' She picks up her keys from the shelf above the radiator, pulls the scarf from her head, letting her hair fall, then closes the door behind her.

51

NICK

July 2000

'DO YOU WANT A GAME?' NICK ASKS AS ALEX SAUNTERS into the barn.

He carries on batting the table tennis ball against the raised end of the table. Alex wanders past him and picks up a child's cricket bat he finds leaning against the wall.

'Alex,' Nick repeats. 'Do you want to play table tennis?'

Alex doesn't respond, doesn't even look at him; in fact he hums to himself, like he's the only person in the room. Then he turns round and walks out. Nick smashes the ball one more time, then lets it bounce past him and get lost amongst the bikes and sleds, croquet mallets and other garden paraphernalia that the Moodys store in here. He looks at the door, baffled, then goes after Alex. Outside the kids are setting up a game of rounders. He joins them. Taisie doesn't look at him, none of them do. There's an odd taste in the atmosphere. He's beginning to see a pattern here.

'Me and Alex will be captains,' Taisie says. 'I pick Pansy.'

'Freya.'

'Rory.'

'Taisie! I wanted to be on your team,' Izzy protests.

'Well you can't. You're on Alex's team.'

'Anyone want an uneven number?' Nick says, smiling from one to the other. No one catches his eye.

'Right,' Taisie says. 'Heads we bat first.'

He wanders over to Alex, who's standing with Freya, who also looks as though she'd prefer to be on the other team.

'What's going on?' he asks.

'Izzy,' Freya calls. 'Come on. Get over here.'

He can feel how conscious she is of his presence. She's trying to behave normally, but it's like she's suddenly been thrust on to the stage and asked to recite a poem in front of the whole school.

'Is no one talking to me? Is that it?'

He waits, then shrugs and wanders up to the terrace and sits on the steps, shading his eyes, which he keeps trained hard on Taisie, because he knows this is down to her. He picks at the grass, wondering how long they're going to keep it up. The ball comes his way, hitting the ground and rolling to within a few feet of him, and Izzy comes running after it. She's a crap runner, slow with an awkward, rolling gait. When she gets to him, she stoops to pick up the ball.

'Are you not speaking to me either, then?' he says.

She looks right at him. It's an almost physical relief to be looked at and seen. She then turns and runs back. He holds her expression in his head and studies its different facets. Apologetic. Defiant. Embarrassed.

GRACE

Monday, 16 April 2018

THE AFTERNOON IS WARM AND SUNNY, THE MAGNOLIA at the end of the road heavy with pale-cream and pink flowers, some petals already strewn on the pavement. Anna and I walk to the parade and she steers me into the cafe, buys us both a coffee and carries them to a table. I peel off my jacket and hang it over the back of the chair. It feels unnatural, as though the scene has been theatrically staged. Anna pulls her hair behind her shoulders, then rests her elbows on the table and weaves her fingers together.

I study her in a way I haven't before, as though she's a potential rival. That she is attractive is beyond argument, but hers is not an easy face to look at; she's challenging, too sexy, maybe; I don't know. She has long black glossy hair, smoky eyes and full lips. Her cheekbones are pronounced, her jawline elegant. I find her both alluring and off-putting. I think most men would just find her alluring. Or scary. There is something sensual about her, and I suppose that's what makes me uneasy.

She uses her hair as a flirtation tool, flicking it back with her hand or a toss of her head, leaning forward so that it drapes over her face, winding a lock of it around her finger.

'Do you think he's left you?' she asks, looking at me oddly. She's probably wondering why I'm confiding in her and not in Cassie.

'I don't know. He went out on Saturday evening and he hasn't come back. He's not answering his phone.'

'Have you checked the hospitals?'

'Yes, and I've reported it to the police, but they think he'll be back. According to their checklist, he's just left. Look, I wouldn't ask you this—'

I stop dead. I should have thought this through. If I tell her, then she's going to take herself off the app. I want to keep her there, trapped on my screen, where I can keep an eye on her.

'You wouldn't ask me what?'

I'm thinking on my feet, but luckily that is one of my skills. 'When he came back from his trip to the shops on Thursday evening he said he'd met a mum from the school and that they'd had a conversation. From the way he described her, it sounded like you. It's a long shot, but he was a little taciturn afterwards, and I thought it might have had something to do with what's happened now.'

She raises her eyebrows. 'And what did he talk to this mystery woman about?'

'I don't know. I didn't get that far.' I rub my eyes and yawn. 'I was distracted.'

'Well, I haven't got a clue. I'm not even sure I'd recognize your husband. You haven't introduced us.'

'We're not married. You must have met him.'

'Nope.' Her smile is quick to arrive and quicker to depart; a sharp tightening of the muscles at the corners. 'It's tough being an attractive single mother. Other women feel threatened.'

'I'm not . . . I don't . . .'

'Oh, I'm not accusing you in particular. It's just a general thing, a feeling I get when I walk into a room. If I'm invited to a party I have to be careful not to let myself be monopolized by any of the husbands. I can feel their wives twitching, you know, and I can tell when they're about to wander over, slide their arm through his, kiss his cheek, and draw him away.' She puts on a mimsy voice. ' "*Oh darling, you must meet so-and-so.*" It's a whole production.'

It's so believable. How would I feel if Nick spent too long talking to Anna? Not great, frankly. I might find the way she plays with her hair irritating, but I don't think Nick would. One hundred per cent I would go up and put my arm round him.

'I don't want their bloody husbands anyway. God. I can't think of anything worse.'

'What happened to Kai's dad, if you don't mind me asking?'

'Prostate cancer,' she says. 'Three months from diagnosis to death. I barely had a chance to get used to the idea before he was gone. I was widowed at twenty-eight.'

She says it so bluntly that I'm thrown for a second, but then I realize it's a defence mechanism.

'I'm sorry. How old was Kai?'

'Five. Old enough for him to have memories.'

The door to the cafe opens and Cassie comes in. She holds it open while Kit, another of our friends, manoeuvres her baby's bulky pram inside. They spot us and wave. I reach for my jacket.

'I'm going to go,' I say to Anna as they inspect the array of cakes, flapjacks and brownies. 'I need to phone Nick's parents. I should have done it yesterday, but I thought he'd walk through the door. I can't believe he hasn't. Thanks for listening, and sorry I had to ask you that. I know it's ridiculous.'

'You can talk to me any time. Will you text me if he comes back? I'll be worrying.'

I hook my bag over my shoulder. 'Please don't tell anyone about this.'

'Of course I won't.'

'Right. Well, thanks.' I feel as bewildered as I did when I stood on her doorstep an hour ago.

'Hey, don't leave,' Cassie says, turning to me as she pays the cashier for a pot of tea and a flapjack.

'Sorry, I need to get back to work.'

She gives me an odd look, glancing past me to where Anna appears to be texting frantically. 'Evan's been trying to get hold of Nick about a Chelsea match.'

'He's not well.'

'Oh, I'm sorry about that. What's up?'

'Food poisoning, he thinks. Sorry, I have to dash. I'll tell Nick about Evan.'

Nick has been gone for thirty-six hours. I call the police but the officer I spoke to on Sunday is in a meeting and no one else can update me on progress. She calls me back fifteen minutes later and I tell her about the mini-mart CCTV. She says they'll look at it, if necessary.

'Can I suggest you use social media? Get the word out. It can produce results. People will be interested in a successful City man going missing. Maybe speak to the *Metro* or the *Evening Standard*?'

I freeze. 'No,' I say too sharply. 'Please don't involve the press. He wouldn't want a fuss made.'

'But Ms Trelawney, we have limited resources. If you put out a plea to Nick to contact you, or someone else if he doesn't want to do that, just to reassure us all that he's alive and well, it can't do any harm.'

'I'll think about it.' I hope she can't hear the note of panic in my voice. 'And you won't talk to them before I do, will you?'

She hesitates. 'If that's what you want.'

'It is.'

I release my breath as I disconnect the call. An image flashes into my mind, unwelcome and quickly thrust away. A knife. Blood. A gasp of pain and surprise. The last thing I need is the press digging into my past.

TAISIE

July 2000

THREE DAYS IN AND TAISIE FELT SO MUCH BETTER. IT was a little to do with Nick and a lot to do with his father. Unlike the boys her age who tried too hard, Tim was just Tim. He had this magnetism, this aura. She had sort of forgotten how old he was, or she'd matured since she'd been here, and maybe he had even regressed. The twins were dead impressed that he was in the music business, and kept wandering past him in their bikinis, singing snatches of pop songs, hoping he'd discover them. He managed a couple of bands that Taisie had slightly heard of, but he knew EVERYONE. The stuff he came out with: even Lorna's eyes were out on stalks.

The first evening that Taisie spoke to Nick at dinner time, he had been so surprised he almost jumped out of his skin. He hadn't been expecting it at all. She just said, 'Can you pass the salt, Nick?' and he looked stunned, like she had been away for three years. He got the picture quickly enough. He only existed in the company of adults. He was sitting opposite her and next to

Izzy, who was so relieved to be able to talk to him she was chatting like a magpie. It was obvious she had a crush. So sad. Nick was hardly going to be interested in a pale little thing like her.

'A restaurant,' Angus was saying. 'What kind of restaurant?'

Tim lit up, like he'd been given his cue. 'Rock themed. I've got some great people involved, producers and musicians who want to put their name to it. Obviously, Tom Gale is my big endorsement.'

'Restaurants are extremely risky,' Angus said.

The voice of doom. Taisie glanced at Nick automatically, forgetting they weren't communicating. The twilight heightened his resemblance to his father. It made her stare. He caught her eye, then looked away, back at Angus. She felt a stab of unhappiness.

'But there are an awful lot of them doing well,' her dad said. 'It's a risk, but I think Tim's plans are really interesting. It's a zeitgeisty kind of place.'

Angus leaned back in his chair, his shirt collar falling away to reveal a tanned throat and lots of chest hair. In the swimming pool the hair on his shoulders would float on the surface while he swam. Taisie was ashamed of her fascination with this. It had never bothered her as a little child.

'Zeitgeisty, Sean?' he repeated.

'Yes. Catching the wave.'

'And what about when the wave's gone?'

Tim laughed. He had a sexy laugh, sort of throaty and gravelly. 'We catch the next one, my friend.'

Angus flinched, but Tim seemed not to notice, or if he did he didn't care.

'Realistically a new, gimmicky restaurant has a two-year life. Once that's over, it's rebranded, overhauled, renewed. And off we go again.'

'With more costs,' Angus said.

That's when Cora finally chipped in. 'Vision, passion, the willingness to take a risk plus investment, is what makes a man wealthy. Plodding along keeps him comfortable, but dead inside.'

'Hear hear,' Taisie's dad said. 'Well said, Mrs Ritchie.'

Was he flirting with Nick's mum? That was gross. She glanced up and realized that Tim was watching her. He gave her the subtlest smile; a twitch of his lips really – barely even that – but it felt like a secret had passed between them.

GRACE

Monday, 16 April 2018

I DEFER RINGING NICK'S PARENTS FOR AS LONG AS I CAN.
I tidy round with little enthusiasm and minimal energy
and have something to eat. Eventually, I run out of
excuses and begin to feel guilty. No matter what Cora
thinks of my relationship with her son, she is his mother.
I'd prefer to speak to Tim, because he's easier to talk to,
but it's Cora who answers the phone, gushing into the
mouthpiece.

'Grace dear, how are you?'

The question throws me. 'I'm fine. I . . . Have you
spoken to Nick recently?'

'I spoke to him last week. Why?'

I swallow. 'What did you talk about?'

'This and that.' She tuts. 'Is everything all right, Grace?
You sound odd.'

'Sorry. Sorry, it's just . . .' I pause. I can hear her
breathing. I walk out of the kitchen, hoping against all
logic that he'll suddenly appear and I won't have to have
this conversation. 'There's no easy way of saying this,

but Nick went out on Saturday evening and didn't come home. I wondered whether you had heard from him, or even if he had turned up on your doorstep. I mean, obviously he hasn't.'

Her pause is almost as prolonged as mine was. 'When you say went out, do you mean he walked out on you? Have you had a row?'

'No, nothing like that. Everything is fine. He went out for a walk.'

'He goes for evening walks without you?' She makes it sound disreputable.

'Not every evening,' I say. 'But that's not the point, Cora. I don't know where he is and I'm worried.'

'Have you tried phoning him?' She can't quite hide her patronizing tone.

'Yes, over and over. His phone goes straight to voice-mail. Are you sure he didn't say anything unusual?'

'As far as I remember, he was his usual self. Did he have the dog with him?'

Toffee is another of Cora's bugbears. She cannot understand why I've lumbered her son with an ugly little mongrel, when I could have chosen a much more attractive animal with a proper pedigree.

'No. I thought it was a bit odd at the time.'

'Oh dear. This is very distressing. Let me get my thoughts together.' She hands the phone over to Tim, whispering, 'It's about Nick, she doesn't know where he is.'

Nick took me to meet his parents three months after we started seeing each other. He told them about Lottie in advance, wanting them to get used to the idea before they met me. He had also told them that I'd been orphaned at a young age and had spent a year in the care system. I'd argued against it – I came from a world they knew nothing about; one that they would never have expected to brush up against; a world of poverty, benefits and deprivation, but he said it was important to him that I could be myself and assured me that his mother, a lawyer, knew exactly what poverty looked like. I was pathetically anxious to be liked, so I didn't really see the merits of that strategy. If she knew about it, then she wouldn't want me near her son. I didn't say that to Nick though.

Their smiles were in place when they came to the door of their pretty country house. They had left London and settled in rural Leicestershire once Nick had gone to university. Nick was hugged and kissed, and so was I, though Tim's hug was several degrees warmer than Cora's. I was wearing tight jeans and a woolly sweater – nothing controversial – and Nick had bought me an oilskin coat and a pair of hardy walking boots. One of the first things Cora said to me was, 'Isn't that Nick's sweater?' then, turning to Nick, 'Didn't I buy it for you for Christmas, darling? It was rather expensive.' She might as well have said, 'What are *you* doing with it?'

I remember the feeling of the air going out of me, of my eagerness slipping away, of my whole perspective changing. I held tight to my daughter, but any thoughts I'd had on how I'd behave, what I'd chat about, melted to nothing.

I get it; I would worry if Lottie brought home a male equivalent. I was twenty-two, but I felt so much older. I had spent time on the periphery of society, and Cora sensed that even if Tim didn't. There was nothing that they could show off to their friends about, unless it was my grit and determination, so I try not to be angry or to judge. In fact, part of me grudgingly admires Cora. She's made of the same stuff as my grandmother: tough, hard-working and doesn't bear fools easily. But that acceptance has come with hindsight. At the time I was devastated.

When we left, Lottie, normally chatty, didn't speak for the entire journey. Nick and I talked, but there was a constraint between us that hadn't been there before. When we got home he scooped Lottie up, pulled me into his embrace and held us tight.

'We don't have to do that again for a long time,' he said with a heartfelt sigh.

As long as they don't interfere in our lives, I can bear the odd mean-spirited remark without reacting. For better or worse, we're stuck with each other and I will always try to be nice, for Nick's sake.

'Grace?' Tim's voice is deep and resonant, like an actor's. 'What's going on?'

'Oh, Tim.'

It's a relief to talk to him. Unlike his wife, he listens to my story without me feeling like he's holding the phone away from his ear.

'That doesn't sound like Nick,' he says.

'Exactly. It's not like him at all. I honestly don't know what to do next.'

'Have you informed his office?'

'I've told them he's ill. I didn't want to turn it into a catastrophe when he might reappear at any moment.'

'Do you want us to come up?'

'No, that's really kind of you, but not yet. I just wanted you to know so that you'd keep an eye on your phones. He may try and get in touch with you.'

I hear Cora's voice in the background, but not what she's saying. She takes the phone back, and I imagine her nudging Tim away with her hip.

'If there are any developments, I'd appreciate it if you would tell us immediately. This is not all about you, Grace.'

That hurts. It's not the impression I thought I was giving. 'Of course it isn't. Why would you say that?'

'Because thinking about other people has never been your strong point, has it?'

Do not react. She's his mother. She's still trying to get her head round what's happened. I close my eyes, count to three. 'Don't worry, I'll call you if I hear anything at all.'

I unlock and slide open the doors to the garden and step outside. The spring sunshine warms my face. Leaf buds, still tightly wrapped, nobble the branches of the trees; the grass needs its first cut. I turn and look up at the house. It's always seemed so solid, but now I imagine it falling apart, bricks and glass cascading down. He's only been gone a day and a half, and already I'm feeling a chill. It's as though I foolishly assumed that the winter was over, and an overnight frost has attacked the green shoots.

At five, I call Nick's office and tell a few more whoppers. I warn Phillipa not to expect him before Thursday,

66

saying that he's too sick to come to the phone. I lie and lie and lie. When she asks if he's getting his emails, I say no. He hasn't been able to get out of bed. He vomits everything up. He has diarrhoea.

'Surely he should be in hospital,' she says. 'He must be terribly dehydrated.'

'The doctor's coming to do an assessment this evening. They don't want him to come to the surgery, in case it's Norovirus.'

There's a long pause. Phillipa coughs. I wait, my hand gripping the phone, sweating against the plastic.

'All right,' she says slowly. 'I'll call in the morning. Grace, is everything OK?'

'I've spent the past twenty-four hours cleaning up sick, but otherwise everything's fine and dandy, thank you.' Too glib, I think, wincing. 'Sorry, it's been a little stressful here.'

'I can imagine. Well, give him my love and tell him we're coping fine and he's not to worry. Focus on getting better. If we have any problems Lewis will phone him. Hopefully he'll be able to take a call, at least.'

NICK

July 2000

HE KNOWS IT ISN'T REAL BUT, EVEN SO, HE'S TERRIFIED, pinned to the bed by sleep paralysis while snake-headed demons swoop at him from the picture hanging on the wall. It's an oil painting of an elderly woman with a bonnet and the purple weeds of a Victorian widow. In his bedroom at home he doesn't have anything on the walls, no posters or photos. He took them down after the nightmares started.

Nick shuts his eyes tight and imagines his limbs moving, concentrates so hard that it feels as though his mind might burst. His foot twitches first, and with that the demons vanish, and relief floods him. Then he can move his arms, his torso, his legs. He shakes his feet under the sheet, opens and closes his fists, twists his neck from side to side and relaxes back with a sigh.

Sometimes, maybe once every couple of months, his brain wakes up before his body. He's paralysed. It's seriously unpleasant, but it's become so familiar that he can get through it. This additional waking problem is something else, though. The creatures appear real and they come straight for him and, because he's awake but still dreaming, he thinks he's going to die. It's fucking terrifying. No kidding.

He wonders whether Taisie's vindictive, spiteful game is going to go on, or if the others will get bored with it.

He gets up and goes to the loo, peeing for a long time, his hand pressed against the wall. There's no sound yet from downstairs. Back in his room he takes the picture down and hides it in the wardrobe, where it can't bother him again, then twitches open the curtains. It's dawn. With a groan he gets back into bed and pulls the sheet and blanket over him.

Angus clearly does not believe Tim's bullshit stories. He thinks Nick's dad is a jerk and he's already sussed that it's his mum who's keeping a roof over their heads. Angus can see straight through Tim, and the sad thing is, Tim doesn't get it; he thinks he's rolling them all over and tickling their tummies. Can't he see that Angus is successful because he's fucking intelligent and knows a chancer when he sees one?

Apart from the whole 'pretend Nick doesn't exist' scenario, because it hasn't been forgotten, cancelled or deferred, he also has this crap to deal with. It is blindingly obvious that the Moodys are wishing them a million miles away. Why the hell did Taisie's mum and dad suggest they come? Or did his father wheedle an invitation? Despite his and Taisie's families being so close, they've never actually been away on holiday together and it's intense. It's like everyone has turned their emotional dial up a notch. There's a real bromance going on between Taisie's dad Sean and Tim. Jesus, get him out of here. Then there's his mum feeling threatened by Lorna Moody, who is much more attractive. A slender brunette with a pair of oversized sunglasses permanently pushed up into her hair.

The only person in this entire place who is on his side is Izzy. She's the only one with the guts to deviate from Taisie's strict instructions. It's all about loyalty with Taisie. He knows because Izzy told him that she's practically blackmailed every one of them into this.

The days seem endless, the heat turns sultry, pressing in on him so that Nick finds himself longing for an autumnal breeze. He gradually grows accustomed to sitting in a silent vortex while the others enjoy themselves around him. It's a bizarre kind of kaleidoscope with him in the centre feeling both acutely self-conscious and invisible. Sometimes he touches his skin, presses his fingers into the muscles in his thigh or arm, so the pain will remind him that he's there, not trapped in a claustrophobic dream.

He could shrug it off – Angus is great to talk to, really interesting and sound, but he's often in his study working; Nick thinks he's probably avoiding his father – but it's getting him down. When people deliberately shut you out, when they walk past you as though you aren't there, when they talk through you and over you, it starts to make you doubt your own worth. It's so fucking stupid. All because Taisie can't bear the fact that he might not fancy her. Of course he does, but it's not a particularly comfortable feeling. It feels wrong, bordering on incest.

But the worst thing is the way she behaves around his dad. He's known her since she was a toddler. He's seen her naked in the paddling pool, for Christ's sake. The whole thing makes him sick. Tim humours her up to a point, but fortunately he has the sense not to respond, at least most of the time. When she gets all flirty with him, his dad starts mucking around with the younger kids, and has them in stitches.

That morning, watching his father charge round the garden with Alex on his back, chased by Rory and Izzy, Nick had never felt so lonely. He had watched the girls covertly as they lounged on a rug, painting their toenails, about twenty feet from him, and their laughter grated so much he had to go inside. In the cool of the library, he felt as though he was hiding from himself as much as from them.

GRACE

Monday, 16 April 2018

THE SUPPER TABLE IS SET FOR THREE. LOTTIE IS DOING
her homework while I shake risotto rice on to the scales.
Two ounces each; six ounces. A chopped onion sizzles
gently on the hob and the kettle has been set to boil for
the chicken stock. In the oven, three pieces of chicken
breast are roasting. I've chopped a cabbage finely, the
way Nick likes it, and dropped it into the steamer. Lottie
has already grated a generous pile of Parmesan for me. I
have some wine to hand, the remains of last night's bottle, to add to the stock.

My doorbell rings. Until now I've never noticed how
often it does. Whether it's the post, a parcel delivery or
a neighbour, it rings all the time. I turn the heat down,
then Lottie and I run into the hall. I grab her shoulder
and pull her back. The figure standing behind the stained-
glass windows is tall and thin. It's not Nick. My heart
slams. I'm certain that it's a policeman, come to give me
bad news.

'Lottie,' I murmur urgently. 'Go to your bedroom.'

'But Mum,' she protests. 'Why do I have to?'

'Do as I say, darling. Please don't be difficult.'

She gives me a look of reproach and drags herself upstairs. I wait until she's out of sight and then I open the door to a tall silver-haired man, dressed in a beautifully cut City suit.

I'm so surprised, I lose the power of speech. We've met only a handful of times over the last few years, but he's unmistakable. It's Nick's boss. I stand to one side and allow him in. He bends to pet Toffee.

This is a man of substance, a man to whom people rush to say yes. He is relaxed and yet coiled, friendly and yet intimidating. I remember when we were first introduced, at a work drinks, one of the rare events to which other halves are welcomed; he had taken my hand in his, looked me directly in the eye, nodded his approval, and smiled. It was a smile that covered everything from sympathy because I was out of my depth, to an understanding that I was an outsider. The smile said that he would keep my secret, he was on my side. He knew nothing about me, of course, he just instinctively understood people. I'd felt quite wobbly when he finally let me go and went to greet someone else. 'He likes you,' Nick had grinned. 'Yeah, well.' I brushed it off. 'It's you he likes.'

'So how is the invalid?' he asks now.

His presence is so strong that my voice trembles when I speak. 'He's asleep. He had a bad night.'

Without waiting for an invitation he strolls into my kitchen. 'Lovely place you've got here.' He slides open the garden doors and steps outside. I follow him nervously, pulling my long cardigan around me. 'You've done a lot of work on it, Nick tells me. It's certainly paid off.'

'Thank you.'

I look back at the house. It is impressive, without a doubt. The modern kitchen extension could have been an uncomfortable juxtaposition, but the heritage-cream paintwork connects it firmly to the wooden window frames. I lift my gaze to the top floor and see Lottie peering out. He's seen her too, and he gives her a cheery wave. It's strange that he's turned up here. Not normal boss behaviour, even if they do have an excellent relationship.

'So, what's wrong with him?' he asks.

'Some kind of virulent tummy bug,' I respond instinctively. It makes no sense, but I pray that Nick doesn't pick this moment to come home. It would be so embarrassing.

'Can I see him?'

'I don't want to wake him. I'll get him to call you. This is a bit out of your way, isn't it?'

He smiles and his teeth gleam. 'I'm due for dinner round the corner, and as I had some papers I wanted to give Nick, I thought I'd drop in and see how he was doing.' He holds up his briefcase, as if to prove it.

'You can leave them with me if you like,' I say. 'I wouldn't want to make you late.'

'I've got a bit of time. I don't suppose I could have a drink? It's been a long day and I need to fortify myself before supper.'

I doubt that's true, but I fetch a beer, pop the lid and hand him the cold bottle.

He stands with his feet apart, towering over me. 'Nick was in an odd mood on Friday,' he says. 'So, I was concerned that the no-show today might have had something to do with it.' His head tilts, as if he's trying to gauge my response.

'Not at all,' I say, blushing. 'He's genuinely ill. Vomiting, diarrhoea and a horrible headache.' I'm hoping that a graphic description will get him out of the house. 'What do you mean, an odd mood?'

'Subdued. Did he say anything to you?'

I shake my head. 'No. Well, he may have said he'd had a stressful day.'

'Does he share his worries with you? Would he tell you if something was wrong? I try not to bore my wife with the day-to-day aggravations, but if something is genuinely bothering me, she's very good at winkling it out. And helpful. Do you help Nick?'

His dark eyes, under the silver brows, probe for the truth. Does he sense that I'm lying?

'Not really. Look, I'm sorry to rush you, but I'm in the middle of getting supper ready.'

I glance inside, my body language clear. A polite request for him to leave. I wish I could tell him the truth, because he might be able to help, but if Nick has had some sort of emotional breakdown he wouldn't want him to know.

And if he doesn't come back?

But I won't think about that.

After he's gone, I make the risotto and steam the vegetables, but the chicken is spoilt, overdone and stringy.

Lottie and I chew disconsolately, leaving most of the chicken on our plates. Nick's plate is covered with a Pyrex bowl to stop the food drying out. I'll have it for lunch tomorrow. We don't talk much, and I hate and resent the silence that has fallen between us. Lottie has always been chatty and open, but right now her body language is that of a teenager, withdrawn, folded in on herself. I badly need a hug, but I daren't ask.

'Lottie, I've told Nick's work that he's ill. OK?'

She pushes her plate away and looks at me. 'Is he?'

'No.'

'Then why did you—'

'I thought it was best.'

'Can I tell Hannah?'

'No, not yet, sweetie. I don't want everyone knowing our business.' Now I sound like my grandmother.

I have a horrible thought. I jump up and go to the fridge to look at my calendar. Tomorrow is Tuesday. There's a coffee morning and it's happening at my house. I'd totally forgotten about it. My mind spirals into panic. It's too late to cancel, and what would I say anyway?

I should have made brownies. They'll have to make do with shop bought. I've got bigger things to worry about.

TAISIE

July 2000

IT WAS THE END OF THE FOURTH DAY; AN AFTERNOON spent lounging around with the Moody twins talking about boys, gossiping and sunbathing, exhausted by an enforced cycle ride that morning. The adults banged on about how beautiful it was, but scenery was so not her thing. She'd seen it before. She knew Izzy was breaking the Nick rules whenever she could, but it was too hot to get worked up about it.

Secretly, what Taisie liked about those balmy evenings was the temporary cessation of hostilities between her and Nick, with him restored to visibility by the presence of their parents. It was bittersweet. Sometimes, when he looked unhappy, he reminded her of when they were younger. She wished she hadn't started this stupid game, because it was making her miserable, but she couldn't stop it, not without losing face. She wanted her friend back. Unfortunately she had probably pissed him off so thoroughly that he would never trust her again.

Besides, what she had felt for Nick paled in comparison

to how his father made her feel. She eyed Tim across the scented candles that had been placed around the table to discourage wasps. He was carving into his steak, cooked on the barbecue to perfection by Angus, his eyes bright as he laughed at something Lorna said. Taisie stared at him, wondering whether he could feel the electricity like she could, whether his senses were alert to her, and when he suddenly caught her eye she felt it like a lightning bolt. The fact that it was wrong made it all the more exquisite. This was the urgent, yearning side of love. Forbidden and taboo. It was OK to dream.

Taisie, Nick and the twins were allowed one small glass of wine each, because they were on holiday – no one realized the twins were used to alcohol. They'd told her that it was smuggled into their boarding school all the time, in soft-drink bottles, protected by ski socks wrapped in articles of school uniform. But as the adults drank more, they became less bothered, and didn't notice that the kids were helping themselves.

Nick was pissed, Taisie could see that. She could also see that he was building up to something. To have a go at her, probably. He was sitting at the end of the table, with Izzy on his right and Pansy on his left. Taisie was sitting between Alex and Pansy with Freya opposite her, and Rory was at the other end with their mum because he was falling asleep.

Nick hadn't spoken to Taisie all evening, concentrating his efforts on Pansy and Izzy and enjoying himself. Taisie pretended she didn't care, but Pansy was flirting with him, batting her eyelashes and giggling like an idiot. Taisie narrowed her eyes. Izzy had a fit of giggles, spitting out her water, and Pansy rocked back in her chair and stretched her arms up behind her head. It was pretty overt, but Nick seemed not to notice. When Izzy got up to go to the loo, Taisie slipped into her place. Nick turned from Pansy and raised his eyebrows.

'What do you want?'

'Nothing.' She chewed at her bottom lip. 'Just wondering.'

'I didn't realize you had the capacity for thought.'

Pansy burst out laughing then shut up quickly at a killer look from Taisie.

'You can talk.'

'But apparently I can't be heard,' he retorted. Then he turned his back on her and put his bare feet up on the strut of Pansy's chair.

Taisie's eyes pricked with tears. She hated him.

The children tidied up after supper, the boys on washing-up duty while the girls cleared the table. Taisie made her way round to where Tim was sitting and let her hip lightly brush his arm as she leaned to take his plate. When she came back out, she plonked herself down on the vacated chair beside him and picked up a half-full glass of wine. Her mother stared at her until she caught her eye.

'I think you can do without that, don't you, darling?' she said.

Taisie held the stem of the glass tightly and raised it to her lips. The wine had warmed and tasted horrible, but she drank it anyway.

'For goodness' sake, Taisie, don't be so immature.'

'Come on, Jess,' Tim said. 'Cut her some slack. We're on holiday, and she's practically an adult.'

Her mother softened, as she always did around Nick's dad, behaving like a cat being stroked. Taisie pushed the glass away. It was late, and she felt drowsy. She stared at the moths flitting round the candles, then dropped her head on Tim's shoulder. Through half-closed eyes, she saw both Nick and her mum watching. Good.

'Sleepy, kiddo?' Tim asked.

'Mmm.'

'Taisie,' her mother said. 'You haven't finished clearing the table yet.'

There was an edge to her voice that made Taisie's hackles rise, but she got up anyway and picked up the salad bowl, leaning across Tim to get at it. She swung her hips as she walked away, thinking of his eyes on her denim-covered bottom and tanned legs, but when she glanced over her shoulder he was leaning back so that he could talk to Sean behind Lorna Moody. It was her mother who was watching her.

GRACE

Tuesday, 17 April 2018

THERE ARE FIVE OF US SITTING AT MY KITCHEN TABLE,
a plate of Tesco's brownies between us; five young mothers, well dressed, well groomed, attractive and vivacious.
We know each other well, and gossip comfortably about
school, family, extensions, Polish builders, planning
applications and paint colours. At least they do; I listen.
I'm cold, even though the sun is shining through the wall
of windows and the others have shed their jackets and
jumpers.

There's Cassie, my closest friend, a stay-at-home mum
to Hannah. Cassie has fine brown hair which she keeps
twisted up with a butterfly clip. She's kind and can be
over-serious. She is not the life and soul of the party, but
that suits me fine. With her are Susanna, bossy and
manipulative, and Mara and Kit, both bright, cheery
women with smart cars, photogenic children, diamonds
on their fingers and Instagrammably beautiful lives. I
often wonder how I found myself here. It wasn't meant
to be like this. Not that I'm complaining; I'm safe and so

is Lottie. At least we were until Saturday night. Now I'm scared again, anxious about what might happen. I feel like those people who are urged to evacuate their homes because the wildfires might reach them. No certainty of outcome whichever decision they take.

We were expecting Anna, but she called and cancelled, and I was glad. It's hard enough trying to hide what's going on around here, without putting pressure on her as well. This is not her problem.

'I noticed Nick's done zero steps since Saturday,' Kit says after I've told them all that he's ill. 'Poor thing.'

I even took up a cup of coffee, to be extra convincing. It's growing cold beside our empty bed.

Mara laughs. 'Yeah, I saw that too. I was going to tell him to get off his backside. I'm glad I didn't.'

'He wouldn't have minded,' I say.

I should tell them the truth, the secrecy is ridiculous, but when I look round at their smiling faces the words won't come. The mantra I grew up with, from both my mother and my gran, was: don't tell other people our business. The reaction would be violent if I did.

'Are you sure you can't sacrifice a couple of hours a week, Grace?' Susanna asks. She is after parent-readers.

As the class rep, it's Susanna's job to throw out a net for volunteers. I would like to help very much, but it's impossible.

'I'm really sorry. I can't tie myself down to being somewhere at the same time every week. I wouldn't be reliable enough.'

Cassie gives me a searching look. Because I work

82

from home when I'm not visiting a site, friends and neighbours, and even the school, assume I'm available. But that's not the real problem. The real problem is a little more complex.

I can feel my colour rise. 'Sorry,' I mumble, biting into a brownie. The intense sweetness of the chocolate bursts in my mouth, making me feel better, less absent. 'So, we were going to talk about the school fete. Can I put my hand up for the book stall? I'm happy to do a couple of stints on the bouncy castle as well.'

The bouncy castle is the short-straw job, the attraction where most of the tantrums occur and the bulk of the injuries are sustained. I know she'll be grateful enough to forget the other thing.

Susanna opens an Excel spreadsheet on her laptop and starts tapping in requests. After that bit of admin we go back to more comfortable topics of conversation.

'It's a pity Anna couldn't make it,' Mara says. 'It would have been an opportunity for her to get to know us better.'

'Did she say why she pulled out?' Cassie asks. 'Only she seemed so excited about it last week. I had the impression she wanted to get involved.'

'Perhaps she had to work,' I say.

'Perhaps she figured out she would be given jobs to do,' Susanna says.

'What do you think of her?' Kit asks.

There's a silence and I imagine them trying to think of polite ways to disguise a bitchy comment. Kit has her three-month-old baby with her, draped fast asleep on his tummy over her knees, his face pointing towards me. I ache to stroke his silky hair. I want another one. It's time.

'She seems very pleasant,' Mara prevaricates. 'She just needs to bed in a little. Kai's an absolute delight though, isn't he? So interested and chatty. Leila adores him.'

Kit pours herself a fresh mug of coffee and adds a splash of milk. She stirs it and her spoon clinks against the china.

'Anna's a man's woman,' she says. 'I mean, she's friendly enough, but when she's talking to you it's as if she's got her radar out in case a likely prospect hovers into view.'

'Oh, I don't think that's fair,' Cassie says. But she smiles. 'She is a bit of a flirt. Remember that drinks party at the Filbys'? You and Nick weren't there, Grace. Anna was wearing this killer dress and kept swishing her fingers through her hair. I think it's insecurity though, don't you? She's trying to make an impression. We've all known each other for donkey's years but she's starting from scratch. It's nerves.'

Mara brushes a crumb of brownie off her left breast. 'She'd better not start feeling nervous around John.'

Kit snorts with laughter, spraying coffee.

'Look, she's not here to defend herself,' I protest. But I'm laughing too. John is short and plump. He's a lovely guy, but not someone a woman like Anna would have any interest in.

'She's more likely to feel nervous round Nick, don't you think?' Susanna says, giving me a mischievous look. 'He's so handsome.'

'And such a lovely guy,' Mara says. 'You're very lucky, Grace. I hope you know that.'

'Shall I make some more coffee?' I squeak.

I go into the kitchen to make a fresh cafetière and while I wait one of Mrs Jeffers' cats, the tabby, stalks across the garden. I bang on the glass. It treats me to a haughty glance before continuing on its way. It reminds me of Nick's boss.

Cassie follows me. I don't look at her, but I can feel her eyes on my profile. I pour water into the kettle, put it on the stand, then lean against the counter and drop my head.

'Grace . . .'

'I need to tell you something,' I say.

She sighs and puts her hand on my shoulder. 'It's OK. I already know about Nick walking out. Lottie told Hannah.'

I turn and stare at her, aghast, the slow heat of mortification spreading from my neck to my cheeks. 'You knew? You let me carry on with that ridiculous performance . . . How could you do that?'

Her face contorts in a grimace of apology. 'Hannah only told me this morning. I didn't want to embarrass you in front of the others.'

I put my head in my hands. 'So who's Hannah told?'

If they all sat there, inwardly smirking, while I babbled on about my invalid boyfriend, I don't think I'll be able to face any of them again.

'Don't worry, no one else yet – Lottie swore her to secrecy. But it's only a matter of time. The sooner you talk to Mrs Shaw the better. I'm sure she'll see you today if you call her.'

I rock back my head with a groan. 'I'll go in early this

afternoon. Don't worry about picking up Lottie today. I'll be there.'

'There's something else.'

'What?'

'It might be nothing.'

'Cassie,' I say sharply, and she flinches.

'OK, but don't bite my head off. I wasn't sure I should say anything. But Evan saw Nick last Thursday evening, talking to a woman.'

I shrug. 'Nick's always bumping into acquaintances.'

'Yes, I know, but Evan described it as an intense conversation. He only saw her from the back and from a distance, so he has no idea who it was. Apparently, she touched him, and he jerked away like he'd been burnt.'

The shock hits me like a wall, but I hold it together, trying not to avoid my friend's gaze.

'How odd. Actually, he did say he bumped into someone. A woman he knew from uni.' I blurt out the lie, smiling brightly, but hot with annoyance and shame. 'Maybe it was an old flame, you know, for him to have reacted like that. Did Evan say anything else about her? The colour of her hair? Her height? Her body language? What was intense about it?'

'I didn't mean to imply anything. Really, Grace. I'm sure Nick isn't, well, you know.'

'I don't know, actually,' I say.

'Well . . .' She pauses, biting down on her bottom lip. 'Uh . . . that type, I suppose.'

I wait, my eyebrows lifted.

'I did ask Evan questions,' she says. 'Obviously I did.

But you know what men are like. They don't clock things the way we do. So annoying!'

As the women leave, chatting in the front garden while Kit settles the baby into the pram, Douglas, my ex, walks up to the door and greets them all by name. He knows them as the parents of Lottie's friends, and they think he's marvellous – even Cassie, who understands a little more about our relationship than the others do, can't help getting a little giddy round him.

'What are you doing here?' I ask, once everyone's gone.

'Can I come in first?'

I shrug and move to one side.

'I had a text from Lottie.'

'I told her not to tell anyone at school. I should have . . .' I stop, realizing too late where this is going.

'You should have told her not to tell me?' His expression hardens. 'Do you often ask her not to tell me things?'

'No,' I flounder. Because of course I do.

I walk ahead of him into the kitchen so that he can't see my face. Tears irritate my ex.

'Grace?' His voice is sharp.

'Give me a moment.' I splash my face with water and wipe it on a clean tea towel, then turn to face him, back in control. 'I didn't want to make it into something it isn't, in case he comes back. What did Lottie say?'

He pulls his phone out of his back pocket, manoeuvres it with one hand and shows me the text.

Hi Dad. Something weird happened. Nick's gone missing and Mum's really upset. I don't know what to do. Lottie xx

'Who else have you told?' he asks.

'No one except Nick's parents and the police.' It's a small fib, but he'll only be offended if he discovers I confided in Cassie and Anna rather than him. 'You know what people are like round here. They'll think he's left me.'

'And he hasn't?'

I glare at him. 'No, course he hasn't. Not on purpose at least.'

'What did the police say?'

'That it's too early to send out a search party. They thought I was being hysterical. If he hasn't reappeared by Thursday, that's when they said they'd take it more seriously.'

'Big of them,' Douglas says, crossing his arms and leaning a shoulder against the wall. Douglas always wears black: black jeans, black jacket, black shirt. It suits him because he's so skinny, but it also makes him look like a drug dealer. 'What can I do to help?'

'You could take Lottie somewhere fun this weekend; distract her.'

'Sure. No problem. What about money?'

'What about it?'

'Well, have you got enough?'

I fizz with irritation. 'I do earn a living, Douglas. I'm fine for the time being, and Nick will be back before it gets to the stage where we're in trouble.'

'So, when did he go? Did you argue? There must be a reason why he's disappeared.'

'Of course there's a reason. Don't treat me like an idiot.'

'Calm down.'

'I've got to go to work, Douglas.'

He comes closer, reaching past me to take a glass from the cupboard. He fills it with water and drinks it in one go, before rinsing it and placing it upside down on the drainer.

'Are you picking Lottie up from school on Friday?' I ask, pointedly moving towards the door. Sometimes he has to come here instead, if he's running late.

'Can we take a rain check on that?'

'Fine.' He touches my shoulder briefly, before strolling out into the warm April morning. The door shuts behind him, but not firmly enough to engage the lock. I give it an aggressive shove.

Sometimes I hate Douglas. I see him regularly because he has Lottie every other weekend and for part of the holidays. She idolizes him, and that's a worry. When I was with him, it was made abundantly clear I could be a better version of myself, and that that was something I should desire and work towards. Every day I failed a little bit more. I don't want that for Lottie. Nick's influence is healthier. It wouldn't occur to him that I could be anything other than the woman he wakes up to every morning, with her mussed-up hair and smudged eyeliner; the woman who wears his Chelsea T-shirt to sleep in and refuses to buy her own socks because men's are better; or that Lottie could be anything but Lottie: imperfect but beautiful, funny and wise.

My job is to mitigate my ex's influence on our daughter; to ensure that she knows it's OK to fail, important even, and that she doesn't have to be anything other than herself to be loved.

I put on my leather jacket and zip it up, frowning. For all my detachment, my constant analysis of his character, my efforts to stay one step ahead, he can still get under my skin. It's hardly unexpected, given our history, but that doesn't make it any easier.

When I was sixteen, after a year in care, I found myself slipping through the cracks. Gran was dead, Mum was dead. I had made a handful of friends in the children's home but when I left I wanted to draw a line under that phase of my life. I didn't have a job, I hadn't had much of an education, but I knew that I had a brain, I just didn't know where or how to use it. I ended up homeless, sleeping in shelters if I was lucky, on the streets if I wasn't. Then I met Douglas.

He was training to be a lawyer and, in the little spare time he had, he volunteered at one of the shelters I frequented, dispensing free advice. He must have seen potential, because he went out of his way to help me and later, once I was more or less on my feet, we became involved. He seemed so sophisticated even though he was only twenty-five at the time. I understood that he liked the idea of moulding me, but at that point, he was all I had, and I clung to him. It fell apart the first time because he was unfaithful.

But that's only half the truth. My reaction crossed a line. I don't know why he took me back, unless he took pleasure in knowing I was cowed. I had put him in hospital, after all.

I drop my face into my hands, unable to relive those events without catching a wave of humiliation and pain. I was a shell, someone who absorbed everything thrown

90

at her, who lived for and through another person. I belonged to Douglas.

It was only when I got pregnant that things began to change.

Douglas took the news badly. I didn't expect that at all, and I panicked. I considered an abortion, couldn't go through with it and almost gave Lottie up for adoption, but something stopped me, some inner strength that I hadn't been aware I possessed. Douglas had encouraged me to be better. Well, I would be better. A better mother than I had been blessed with.

I left him, moving into a rented one-bedder in Catford. It was above a Balti restaurant and the cheapest thing I could find. Below my bedroom window the air-conditioning unit rumbled and the smell of curry drifted in. There were rats too, in the space behind the building where the bins were kept; I'd hear their squeaks and scurrying when I woke in the night. I remember sitting in that place, in the summer heat, breathing in stale spices, Lottie fast asleep in my lap, her eyelashes fluttering, her cheeks pink – my perfect child in this shitty place – and when I found a rat under her cot, I knew I had to get us out before she became aware of her surroundings, even if it meant crawling back to Douglas.

This third attempt at a relationship faltered because although I was grateful, I was no longer submissive; Lottie had put fire in my belly. Douglas didn't like that and said he was bored. That stung, but it made things easier. Despite his initial reluctance to be a father, he worshipped Lottie so, as long as I shared her with him, he appeared to be content to let me go. I met Nick nine months later.

But it wasn't as simple or unstrained as it first seemed. Nothing ever is with Douglas. He knows the worst of me and thinks it gives him permission to retain that paternal familiarity that infuriates Nick, who is no fool. It's as though Douglas allows me to be with Nick while he retains ultimate ownership. As he demonstrated today, it's in his body language and it's in the subtle nuances of what he says or doesn't say.

And yet, when he left me just now, it was like a cold breeze blowing through my house.

NICK

July 2000

HE'S LYING ON A RUG, LISTENING TO THE CLIPPED TOCK-
tock of ping-pong balls coming from the barn. The sun
is beating down on his bare back, hopefully doing his
spots some good. The book Angus has loaned him,
The Prince by Machiavelli, isn't quite the distraction he
needs, but he's determined to read it anyway because he
doesn't want Angus to think he's a lightweight. He lives
for the evenings, when they're all gathered around the
big table on the terrace and Taisie has no power. He's
surprised at how long she's been able to keep it up, not
to mention maintain her sway over the others. And he's
beginning to wonder about himself. Is he who he thinks
he is, an ordinary boy, or is he the way she seems to see
him? Like the kids that get bullied at school because
they've made the mistake of showing weakness. He's
never felt that doubt before, the kind that eats away at
your confidence. It feels like a sickness, not a mental
state. It's not that he's upset, though of course he is; it's

something that goes deeper, that feels like it's growing into him, like scar tissue.

A shadow falls over his chest and face, and he turns his head, squinting into the sun. It's Taisie.

'What do you want?' he asks.

He raises his eyes to the frayed denim shorts and the halter neck top. Her hair is tied up messily.

She doesn't answer, just wanders off. He watches her feet in the grass, crushing daisies, her bare tanned legs, the tie-string that hangs between her shoulder blades bouncing. Does she want him to follow her, or what? How is he supposed to interpret the message? She's The Prince and the rest of them are her Dominion. Probably best she doesn't read the book. It might give her ideas.

He refuses to react to her crap and turns the page, and then dozes for a while, waking up to feel something tickling the backs of his knees. He lifts his shoulders off the ground and twists. Izzy is sitting next to him. His legs are strewn with daisies. He sneezes and half of them jump off.

'You were fast asleep,' Izzy says.

'Where are the others?'

She shrugs. 'Somewhere. Taisie's being weird,' she says after a pause.

'Are you supposed to be speaking to me?'

She leans back on her hands and raises her face to the sun. Izzy is nothing like her big sister. Where Taisie is obvious, with her generous lips, ski-jump nose, large eyes and thick, shiny hair, Izzy is small and inward-looking. It's hard to describe, but where Taisie's presence fills a room, Izzy's barely touches it. He's known her since she was a baby, though, so he knows that there's a mischievous side.

He jumps up and pulls her up with him. She executes a perfect cartwheel.

'Piggyback, Shrimpy?' he says.

'Don't call me that.'

'Why not, you are a shrimp.'

He lowers himself and she wraps her arms around his shoulders, her skinny legs around his waist and they take off up the garden, Izzy shrieking and Nick laughing. It's the first time he's laughed since he got here, if you don't count the fake laughter. When they come round the house, Taisie is standing in the doorway with the twins and he feels the sudden tension in Izzy's body, the cold front coming from her big sister. Izzy wriggles, and he allows her to slip from his back. She leaves him with a smile of regret that barely makes up for it and goes to them. They walk back into the shadowy darkness of the house, leaving him standing there feeling like a plonker. He closes his eyes and imagines himself under Westway, standing on the lip of the half-pipe waiting his turn, before dropping over the edge, knees bent, arms out, looking over his right shoulder, one hundred per cent focused, rocketing round the inside of the curve with the sweet clatter of wheel bearings filling his ears.

GRACE

Tuesday, 17 April 2018

AND NOW, AFTER DOUGLAS HAS LEFT, I'M IN SOUTH Kensington showing prospective tenants around a house: a French couple with three small daughters. It's the kind of house that makes your mouth water, with a white stucco facade, pillars and a big, shiny door knocker in the shape of a lion's head. I tell them about the area, the schools, public transport, where to get the best coffee. They love the high ceilings and classical coving, adore the fireplaces, love the kitchen, and coo over the bathrooms. They need somewhere immediately, which is great for Rupert, but means added stress at my end.

As they confer, in their own language, my mind strays back to Saturday, trying to remember every word we said, every fleeting expression on Nick's face. Apart from his proposal, the most significant thing that came up was that his work no longer made him happy. He was fed up with the treadmill, with making money for money's sake. Could that have had something to do with it? Was there something more to his mood, something that happened at work to trigger a change in his thinking, that perhaps opened his eyes? Maybe he had already decided to walk away. I shouldn't have allowed the conversation to end there. I should have dug deeper.

I wrap up the viewing quickly, anxious to get to the school by three, in time for my appointment with the head.

Mrs Shaw comes to pick me up from the school office, where I've been sitting on the chair normally reserved for sick children, my phone in my hand, listening to the secretary and Mrs Shaw's PA gossiping. The head-mistress of Cedar Heights could be a politician or a newsreader with her bright, boxy jackets, obedient hair and unflappable eyebrows. When I arrived, the admin staff had been overly familiar, calling me Grace, their eyes alight with interest, from which I understood that the grapevine had been working overtime. They couldn't quite bring themselves to ask direct questions, but I fielded several indirect ones before resorting to my emails. I zone out their voices and the sound of a netball match going on in the playground and try to focus.

Cedar Heights is a popular, two-class-entry primary school. The building is red-brick and two storeys high, with an enormous hall that does service as gym and dining room, the trestle tables and benches stacked away after lunch. The head's office is up one flight of stairs, next to the girls' loos. A child bursts out as we pass, stopping to gaze up at us before running downstairs.

'Walk, Amelia,' Mrs Shaw admonishes her.

Amelia walks, so slowly she could be on her way to the guillotine. She reaches the bottom, jumps the last step and skips off.

Mrs Shaw's office is sun-filled and too warm. At her invitation I take a seat on the sofa and she sits down on the matching armchair. This is where parents are coaxed, seduced, rebuked and reassured.

'Now,' she says. 'Why don't you tell me exactly what's happened?'

After I've explained the situation, we discuss how the school is going to support Lottie. She asks me whether I'd like her to refer the family to social services to see what support they can offer, but I decline the invitation, trying not to let my horror show.

I'm relieved when the bell rings to signal the end of the day. Mrs Shaw stands up and we shake hands. She opens her door, says something encouraging, and I go back out to where the classes are lining up; row upon row of little girls in pale-blue gingham dresses and white socks and little boys in shorts and blue shirts. As I cross the playground, towards the gate, children and teachers turn to watch and I don't think it's me being hypersensitive, but it feels like the walk of shame. From the street, the other parents are watching me too. Everyone is, even the dogs tied to the railings.

The caretaker lets me out and pulls the gate shut behind me and I stand in the crowd of parents and nannies, my gaze fixed on the big red-and-blue clock. The minute hand moves excruciatingly slowly.

I feel a light pressure on my arm and find Cassie beside me. I catch her eye and she shakes her head with a grimace and pulls me to one side. We walk as far as the corner before we speak.

'I had a call this afternoon asking whether the rumours are true,' she says. 'Apparently one of the children went home sick and told their mum what they heard in the playground. It spread like wildfire. I'm so sorry. I've tried to nip it in the bud, but I think everyone's assuming Nick's left you.'

I wrinkle my nose. 'I've made it worse for Lottie.'

'It'll blow over.'

I bite my lip and turn round, and several well-groomed heads swivel the other way.

Lottie sees me and goes still, her expressive face questioning. When the gates open and we surge forward, she is practically jumping, her hand stretched out to shake her teacher's. She runs up to me with Hannah close behind her and I immediately see that her eyes are red, her cheeks blotched. She looks so forlorn that I almost weep. I hug her, and she clings to me.

'Has Nick come back?' she asks, her voice muffled by my quilted jacket.

'No, sweetie, I'm sorry, but he hasn't. Come on, let's go home.'

Hannah is shuffling her feet. She looks up at her mother, then at me. 'I didn't mean to upset her,' she says. 'I only told Leila.'

'Don't worry about it,' I say with a bright smile. I don't want her to feel awkward around me. Lottie needs her friends. 'It doesn't matter in the slightest.'

NICK

July 2000

LATER ON, THEY GO DOWN TO THE RIVER WITH HIS dad, Angus and Sean. Jess, Cora and Lorna go shopping in Totnes. Nick wishes the girls had gone with them. It would have been more fun.

Izzy is ignoring him again. He feels sadder about that than anything else. That she is so under Taisie's thumb is scary. Even Alex, who he thought was reasonably normal, hasn't got the guts to defy his sister. This is a family he has practically grown up with. He's been in and out of the Wellses' house since before he can remember; he's bounced on their beds, watched cartoons on their sofa, slept top to tail with Taisie. He's seen her throw up spectacularly after eating a whole packet of those pink wafer biscuits. And now, it's as though they don't know him. They're keeping up this ridiculous charade, and the frustration feels as though it's bubbling in his stomach. His spots have got worse, when they should have got better in the sun, and all he does is look forward to his next meal.

The river is benign, though they've been warned that it can be treacherous when it's swollen. He sticks with the adults; the kids are no use to him. The girls swan around in their bikinis as if they own the place; which of course Pansy and Freya do.

Nick is sitting on the bank talking to Angus when Taisie and Pansy swim over to his father and attempt to dunk him. There's a whole load of squealing and flailing around and then the others get in on the act. The girls' skin is slippery and gleaming and their curves, both hidden and enhanced by their swimming costumes, still come as a shock. Pansy catches his eye and raises her eyebrows and he looks away, uncomfortable. They're doing it on purpose, Taisie playing up to his dad, wrapping her wet arms around him. The boys are like over-excited puppies. His father extricates himself, then gets hold of a sobbing and spluttering Rory, who has accidentally been ducked under water in the mayhem, hitches him on to his back and carries him out, dropping him down beside Nick. He stands over them, laughing and dripping wet, water running in rivulets through the hairs on his chest and legs. Nick has to admit, sometimes his dad looks like a god. It's obscene for a parent to be that attractive, and not exactly great for him. He's conscious that comparisons are being made. Taisie gets out and starts making a fuss of Rory. Nick shuffles away and sits further downriver, lying back with a groan. He's had enough. He wants to go home.

The breeze becomes wind, rippling the water, and seconds later a drop of rain hits his forehead. The atmosphere is tinged with yellow as thunder rumbles and bruised clouds gather. The rain comes hard and fast, drenching them as they run back through the woods and across the lawn and tip inside. Nick retreats to his room and closes the door, jamming it with a chair, then he gets under the covers and masturbates with a picture of Taisie standing naked, up to her thighs in the river, her body slick with water, in his head.

GRACE

Tuesday, 17 April 2018

OUR HOUSE IS SET BACK FROM THE ROAD BEHIND A low red-brick wall with black railings. The front garden is paved in York stone divided geometrically by low box hedges. It was much admired when I first created it, after seeing something very similar in a garden in Chelsea.

Sometimes I feel such a fraud. The women round here know very little about me. As far as they are concerned I've only existed since Lottie started at Cedar Heights Primary. They think I'm this sorted woman with an enviable job in property and a wealthy banker partner; a woman too busy and in demand to give up her time to read with the children. If only they knew. Volunteering at the school, whether it's reading with the kids or doing lollipop lady duty, requires a criminal record check.

Under the window is a wooden bench, silvered with age, that no one ever sits on. Its job is to look pretty and rustic, which I have a feeling might be a little pretentious, but I like it, so I don't care. I don't see its two

103

occupants until it's too late to turn round. And where would I have gone anyway?

'Hello,' Cora calls, as I cross the street. 'Now, I know you said not to come, but I couldn't sit still.' As if to prove her point, she's up and off the bench, hurrying towards me. 'Have you heard anything?'

Tim strolls over, looking handsome and a little seedy, with his stubbly chin and floppy hair; the ageing public schoolboy. Lottie runs to him and he scoops her into a bear hug. I feel a little envious. I could do with a hug right now, and Tim's greetings are so enthusiastic.

Tim is like Nick, a tall man with broad shoulders. Cora is around five foot six, with thick, wavy blonde hair. She always wears trousers – I don't think I've ever seen her in a dress or a skirt, even at a function – and favours expensive fabrics and classics. Cora in the winter is all muted cashmeres, in the summer subtle beach tones; white trousers with stone-coloured tops that drape and pleat in a way that flatters her figure. Today she's wearing a calf-length, silver quilted coat. They both have wheelie cases – his black, hers navy. I try to hide my dismay, but Tim gives me a wry smile.

'No, but I'm about to call the police now,' I reply. 'You really shouldn't have come all this way.' It's a good three-hour drive from their village.

'We thought we could make ourselves useful,' Cora says. 'Presumably you have work? We can stay here in case something happens.'

I stand at the gate, my bag clutched against my stomach. 'Well . . .'

'Nick might turn up while you're out and need our help.'

'That's very kind, but if he's in trouble I'm not sure he'd appreciate a welcoming committee. He definitely wouldn't want any fuss.'

'I'm not fussing,' she says. 'I'm concerned for my son.' She looks me up and down. 'You're looking well, Grace.' The slight tightening around her lips tells me it isn't a compliment.

'I've been at work,' I say, stung. 'I'm wearing make-up. I've barely slept.'

'Of course. I didn't mean anything by it, dear. I'm sure you're worried sick.'

'Worried and confused,' I say.

Tim pats my shoulder. 'Of course you are.'

'The thing is,' Cora explains as she hustles past me, the wheels of her suitcase clacking on the path, 'we were meant to be staying with friends for three weeks, and we've rented our house out with Home Swap. Have you heard of them? Our neighbours use them, so we thought we'd give it a try. They clean before and after and you get a lot of money. Last time we did it the place was cleaner than we left it. Wasn't it, Tim?'

'Spick and span.'

'Only the problem is, our friends have rather let us down. A family crisis, apparently. So, we've nowhere to go, and since you're in this fix and we're so worried about Nick, we thought we could turn a disaster into an opportunity.'

An opportunity? I am speechless. I fish in my bag for

my keys. Are they going to stay for the full three weeks? Nick wouldn't have allowed that; they would have driven him insane.

I do have to go to work tomorrow, a contract signing and a last check on a house in Chelsea before an American tenant and his family take up residence, but there's no need for Tim and Cora to stay. I'm always back in time for Lottie and on the rare occasions that I'm not, Cassie takes her home.

'Nick wouldn't have objected,' Cora says.

'I don't object,' I say. 'I'm just a bit surprised. You should have let me know.'

'You don't mind, do you?' Tim asks. 'We'll keep out of your way.'

I wonder how they plan to do that. Stay in their bedroom?

'We have plenty of London friends to catch up with,' Cora says, following Lottie inside. 'Not that I feel in the slightest bit sociable, but I think the three of us sitting round waiting for the phone would be too morbid.'

'Four of us,' Lottie says as she slides her rucksack off her shoulders and drops it to the floor.

'Lottie, why don't you go up to your bedroom for a few minutes and let your mother and me talk.'

'I want to hear what you say. And I'm hungry.'

I glance at Cora, my eyebrows raised. Lottie goes into the downstairs toilet and closes the door behind her.

'I just worry,' I whisper, 'that you two suddenly appearing is going to make Lottie think it's worse than it is.'

'How much worse can it get?' Cora demands. 'My son has gone missing.'

106

I walk into the kitchen and pick up the kettle, angling it under the tap. 'According to the police,' I say above the sound of water gushing, 'Nick is "absent", not missing. He won't be missing for at least another twenty-four hours. Until that time, please could we underplay this, for Lottie's sake? I understand why you've come – you're anxious – but she's upset enough as it is, and this is just adding to the drama.'

'Excuse me—'

'Now, Cora.' Tim steps forward, like a referee coming between two warring footballers. He takes the kettle from me, places it on its stand and flicks the switch. 'There is nothing to be gained by upsetting each other. Let's sit down and talk this through. Have you eaten anything, Grace?'

'Not a lot.'

Trust Tim to be the one to notice. He leads me to a chair and sits me down, then makes me a cheese and chutney sandwich. I am so close to tears that his kindness almost pushes me over the edge. Lottie comes in, takes two slices of bread out of the packet and puts them in the toaster.

We sit in silence round the kitchen table while Lottie eats her toast, then when she starts removing the contents of her book bag, Cora finally loses patience.

'Lottie, please. Go and do that in the sitting room or your bedroom. I'm sorry, dear, but the grown-ups need to talk.'

'Mum,' Lottie objects, her jaw set.

'Sorry, darling. Just for ten minutes.'

She scowls, but she does as she's told. I follow

107

her into the hall, feeling guilty for not sticking up for her.

'It's not her house,' she says fiercely. 'She can't tell me what to do.'

I close the kitchen door. 'Shh. Keep your voice down. She's just worried, Lottie. She's Nick's mum. We have to be kind to her.'

'She's not always kind to you.'

I pause, surprised. I didn't think it was that obvious. 'That's just her way. She doesn't mean it.'

I speak to the police and am told that the detective in charge of Nick's case is out. Even though I press for information, I'm put off. But at least I have a meeting now; with a DI Marsh.

Cora has been listening to every word. 'You should have let me make that call,' she says. 'I know how to deal with them. I'd better come with you tomorrow.'

Toffee trots over and puts his paw on her knee. She removes it and brushes imaginary dirt off her trousers.

'No,' I say. 'I'm going on my own.'

She sighs. 'If that's the way you want it. Now, tell us everything that's been going on.'

'I don't know where to start.'

A wave of sadness catches me off guard. What if he doesn't come back? What will I do without him?

'Why don't you start from the beginning,' Tim says.

The thought of going through it again makes me well up. I've held it together since Sunday for Lottie's sake – I even managed not to cry in front of my friends – but I'm struggling now.

Tim gets up and pulls me into his arms, which makes it worse because, like his son, he possesses broad shoulders that are designed for crying on. His sweater muffles my sobs. Then Cora's voice breaks through Tim's murmurs of sympathy.

'Pull yourself together, Grace. Your hysterics aren't going to help Nick.'

Tim's arms loosen, and I turn, wiping my eyes on my sleeve.

'Right,' Cora says. 'What happened?'

I splash cold water on to my face and dab it dry with a clean tea towel. 'I don't know. I've gone over and over it in my head, but it doesn't make sense. We spent a lovely day together. Then in the evening he said he wanted to go for a walk. He didn't come back.'

'It's a little odd to go out for a walk without the dog, don't you think? And why didn't you go with him?'

'I had just run a bath. And I honestly don't know why he left Toffee behind. It did seem strange at the time.'

'It implies that he knew he wouldn't be coming back, doesn't it?' Cora says.

I sigh heavily. 'I already feel bad enough, Cora.'

'I'm sure it's nothing you've done,' Tim soothes me. I feel the glance he throws at his wife. 'We want to help. People don't walk out on their families for no reason.'

'He hasn't walked out on me.'

'Well, that's what he appears to have done, isn't it?' Cora says. 'He's left the house and not come back, not left a note, not called you or sent a message. We need to examine why that might be. If you've quarrelled, you'd better tell us.'

'We haven't quarrelled.'

'Maybe he's under pressure, financially, I mean, and hasn't been able to tell you.'

I shake my head. 'I know all about our finances. Nick doesn't keep any secrets from me. Any pressure is shared.'

She snatches at that. 'So, there has been pressure?' She looks around. 'There must be a problem if you can't afford help.'

'Cora,' I say, riled. 'This is my house and I like it the way it is.'

I don't have help in the house, despite its size, despite my and Lottie's tendency to create mess, despite Nick's careless attitude towards our possessions, because I don't want it. Gran was a cleaner and the stories she would come home with were a source of wicked delight to me. I loved the gossip, loved it when her lip curled in disgust at someone's nasty habits, loved her huffs of exasperation, loved her bitchiness. That's why I'd rather live with dust, thanks all the same, than have someone judge me and mine.

'Right,' Tim says. 'Let's go back to what happened at the weekend. Did he say anything? Did he appear worried or preoccupied? Was there anything at all that was different?'

'Yes, there was.' I look at them both. Tim nods encouragement, Cora waits, alert. 'Nick asked me to marry him.'

Neither of them say a word, but Cora's face is a picture of dismay.

'I said yes,' I add.

'Well,' Tim rushes forward and hugs me. 'That's wonderful news. Congratulations.'

'Thank you.' My voice sounds hollow.

I glance at Cora over his shoulder. She's smiling thinly. 'I'm so pleased,' she says, sounding anything but.

I've imagined this moment, without Nick's unexplained absence, of course, and thought about how they would react and how I'd respond. I knew it would be hard, but I didn't foresee the physical ache that would come with Cora's lack of enthusiasm. I've never really had a mother – at least not a fully functioning one – and Cora is not going to fill that space.

'So you see,' I say, my smile wavering, 'we are very happy. Everything's been going well. That's why it's so strange.'

Cora pushes back her chair and gets up. She goes to the sink, rinses a cloth under the tap, then starts to wipe down the surfaces.

'Cora, there's no need to do that.'

'Come and sit down, darling,' Tim says. 'That can wait.'

'I have to do something.' She holds the cloth in both hands, twisting it. 'My son has inexplicably disappeared. Good men don't do that without a reason.'

'But he *has* disappeared,' I point out, 'and he is a good man.'

'In that case, he has secrets, Grace. There must be something he hasn't told you.'

'Nick's as straight as a die,' Tim says. 'There's no way he'd do anything that wasn't above board.'

We get through a desultory supper, then Lottie finishes off her homework while I run a bath. Immersed in hot water, I let the tears dribble down my face. They tickle, and I blot them with the hot flannel. I feel as though I've let the enemy into my house. Cora is toxic, and Tim, a pussycat compared to his wife, tends to say what he thinks people want to hear. What do they hope to achieve, apart from making me feel stressed and defensive? I bend my knees and sink deeper into the water, holding my breath as my face is submerged. I keep my eyes wide open. The ceiling shimmers and dances. I come up again when my lungs start to strain. We lead such a normal life. It's me and Nick, and Lottie and Toffee; it's suppers together and walks in the park.

On Saturday afternoon he asked me to marry him, and that evening he went out and didn't come back. Did he know what was going to happen? Maybe he did. Cora is right: why else would he have left Toffee behind? My head is swimmy from the heat. He must have been going to meet someone. I have a glass of wine beside me. I reach for it with wet hands and drink it slowly, letting reality sink in. Nick Ritchie has left his family in limbo, with no clue, no information, no signpost. One moment he's here; next, he's gone. He could have hired a car or caught a train or a plane. Oh shit. A plane. He could be out of the country. His passport. I almost go flying when I get out of the bath. I dry myself off, throw on the trackie bottoms that Nick thinks are hideous, a tee and a long cardigan and pad down to his study.

The large brown envelope containing our passports and birth certificates is kept in the bottom drawer of his desk. I delve inside. Three passports. I slump in the chair, not knowing whether what I'm feeling is relief or horror.

Nick's screensaver is a photograph of me and Lottie on a near-deserted beach in Cornwall, towels wrapped hastily round us, faces still wet from the sea. I type in his four-digit passcode and the image disappears as I'm welcomed in.

Hello Nick

Most of Nick's emails are work related, and I've seen them already. There are several from Evan from last week, trying to arrange a trip to the Queen's Arms to watch next Saturday's Chelsea match. But there's something new. A message from an Alexander Wells.

Hi Nick. We still OK for Wednesday morning? Probably easiest if I meet you in the Starbucks on the corner of Eastcheap. 11 a.m. It would be really helpful for me to talk to you about what happened. If there's one thing I've learned, it's that you've got to face up to things, or they bring you down.

   Alex

I click on reply and begin to type a message letting him know that Nick won't be meeting him tomorrow, then I slowly delete it. I respond instead with 'See you there.'

What does Nick have to face up to? I've never heard of Alex Wells. All I know is where he is going to be at eleven o'clock tomorrow morning. And – my heart races when I think this – Nick might turn up for the appointment.

Lottie pokes her head round the door.

'Can you come and kiss me goodnight?' she asks. 'It's nearly nine o'clock.'

'Is it?' I say, surprised. 'I'm sorry, darling. Have you cleaned your teeth?'

I follow her into her bedroom and read a chapter of *The Amber Spyglass*, although my mind is elsewhere and the words make little sense.

When I come downstairs, Tim and Cora are on the sofa in the sitting room watching the television. Cora has taken my spot and Tim is sitting where Nick normally sits, with the little table in front of him where Nick's phone and bottle of beer should be, so I have to sit alone on the armchair. They aren't touching. When Nick and I sit there, even though I frequently lean into the corner, my feet are always against his thigh. I yearn for that physical connection, miss it so badly it burns.

TAISIE

July 2000

IT RAINED ALL NIGHT, BATTERING DOWN ON THE ROOF directly above them, bouncing off the skylight. It was like trying to sleep in a war zone, or in the middle of a fireworks display. Taisie couldn't get comfortable on the lumpy camp bed and resented Freya and Pansy for sleeping so soundly. She didn't know how they managed it, but they came here in winter too, so maybe they were used to sleeping so close to the elements. Taisie kept replaying that moment from earlier, Tim carrying Rory out of the river. She wished it had been her. She imagined herself draped barely conscious in his arms, pressed against his chest, water dripping from them. He would have laid her down gently but urgently and given her the kiss of life, his warm, firm hands on her skin.

Oh. She had an idea. She lay on her back thinking as flashes of lightning sent ghostly shapes darting across the room. After a few minutes she decided to check how

Izzy was coping. Her sister didn't like storms. She dragged the musty old eiderdown round her shoulders and went downstairs.

Izzy had her own bedroom because she refused to share with Alex and Rory. Taisie was on her side there. She would rather pull her nails out than put up with those two. She pushed the door open.

'Are you awake, Iz?'

'Taisie?' Izzy's voice came out of the darkness.

As her eyes adjusted Taisie saw that Izzy's were wide open, her fingers clutching the sheets at her throat. Her sister reminded her of Helen Burns from *Jane Eyre*. Taisie wrinkled her nose at the duck-down pillows. They smelled like they'd been around for half a century – knowing the Moodys and their sacrosanct heirlooms, they probably had – and the feathers tended to stick through and scratch your cheek.

In the darkness, Izzy perched beside her, leaning over her skinny knees and picking at her sky-blue toenail varnish.

'I want you to do something for me,' Taisie said.

'What?'

'I need to stop the game with Nick, but I can't just go up to him and say it's over. I need a distraction to get me out of this mess without losing face; something dramatic that'll make me look good. They all hate me, even Pansy and Freya, although they pretend they don't. It's gone too far, Iz. No one will forgive me unless I do something amazing. If you help me it'll all be forgotten, and we can go back to normal and start having fun.'

116

'You mean we can play with Nick again?'

'Yes, of course. If you do what I tell you.'

She woke because Izzy was shaking her. 'I don't want to do it.'

She stretched out, yawning, her thoughts muzzy. 'Nothing's going to happen to you. I promise.'

'Why does it have to be me? Why not Rory?'

'Because I asked you. But you obviously don't care about me.'

'Of course I do. That's not fair.'

'You'd rather be with Nick bloody Ritchie.'

'No I wouldn't!'

Wide awake now, Taisie sat up. Her eiderdown had slid to the floor. She reached for it, and pulled it round her like an Indian squaw. 'Yes you would. You don't want to help me, but you'd do anything for him even when you know that he's a two-timing bastard.'

'I can't just stop liking him.'

'Why not? I have. Do you have a crush on him, Iz?'

Izzy's eyes filled with tears so Taisie held her. She could feel her knobbly spine. She wondered what it felt like to be so fragile. Men loved that, didn't they? It was a pity she was so robust.

'It's nothing to be ashamed of, Izzy. I had massive crushes on boys when I was your age.'

'Did you?' Izzy hugged her tighter, pressing her cheek against Taisie's.

'Yes, of course. When they didn't love me back, it felt like the end of the world at the time, but now when I remember, it makes me laugh. You think you love Nick,

117

but you don't really. He's been in your life for ever and right now your hormones are all over the place.'

It struck her that it should be their mother having this conversation, but it felt good to be needed. It made up for some of the shit she'd had to take recently.

She lay with her face so close to her sister's that she could feel Izzy's toothpaste breath on the tip of her nose. 'You were such a scrawny little baby. It was like your eyes were too big for your head.'

Izzy snuggled into her embrace. She loved this story.

'When you were sick I spent every moment I could with you. You almost died, but I willed you to pull through. I wanted you to survive so badly. I felt so protective about you. I still do. I wouldn't let anything happen to you, Iz. You do believe me, don't you?'

'You'll be right behind me?'

'Yes, of course I will.'

'When will we do it?'

'Dunno. Tomorrow, probably. Depends if this lets up, I suppose.' Taisie yawned and tried to get comfortable. 'Go to sleep now, Izzy.'

'It will be all right, won't it?'

'Of course it will. I've always looked after you, haven't I?'

'Yes.' She didn't sound convinced. 'Taisie?'

She had nearly nodded off. She rolled over on to her side. 'What?'

'Nothing.'

She lay watching Izzy until her breathing deepened, then she stroked her hair in the darkness, spreading it on the pillow and weaving her fingers through it, before falling asleep herself.

GRACE

Wednesday, 18 April 2018

I WAKE FEELING HEAVY AND DRAINED OF ENERGY, AS IF during the night something has sucked the blood from my veins. I touch Nick's side of the bed, running my hand over the shallow dip made by his body, then pull his pillow across and breathe it in. Without him here, I'm so much less, although I know I shouldn't feel that way. I hope he would feel the same about me. I miss him and I'm desperately worried. What if he doesn't come back? What on earth will I do without him?

I won't think about that now, not when it's morning and there is Lottie to reassure. It's vital to carry on for her sake; vital to fill in that form for the school trip to the Science Museum, vital to sign her homework diary, vital to check she has the correct kit. Vital is what gets me up and doing the things that need doing.

A toilet flushes and I remember that Tim and Cora are here. I lie back and pull the covers up over my head. Cora is an early riser, which means I'll have to face her over breakfast. I wait for a few minutes then reluctantly get out of bed and head downstairs. She's making coffee. I mumble a good morning and get a clean mug out of the dishwasher and drop a teabag into it, then I go upstairs to make sure Lottie is awake. Somehow or other, I choreograph the morning so that Cora and I spend limited time in the same space, and as soon as Hannah and Cassie have whisked Lottie off, I get myself ready and go out.

I finish up in Chelsea at twenty past ten, then jump on my Vespa and whizz into the City for my meeting with Alex Wells. I locate the Starbucks and go inside. It's full of suited businessmen and women.

I don't have a clue who this man is, let alone what he looks like, or his age. There are several tables taken up by single men working on their laptops, phones to their ears. The place is bustling and noisy. I look for someone watching the door, like me. The waiting makes me jumpy.

Nick doesn't come, but I soon find a candidate for Alex Wells. The young man is holding a book, but not reading it, and is as interested in who's coming through the door as I am. I approach with my coffee in my hand and hover near him until finally he glances up. Not recognizing me, he pretends to go back to his book.

'Excuse me,' I say. 'Are you Alex Wells?'

This time he scrutinizes me. 'Yup.' His tone is evasive but curious at the same time.

'My name's Grace Trelawney. I'm Nick Ritchie's girlfriend.'

'Oh.' He frowns in confusion. 'He's meant to be meeting me.'

'I know, I saw your email. That was me who replied. Do you mind if I sit down?'

He looks bemused. 'No, not at all.'

He dabs at a spill of coffee with a paper napkin. I take the seat opposite him, put my helmet on the floor beside me, and unzip my bike jacket.

'Is Nick with you?' He looks round at the counter, as if hoping to see him there.

'No.' I hesitate. 'I don't actually know where he is. I haven't seen him since Saturday evening. I came to meet you because of your email. I hoped he would be here. I'm extremely worried about him. I thought maybe—'

'I don't know where he is.' His response is as quick as a flash, and he already looks as though he wishes he could take it back. 'I mean, I thought he would be here, but as you can see, he isn't.'

'What was it you wanted to talk to him about? I don't mean to pry, but I'm desperate. I live with him, you see, so it's not as if he just hasn't called me. He went out for a walk and didn't come home.'

'Shit.' Alex has gone sheet white. 'What do you think . . . I mean, you don't think he's done something stupid, do you?'

'Why do you say that?'

'Oh. No, sorry. No reason.' He hesitates. 'It's just a question you ask when people vanish.'

'Well, I don't think that at all. I'm just looking for connections. Can you at least tell me why you asked him here?'

He looks like he wants to leave but I pin him to his seat with my eyes. Outside, the street is busy; a sea of taxis, delivery vans and bicycles. People walk with purpose, their minds focused, phones to their ears. Slowly, Alex turns to face me again.

'I felt like reconnecting. I haven't seen him in years. There's nothing else.'

I put my phone on the table between us and show him his email. He reads it and shrugs.

'This doesn't look like nothing to me,' I say.

He swallows hard, his Adam's apple rising and falling. 'I thought he might be able to help with my recovery.' He pushes the plastic lid from his coffee across the table with the stirring stick.

'Your recovery from what?'

His eyes narrow as he looks at me. He's weighing up how much to tell me, how much I already know. Which only makes me wonder how much he plans to leave out.

Then he releases his breath. 'My sister drowned when our families were on holiday together.'

I don't know what I expected, but nothing like this.

'I'm so sorry.'

'I thought I was OK, but lately . . .' He shrugs but his hands are shaking.

'What was her name?'

'Isabel. Izzy. She was thirteen.' His eyes are full of pain. 'I'm surprised Nick hasn't told you about it.'

Me too. This must have been a significant and life-changing event for him. I thought he trusted me. My face heats. I press on to cover my bewilderment.

'In your email you hint that Nick needs to face up to things. What did you mean by that?'

'Nothing. To be honest, I was drunk when I wrote it. I only meant myself. My psychiatrist encouraged me to get in touch with him.'

I look at him sceptically. 'There's no suggestion that Nick should feel bad about your sister's death? That's not what this is about?'

'Absolutely not.'

'How did you find him?'

'Through LinkedIn.'

'And when was this?'

He finally realizes that his trembling hands are giving him away and puts them on his lap. 'Last Friday.'

'Prompted by your psychiatrist?'

'That's right.'

'So it's a coincidence that he vanished on Saturday night? You don't think getting in touch triggered something?' It's my turn to swallow hard. 'You don't think Nick might have felt responsible?'

He gives a bitter laugh. 'We all do, one way or another. But we shouldn't. Our parents were supposed to be in charge, but they were getting pissed and generally trying to forget we were there. There was all sorts of shit going on; Nick's dad making the females behave weirdly. But I presume you know what he's like. He was loving it; the cockerel amongst the hens.'

'Do you think that's what was troubling Nick? He thinks his father's to blame in some way?'

'I doubt it. If Nick read something else into it, that's his problem. I wish I'd never got in touch with him.'

123

'But you did, and now he's gone.'

'Listen, that has nothing to do with me.'

He opens his wallet and fishes out a photograph. I take it from him. It's of a young girl. A head-to-waist shot. Someone else's arms are draped around her shoulders, but the picture has been cropped to the size of a credit card, so that only the little girl features. She looks happy – she's grinning – but there are blue shadows under her eyes, and her lips are chapped. She doesn't look healthy. I hand it back to him and he carefully replaces it in its pocket.

'It seems odd that Nick's never told me any of this.'

'He probably wanted to forget it. I did too. It seriously screwed our family up. My older sister went completely off the rails. She was never home, and a pain in the arse if she was. She . . .' he checks himself.

I wait, but he doesn't finish the sentence. 'God. Poor thing.'

'Yeah, well. Fifteen is a bad age for your life to go tits-up. She hasn't spoken to any of us since she left home. We hear things occasionally. She married some guy, but he topped himself.'

I wince at his terminology. 'I'd like to speak to her.'

'Be my guest. I don't know where she is, though.'

'You've never tried to find her?' Some brother he's turned out to be.

'She's made it clear that she doesn't want us near her so . . .' He raises his hands. 'You'll have to do some digging. Her name's Taisie Wells. Taisie short for Anastasia. I suppose she might have taken her married name, though.'

'Thanks.' I say drily. I start to get up.

'So you really have no idea why Nick left?' Alex says.

'Nope.' I pull on my jacket. 'Is there anything else you want to tell me?'

He stiffens, scratching at a dried smear on the table, and looks as though he's hoping for a waitress to come and clean it and rescue him from me, into the bargain. When no one appears, he pushes his cup away and picks up his phone, activating it and glancing at the screen. No messages. No excuse from Nick for not turning up.

'No.'

I don't believe him, and it must show on my face, because he frowns as though he's remembering something. It feels a little like play-acting to me.

'Actually, there is something. When I spoke to one of the others who'd been on that holiday, she told me something interesting.' He stops fiddling with his phone and looks directly at me. 'But it can't go any further than this room.'

'That's fine by me.' But not a promise, I add silently.

'Back then, Tim was starting a restaurant, but his main investor pulled out. I can't remember his name, but anyway, that doesn't matter. What matters is that it turns out it was Angus who warned this guy off; basically told him that it was dodgy. The restaurant folded pretty quickly after that. I doubt Ritchie's would have succeeded anyway, but I'd imagine that put the knockers on it.'

'Angus?'

'Angus Moody. His family owned the house we stayed in that summer.'

My stomach flips. 'But he's Nick's boss.'

'Shit, is he?' He pauses, looking suspiciously like a man trying to work out what this means, but if I've learned anything in the last twenty minutes, it's that thinking on his feet is not Alex Wells' strong point. 'Angus spent a lot of time talking to him, so maybe they stayed in touch.' He smiles ruefully. 'I wish he'd given me half the advice he gave Nick.'

All I know about Angus Moody is that Nick did an internship with his company before he went to university. Three years after graduating Nick was head-hunted by Angus from HSBC. I had no idea that their connection went back further than that. Why wouldn't Nick have told me? He talked about him often enough.

'Can we backtrack a little? How did you all know each other?'

He looks at me as if I'm slow. 'Angus and his wife Lorna are old friends of my parents.'

I rub the space between my eyes. If Angus was instrumental in ruining Tim, that would have crushed Nick if he found out.

'He tried to warn Mum and Dad, but unfortunately they ignored his advice. I was supposed to keep it quiet, but . . .'

I look at him steadily and he flushes and shrugs.

'But you told Nick? Is that it, Alex? You told him that Angus Moody killed off his father's dream?'

'I thought it would help.'

I grit my teeth. Talking to Alex Wells is like wading through treacle. 'And this was on Friday?'

'Yes. Is it important?'

126

I close my eyes for a second. The noise of the baristas taking orders, the hiss of steam and clunk of stainless steel bombard me. When I open them Alex is looking at me anxiously.

'It might be,' I say.

'It affected us too, you know. We lost a shedload of money. Dad was overly impressed with Tim and couldn't see past his bullshit. When the restaurant folded, Dad felt like an idiot. He was embarrassed. Tim never said sorry; he just walked away from it. Dad's never forgiven him for that.'

'Will you tell him about Angus?'

'I don't know. I don't see what it would achieve, apart from reminding them of a horrible time.'

I debate whether to mention the visit that Angus paid me on Monday evening. I need to think what it means, in combination with this new piece of information, but I don't believe his story about the supper party. His appearance on my doorstep was so outlandish.

'When was the last time you spoke to Angus?'

'God, I've no idea. Mum kept in touch with Lorna for a while, but it was all so painful that they kind of let the friendship slide.' He shrugs. 'Ten years or more? Sorry. I don't remember.'

As I leave, he says, 'Say hi to Cora from me. I was fond of her. I missed her when we moved out of London. The Ritchies were a big part of my childhood.' He hesitates, then adds, 'Are you and Nick married?'

'We've just got engaged.' I like the way that sounds.

'Pity,' Alex says. 'Legally, you'd be on a stronger footing

if you were. In the current circumstances, I mean.' He sees my horrified expression and grimaces. 'Sorry. I'm a lawyer. It's the way my brain thinks.'

My answering laugh is dry; more cough than mirth.

As I walk away, it's Angus who occupies my thoughts, not Alex. There were four reasons why he might have come to see me. He genuinely cared about Nick; he was suspicious that Nick was lying about why he was taking time off; that perhaps he'd taken an impromptu holiday; he knew Nick wasn't there. His visit was a taunt or a threat of some kind. An implication that he's watching us.

I smile. Things must be bad if I'm weaving conspiracy theories. Angus came because he was 'just passing', and he wished to show concern for an employee he values.

Of course, there were the mythical papers he said he had for Nick and which he didn't leave behind.

'Where's Cora?' I ask Tim.

'She's putting her feet up for an hour. It's a strain, all this.'

He gives me a glum smile and I nod, noticing the invisible eye-roll, the way he looks at me as though we both know what she's like. For some reason it annoys rather than pleases me. Cora may be difficult, but she's his wife. He should be loyal.

She must have heard me come in, because she appears, refreshed from her nap, just as Tim is asking me where I've been.

'To see Alex Wells.'

'Oh?' Cora says. Their surprise is evident. Tim looks nervous.

'He'd arranged a meeting with Nick, so I thought I'd go along and see what it was about. Alex has some stuff he's working through. He's been in therapy. He wanted to talk about his sister.'

'Well, of course, that was a tragedy,' Tim says.

'He thought Nick might have unresolved issues. Alex certainly does. I got the feeling that no one talked about it properly after it happened. That you dealt with it by losing sight of each other.'

Tim sighs. 'Yes, that's true to an extent. We did lose touch with the family. It was so incredibly difficult, so painful. It's not a nice thing to admit, but I was relieved when they moved away. How is he?'

'I don't know him, but he seemed uncertain, in a bit of a rut, maybe. The impression I got was that he was trying to move his life forward by tracking Nick down. On the other hand, it's hard to believe that the timing was a coincidence.'

'It certainly seems odd,' Tim says.

'Why wouldn't Nick have told me about this?'

'Perhaps he thought you wouldn't understand,' Cora says. 'Or that you would play it down in some way.'

'He knows I'd never do that.' I swallow back the hurt and instinctively fight back. 'What about you two? Alex told me about the restaurant. About losing your friends' money. He didn't think you cared.'

'Of course I did,' Tim protests. 'I felt terrible. But it was business. You win some, you lose some.'

'Do you?'

He ignores my tone. 'Nick was going through adolescence. He was very up and down at the time. After the accident he withdrew. He was diagnosed with depression the following year.'

Depression. There's too much to take in; I pull out a chair and sit down hard.

'I'm sorry, that's obviously a shock to you.'

There's a long silence. After a few moments, I take a deep breath and look up. 'How did she drown?'

'No one knows,' he says. 'It was one of those things. We didn't even know she was outside.'

'Do you think it might have something to do with what's happened?'

'We don't know,' Cora says. 'We're just looking for something to explain the unexplainable.'

TAISIE

July 2000

THE RAIN KEPT UP THE NEXT DAY, SO THEY SPENT THE morning in Totnes visiting the museum, where they had to suffer the humiliation of dressing up as Victorian children. After that they shopped for food.

The car journey back was a nightmare, because Nick managed to work things so that he was sitting next to her. Actually, Taisie suspected it was the twins' fault. They were sitting in the back, whispering and giggling. It was precisely the sort of situation they would find funny. Izzy sat in the front. The little boys had gone in Cora's car with Lorna. Obviously, her mum orchestrated that arrangement. She didn't want to be cleaning mud off the seats, and the ancient Volvo Estate Lorna and Angus kept down here was filthy anyway. Last time Taisie sat in it, she got straw stuck to the backs of her thighs.

Back home, they fell out of the car and sprinted to the house. Not that it made any difference. They were all soaked to the skin anyway. God, what a waste of time that was. The only people enjoying themselves were Rory and Alex, who were so easily pleased it was pathetic.

'Find something to do,' Lorna said, as soon as they were inside.

Taisie and the twins wanted to go upstairs and chill, but no, they had to 'do' something that involved 'all of you' and not 'leave anyone out'. As if they hadn't wasted an entire morning doing exactly that.

'Let's play Sardines!' Rory shouted from the downstairs toilet.

Taisie rolled her eyes and glanced at Pansy. She rolled hers back.

'I think that's a wonderful idea,' her mother said.

'Are you going to play too?' Taisie asked, raising her eyebrows to make it obvious she was being sarcastic.

'I don't think so, darling. We'll tidy up downstairs.'

The three men wandered out of the kitchen, holding half-drunk bottles of beer. Taisie looked such a mess, standing there in her socks and damp clothes. Tim barely looked at her. Yesterday he said that he must introduce her to Tom Gale because they'd get on like a house on fire. She had wanted to ask why, but her mum had flicked a stony glance her way. She had returned it with a scowl. What was her problem, for Christ's sake?

She risked a quick glance at Tim, but he was messing with Rory, his hand on her brother's head as he flailed with his fists, giggling hysterically. Tim was brilliant with children. It was scary how hard she was falling for Nick's dad. Now she couldn't stop thinking about him. At least it took her mind off Nick. He was so immature.

'What about the dads?' Pansy asked. 'Are you going to play Sardines, or sit around drinking beer all afternoon?'

'Don't be cheeky,' Angus said.

Taisie's father clapped his hand on Tim's shoulder. Taisie groaned inwardly. He was pissed. Great.

'Go on, kids. Make yourselves scarce. Give us a break.'

'Another one?' Lorna said wryly.

But she was on the men's side. Taisie turned to the others. They were waiting for her to make the decision, as usual.

'Come on, then. We might as well. *Ip dip sky blue, who's it, not you . . .*'

133

GRACE

Thursday, 19 April 2018

BEFORE I HEAD TO THE POLICE STATION, I CALL PHILLIPA at Financial Logistics. Since Nick is now officially missing, I can't put it off any longer. She's sympathetic, but what happens next is not up to her.

'I'll need to speak to Angus,' she says.

Ah, Angus, I think. The man who, unbeknownst to me, has known Nick since he was a teenager. I'd love to know what the policy is for when employees vanish into thin air or if they even have one. I presume this isn't something they've had to deal with before, but you never know.

'OK.'

She must have heard the tremor in my voice because she offers to wait until Monday.

'He's taking a long weekend and he's already left the office,' she says. 'And he hates being disturbed at home.'

'Thank you.'

'A lot can happen in three days. Hang on in there.'

After I put the phone down, I feel oddly distant, as

though I don't belong here any more. I'm the woman whose boyfriend has apparently vanished into thin air. My house isn't empty, but the atmosphere is hollow. Absent, I keep thinking. There's no smell, no shadow, no noise from the shower, no extravagant sneezes. And in bed at night I'm alone.

Leaving the Vespa in the Asda car park, I walk along the busy high street to the police station for my appointment with DI Marsh. The detective is in his early forties, balding, his head shaved. He has a raised mole at the side of his nose, near his right eye, that I have to keep telling myself not to focus on. He briefly outlines what's been done so far, warning me not to expect much because it's too early in the process. He has one of his officers checking local CCTV footage but so far there have been no sightings beyond the Queen's Arms.

It's bewilderingly noisy in here; officers on the phone, phones ringing incessantly, conversations and banter. Marsh ignores the cacophony and focuses on me, and soon has me settled in the bubble of his attention.

I tell him everything I know, from the death of Alex Wells' sister to the business with Nick's boss. I mention the In-Step app and Anna, even though I'm a little ashamed to, because it makes me feel like a stalker.

'I'll make a note,' he says. 'But it seems to me that there are good enough reasons for all of this. People do go into therapy years after an event and they do try and track down the other people involved. Something will trigger a need, it may be a decade or even four decades later, but it can be a force that's too strong to resist.'

'But what if the trigger for Alex getting in touch was also the trigger for Nick's disappearance? Alex told me a bit about the dynamics of the three families that summer. There were underlying tensions. And what about Angus Moody's involvement? He scuppered that restaurant. Nick knew nothing about it until Alex told him. He would have been extremely angry.'

'Ms Trelawney, what you're talking about is life. Restaurants go under. Your partner works in banking. I'm sure he has a healthily pragmatic view about the vagaries of any business, and restaurants are particularly risky. I very much doubt he would blame his boss for making what appears to have been a sensible decision. Presumably Moody hasn't got where he is today without being able to spot a bad bet when he sees it.'

'I know, but—'

'I understand that you're frightened, but try to be rational. Nick has walked out. No one has seen him, as far as we know, but that doesn't mean he isn't staying with a friend, trying to get his head straight. Something will have shaken him so badly that he feels he can't face his family, but that doesn't mean he's in any danger. In fact, the most likely scenario is that he's holed up somewhere. You have to be patient and have faith. From what you tell me, Nick has plenty of common sense. He doesn't sound like the sort to misjudge a situation.'

'I know something's happened to him. You have to believe me.'

In my distress I squeeze my hand round the white plastic beaker I've been holding, and it collapses in on itself. Water splashes over my coat, trousers and the back of

Marsh's desk. I leap up and try to mop up the mess with my sleeve, but water trickles around the base of his keyboard and soaks into a pad of paper. Marsh remains calm, moving everything to one side. Another officer hands him a box of tissues. He pulls out a wad and dabs at the mess.

'I'm so sorry.'

'Don't worry about it.' He dries a pen and puts it to one side.

'Will you speak to Nick's boss? He's out of London, but his assistant will have a contact number for him.'

'Do you think he'll be able to shed some light on what's happened?'

'I have no idea. I thought I knew everything about Nick, but it appears I don't. For all I know, he's embezzled the company's millions.'

Marsh's eyes show a flicker of interest. 'Has he been spending large sums of money recently?'

'I was joking. Nick's very careful with his money.'

Back at home, I put on one of Nick's sweaters. It envelops me and I can smell him in the soft wool. Tim and Cora are out, and it's such a relief to have the house to myself that I feel a surge of physical happiness as I reclaim my space. Armed with a coffee, because I need as much caffeine as I can get to mitigate the effects of a succession of bad nights, I push open the door to Nick's study, half expecting to find him there. He's not, of course. I run my fingers along his shelves, pick up the photograph of me and Lottie and set it back down. I take his seat, swivel it round and settle myself at his desk.

I force my mind back to the days before Nick vanished. There were several significant events: he had a nightmare that terrified him; he asked me to marry him; he was contacted by Alex Wells. And one seemingly insignificant event – the one thing that Marsh showed no interest in – he went for a walk and paused at the same time as Anna Foreman. She could have been somewhere else entirely. Kai was at Hannah's sleepover too, so she may have taken the opportunity to have a night out. It could be nothing, but now that I know Evan saw him with a woman, I don't think it is; I think it may be everything. My gut feeling is that this has something to do with the part of his past Nick has kept hidden from me. The part that spills over into his dreams from time to time and causes those horrible hallucinatory visitations.

A woman. The thought leaves me breathless with anxiety, it sends heat racing up into my face. It sickens me. I ram my feet into the carpet and stop moving.

Stop it. Stop thinking this way. For heaven's sake, if it was something like that, I would know by now. Think about practicalities. I cannot afford to let things slide, not with Lottie to consider. And Nick wouldn't want me to either; he'd tell me to pull myself together. There is a very expensive roof over our heads and it's up to me to make sure it stays here.

I have a good idea of the general day-to-day stuff, and I know that our mortgage costs us four hundred pounds a month. He has a company car, but my little runabout is on a lease, and he pays that too, with its insurance, MOT and tax. I cover the costs of my Vespa. What I earn from my job pays for our supermarket bills and our immediate needs, but not the Direct Debits or standing orders.

Beside me Toffee gets bored and curls up, makes a soft snuffling noise before burying his muzzle in his paws. I wish I could do the same. Outside a gust of wind sends pink blossom swirling. I lean over the monitor to watch the flurry drift on to the lawn, then sit down again with a thump. Toffee whines, confused.

'Settle down,' I say, and go back to my calculations.

Twenty minutes later, I push the chair back and weave my fingers through my hair. Ball park, our joint out-goings add up to a vast two and a half grand a month if I factor in everything I can possibly think of and add a hundred for contingencies. And that's not counting the money Nick gives his parents. It's amazing how much we spend without even thinking about it. We're not extravagant – Lottie's school is a state primary and we only have one foreign holiday a year – but there's no way I can support us on my income alone.

'Nick.'

I mutter his name without thinking, but unfortunately it has a galvanizing effect on Toffee, who jumps up and hurtles downstairs. I run down after him and find him quivering by the front door. I sink down beside him, pull-ing him into my arms.

'Sorry, darling.'

I rub my cheek against his knobbly head. I try to pic-ture Nick coming through the door, dropping his keys, calling out, bending to push an ecstatic Toffee out of the way. His image is frustratingly insubstantial. I'm having trouble picturing him without a photograph in front of me. How could that have happened so quickly?

And if he doesn't come back? If he's dead, if the police start looking at me? Maybe they are already. I think back to my meeting with Marsh; I didn't get the sense he knew about my past. Maybe I'm safe, for now. I can imagine his eyebrows hitting the ceiling when he does find out.

I clasp my hands together and mutter into my knuckles, 'Come home. Please, Nick. Come home.'

If he doesn't, then they'll take a closer look at me.

NICK

July 2000

RORY, SINCE HE INSISTED ON THE GAME, IS THE FIRST to hide, but instead of looking for him, Nick makes himself a sandwich and takes it up the back stairs with his book to an alcove he's found on the turn of the landing. It goes under the eaves and around the corner for a few feet. A bare bulb provides enough light to read by. At the back there are dusty carrier bags full of yellowing papers and an abandoned wasps' nest with the odd desiccated carcass strewn round it. He brushes them away with the book. It's muggy, the built-up heat combining with the rain. A sweet smell is overlaid by the dust burning on the light bulb.

Nick pulls the door to. The others are pounding round the house. Someone opens the door and he looks into a pair of bright blue eyes. Pansy's. She hesitates, then closes it.

There's a whisper, then Taisie says, loud enough for Nick to hear, 'God, what a loser. Why doesn't he hang out with your dad? He's been clinging to him like a limpet all week.'

'Come on, Taisie, that's not fair. Who else is he meant to talk to?'

'I don't care. I just know that if I have to look at those pulsating spots for one more day, I'm going to top myself. He makes me feel sick.'

He holds his breath and shrinks back into the shadows, feels a spider's web tickling his ear and bats it away. Their voices fade and he opens his book, already regretting bringing Machiavelli rather than Bernard Cornwell, and has to force himself to stay awake. There's a movement behind the door, a thud and shift, and he braces, hoping it's Alex or Rory. But it isn't: it's Izzy.

She puts her finger on her lips, then crawls in and tucks herself into the small space beside him, bare skinny knees pressing against his hairy shins, before reaching for the door and pulling it shut.

'What's up, Shrimpy?' he says.

'Taisie's going to stop soon.'

He pretends not to know what she's on about. 'Stop what?'

'You know. This. The *Invisible Nick* game.'

'Oh that,' he says. 'I don't care about that.'

'It's hot in here.'

'It stores heat,' Nick explains. 'It's like there's days of it packed in.'

The rain patters on the tiles above them, a constant, comforting sound.

'It feels like we're on a boat,' Izzy says.

'It does.'

She yawns and leans against him, and he tilts his head against hers. Her hair is silky and smells of grapefruit shampoo.

'Do you still like Taisie?'

Nick shrugs. 'Yeah. I suppose.'

'She's being mean.'

'Sometimes girls do that.'

He's beginning to feel sleepy too. He closes his eyes and drowses. The rain keeps falling, the smell of the eaves, musky and hot, mingles with the smell of the child nodding off against him. He slips into a dream in which he's swimming downstream and the Moody twins are running along the riverbank, barefoot, tripping and skidding in the mud, crying out to him to be careful. Then someone says, 'Where's Taisie?' and he panics, doggy-paddling round and round, his feet thrashing beneath him, looking for a head bobbing in the water.

He tumbles out of the dream with a cry. There's a creature crawling out of the tightest angle of the eaves, reaching for him with its gnarled hands. It makes a grab for his ears, and he falls back, banging his head on a rafter, but not before it's glued its mouth to his. He pushes it away and feels the small bud of a pre-pubescent breast under his hand. Someone shrieks and he surfaces, disorientated and grappling for a way out. He knocks his head on the hot bare bulb and it swings nauseatingly. Izzy is hitting him, shouting in his face. 'Get off me! Don't touch me.'

She pushes open the door and tries to pull herself out and he isn't together enough to explain that it was just his weird problem. How would he have explained it, anyway? He hasn't even told his mum and dad.

143

But this is the first time it's touched him. In disgust, he rubs his wrist across his lips, then goes very still. Oh shit. Izzy.

Izzy is scrabbling to get away from him, crawling out of the cubbyhole door.

'Izzy,' he says, catching at the hem of her jeans. 'Sorry. I didn't mean to scare you.'

But it's too late, she's gone.

GRACE

Friday, 20 April 2018

THE WEEKEND IS IMMINENT, AND WITHOUT LOTTIE acting as a buffer between me and Nick's parents, the prospect is dismal. Douglas texts to say that he'll pick Lottie up from the house, not the school. I mentioned that Tim and Cora were here and he's curious, never having met them before.

Half an hour later, he's outside the front door. I bring him into the kitchen where Cora is reading a book and Tim is scrolling through an article on the iPad. I introduce them and Tim jumps up, a hand outstretched. The men couldn't be more different; Tim with his big bones, swept back salt-and-pepper hair and handsome, patrician face, has always seemed benign to me, like a 1940s film star. Douglas, thin as a rake, heavy-featured, with his sensual mouth and hard gaze, is intimidating.

I make tea while they chat, covering innocuous subjects like the trouble Tim is having setting up broadband in their Leicestershire home, Cora's mother's deteriorating health and the way other people's dogs are so badly behaved compared to Toffee, Cora pretending to be fond of my unprepossessing companion. She's flirtatious, her voice earnest and interested. She is trying to impress, not knowing how unlikely she is to succeed.

I set mugs and a plate of biscuits down in front of them. Douglas pats the seat beside him, but I shake my head. I stand leaning against the counter, my mug in my hands.

'How are you feeling?' he asks.

'I don't know. Numb, I suppose. I don't seem to be getting any answers.'

'I don't think you're dealing with the police particularly well, Grace,' Cora says. 'If you'd let me speak to them we might get a little further. They would be more likely to pay attention to someone of my background and experience.'

I'm used to veiled reminders of my deficiencies from Cora, but she still gets under my skin. 'I'm sure that'll come in handy,' I say with a tight smile. 'But I don't want to go in with all guns blazing quite yet. I don't want to antagonize them.'

'Don't be wet. Every day that Nick doesn't come back it becomes a little more likely that he won't. You do know that, don't you? Time is of the essence.'

'Of course I know.'

'If you don't ask, you don't get. We have to put pressure on the police and get them to prioritize Nick. I know how these things work.'

Douglas puts his hand on the table, splaying his fingers. He looks at Cora thoughtfully. 'I think Grace understands perfectly well. You're right though, she does need help.'

Cora glances at me to see my reaction. I shrug.

'However,' he continues. 'In my view, that help would be better coming from me.'

'From you?' Her head snaps round. 'You're not even related to Nick.'

Tim breaks his biscuit in half and dunks a corner into his tea. 'I think it would be helpful if we were all on the same page,' he says, smiling. 'You're doing incredibly well, Grace, but I do think Cora and Douglas have a point. You need to let someone else step in, someone with legal expertise who can put pressure on the police.'

'I practised law for six years,' Douglas says.

'What made you give up?' Cora asks.

'I didn't much like the people I was having to deal with.'

'Personally I try not to judge.'

'I find that hard to believe. You're pretty judgemental of Grace.'

I watch this interaction, torn by anger and compassion. I know why Douglas left the law. He had been a father for three years when he was asked to defend a man accused of abusing his thirteen-year-old niece. He won the case despite being certain that his client was guilty. The girl committed suicide three months later. After that, Douglas worked for another year and then he resigned. Maybe if he hadn't had Lottie, he could have viewed it dispassionately, but she changed him. Despite all the things that drove me away, I cannot fault him as a father.

'I suspect you weren't up to the job,' Cora retorts, her

earlier pleasantness forgotten now that Douglas has dared to defend me.

I study my fingernails, not wanting to get caught in the crossfire.

'I don't have to explain myself to you,' Douglas says. 'The way I understand it, you barely tolerate Grace and you blow hot and cold with my daughter. If Nick isn't found, I'll personally see to it that you don't get access.'

I'm so surprised at the turn this conversation has taken that I intervene. 'Douglas. This isn't the time.'

'Now come on,' Tim says, visibly bristling. 'I'm extremely fond of Lottie.'

'Are you?' Douglas sneers. 'All the more reason.'

'I beg your pardon? What the hell are you implying?'

Tim is at least twenty-five years older than Douglas. All the same he squares up to him, shoving his chin out. Tim is all bravado, but he isn't nasty. Douglas is; he won't scruple to hurt the older man, to put him in his place.

'Please stop,' I beg them. 'Quarrelling is not going to help Nick.'

'I'm not implying anything,' Douglas says smoothly. 'Let's move on, shall we?'

Cora sends him a suspicious look, then nods agreement and just as suddenly as it came on, the tension recedes.

'We need to be calm and think this through,' she says. 'I have contacts in the police force, and I know how these things work. I'll liaise with them.'

'No,' I say. 'I'm talking to them on a daily basis. I don't think you telling them how to do their jobs is going to help. I need them on my side, so it makes sense for me to build a relationship with the detective.'

Douglas twists round so that he can look me in the eye. 'You always did insist on doing everything yourself, Grace. But this is not the time to dig your heels in. You need my help.'

'Thanks for the offer, but you'll know if I do, because I'll ask you.'

He scrapes his chair back and stands up, moving towards me. 'How many times do I have to remind you that anything that impacts on my daughter's well-being is my business? I want you to keep me informed of every development. I don't care if it turns out to be irrelevant, let me know. There are things I can do.'

'What things?' I ask.

'Of course you'll be kept informed,' Cora says before he can answer. 'Naturally you're worried about your daughter. Tim and I respect that, but really, apart from giving the family moral support, I don't think it would be appropriate for you to be involved in any official business.'

'Appropriate?' Douglas says dangerously quietly.

She sighs. 'Well, it does rather smack of you getting your feet under the table while my son is out of the way.' She pauses, her smile deceptive. 'Why exactly are you here? What is it you want?'

'I could ask the same of you, Cora,' I interrupt. She's playing games with him, trying to be clever. She has no idea who she is dealing with. 'You can just as easily keep an eye on things from Leicestershire.'

'Yes, Cora,' Douglas drawls. 'What is it you want to contribute that can't be done from home?'

'I don't have to explain myself to you,' Cora sniffs.

'Right, that's enough,' I say. 'Lottie's going to be back any minute. Please can you get it into your heads that I do not need to be looked after. I want Nick home and I want my life back the way it was. I certainly don't need anyone telling me what to do.'

As if on cue my daughter bangs on the door. Toffee leaps up with a sharp bark and Douglas pushes back his chair, treating Tim and Cora to a smarmy smile as he leaves the room. I follow him, picking up the rucksack I packed for her earlier. Lottie submits to a hug, then Douglas suggests she says goodbye to her grandparents. This shows surprising generosity on his part, considering that up until a minute ago they were at each other's throats, but when she goes through to the kitchen, he turns on me.

'I don't want you leaving Lottie alone with that man.'

'What are you talking about? They adore each other.'

'Don't you think he's a bit over-familiar?'

'No, I do not.' A cold trickle runs down my spine. All it takes is a germ of doubt these days. 'You have a filthy mind, Douglas. Tim is her grandfather and he has never behaved inappropriately. You're paranoid.'

'Maybe I am, but better safe than sorry. Don't forget I'm her father.'

'I'm hardly likely to. What the hell is the matter with you? Are you so jealous of what I have that you want to destroy it?'

'Listen to me, Grace.' Douglas responds. 'Those two are out to cause trouble. I'm just giving us leverage.'

I open my mouth to object, but the door opens. Lottie looks from one to the other of us.

'Hey,' Douglas says. 'You ready, Munchkin?'

'What were you talking about?'

'Nothing,' I say, handing over her rucksack with a kiss. It's scary how perceptive my daughter can be. 'Be good for Daddy.'

Cassie calls. 'Are you coming tomorrow evening?'

I walk upstairs with the phone. Cora has big ears. 'Coming where?'

'Cherry's party. I'm sure it's the last thing you want, but I thought I'd ask. It might do you good.'

I remember now. The invite was issued a couple of weeks ago. Cherry is about to be forty; most of my friends are ten years older than me. It doesn't matter, except that, in many ways, I feel so much older than them. She's having an official party to celebrate next week, to which Nick, Lottie and I are invited but won't be going. Tomorrow is the unofficial celebration; the one where Cherry reverts to her early twenties and shrugs off the cloak of motherhood.

'Anna's coming,' Cassie adds when I don't immediately answer. 'Cherry thought it would be a good way for her to get to know us. We'll get her pissed.' She giggles.

I bite my fingernail, thinking about Anna letting her hair down, maybe opening up a little, maybe even admitting that she met Nick that evening. 'Yes, OK. I could do with getting out of here.'

'Good girl. And if something happens, we'll stick you in a cab home.'

TAISIE

July 2000

SHE CAME UP TO THE ATTIC, NOT TO HIDE, BUT BECAUSE she didn't want to play out of principle. She was too old for stupid games. The window was open, the curtains billowing and the rain coming in, the windowsill pooled with water. Taisie ran to close it, banging it shut, and jumped, her hand flying to her chest. Izzy was hiding between the bed and the wall, tear-stained and pale.

'Bloody hell, you gave me a fright! What's the matter?'

Izzy rubbed her face, leaving a smut below her left eye. 'Nothing.'

'Bollocks. Tell me what's happened. Has someone said something to you?' The boys could be mean to her. Rory told her she was ugly once.

'No.'

Taisie tried to pull her out, but Izzy shrank back, so she sank to the floor and put her arm around her sister's thin shoulders. The bare boards tickled her sunburnt thighs. 'So what is it?'

Izzy curled her body over her knees. She smelled of

attic dust and BO. She was growing up. Taisie would have to have a chat with her about personal hygiene, since their mother evidently wasn't going to.

'What is it, Izzy?'

'Leave me alone. I'm not telling you, OK?'

'Yes you are. I'm your big sister. I care about you and I can help.'

After a second, Izzy spoke, but so quietly Taisie had to strain to hear. 'He kissed me.'

Her chest tightened. 'Who kissed you?'

'Nick. And he put his hand here.' She touched her right breast.

Taisie went still. '*What?* That wanker. I'm going to tell Mum.'

'No, don't. Please, Taisie. Don't say anything. It's embarrassing.'

'You have to tell her yourself, then.'

'No! I won't, and you mustn't. Promise me, or I'm not going to help you. And I won't speak to you ever again.'

Taisie held up her hands. 'All right. Don't be so melodramatic.'

'I'm not melodramatic.' She folded her arms across her chest and stuck her bottom lip out. 'Can we do your plan now?'

'Don't be silly. It's belting out there. We can do it tomorrow.'

But Izzy was adamant, fists tightly curled, her body shaking, an explosion building inside her, like a toddler about to throw a tantrum. 'It's not cold. And I want to do it now.'

Above them the rain battered the skylight, but Izzy

was right, it was warm and muggy. Taisie had played the scene out in her mind many times since last night, imagining her mother's face, her relief and gratitude, her pride in her eldest daughter. It would go down in family lore. The idea of not doing it, of letting the opportunity slip away, was too tragic to entertain. And Izzy being so upset helped; she could blame it on Nick. It would serve him right.

'Let's go through it one more time, then,' she said. 'You go to the river. I'll be right behind you. I'll shout from the woods so that you hear me coming and have time to go in. You swim out a couple of yards and then you scream – don't go any further and make sure you can still touch the bottom with your toes. Then I'll save you. You've got to act it properly though, Iz, in case anyone sees, or there's no point doing it at all. So no laughing, especially when I carry you back. Mum's got to believe you were really in trouble.'

Izzy was practically jumping with impatience. 'I won't. I promise. I'll tell Mum that I thought I was going to drown and that you were amazing.'

Taisie hugged her. 'I will be amazing. Don't you worry.'

A scream, followed by a burst of laughter, startled them. A door slammed. Taisie and Izzy crept out on to the landing, then took the back stairs into the snug and to the old scullery door.

'Go,' Taisie said. 'I'll count to sixty and then I'll come after you.'

Izzy scooted off, pulling her cardigan over her head to protect her from the rain, and Taisie counted, eyes closed. As she stood there, two cool hands covered her eyes, making her cry out in irritation, thinking it was Alex or Rory. But as soon as she tried to pull them off, she knew who it was. The hands were far too big and clean-smelling to belong to either of her brothers.

GRACE

Saturday, 21 April 2018

'ANOTHER ONE?' CORA COMMENTS AS I POUR MYSELF A second glass of white wine.

I can feel myself blush. I put the bottle down, my glass half full. I only wanted to dull the voice in my head.

'What time are you going out?' she asks. 'You don't want to turn up already tipsy. It isn't dignified.'

'I'm not going out.'

I said yes to Cassie on impulse, but I've had time to think better of it. I'll only want to turn round and go home the moment I've got there. I've already texted Cassie to let her know. She understands.

'Really?' Cora says, not bothering to hide her disappointment. 'Is it that detective inspector? He's not going to think any the worse of you.'

'It's not the inspector. I just don't feel up to it.'

She looks at me through narrowed eyes. 'Won't you be letting your friends down?'

'They'll understand.'

She wanders over to stand where I usually do, her back against the counter. She even echoes my posture, arms loosely folded around her stomach, the small of her back against the edge, one ankle crossed over the other. The hostess's perch.

'What a shame.'

Tim appears, wearing Nick's leather slippers. 'You haven't got your face on.' To give him credit, he doesn't look as disappointed as his wife.

'She's not going out after all,' Cora says. 'I've told her she should.'

'Of course you should,' Tim says. 'It'll perk you up. You don't want to spend your Saturday night hanging out with the oldies.'

'You need your friends, Grace,' Cora says. 'Don't push people away.'

It's the first thing she's said to me that I agree with. Since last Sunday, apart from the coffee morning that I floated through like I was on an acid trip, I've avoided my friends. I can't believe it's only been a week. It feels like a month has gone by. My phone beeps to tell me I have a message. I glance at it. It's from Douglas, and my stomach drops. It must be about Lottie.

Lottie told me Tim's been reading her bedtime stories. I don't want that happening again.

I glance up at Tim. He's decanting Toffee's food into his bowl.

I type back. *You're being paranoid.*

I'm being careful. This isn't a suggestion. This is what I expect you to do. Do you understand?

I don't answer at first, because I don't know what to

say. Instead I scrape my chair back and take my glass to the sink, tip out the dregs of my wine and wash it up. On second thoughts, I can't stay here.

Cora brightens when I tell her.

It feels all wrong to be dressing up, but I make myself flick through my clothes. I pick skinny black jeans, a silky green top with the corners of the shoulders cut away in two large scoops, another scoop for my cleavage; the highest heels I possess, lifting me four inches in a pair of studded black boots. I wet my hair, rub in some mousse and blow-dry it upside down. I put make-up on, add a brighter lipstick, stare critically at my reflection and wrinkle my nose. Trying too hard, it makes me look like I want people to think I don't care. Douglas hated it if I overdid it. He said it demeaned me. Nick isn't keen either, but he's kinder about it. I brush the oomph out of my hair and tone down the lipstick. My phone dings and I pick it up, expecting it to be Cassie or one of the others, but it's Douglas. I never responded to his last message. He won't like that.

So? his text says. *Have you finished mulling it over? I need to know I can trust you, Grace.*

I tap out a curt response.

Lottie would tell me if there was anything about Tim that made her feel uncomfortable. She certainly wouldn't willingly spend time with him. You don't have to worry.

He doesn't reply.

'My goodness, don't you look stunning,' Tim says when I totter downstairs.

* * *

158

I get into the people carrier, hired for the occasion, squeezing into the back row between Mara and Cassie, while Anna sits between Cherry and Kit. Susanna sits beside the driver. I note Anna's easy familiarity with these women. I didn't know she'd become so pally with my friends. Then I spot Mara flicking Kit a glance. Anna is pissed. She must have had a drink or two before she came out. I feel for her; she's nervous, keen to be seen as fun, to be part of the in-crowd, so scared of missing out that she's overcompensating. I resolve to be extra nice to her.

We head north through South London, over Waterloo Bridge and up to the West End where we tip out into the noisy gaiety of Soho and saunter into Astra. It's a long time since I've done anything like this, a long time since any of us have. The noise blasts us as we mince down the stairs on our silly heels, a heavy beat that vibrates through my body and lifts my spirits.

Cassie puts her mouth close to my ear. 'Any news?'

I shake my head and pull away, get to the bar. We order luminous cocktails, cram round a tiny table, sharing squat, velvet-covered stools and yell at each other. I demolish a delicious, icy banana daiquiri, enjoying the intense hit of sweetness and alcohol.

Anna starts to sway in time to the music, glossy hair falling forward as she hunches her shoulders, closes her eyes and dips her head.

I stand up. 'Want to hit the dance floor?' I survey the group. 'Anyone?'

They look at me oddly. No one expects me to be the life and soul.

* * *

159

The speculation begins when we sit down again, fresh drinks in our hands. My companions seem to think it's acceptable to theorize, to suggest, to repeat anecdotes that are no more than urban myths, unaware that my mind has already covered every possible scenario. But even if it hadn't, the onslaught feels like an attack.

'Did you read that article about . . .'

'God, how well do we know our husbands?'

'What about old girlfriends? Have you checked none of them have been in touch?'

'I heard about this girl, well, woman really . . .'

'Grace, you mustn't blame yourself . . .'

'Do you think the police will want to talk to any of us?'

All this yelled above the pumping dance-floor beat. Some of it I don't catch. I answer the questions, but they're so intrusive that I begin to feel as though I'm under siege. The only person not part of the barrage is Anna. She's quieter now, her energy apparently burnt off. From time to time I feel her eyes on me.

'Was your sex life still good?' Cherry says.

Granted, this is her party and she's hammered, but that question is too much. I shout that I'm going to the loo and stagger off. A man comes out of the crowd, drunk and leering, putting himself in front of me, his hands spread wide, mouthing a question. *Dance with me?* I recoil instinctively, my ankle buckles on its high heel, and I go down, sprawling across the floor. Someone laughs, and Anna leaps to my rescue, pulling me up and helping me hobble to the cloakroom. She pushes me through the cloakroom doors.

I shut myself into a cubicle. Other people bang in and out, using the loos, gossiping through the partition walls, while I lean on my knees with my head in my hands.

Anna taps on the flimsy door. 'You coming out?' She pauses as a woman bangs into the cubicle next to mine and retches. 'It's not exactly five-star luxury in here.' Her voice is fuzzy at the edges.

'Dunno. I might do when they've all left.'

She laughs. 'Come on. Let's get our coats and sneak off. They won't be bothered.'

I open the door and go to the sink, turning to smile, grateful that she understands. 'I'm not dragging you away when you're having a good time.'

'I've had enough.' She pulls her fingers through her hair and yawns. 'You all know each other so well and the drunker you get, the cosier you become. I'm better off leaving before it becomes obvious I'm the lemon.'

'Anna! You are no such thing. I don't feel part of it tonight either. I'll stay if you want me to.' I'm prepared to hang around for another half-hour if my presence gives her confidence.

'No. Really, I'm done.'

'OK. But we're not sneaking off. We'll say goodbye properly.'

In the event, I acknowledge that Anna is right. They don't mind her being there, are pleased she came, but are equally happy that she's leaving them to it now. As for me, Mara reaches out and takes my hand, and the others jump up and surround me, insist I call if I feel down and if there is anything they can do to help, I

161

mustn't hesitate, and they will have Lottie whenever. No problem. Only say the word.

'Call me,' Cassie says, and I can see that she's hurt that I've chosen Anna to lean on. But the truth is, I've recognized in Anna someone as torn to pieces and patched-up as myself.

I open my eyes. I must have dozed off. 'Where are we?'

'About to cross the river,' Anna says.

I lean forward as we sweep on to Waterloo Bridge, so that I can enjoy the light show. The drink must have made me maudlin because the Millennium Wheel moves me to tears, and so does the white dome of St Paul's and the skyscrapers with their aircraft-warning lights, like a cherry on top, and the cranes rising like aliens from the streets.

'So, tell me about Lottie's father,' Anna says. 'What happened with him?'

'I was too young. It didn't work out.'

'But you must have loved him, to have his child?'

I pause. 'I think it was more infatuation.'

'On his side or yours?'

I smile. 'On mine. Douglas doesn't get all hot under the collar about love and romance. I was desperately young when I met him and had a lot of growing up to do. I stayed until I saw that what I was doing was growing into the mould he'd made for me. I needed to find out who I was, for myself.'

'Have you ever wondered whether it was you, not him?'

'I don't understand.'

'I mean, if you were projecting your own lack of

self-esteem on to him. That it wasn't him you weren't good enough for, but yourself?'

It's an odd thing for her to say but I give the question some consideration. Have I blamed my own failures on him? My self-esteem was dangerously low when we met, but the momentum to improve came from Douglas, not me.

'Admit it,' she says teasingly. 'He was actually good for you.'

'Are you serious? Or are you playing devil's advocate?'

She laughs. 'Devil's advocate. He and Lottie have a lovely relationship, don't they? She's so lucky having two dads. I wish Kai had Ben.'

A silence falls, and I almost doze off before she speaks again.

'Does Nick mind you seeing so much of your ex?'

I rub the crick out of the back of my neck. I feel blurry, and not really up to this conversation. 'I wouldn't say he's Douglas's biggest fan, but he knows how much Lottie loves him and he wouldn't mess that relationship up for the world.'

'Why did you split up?'

'What is this? The third degree?'

'Sorry. Don't tell me if you don't want to.'

'I don't suppose it matters.' I blow out a breath. 'Among other things, I caught him in bed with another woman.'

'Shit,' Anna says. 'That must have been awful. Why on earth did you go back to him?'

Did I tell her that? I must have done. I'm so tired, I can't remember exactly what I've said.

'Good question.'

'Sorry,' she says. 'I'm incurably nosy.'

I smile. There's something about being drunk in a cab that invites intimacy. It's seductive. 'My life had been chaotic; Douglas gave me rules, he gave me structure and he had expectations.'

'You haven't mentioned love.'

I don't answer, because I can't. I didn't know what love was back then. I look out of the window, feeling a sense of relief as we leave Battersea behind. We're on the home stretch.

'He was a substitute parent,' Anna supplies. 'I can understand that.'

I drag my gaze away from the windows of a bus going in the other direction. 'You can?'

'Ben was a lot older than me.'

'What was he like?'

'He was serious, and kind. Very bright. How did you and Nick get together?'

A neat deflection. 'At a charity bash I was helping to organize. The company he works for were major contributors. They still are. He changed my life.'

I feel her eyes on my profile and glance at her. 'What?'

'First Douglas and then Nick. Do you always need a man to change your life? Sorry,' she says, after a pause. 'That was unfair.'

'No, you're right. I met them both at low points and they helped me get on my feet. I . . . um . . . I had been in care before I met Douglas, you see.'

'Oh.'

I don't look at her, I don't need to. I can hear the surprise in her voice.

164

'I'm not what I seem,' I say with a smile that feels weirdly coy. 'This is all a facade.'

'A good one,' she deadpans. 'I thought you were the perfect South London yummy mummy.'

I laugh. 'Hardly . . . Anna, none of my friends knows about this, so please don't talk about it.'

'You haven't told Cassie? I thought you were so close.'

I feel a stab of guilt. 'We are, but that time is behind me. I don't want it seeping into the life I've got now.'

'No one would even care, Grace. They'd respect you for it.'

'Still, please don't say anything.'

'I won't say a word; I promise.' She takes her phone out of her bag, swipes the screen then puts it back, turning to me eagerly. 'And I get it, I really do.'

'Thank you. Nick needed me as much as I needed him, you know,' I add, wanting her to know that it wasn't only me who needed saving. 'He said it had been years since he'd felt so happy. He told me once that he couldn't believe I'd chosen him.'

'Really?' She sounds disapproving. 'He sounds needy. Like your little rescue dog.'

'He isn't like that at all,' I protest. 'He's the strongest person I know.'

Or I thought he was. I look down at my hands and a tear drops into the dip between my knuckles.

'What if he's left me? What if it's something I've done?'

'Don't be silly; you couldn't have done anything so bad that he'd leave without telling you why. That would have been the act of a coward.'

165

I dart a look at her as the cab turns into Camomile Avenue and she fumbles in her bag for her keys, but there's nothing apart from concern and sympathy registering. Even so, the moment sent a shock wave through my body, because in that split second I believed she knew what I had done. It was a gut feeling caused by an almost imperceptible change in her tone. A tiny ripple that disturbed my subconscious.

But of course she doesn't know; she can't do, because the only person who knows is Douglas.

I stagger through Sunday morning, hungover and miserable, keeping to the sanctuary of my study or reading in my bedroom. I listen to Tim and Cora's movements, the little conversation they have, the hum of the radio or television, footsteps, the clink of cutlery; sounds that once upon a time meant Nick was downstairs. At lunch they go out to visit friends and I come downstairs to root around the cupboards and fridge for comfort food, hoping to feel relief, but feeling weird in the empty house. I give myself small jobs: I wander round with a damp cloth dipped in washing-up liquid, cleaning the finger marks off the light switches; I put on a wash; I go through my diary for the next week; I finish typing up an inventory that should have been in on Friday; I take Toffee for a walk, driving to a park a couple of miles away so that I don't bump into anyone I know. I feel like I did when my grandmother died. Dumb with misery.

That evening, I find Cora sitting white-faced on my sofa, a photograph of Nick in her hand. This is real. Her son may not come back. For the first time, I feel genuine

166

sympathy for her. We are both in pain. I wouldn't wish this situation on my worst enemy.

I sit down beside her and reach out, my hand hovering above hers before taking it. We never touch each other; the closest we've ever come is an air-kiss. It feels unnatural, and unnerving.

'He'll come home,' I say.

She drags her hand out from under mine and wedges it between her knees. 'He's all we have.'

Her tone of voice is odd, and I can't help wondering if there's a double meaning to her words. I think about the money that's been leaving Nick's bank account for God only knows how many years. He is all they have between them and what? Losing their home? Destitution? I have no idea how desperate they really are.

NICK

July 2000

HIS BODY FEELS HEAVY. HE SHAKES HIS HANDS, MOVES every limb to unlock his joints, then crawls out of the eaves space and crouches at the top of the stairs listening to the house. He hears Rory squeal with laughter, and thudding footsteps. Then he frowns and touches his lips, the wisps of his dream dissipating to reveal which parts were real. Izzy kissed him while he slept. Shit.

He crawls on to the landing and looks out of the window, in time to see her vanish round the side of the swimming pool changing room. Christ. Why did girls have to be so dramatic? He'd better check she's OK. He runs down the stairs unseen, listening for the adults as he grabs a raincoat off the hook in the boot room and shoves his feet into wellington boots. The murmur of female conversation makes him hold his breath, but no one appears. He lets himself out through the side door and runs, enjoying the cooler air and the rain on his face after the oppressive stuffiness of the cubbyhole.

His feet leave dark imprints in the grass, then wet patches

on the paving that surrounds the swimming pool. The rain breaks the surface of the water, thousands of rings spreading. A dead wasp undulates, buffeted by the wake of an ever-expanding circle. He runs on, holding his breath as he passes the fermenting stink of the compost heap and ducks with relief into the shelter of the woods.

He calls Izzy's name but there's no answer, just the rhythmic sounds his feet make as they hit wet mud and leaves, and his breath as it puffs in and out of his lungs. He stops, his hand pressed against a tree, doubled over with a stitch, panting. The river is audible above the rain now. He sets off again, following the path until Izzy's skinny figure appears through the trees. She has her back to him.

'Izzy!' he shouts. 'Iz!'

She turns slowly, squinting at him through the rain. It's hard to make out her expression, but he smiles anyway, wanting to reassure her that they're still mates; to reassure himself.

'You look like a drowned rat,' he says, walking towards her.

As he comes closer he sees fear written on her face. It stops him in his tracks. Does she think what happened in the cubbyhole was his fault? Is that what she's going to tell the adults when they want to know why she's dripping wet? Shit. He's got to make sure that doesn't happen. No one's going to believe his story over hers, because no one is on his side apart from his parents. Possibly Angus too, he thinks, but even Angus might not support him when he sees the state Izzy is in. He takes a step forward and she screams at him to go away.

GRACE

Monday, 23 April 2018

'DRAWN A BLANK THERE, I'M AFRAID.' DETECTIVE
Inspector Marsh has come to see me after interviewing
Nick's boss. 'There's been nothing irregular – the company accountants have been scrutinizing any transac-
tions Nick's been part of. They've been at it since Thursday
and have found nothing to suggest any illegal dealings;
so far, at least. I think you can rest easy on that score.
Nick was a model employee: intelligent, trustworthy and
exceptionally good at his job.'

I don't feel relief, because I never doubted Nick's integrity, but I'm glad it's been officially confirmed. It's a tick
in a box. The police can move on to the things that really
matter, the things I've been insisting are relevant.

Marsh tugs Toffee's collar absently. The dog gazes up
at him.

'You've been around the block, haven't you, boy?' he
croons, running the pad of his thumb over the inch-long
scar that crosses Toffee's nose, while my fickle little
mongrel gazes at him slavishly. 'I'm sure I've arrested

someone who looks just like you.' He twitches the file again. Opening it and flicking through the meagre sheaf of papers, as if something useful might appear. 'What about your female friends?'

'What about them?'

'We can't rule out the possibility that there's a woman involved.'

'I think I'd know if he was having an affair. I definitely would if it was a friend.' I draw up a mental list. Kit, Mara, Susanna, Cherry and Cassie. Of all of them Cassie is the one Nick knows best, the one I'm closest to, but she's not the type. I wouldn't believe it of any of them. And Anna, of course. She's never far from my mind.

'What about casual liaisons?'

'Highly unlikely.' Nick goes on business trips, but I can't imagine him sneaking into a female colleague's hotel room or picking up someone in a bar.

Marsh looks at me pityingly. 'He left the family home only hours after asking you to marry him. Maybe it's as simple as a case of cold feet.'

'A bit extreme, don't you think? Nick is honest. He would have said something.'

'Men can be cowards when it comes to women.'

'It has nothing to do with that, nothing directly at least. It's to do with the past. I'm convinced that the holiday, those three families getting together, and a child dying, is at the heart of this. Something threw Nick so badly that he had to leave. The brother of that little girl got in touch with him, and two days later he was gone.' *Day Zero*, I think suddenly; and it fits. The day of Nick's departure now has a name. 'How much more do you need?'

Marsh gives Toffee a pat, scratches his nose, then picks up his phone. 'I'll be having a chat with Lorna and their daughters tomorrow morning. But not formally, you understand. The trouble is, Ms Trelawney, we have no evidence that a crime has taken place, so any interviewing or following up has to be fitted in alongside more pressing investigations.'

When he goes, he takes Nick's computer and laptop with him, loading them into the boot of his car. I wander back up to Nick's study and gaze at his empty desk. I'm losing more of him by the day.

Later, while I'm in John Lewis looking at flooring for work, I get an email from Nick's company. In the Subject box it says Re: Absenteeism. It had been sent to Nick, cc'd to me, presumably because they knew there was a good chance it wouldn't reach him.

23 April 2018

Dear Nick

We regret to inform you that your employment is being terminated, effective from 31 May 2018 unless you return to work with an acceptable reason for your absence by Monday, 30 April. This decision has been reached with great regret.

Upon termination, all benefits associated with this position will cease to be valid. You are requested to return your company car, laptop computer and any other property belonging to the company before 31 May to the Human Resources department. If this is not done, the property will be collected from your address on 1 June 2018.

Please keep in mind that you are bound by our confidentiality policy. Any information that was received during the course of your work, regarding our customers, company, partners, etc. must not be disclosed to any party. Such information must also be deleted from all personal devices. In addition, you have signed a non-solicitation clause as part of your employment contract. This binds you until the date specified.

You are entitled to your salary up until 31 May 2018. Severance pay will amount to £9731.00 and will be paid on 30 June 2018. Because you are in breach of the terms of your contract, you will not be entitled to any other compensation.

This decision is non-reversible. We advise you to refer to our disciplinary action policy. If you have questions or would like any clarification, the Human Resources department remains at your disposal for up to seven working days after your last day of employment.

Yours sincerely
Philip Colville
Head of Legal
Financial Logistics

Monday, 30 April is next week. I cannot believe that after all his loyalty and hard work, and frankly, all the money he's made for that company, they could send this, without even a phone call. The tone of the email is so cold.

I push open the doors to the stairwell where it's quiet, away from the busy shop floor, and call the office. I get Phillipa on the phone. I'm spitting I'm so angry.

'I know,' she says. 'We're all absolutely horrified here. The police came in, Management called a meeting and that was that.'

'They're total shits. Can you put me through to Angus?'

'I can't, Grace.'

'I'm sorry? I don't understand.'

She breathes out. 'He's asked me not to. He will get back to you, only not today. He wants you to have a chance to absorb it first.'

'Oh, lovely. He doesn't want a messy scene. What a coward.'

'Grace, please don't overreact.'

'Overreact! Nick has only been gone a week and I get this?'

'You should have been honest from the get-go,' she sighs.

'I know,' I say, swallowing my anger. This is not her fault. 'I'm sorry, I really am, but I was trying to protect him. Why didn't you warn me about this?' She and Nick have worked together for five years. We went to her wedding.

'He may come back,' she says. Her voice becomes conspiratorial. 'Look, Grace, I don't know what's going on, but Angus and Nick had a massive row on that last day.'

174

My nerves tingle. 'You didn't tell me.'

'I couldn't. Discretion is highly valued here. I wouldn't dream of gossiping about conversations between Angus and his employees.'

I reluctantly decide it wouldn't be politic to ask her why she is now. 'What did they argue about?'

'I don't know. I walked into Angus's office and walked straight back out again. They were right in each other's faces.'

I remember now that he was at home when I got back from school with Lottie on that Friday. He claimed he had left work early because he had a presentation to focus on. Is this the real reason – that he needed to draw a line between the blistering row with his boss and his home? If so, why didn't he want me to know about it? Surely that's what being someone's partner is all about.

'Grace?' Phillipa says.

'It's OK. Thanks.'

I end the call and run down the stairs and out through the back of the shop to Cavendish Square where I've parked the Vespa. I check my watch: it's just gone one o'clock. It's my week for school pick-ups, but if I hurry I can get to the City and still be back in time.

175

TAISIE

July 2000

'NOT PLAYING WITH THE OTHERS?' TIM SAID.

Taisie's eyes were glued to his face. She seriously thought she might collapse in a heap. 'I'm pretending to. But it's a bit childish for me.'

He laughed, and she laughed back, although she was worried that he was laughing at her, not with her.

'You are so charming,' Tim said.

'I'm not really. I'm actually a nightmare. You should talk to Mum. Well, actually, you shouldn't.' She was babbling, nervous as hell, caught in his gaze.

'Well, if you're a nightmare, you're the fun sort,' he said.

Taisie shivered happily. He didn't say anything else and she couldn't think of anything to say. She waited, feeling like an idiot, thinking she should go, calculating where Izzy would be, but wanting a few more seconds of this agony. Then he made an odd groaning sound, as if it was a huge effort to keep his hands off her, and that clinched it. With more confidence than she felt, she touched his cheek and he grabbed her hand and pressed his lips into her palm. Oh my God, she thought, the feelings that pulsed through her ... she couldn't describe, but her knees practically buckled.

'We can't stay here,' he said. 'We'll be found.'

He stuck his head into the hall, checked there was no one around, then propelled her across the parquet floor and into Angus's study, his hand on the small of her back.

'No one would dare come in here,' he said, closing the door.

She stood, frozen, her heart thumping, unsure what exactly was going on, whether she wanted it, or whether she should get away.

'Anastasia,' he murmured.

The way he said her full name sent shudders through her. He pulled her in to him and kissed her on the lips. First softly, then harder, his tongue pushing between her teeth. When his hand crept under her top, touching the underside of her breast, she thrust him away, shaking her head, suddenly shy.

'What's up, baby?'

'I didn't think you liked me.'

She bit her bottom lip, and he tipped her chin up with his finger.

'You're fishing for compliments. You know perfectly well that I haven't been able to take my eyes off you.'

He bent to kiss her again, and she kissed him back, letting her tongue press tantalizingly against his before wriggling out of his clasp.

'I'm sorry,' she said. 'I'm really sorry, but I've got to go.'

She looked at the door, then back at him, imploringly.

Izzy would be at the river by now, waiting. She wished she hadn't let her go. She hadn't thought it through, only dwelt on the glorious aftermath. What if Izzy got impatient and came back to the house? Their parents would want to know what she'd been doing outside all by herself. Izzy caught colds easily; Taisie would get the blame.

'No, I'm the one who should be sorry, sweetheart.' Tim held her against him and kissed the top of her head, murmuring, 'God, you drive me crazy.'

She put her hands against his chest and pushed him away reluctantly. He smelled so lovely, she wanted to bury her nose in his shirt.

He dropped his hands with a sigh. 'Are you cross with me?'

'No!' She could hardly be cross with him when her lips were throbbing from his kiss. 'I liked it. I've never been kissed like that before.' She blushed, embarrassed at how naive she sounded, but the hungry look on Tim's face reassured her. She was already anticipating the possibility of more.

He smiled softly, took a strand of her hair and carefully tucked it behind her ear, brushing her cheekbone with his fingers. 'I care very much about you, Anastasia. But we need to keep this secret.'

'I won't tell anyone. I swear.'

178

GRACE

Monday, 23 April 2018

THE OFFICES OF FINANCIAL LOGISTICS ARE OFF
Fenchurch Street. The lane is so narrow that I have to
leave the Vespa on the main road, and I don't get much
of an impression of the building as I approach, just my
reflection in the glass wall. I enter through revolving
doors into a cavernous space and walk up to a shiny
desk manned by three receptionists. It's an old-fashioned
concern dressed in sparkly new clothes. They moved to
this building a year ago, but Nick preferred the familiar
scruffier offices down the road.

I head over to the desk because I've been clocked by
the security guard, his attention drawn by my shifty
behaviour. I place my helmet on the polished glass surface and ask for Angus Moody. I am still fuming. I
understood the message behind the standard format.
Let's draw a tidy line and move on. Well, I am not a tidy
person.

The receptionist studies her monitor. 'Do you have a
meeting? I don't have a note of it.'

I feign surprise that she could possibly doubt me. 'Yes, I do. One thirty.'

'I'll call his PA,' she says. 'She'll be able to help you.'

That's the last thing I want. 'That won't be necessary,' I say, maintaining my professional demeanour. 'I'll give him a call.' I turn on my heel, trying for an air of offended aplomb and march to the revolving doors. As I go out a group of men and women come in, so I keep going round, following them back inside and trying to camouflage myself in their midst. The security guard isn't fooled and eyes me with hostility, moving forward as I hurry to the lifts. As luck would have it, one set of doors sweeps open and I dart in, cramming myself into the corner. The group get in with me, the doors closing before the guard can reach them, and the last thing I see is him glaring at me and lifting his walkie-talkie to his mouth.

I scrutinize the brushed-steel buttons. Someone presses five, someone else presses eleven.

'Oh damn,' I say. 'She told me which floor Angus Moody is on, but it's gone out of my head.'

'Fourteen,' someone says, and presses that button.

I release my breath. After the excitement, reality hits. The security guard will by now have asked the receptionist who I'd wanted to see and will have relayed that message upstairs. Someone will be waiting for me. My stomach rumbles loudly, demanding lunch, and everyone pretends not to have noticed. I watch the numbers rise, then on impulse get out at the eleventh floor.

'You wanted fourteen,' the helpful man says. 'This is eleven.'

'I need the exercise,' I say with a smile, as the doors close again.

I find the door to the stairwell and walk up three flights to the top floor, inch open the door and peer out. There are two people conferring outside the lifts. The security guard and Phillipa. I wait until they step forward, the lift door opening, and then I dart out and walk down the carpeted corridor, spot the ladies' room and go in. I count to ten then open the door a crack. There's no one there. I hurry down the corridor, noting the portraits hanging on the walls, the dark-grey carpeting, the masculine feel of the place. I knock twice at Angus Moody's door, a loud, confident rap and turn the handle before anyone inside has a chance to respond.

Moody is on his phone. He watches me walk in and carries on with his conversation. He shows no surprise, so he must have been warned. I stand in front of his desk, feeling like an idiot, revved up and deprived of my moment.

He finishes his call. There's a knock and Phillipa comes in, looking flustered, but Angus waves her away. He waits until the door is closed, then smiles at me.

'What can I do for you, Grace?' His voice is suave, unflustered, reminding me of Douglas.

I have no preamble, no way of working up to what I need to say, so I dive right in.

'Nick has worked for you for years. What were you thinking?' To my horror, tears well in my eyes. I swipe them away. 'Do you have no feelings? He's missing; he could be hurt, or sick or worse. I'm going out of my

mind with worry, and you send *this*. It's a standard letter, for God's sake.' I fumble clumsily in my bag, pull
out my phone, make sure the letter is on the screen and
place it on the desk in front of him, push it closer with
the tips of my fingers.

He runs his eye over its contents. 'Take a seat.'

'I don't want to sit down. I want an apology and a
retraction.'

'Sit, Grace.' His voice is kind, but firm. 'Please,' he
adds.

I feel like a surly schoolgirl, but I do sit, perched on
the edge of a leather chair. His manner is soothing,
avuncular.

'You came to our house,' I say. 'You came to see him.
What was all that about if he means so little to you?'

'I was genuinely concerned, and I was in the area.'

'A bit of a coincidence, wasn't it?'

'Not really. We visit those friends regularly. Look,
Grace, I am very sorry this has happened. And I whole-
heartedly agree with you, the email is crass and
insensitive. It should never have been sent.'

'No, it shouldn't.'

Despite myself, I am calmed. There is so much understanding in his voice that I'm lulled into thinking he's
about to metaphorically rip the letter up and retract.

'But this isn't a charity,' he says. Disconcertingly, he's
still smiling. 'And I can't treat Nick differently from anyone else in my employ. It wouldn't be ethical. He's failed
to let us know that he won't be in. He's missed crucial
meetings and deadlines and in doing so has caused the
firm, and me, embarrassment. I'm being generous in

182

allowing him until the end of the month to give me a satisfactory explanation.'

'How can he give you that if he's in trouble?'

'We don't know that he is.'

'You've had a visit from the police. That's a big clue.'

He sighs and picks up his expensive-looking pen, then lays it down again. 'Nick is probably having a midlife crisis. He's gone off to find himself, revisit his youth. For all you know he's sunning himself on a beach in Thailand. He won't be the first man to do that. Maybe he wanted out of the relationship but was too much of a coward to tell you to your face. Surely you've considered that?'

I stare at him, outraged. 'You couldn't care less, could you?'

'Of course I care,' he says. 'Please tell me what I can do to help you.'

'Tell me what you and Nick rowed about that Friday.'

He looks surprised. 'We might have disagreed. We do from time to time. I consider it part of running a healthy company.'

I shake my head. 'No. Phillipa says you had a massive row.' I feel a twinge of guilt, even as I say it. I shouldn't have named her specifically.

He sighs. 'We argued about an unhappy client. It happens. Water under the bridge. Obviously, I can't go into details.'

'Obviously.' I cross my arms and hold his gaze, refusing to be the first to look away. 'I'd like you to ask Phillipa to give me access to Nick's emails and search history.'

He laughs out loud. 'You can't seriously believe I'd do that.'

'I just want to see if there's anything personal in there, anything that might help find him. Phillipa is welcome to see what I look at. You owe him.'

He raises one eyebrow. 'That's a strange logic. The police have already had a look. They didn't find anything particularly helpful.'

He smooths his silver hair back, lifts his glasses and rubs his eye with his fist. The gesture makes him look younger, more approachable.

'Nick loves this job and has great respect for you. He would never have done this voluntarily. Something has happened to him.'

He lifts an eyebrow. 'Clearly.'

'I know that you've known Nick since his teens. Why would you have kept that secret?'

He looks as though he truly pities me. 'It's no secret, unless Nick had some reason for not telling you. I'm surprised he hasn't.'

So am I. I try something else. 'Can you tell me anything about that holiday, when Nick's family came to stay? I've talked about it with his parents, but they haven't been able to tell me much. I know you were kind to him.'

He hesitates, then nods. 'He was having a tough time. Particularly from the older girls. I felt sorry for him – I hadn't forgotten what it was like to be an adolescent boy. It was three against one, poor kid. So I talked to him and encouraged him. It wasn't a chore. I liked him.'

I throw down my final card. 'And yet you still pulled the rug out from his father's restaurant business.'

To my surprise he laughs. 'Christ, not that again. Business is business. I would hardly be the CEO of my own hedge-fund company if I allowed sentiment to get in the way of decision-making.'

'So you don't care?'

His eyes pierce through me. 'Not about that, no.'

I nod slowly. 'And Izzy Wells' death? You cared about that, I presume?'

His eyes turn to flint. I've gone too far. Of course he cares.

'I apologize,' I say quickly. 'That was uncalled for.'

He waits before responding, then shrugs. His voice is curt, and I can feel the emotion reined in. 'It's the worst thing that's ever happened to me. It changed everything; ruined lives.'

He clasps the back of his neck and rubs it. His body language has been so spare until now that the gesture is shocking. He's been so careful not to give anything away. Maybe he's human, after all.

'What made you offer Nick a job?'

'He got in touch about interning with us a couple of years later. I didn't think I wanted any reminders, but in the end I agreed to see him, and I was glad I did. None of it was his fault, and he didn't deserve to have what happened affect his future. After university he worked for HSBC, and after that I took him on.'

'And now you've fired him.'

He sighs. 'Grace, I'll see what I can do. Of course, if he comes back before the end of the month, there won't be a problem. Beyond that, well, let's take one day at a time.'

'I've got to go.'

He gets up, pulls his jacket off the back of his chair and puts it on. He holds the door open for me and I follow him in silence back along the corridor to the lift. To my surprise he gets in with me and sees me all the way to the ground floor. Maybe he doesn't trust Phillipa.

'I very much hope things turn out well,' he says as he shows me out. 'I've always been fond of him.'

TAISIE

July 2000

'TAISIE.'

She stops in her tracks, her heart slamming.

'What were you doing in Angus's study? You know you're not allowed in there.'

Her mother was at the bottom of the stairs.

'I was hiding.'

She hoped to God Tim was listening and wouldn't come strolling out. Her lips felt bruised and swollen, and if the light hadn't been so bad in the hall she was certain her mother would have seen.

'It's out of bounds. You should know better.'

'OK, fine. Can I go now?'

She had to get to Izzy. The poor thing would be drenched, waiting for Taisie to appear. As long as she hadn't gone in already. Taisie was sure she had told her to wait until she heard her coming. She distinctly remembered saying that.

'Actually, no. While you're here. I need a quick word with you. In private.'

'Oh, not now, Mum.'

'Now,' her mother said sharply. 'Do as you're told.'

She rolled her eyes, but she followed her mother into the library. She wondered what was up. Mostly, her mother had no idea what was going on in Taisie's head and tended to assume she was fine because she was the oldest. Taisie's job was basically to set an example to her younger siblings and generally keep out of her mum's hair. She was all lovey-dovey when it suited her, but it was so unnatural it was embarrassing.

'Now don't fly at me, Taisie.' Her mother sat down on the sofa and patted the seat beside her. 'But I need to talk to you about your behaviour.'

Taisie remained standing. She was tense and twitching to go. 'My behaviour?' She stressed the second word, putting a question mark at the end. Nick must have moaned about her. She never had him down as a snitch.

'Your behaviour around Tim.'

Her stomach flipped. 'I don't . . .'

'Taisie, please. You're old enough to know precisely what you're doing. Listen, darling, I remember what it's like to be a teenage girl, to discover that you have sexual power, but you should tone it down. Considerably.'

Taisie drew in a sharp breath. 'What are you talking about?' Did her mum know where she had been?

Her mother smiled, giving her that look; the one that told Taisie she thought her eldest child was being deliberately obtuse. She probably did that with clients too, and colleagues. Bet she was popular at work.

'You've been flirting with Tim and it's beginning to embarrass us all. He's behaving very well in the circumstances, but it's obvious that it's awkward for him. And think about how poor Nick must be feeling. He must be mortified.'

'Oh my God.' Taisie curled her lip. 'Get off my case, Mum. Number one, I don't care what Nick thinks, and number two, that's gross. I've known Tim all my life.'

'Taisie.'

'I suppose I should be grateful,' she hissed. 'It makes a change from being totally ignored.'

'Now you're being ridiculous.'

'Right. Yeah. Silly me.'

Her mother hesitated, as if weighing up whether there was any point in continuing the argument, then said, in her best this-is-over voice, 'I'm glad we had this talk. So that's all clear then.'

'It's clear that you're jealous of me,' Taisie muttered.

'What did you say?'

'Nothing. Is that it?'

Her mother paused for a heartbeat, then raised her hand and flicked her fingers at Taisie. 'Yes. Off you go.'

God knows how many minutes had been wasted by her mother's lecture. She started to run, splashing through puddles, slipping on wet grass, throwing herself through the gate into the woods and down the churned-up footpath. She ran until it felt as though her lungs would burst, until she developed a stitch like a burning knife in her side. She doubled over, gasping for air. When she had her breath back she yelled Izzy's name and set off again, clutching her waist. Half a minute later, scratched and wet and muddy, she burst into the clearing and ran down to the river's edge.

'Iz? Izzy? Where are you?'

Taisie stood there, stumped. Izzy must be playing a trick on her, paying her back. There was no other explanation, no acceptable one anyway. She hadn't gone into the river, she had doubled back and was warm and dry and safe in the house. She walked down to the river's edge and stopped short.

Her sister's shoes were placed neatly side by side. But there was no sign of Izzy. No sign at all.

GRACE

Monday, 23 April 2018

WHEN LOTTIE AND I COME IN, HAVING DROPPED OFF
Hannah, Leila and Kai at their respective houses, Cora
is reading a book in the garden wrapped up in Nick's
sweater, the one I like to wear, a soft tartan rug over her
lap. Tim is on his knees beside the flower bed pulling
up a new crop of weeds, Toffee beside him sniffing
around, a robin looking down at them from the trellis.
It would be an idyllic scene if it wasn't my garden and
my rug and my dog. The house feels like a country under
occupation.

'Have you had a productive day?' Cora asks, putting
the magazine down. 'It's been lovely and quiet here.'

'I've done everything I needed to.'

Do I tell her about the email and my meeting with
Angus? I think I ought to, but I can't bear the idea that
she'll think her son wasn't valued. She's so proud of him. I
can't do that to her, not when I'm about to ask her to leave.

'Cora.' I take a deep breath. 'I'm sorry, but this isn't
working for me.' I wince inwardly, anticipating the fallout.

It's the right thing for me and Lottie. This weekend proved it. I felt unwelcome in my own home.

'What do you mean?'

I sit down on one of the wooden chairs and lean forward. 'You and Tim being here,' I say as gently as I can. 'I know how you're feeling, and that you're as worried as I am, but this is my home, and I'm feeling invaded. Things are difficult enough without having to worry about guests.'

'You surely don't see us as guests,' Tim says, his knees clicking as he stands up. He brushes dirt off his hands. 'We're family and we want to help.'

'I know you do, but I'm all right. Honestly.' I have coped in the past, I can cope now.

'Be that as it may,' Cora says, looking at me as though I'm a sulky teenager. 'Our house is unavailable, and I hardly think Nick would want his parents out on the streets.'

'Surely you can afford somewhere to stay. Airbnb?'

'I must say, I think you're being very unkind,' Cora says. 'You're not the only one going out of your mind with worry.'

'Please.' Even though I know it's futile I have to try and get through to them. 'I want to be on my own. Can't you understand that?'

'Oh, Grace,' Tim says. 'Don't shut yourself away.'

'I'm not shutting myself away, I just can't cope with having other people around.'

'We're hardly other people,' Cora sniffs. 'We are Nick's parents. We have a right to be here. If he's—'

'Cora,' Tim says. 'That's enough.' There's a warning in his voice that makes my nerves stand on end.

'If he's what?' I say. 'Dead? Well, he's not. All I'm asking is that you be a little more understanding of how I'm feeling.'

Cora contemplates me. 'This is not about you, Grace. It's about Nick.'

I speak carefully, trying to avoid outright antagonism at the same time as making myself perfectly clear. 'I understand that, and of course I respect your right to know what's going on. But I can call you if there's a development and you can come straight back.'

She sighs deeply, shaking her head, as if I'm a child who doesn't get it. 'I feel closer to him here.' A tear slides from her eye but she doesn't seem to notice it.

'Wouldn't you want to stay if it was Lottie?' Tim says.

'Why do you have to make it so hard for me?'

'In what way are we making it hard?' Cora demands. 'We're here if Lottie needs to be looked after. We help with the housework and we're happy to chip in for bills if you're having problems.'

'I'm not.' Not yet, at least. I have a nasty feeling I will if Nick doesn't come home before Angus's deadline. Not that these two would be much help. The idea of them 'chipping in' is laughable. If I could, I'd cancel that Direct Debit. 'I can't relax.'

'Oh well, if it's a question of relaxing . . .'

'I didn't mean that. I'm not going to put my feet up the moment you've gone, but you're making me tense. I don't want you tidying up after me and sitting in judgement while I try and get on with my life. This is my house.'

'We understand,' Tim says, glancing at Cora to check she's in agreement. 'And we promise we won't interfere

193

any more. We'll try to stay out from under your feet, but please let us help.'

'We're family,' Cora adds. 'We should stick together.'

'Are you including me in that?' I ask.

She doesn't dignify the question with a response.

I go indoors, stomp upstairs and lie down on our bed. I haven't been able to change the bedclothes since Nick went, and I pull his pillow on to my chest and hug it. Tears trickle down my cheeks, tickling my ears, drying on my neck. I wipe them away and turn on to my side, cradling the pillow and smothering my sobs.

There's a knock on the door. Tim comes in and the mattress dips as he sits down beside me. He puts his hand on my shoulder. I push the pillow away and sit up, shuffling up to the headboard and wrapping my arms around my knees.

'Grace, my dear.'

I turn my head and contemplate his handsome face. Nick looks like him, but his bone structure is softer, less pronounced, his eyes and mouth more like Cora's. I remember what Alex said about all the girls having crushes on Tim that summer. It's not unusual for teenage girls to be infatuated with men in positions of authority, but Tim isn't a danger to Lottie. I'd know. For one thing, my daughter isn't scared of speaking out when something's bothering her. Douglas is stirring where there's nothing to stir.

Tim sighs and smiles. 'If you're going to keep things on an even keel, you need backup.'

'But not the sort Cora provides. That's more like a stab in the back.'

'I'll keep her in order.'

'Tim, look. Don't get me wrong, I'm fond of you, you're Nick's dad and you've always been kind to me, but Cora . . .' I curl my hands into fists. 'It's not very comfortable having someone in the house who openly dislikes me.'

'She doesn't dislike you. She's just not a woman's woman. And she's desperately anxious.'

We sit in silence, both of us looking at our hands.

'We're all hurting,' Tim says eventually. 'We're all a little lost without Nick. Let's calm down and take things one day at a time. For all we know, Nick might walk back in here tomorrow.'

I sniff back my tears. 'He'll get a rollicking if he does.'

'That's my girl. So we're all good?'

I nod, defeated.

After he's gone I throw myself back on the bed with a sigh of frustration. My phone rings. I reach for it, automatically checking the caller display for Nick's name. It's Marsh.

'Did you get my message?' he asks.

I sit up and drop my feet over the edge of the bed. 'No.'

'I spoke to Mrs Ritchie. She said she would pass it on.'

I close my eyes for a second. 'She didn't. What did you want to talk about?'

'It was just a quick update. We're following up a couple of leads and I wanted to let you know.'

'What leads?' My heart thuds as adrenaline shoots through my veins.

'A possible sighting at Paddington station.'

'Paddington? He must have been heading to Devon then, surely.'

'Possibly. There's plenty of CCTV, so we should know one way or the other soon. We're looking into the information Evan Morgan gave us, trying to discover who the woman was he was talking to on the parade. We've talked to everyone on the class list you gave me, but none of them have admitted to being her. Do you have any idea?'

'No. None. Did you speak to Anna Foreman?'

'Yes. She said it wasn't her.'

'OK.' I don't know what else to say.

'Are you certain that Nick wasn't having an affair?'

'Absolutely certain.'

He sighs down the phone. 'OK. Call me if you can think of any reason why he might have met this woman. And I want you to think hard about Nick's behaviour over the last month or so. He may not have walked out on impulse, he may have been building up to the decision for a while. If he's kept quiet about that holiday, there may be other things that he's been keeping from you.'

'Then why propose?'

'I can't answer that.'

Neither can I. 'Can you do me a favour? Next time you can't get hold of me, don't speak to either of the Ritchies.'

I walk slowly downstairs and stand at the kitchen door with my hands on my hips watching Cora leafing through a newspaper until she notices I'm there. She looks up at me over her glasses.

'I thought you were taking a nap.'

'I've just spoken to Marsh. Apparently, he asked you to pass on a message. Why didn't you tell me?'

She sighs. 'I would have done, but the shock of being asked to leave put it out of my head.'

She goes back to the article she was reading, and I stand at the sink, bristling with resentment, before saying quietly, 'You went behind my back, Cora.'

'I did no such thing. Will you please calm down? You're beginning to sound mad. I meant to tell you earlier, obviously, but you started having a go at us, so I decided it would be tactful to wait until you were in a better mood.'

I only hear the word 'mad'. It takes me flying back to the worst night of my life, to the flat I used to share with Douglas. To a woman screaming that word at me, to blood pumping from a deep wound. I screw my fists up tight and leave the room, sit on the stairs and call Nick's number to hear the recording of his voice. I check In-Step to see if he's moved. He hasn't. There's a big fat zero beside his cartoon bird, as there has been every day since that Saturday. Below, I see that Anna isn't moving either. So she's probably at home. I need to talk to her again about that Thursday evening. I still think she's the woman Evan saw, and I'm determined to prove it. It's too late to go round there today, and I don't want to broach the subject with Kai in the house. I'll talk to her in the morning.

NICK

July 2000

THE GAME HAS FINISHED, JESS IS BUTTERING CRUMPETS while Lorna sets out an assortment of chipped plates and mugs. The rain has finally stopped, the sun slow-winking in and out of view from behind fluffy clouds. Izzy hasn't come back yet and he's not sure what to do, whether to say anything. He doesn't think anyone saw him come in.

He watches the three older girls through the door to the snug. Pansy and Freya are on the brown corduroy sofa, Taisie lounging on a beanbag at their feet while Freya plaits her hair. The twins are singing show tunes, Jess joining in with a little too much gusto from behind him. It's like a scene from a painting transposed into modern life. Three nymphs. In the painting Taisie would be in the water. Then she turns her head, catches his eye and it's not the same snarling hostility he's become used to over the past week; it's not the old Taisie either. It's like she's taken off her carapace. She looks lost and anxious and he's suddenly sorry that he allowed himself to be targeted by

Rosa, that he didn't take the hint. He had kissed Taisie at the barbecue and then chosen to pretend it didn't happen. He had been confused, a little repulsed, angry at himself, scared of starting one thing and destroying another. Shit. This is his fault. All he needed to do was apologize and none of it would have happened, the summer wouldn't have been spoilt. Izzy would be sitting here eating crumpets with them, giggling, instead of sulking.

He's getting really worried. It's his fault she's outside. He scared her. Should he have said something, done more, grabbed her hand and dragged her home, told her not to be silly? What if she isn't playing a game, what if she's punishing him? She won't go in the water; why would she? But in that case, where the fuck is she? He doesn't want to have to explain what happened, because they'll look at him like he's mad, but maybe he should say something. He opens his mouth to speak but is forestalled by Rory.

'Where's Izzy?'

'Must be still hiding,' Nick says, relieved.

'One of you ring the bell,' Lorna says.

Rory leaps up and dashes to the front door. The peal is loud and long, designed to call errant children in from the fields and woodland beyond the garden.

Listening to it fade out, Nick feels a knife-twist of guilt, though there is no reason why he should. Izzy kissed him, mid-nightmare. It was hardly his fault. He wishes she had listened to him, though.

'Go and find her, would you, Alex?' Jess says. 'She won't want to miss out on these.'

Alex pounds up the stairs and along the landing,

shouting for his sister. His footsteps echo through the house. No one speaks.

'I can't find her,' he says, standing in the kitchen door, panting.

Jess frowns and Nick's nerves prickle. The three girls slowly stand up and come into the kitchen. Lorna smiles and says she'll be around somewhere. 'Perhaps she went outside. Why don't you all go and look for her? Spread out.'

Rory and Alex glance regretfully at the crumpets, butter melting through their perforations, and Lorna offers them to Nick with a smile.

'Take them with you.'

Within seconds the plate is empty. Nick sprints out of the back door with the others. They fan out across the garden, the younger boys towards the barn, Nick to the woods and the older girls to the swimming pool with its clapboard changing room.

He's on his own, running along the path, deliberately obliterating his own footprints, rain dripping from leaf to leaf before landing on his forehead, his nose, his shoulders. He calls her name as he runs, then reaches the river and stops, short of breath. He's going to address his fitness when he gets home. A six-pack by Christmas. He can hear distant shouts. The river has risen considerably. It must be a metre deeper than it was yesterday, swollen by the torrential rain. Out of the corner of his eye he sees something that looks out of place with the mud and trodden-down grass of the riverbank. He squints and walks towards it. A pair of trainers. He picks them up, turns them round in his hands and looks out across the water, and his blood pounds in his ears.

GRACE

Tuesday, 24 April 2018

OUTSIDE ANNA'S I TAKE A DEEP BREATH BEFORE RINGING the bell. I hear her footsteps, then the door opens. She stoops to pat the dog, then opens the door wider to let us in. In the kitchen she pours water into a plastic tub. Her hand shakes as she puts it on the floor so that it splashes on to the floorboards and dribbles through the gaps. Toffee sniffs around, whines, and comes to sit right up close to me, leaning against my leg. I rest my hand on his shoulder to settle him.

Anna holds the kettle under the stream of water. To her left a regiment of different-sized black knife handles stick out of a bleached wood block. I try not to look at it. When she turns to me, she's smiling.

'Good timing. I needed a break.'

'You're not painting this morning?' She isn't wearing her overalls.

'No. Paperwork, damn it.' She screws up her face in an expression of disgust.

I look around. Anna's kitchen smells of paint and

linseed oil. In the small glass extension there are four child-sized wooden chairs – they look like IKEA – two of them completed, one not started, and the one she's currently working on, sitting on a paint-spattered trestle table. It's painted with the name Thomas and a selection of rockets and stars. The completed pair are for Sammy and Jenna. They've been painstakingly done, the images delicate and detailed.

'What's happened to this one?' I ask, picking up a broken chair.

She takes it off me and inspects it, pushes the loosened rail back into its hole. 'I tripped over it. Nearly broke my leg. It just needs a bit of glue and a hammer.'

'I wish I was as practical as you.'

She smiles. 'I didn't use to be. I've surprised myself. It's a good feeling, knowing that I can manage on my own.'

The kettle clicks, and Anna fills two mugs. She adds milk and puts them on the table. We sit down.

'So, how are you?' she asks. She pulls her hair back, twists it and lets it fall.

I keep my hands on my knees because they're shaking so much. I'm scared of what comes next. On the way over, I scripted what I wanted to say, but I can't remember how I proposed starting.

'Not so good. It's the not knowing that's the worst thing. How can someone disappear without leaving a trace?' I pick up my coffee and blow on it, then sip carefully, watching her over the rim. Toffee barks sharply. I press my hand on his muzzle to shush him.

'Sorry, he's been nervy since Nick went.'

'I've got mice,' Anna says. 'I expect he can smell them.'

'Probably.' I drink some more of the coffee. She watches me, a question in her eyes. She wants to know what I'm doing here. I put my mug down and take a deep breath.

'Anna, you remember I asked you if you'd happened to bump into Nick the Thursday before he disappeared?'

She frowns, but I don't believe she's forgotten. I wait, my eyebrows raised, until a red tinge begins to creep up her neck. I take a deep breath. I need her to believe I know more than I do. I decide to lie; after all, it may be the truth. 'You were seen, Anna.'

'What?' Her mouth stays open. That and her flushed face tell me all I need to know.

'Cassie's husband saw you arguing with Nick.'

There's a long silence, and I don't fill it. I understand that she needs time to adjust.

'OK. Yes. I did see Nick. We recognized each other from the school and said hello. We weren't arguing. I don't know what gave him that idea.'

Finally. I look directly into her eyes. 'Did something happen between you two? Are you having an affair?'

She looks genuinely baffled. 'No! Absolutely not. God, people are such gossips.'

'So you do know him?'

The silence is long and painful. I can see the conflict in her face.

'All right,' she sighs. 'Yes. I knew him a long time ago, but I hadn't seen him in years, I swear. I wasn't even sure if he was who I thought he was. I'd seen you two together and heard you refer to him as Nick, but I was confused

203

because Lottie's surname is Trelawney-Parr. I had no idea she wasn't his daughter until Cassie told me.' She holds my gaze. She seems sincere.

I push my fingers through my hair and groan. 'How long have you known each other?'

'Since I was two. But the last time I saw him, I was in my teens.'

'Brilliant. Jesus, all these people crawling out of Nick's past. Why don't I know any of this?'

'Why would you? We hadn't been in touch since 2000. Does he tell you about all his old school friends?'

'Sorry, that was a stupid question. Listen, do you know an Alex Wells? He would have been a little younger than you, but he went to Nick's school too.'

'No.' She answers too quickly. 'Well, I don't think so. It was a big school. I wouldn't have known the names of the boys in the years below me. Would you?'

I laugh. 'Certainly not.' We're OK again.

Toffee starts to whine so I pick him up, looking round as I do so. A photograph on the dresser snags my attention. I get up for a closer look and feel a cold trickle down my spine. I've seen it before; or at least, I've seen part of it. This one is uncropped, and the person whose arms are so fondly draped around Izzy Wells' shoulders is Anna. Younger but, unmistakably, her. I turn to find her staring.

'I don't understand,' I say. 'Alex Wells showed me this picture. Why do you have it?'

She takes the frame from me and sets it back on the shelf. 'You're going to find out sooner or later,' she says.

I tense. 'Find out what?' But I think I already know.

'Alex is my brother. It was my sister who drowned. It was Izzy.'

My mouth drops open. 'Why did you lie to me?'

Her face is stiff. 'I don't know. Habit, I suppose. As far as I'm concerned, I don't know my family. I haven't spoken to any of them in years.'

I try to imagine what it would feel like if Lottie refused to speak to me. It would be devastating. Anna must feel the same about Kai; and yet she's cut her mother out of her life, and her grandchild's life. She had been through a trauma, but still, why add to their pain?

'What happened?'

I go back to my chair and sit down, lean on my elbows and watch her. She pulls her eyes from mine and looks down, scratching a dried blob of paint from the knuckle of her thumb.

'Do you want the short version, or the long one?' she asks.

'I have plenty of time.'

Finally, she looks up and shrugs. 'Well, OK. I'm the oldest of four. Two girls, two boys. Alex, obviously, and Rory. It's the typical thing, all the pressure on the first baby to be perfect, to speak early, to walk early, to achieve more than the other babies popped out by the women you've met at the NCT. Then two years later Izzy comes along, premature and fighting for life. I was a stroppy, spiky little thing, who didn't like to be cuddled for too long, but Izzy, when she was tiny, would lie on Mum's chest, like she was still inside her. Alex and Rory were princes and Izzy was Mum's little warrior. I slipped between the cracks. So, anyway, I became

205

a disgustingly attention-seeking child, and a filthy-tempered, equally attention-seeking adolescent and when the terrible things started happening – did Alex tell you that Dad lost his money thanks to Tim Ritchie?'

'Yes.'

'Yeah, well. After what happened to Izzy, it almost killed him. I started counting the days till I could go. I finished my GCSEs, packed my bags and went back to London.'

'Where did you stay?'

'With my godmother in Hackney, while I did my A levels. Then I moved out. So what else did Alex say? I suppose he told you all about that holiday?'

'Not much. Just what happened to your sister. It's Nick I want to know about.'

She tilts her head, squeezes her eyes shut and rubs her fingers across the bridge of her nose. She takes a deep breath. 'I gave Nick a really hard time.'

'Why?'

'He'd upset me. I'd caught him kissing a friend of mine and I wanted to punish him. It was one of the reasons I was so keen to talk to him. I wanted to apologize for being such a bitch that summer. It backfired on me big-time. Everyone started to hate me. I would have stopped it all and made friends with Nick again.' She draws a long sigh. 'But then Izzy died, and our family fell apart. I didn't want to talk to any of them. I avoided Nick. I had little to do with my brothers – there was too big a gap between us.'

'What else did you talk to Nick about?'

'This and that. Our children and the school. I told him

that I'd been married and was a widow. He was sweet about that. He said I should come for supper some time. He said you were always having little supper parties.'

'Oh, not that often,' I say quickly. Would Nick have said those things? I suppose he might have done. But then why baulk when I suggest exactly that? It makes no sense.

Her phone buzzes; she swipes and reads the message then glances at me. 'It's Susanna wanting to know how many cakes she can put me down for.'

I nod, not interested. 'I wish you'd told me.'

She fiddles with her hair, rubbing the ends between her finger and thumb, pulling a strand taut across her lips, then curling it behind her ear. 'I do, too. I just didn't want that summer rehashed, to have to explain how appallingly I behaved. Meeting Nick brought it all back.'

'For him, too, I'd imagine.'

'Yes.' She looks as worn out as I feel. 'All I can tell you is that Izzy had a thing about him. She followed him round and she was the only one who refused to obey my rules.'

'What rules?'

'We pretended he didn't exist. Didn't Alex say?'

I think back and shake my head. 'No, he didn't.'

'That is so like him. Well, it went on for days. But Izzy wouldn't stick to the plan. Whenever she thought I wasn't looking, she'd smile at him. She would talk to him if I wasn't in the room. I'm glad of that now. My sister was a kinder person than me. She should still be here.'

'Why was everyone so pathetic? Why didn't they tell you to stop it or ignore you?'

'Have you forgotten what it's like being a teenager? Weren't you ever so in thrall to someone that you'd do anything to be in favour? I'm not proud of how I behaved, but back then the sense of power it gave me was extraordinary. I look back, and I don't recognize that girl as me; but it was. We do bad things when we're young and ignorant, but it doesn't necessarily make us bad adults. Stronger children gang up on weaker children; it's human nature. And down in Devon, in that huge old house, cut off from London and real life, it was like we were on an island. Different rules applied. Nick began to rely on Izzy.' There's a glint in her eye when she says this. 'Maybe the age gap between them became distorted or blurred around the edges.'

I stiffen. 'What're you saying?'

'I'm not saying anything. I'm trying to explain what the atmosphere was like.'

'Were you jealous of Izzy?'

Her eyes cloud. 'No. Not at all.'

'You get him away from your rival and suddenly he's cosy with your little sister.'

She scowls. 'Only because I wouldn't talk to him.'

I press my linked hands against my mouth and look at her over the weave of my fingers. She avoids my gaze.

'Afterwards, I felt so bad about everything, you know. I wanted to forget the whole thing, not mention it. Izzy was dead, so what did it matter how Nick was feeling? But it did matter, and I was ashamed, but too proud to admit it or apologize. Nick looked awful at the funeral, like he hadn't slept or eaten properly since. We had to acknowledge each other, but there was no real communication.'

208

She closes her eyes. I wait patiently, feeling desperately sorry for her, or for that screwed-up teenager at least. She behaved badly, but it all feels so familiar. Usually we can leave our self-obsessed adolescence behind us, but not Anna. She's locked in Taisie's world because of her sister. She'll never escape that summer.

Anna lowers her hands to the table. 'He didn't come back to school in September, and after the fiasco with Tim's restaurant, we moved away. Dad and Mum said it was because they needed a fresh start, somewhere they wouldn't be reminded of Izzy, but really it was because we had to sell up. I didn't hear any more about Nick, and our parents had fallen out big-time, so there was no contact. It hasn't been easy, but I've tried my best to move on.'

It's cold in her kitchen. I rub my arms, and shiver. 'Are you asking me to believe that it's a coincidence that Alex contacted Nick the day after you confronted him in the street?'

'I didn't confront him.'

I shrug. 'According to Cassie, Evan described it as an intense conversation.'

'That was his perception, then. He was wrong.'

'Really?'

She doesn't elaborate. She doesn't need to. It's Evan's word against hers.

'Did you and Alex plan this?'

She frowns. 'Don't be silly.'

The cogs of my mind are turning slowly. 'But you understand why I might wonder, don't you? Alex was looking to heal by getting in touch with the other people who were there that summer. If he managed to get hold of Nick's number, I doubt he'd have had much trouble finding you.'

'Maybe not. But he didn't.'

I watch her closely. 'How do you feel, knowing that he's been in touch with Nick, talking about the past?'

She looks me straight in the eye. 'I feel sorry for both of them.'

'Was there something odd about Izzy's death? Did Nick know something?'

She laughs. 'Oh my God, Grace. Do you have any idea what you sound like? I don't have a clue why Alex chose now to deal with his demons. As for me, bumping into Nick has brought back some unwelcome memories and I'd imagine the same applies to him. We were a shock to each other. Maybe he felt responsible, or guilty, and seeing me triggered a breakdown. I don't know. You're the one who lives with him. What do you think?'

I swallow. 'It seems a little fishy.'

'I'm sure it does. I hope he comes back.'

'When you spoke to the police, why didn't you tell them you knew Nick?'

She blushes. 'I thought I could avoid it.'

'You know that I will.'

'Of course, but there's no need. I'll do it myself.' She presses her fingers into the corners of her eyes, as if she's trying to block her tear ducts. 'I'm sorry I didn't come clean before. I was thrown. I've had a tough time since Ben died, and it's made me secretive.'

'Is it because you don't want anyone to know your husband killed himself?'

She gasps. She might have been ready for questions about Nick, but she wasn't ready for that.

'How the hell did you know?'

'Alex told me.'

She slumps back in her chair and covers her face with her hands. We sit in silence. It's so quiet I can hear the wind rustling the leaves of the tree that overhangs Anna's garden from next door.

'You really know how to drive the nail in, don't you?' She removes her hands to reveal eyes welling with tears. 'I don't tell people my husband killed himself. It's too personal, OK? I'm ashamed that he didn't love me or his son enough to stay. I'm ashamed that I couldn't help him. I'm not going to talk to new friends about that. Why the hell should I? It's my business. My pain.'

The tears are falling hard. She slashes them away with her fist. She's angry and I feel terrible. I move around the table to sit beside her.

'I'm sorry. That was incredibly insensitive.'

She sniffs and swallows. 'Yes, it was. Please can you go.'

'I don't like to leave you like this.'

'I'll be fine.' She jumps up, pulls a sheet from the roll of kitchen towel and dabs her eyes. 'I'd better get back to work.'

At the door I hug her. Her body is slim and warm, but stiff with tension. Her hair smells of grapefruit.

'Wait,' she says. 'How was he? How was Alex?'

'He seemed fine. He's a lawyer.' No need to tell her what I actually thought of him. 'Maybe you should get in contact. I can give you his email address.'

'Maybe. Oh, and Grace? Please don't tell Nick's family about me.'

'Why not?'

'Because I made the break with the past for my own sanity. It's taken me a long time to recover and I honestly don't think I could stand seeing them.'

'I don't know.' It doesn't seem logical to me. This is a villagey sort of place. She won't be able to avoid them for long. 'Cora can be difficult, but Tim's OK. Why don't I speak to him, so that it's not such a big deal if you do happen to bump into each other.'

'No! For Christ's sake, Grace. Don't you understand? I do not want to talk to them.'

I hold my hands up, bewildered by her reaction. 'OK. OK. Sorry. I won't say a word. But, Anna, you do realize that once you've told the police about your connection to Nick, they're going to ask them about you. I can't do anything about that.'

She looks uncertain, but then she nods, adding to my feeling that she's making this up as she goes along, that events are catching up with her, the ripples of what happened to her sister eighteen years ago finally breaking at her feet.

'It's all right. It's my problem, not yours. Leave it for as long as possible, so I can prepare myself.'

'Is it really that bad?'

She lowers her head and I don't hear what she whispers, so I ask her to repeat it.

'Tim seduced me when I was fifteen.'

'Shit. Oh my God, Anna, that's awful. Did you tell anyone?'

212

She shakes her head. 'No, and you mustn't. But you understand why I don't want him knowing I'm here?'

'OK,' I say quietly. 'It won't come from me.'

As I walk back, my head is spinning. Part of me can't believe that the man I've known all this time could be capable of something like that. But the haunted look in Anna's eyes convinced me she was telling the truth. Douglas could clearly see something dark in Tim that I couldn't.

TAISIE

July 2000

AFTER THE TEARS, THE HYSTERIA, THE COMMISERATIONS, the police and the press and the total, drowning, wipe-out misery, it was the day of the funeral. Taisie couldn't believe that she was standing in a church and that her sister's body was in that shiny wooden box with the huge arrangement of bright green foliage and white flowers trailing over the edges. The smell of jasmine, roses and lilies was overpowering. There were so many people it was standing room only, and some mourners had even spilled out into the narrow corridor outside the crematorium chapel. Family, friends, teachers, Mr Wendover, their headmaster, looking shiny and smart in his dark suit, his fluffy wife beside him. Taisie saw him tip up his glasses and wipe away a tear.

Her sister was getting SO much attention. It was almost worth dying for.

Oh God. She could not believe she just had that thought. *I'm sorry, Izzy. I really am, truly sorry.*

But it wasn't Taisie's fault, was it? Izzy knew that if

214

Taisie had known the water level had risen so high she would never have asked her to keep her promise. Izzy wouldn't have gone in if Nick hadn't done what he had. A picture of her sister in tears flashes through her mind and is gone. She wouldn't think about that. She couldn't. Her mind is swirling with dark clouds. She can't fix on anything. What had Izzy said to her before she ran off? That Nick had kissed her? That he had touched her breast? She couldn't picture it. It wasn't the sort of thing he would do. But on the other hand, the truth is too much to handle. There's Tim and the way he made her feel, there's the minutes she lost with her mother's intervention. Surely Izzy wouldn't have gone in like that, not without making sure that Taisie was right behind her? So she must have been desperately upset.

This was horrific, unbearable. She couldn't untangle the strands. It wasn't her fault. It wasn't. So it must have been Nick's. He was angry at them for the way they had treated him. Izzy had been kind and he had taken advantage of a young girl's adolescent crush. Izzy had always been a physical child, prone to displays of affection, hugging, winding herself round you. That's what must have happened. Nick was unhappy, and he got the wrong idea.

She choked on her tears and pressed her hanky to her eyes. Down the other end of the pew Nick was with Tim and Cora. She had caught his eye earlier and he had given her a nod, like he understood. He didn't, but he was going to. She sniffed and turned her head away. He used to be her friend, and she misses that. She can't help looking back to a time when nothing mattered except playing their daft games. She wished none of this had happened, but it had. Izzy was in that coffin and someone had to take the blame.

When it was over, they filed out of their pews to the strains of 'Oops! . . . I Did It Again'. Taisie had chosen it because it was the song of the summer. Inappropriate, but who cared; Izzy had adored it.

Later, back at the house where the mourners had gathered, pressing into their kitchen and tramping through to the garden, Taisie found Nick sitting on the old blue-and-red climbing frame. Their garden felt tiny with all these people crammed into it, and it was hot, the men sweltering in their suits. Nick looked down at her. She climbed up beside him, carefully arranging the hideous, knee-length black skirt her mother had bought her for the occasion and insisted she wore, out of respect. Izzy wouldn't have given a toss. Taisie sat very straight and didn't speak. She looked at Tim instead. He was talking to her grandmother, his hand on her arm, and Taisie was filled with an angry longing. It wasn't Tim's fault; he wasn't to know that a delay of even twenty seconds would have had such a tragic result.

Nick said something, and she pulled herself back. 'What?'

'I think it was my fault she ran off. We were in the cupboard together, and I scared her. I had one of my nightmares, and she was kissing me, but I was still in the dream, so it was like there was this creature trying to suck the life out of me, and I went crazy.'

She knew all about his nightmares, although she didn't really believe in his descriptions. Monsters coming out of the cupboard, springing at his face? Yeah, right. He made them up to get attention, and now he was using them as an excuse for what he did to her sister. She sniffed and pressed the pads of her palms into her eyes, trying not to smudge her make-up. It wasn't her fault, it was his, and he needed to know that.

'So this is all down to you? Izzy's dead because of you?'

Nick jerked. 'What? No. I just mean, she might have been upset because she was embarrassed. I think she had a crush on me.'

'You mean she trusted you and you abused her. And now you're laying the blame on her. She never kissed you, Nick. She was a kid. It was you who kissed her. Admit it.'

'I . . . No. I didn't . . . I didn't.' When he went red, his spots literally glowed.

'You disgust me, Nick Ritchie.' His face was ashen, but she pressed on, unable to stop the surge of bile. She had to make him think he was the last person to see Izzy alive. 'You went too far, didn't you? You—'

'Hey, you two.' It was Lorna, holding a glass of wine, her eyes red-rimmed. 'Don't hide, sweetie.' She put her hand on Taisie's knee. 'I know it's difficult, but your mum needs you. You can hand round nibbles if you don't feel up to talking to anyone.'

Taisie clambered down. She fetched a plate laden with cocktail sausages from the kitchen and wove her way between their guests, listening to snatches of conversation, but mostly people went silent when she approached. After a while Nick wandered over to his mum, but Cora was with some other women, mothers from the school, so he just hovered beside her looking like the spot-encrusted loser he was.

Her throat tightened, and her eyes pricked. She dashed inside and locked herself in the bathroom. There was only one person she wanted to talk to, and that was Tim. She wanted him to hold her, to stroke her, to caress the pain away.

PART 2

GRACE

Wednesday, 25 April 2018

NICK'S DISAPPEARANCE HAS FINALLY CAUGHT THE attention of the press. Tim went out for the paper this morning and wordlessly handed it to me. It isn't a big item; a few column inches to say that thirty-four-year-old Nick Ritchie has been missing since the fourteenth of April. That's followed by a human-interest piece on how many people go missing each year. A set of startling statistics. So far there's been nothing about me, but I reckon it's only a matter of time before some bright spark comes asking questions and discovers that I'm not the conventional mother I appear to be.

I put the paper down and call Marsh to ask whether Anna has been back to see him.

'And?' I ask when he confirms this.

He sighs. 'And I don't know. She thinks you're fixated on what happened eighteen years ago.'

'If I'm fixated, it's because it was a massive upheaval in Nick's life. What if he went back to the place where she died? What if he has some sort of guilt complex about what happened? The police should search the river. Maybe he's in the house or camping out. They were all there; all these people that are, or were, part of Nick's life: Angus Moody, Anna Foreman, his parents. And now Alex Wells.'

'Slow down. Supposing he did go down to Devon, how did he get there? His car is parked in your driveway and there's no CCTV footage of him beyond the Queen's Arms. The Paddington station sighting wasn't him.'

'I don't know. But it's not impossible, is it? Maybe he hitched a lift. Please can you at least look at it?'

He gives in. 'I'll talk to Devon and Cornwall Police for you, but don't expect them to organize a search without a very good reason.'

It's something. I've driven a small wedge in the door. I risk another push.

'I think Nick was so upset by meeting Anna Foreman and her brother, and the memories that triggered, that he may have harmed himself or be intending to.' A lump rises in my throat, causing a break in my voice.

'Has he ever given you reason to believe he's capable of something like that?'

Once upon a time I would have said absolutely not, but now I know about his depression, I've had to rethink our entire relationship. 'It can happen to anyone, surely? Given the right set of circumstances.'

He is unimpressed. 'If we assigned officers to every *what if*, we wouldn't have time to deal with the crimes that are actually being committed. We haven't been sitting on our hands. We've uploaded Nick's details on to the Missing Persons database. We've looked at his computers both at work and at home. We've spoken to his colleagues. We've been through his phone records and his bank and credit card statements. I have a list as long as my arm of things that need my attention and people who need my help. I cannot devote every hour of every day to finding Nick. If he wanted to go back there to kill himself, why not drive, or get the train?'

'Because he didn't want to be found.'

I can almost hear the lift of his eyebrow. I can certainly picture it.

'My point exactly.'

Cornered, I groan. 'It's not that simple.'

'Ms Trelawney.' He sounds exasperated. 'If you know something, you should tell me, even if it doesn't show Nick in the best light. If what you're saying is true, then we need to act quickly.'

What Anna told me – what she implied about Nick and Izzy's relationship becoming blurred around the edges – is hard to articulate, because it goes against everything I know about Nick. I could repeat it to Marsh, but the slightest suggestion that a sixteen-year-old boy assaulted a thirteen-year-old girl, and possibly has some indirect connection to her death, has implications that could be life-changing and career-destroying.

'I've told you everything I know.'

'OK,' he says after a pause. 'I'll talk to Moody again.'

'And the Wellses. You need to talk to Anna's parents.'

He sighs.

'I'm sorry. I'm telling you how to do your job. Please

can you email me Nick's bank statements? I want to go through them.'

I hang up and go in search of Cora. She's in Lottie's bathroom, bent over the bath, a green sponge in one hand, a bottle of lemon-scented cream cleaner in the other.

'You shouldn't be doing that,' I say, trying to sound friendly. 'You know Lottie cleans her own bathroom.'

Cora turns and smiles. 'She's a child. Now, if you want to do something helpful, you could strip our bed. I've noticed you do have some clean linen in the cupboard.'

I stare at her, my mouth gaping. I want to respond, what did your last slave die of? but refrain, instead telling her, politely, what I've talked to Marsh about, and that he's going to speak to her old friends, Jess and Sean Wells.

'I need to talk to Jess first,' she says, dropping the sponge into the bath and getting to her feet. She peels off her rubber gloves and rubs the small of her back.

'I got the impression you weren't on speaking terms,' I say.

She hesitates at the door. 'This is important. We're all involved in this whether we like it or not. Jess and I were close once. I can't believe she won't care about what I'm going through.'

I feel a tiny twinge of compassion for this intelligent, bitter woman, although she evidently feels little for me. It must be sad when you lose a close female friend, sadder than losing a lover. If Cassie dumped me, I'd be devastated.

I follow her downstairs and make us both a cup of tea while she takes the phone into the front room. Jess is obviously prepared to speak to her, because I can hear the murmurings of conversation. I go out into the hall and stand close to the sitting-room door, not quite putting my ear against it, but almost. The floor creaks and I wince, holding my breath.

'Grace thinks he may have gone to Devon,' Cora says. 'To the house ... Why am I calling you? To tell you ... Well, no, I know it's nothing to do with you but ... Jess. Look, I'm sorry, I was just reaching out. It's been so long ... What? No. No, of course we can't. Well, if that's the way you feel—' She breaks off and says, 'Jesus. What a bitch.'

I nip back into the kitchen and pretend to be rummaging through my bag. I glance over my shoulder when she comes back in. 'So, what did she say?'

'You were listening, weren't you?' Cora says.

She picks up her book and, without waiting for her tea, takes it upstairs.

Since I spoke to Marsh, I've been obsessing about Devon. I want to see the place where Anna's little sister died. The more I learn about what happened, the more I'm certain that the waves caused by that summer have followed Nick down through the years. My gut tells me those waves broke on the day he left this house to buy a pint of milk and ran into Anna Foreman. I have nothing against coincidence, but there are far too many for credibility here. Nick and Anna were estranged childhood friends who happened to wash up in the same corner of suburban London. Anna's brother happened to contact Nick the day after she spoke to him. I don't think so.

I sit cross-legged on the sofa, cradling a cup of mint tea, thinking about the logistics. I don't want to stay overnight, not when things are on such a knife-edge here. I'll do the drive there and back in a day. It'll be exhausting but even if I'm not back in time to see Lottie before she goes to sleep, I want to be there in the morning when she wakes up.

The only obstacle is that I'll need permission and that means getting in touch with Angus Moody. I bite my lip. I don't want to ask him if I can have a snoop round his house and land; he could react badly.

Anna, I think suddenly. She can get me in, and she can guide me; she can help me picture what happened to her sister and she can explain the relationships between the various family members. I put my drink down and reach for my mobile. Is this wise? Do I really want to share my intentions with a woman I don't entirely trust? I hold the phone in the palm of my hand. Time might be running out for Nick. I have no choice. It's Anna or nothing.

'But why are you going at all?' Anna says when I explain what I want from her.

'Because it was a significant event in Nick's life that I didn't know about, and I have this gut feeling. I need to see it, to smell it.'

There's a long silence and when she does speak, she sounds as though she might be wavering. 'I haven't seen the Moodys in years. And anyway, they probably won't

226

be there, they're in London or abroad most of the time. It was only ever a summer holiday home.'

'There must be some local person who looks after the place.'

She sighs. 'Well, there's Mrs Burrows. Unless she's retired. Someone in the village will know; everyone knows everyone's business down there.'

'Good,' I say. 'Can you be ready to leave by seven?'

'Grace.' Her voice is taut with suppressed frustration. 'I can't come with you, not at a moment's notice.'

'You owe me.'

'For what?' She sounds incredulous, and I admit, I am pushing it.

'For not telling me you knew Nick.'

'Oh for Christ's sake . . . All right. Fine.'

'I'll come and pick you up. I'm sorry, I'd offer to have Kai here with Lottie, but I know you don't want to see Tim and Cora.'

'Kai isn't a problem. My neighbour will have him.'

'Thanks. You never know, the trip might be good for you too.'

She laughs drily. 'If you dare say the word closure, I'm not coming.'

GRACE

Thursday, 26 April 2018

I STRETCH AND YAWN, SURPRISED THAT IT'S NOT DARK outside, that my clock reads not two or three or four, as it has been since Nick went missing, but five forty-five. Blearily I feel along the row of buttons on top of my radio and cancel my six o'clock alarm. I can't believe I slept so solidly, but perhaps it's because I'm going somewhere and doing something constructive for Nick. I rub my eyes and sit up, throw back the duvet and swing my legs out of bed. I feel refreshed by sleep for the first time since he left.

I chide myself. Nick didn't leave. Leaving is something you do on purpose. Nick is missing, absent, vanished.

I make sure everything Lottie needs is easy to find; she's supposed to organize herself, but now is not the time to stand on principles. The last thing I need is a call from the school secretary demanding I bring in her recorder. I haven't told Lottie that Anna is coming with me in case she mentions it to Cora and Tim, because they'll want to know who this Anna is and why I would want her company. It's ridiculous; Anna's bound to bump into them soon. I can't walk across the Common without seeing someone I know; it's that sort of place. But it's none of my business.

By seven, I'm parked in Camomile Avenue. Anna gives Kai a hug then propels him towards the neighbour's door. I wait until he goes in, then we drive away.

Anna is texting someone. She sends it and drops her phone into the canvas tote that she's settled in the space at her feet, then leans back and closes her eyes. She doesn't want to involve the Moodys, so we've arrived unannounced. If the housekeeper isn't there, Anna knows where she lives in the village.

'Too early for you?' I ask, in a friendly way.

She turns her head. 'Just a little.'

'I don't mind if you nod off.' In fact, I'd like it, at least until I've got used to having her there.

'No, it's OK.'

She straightens up, drinks from the water bottle she's stashed between her thigh and the gearbox and wipes the corners of her mouth with a delicate finger.

I switch the radio on and Anna groans as John Humphrys sinks his teeth into the Transport Secretary. The sun has risen, and although the forecast is that the mini heatwave is over, the sky is brightening.

I check the petrol gauge. Half a tank. I'll have to fill up. Normally, this is something I'd do without thinking; just one of life's chores. I rarely look at the cost of any-thing, let alone a litre of petrol, but since Marsh sent me copies of Nick's bank statements I've had to change my ways. There are various standing orders, but the fifteen hundred pounds a month he gives Tim and Cora sticks out like a sore thumb. It's unsustainable. If Nick doesn't return his account will empty and those commitments won't be honoured. I regret the impulse that led to this morning's trip, but it's too late to back out now. And I need to do this, for Nick's sake as well as my own.

We approach the Moodys' house by way of a long, meandering drive abutted by fields. On one side, sheep lift their heads, ruminating gently as we pass. On the other side the green shoots of some crop or other march along ridges of earth. There's woodland beyond them and the sky above is pale blue broken by wispy strips of cloud. An aeroplane trail streaks across it, its tail softly dissipating. The house is built of grey stone and is cloaked in wisteria. Chimneys rise from a slate roof. I'm openmouthed with envy. It's gorgeous.

Beside me, Anna sits up straighter. 'Quite something, isn't it?'

'It's not what I was expecting at all. I thought it would be smaller. This is so grand. They must have pots of money.'

'This is just their country crash pad. It's been in Lorna's family for generations. You should see their Kensington house. It's eye-watering.'

Out of the corner of my eye I see a slow blush creep up her neck, but I don't have time to dwell on why that might be. I pull up in front, and we get out, eager to breathe the fresh air and stretch our legs. There's a scruffy Land Rover parked near the lawn. Anna marches up to the door and rings the bell. It peals long and loud.

'That's so people can hear it at the end of the garden,' Anna explains. 'Lorna used to ring it when it was time to come in for lunch. We could hear it all the way to the woods and . . .'

'The river?' I say.

'Yes.'

I allow a pause before I speak again. 'You must have missed those holidays.'

She shrugs. 'They wouldn't have been the same without Izzy.'

We are greeted at the door by a friendly woman in her late sixties. Her grey hair is tied back, a baggy sweater swamps her plump figure, and she has green rubber gardening clogs on her feet. She frowns, evidently puzzled, then Anna introduces herself.

She smiles warmly. 'Goodness, you've changed. I thought you were a couple of lost ramblers.'

'Mrs Burrows, this is Grace Trelawney,' Anna says, indicating me. 'Do you remember Nick Ritchie? Grace is his girlfriend.'

'Of course I remember Nick. Are you on your holidays? You should have brought him with you.'

The housekeeper looks from me to Anna, tweaking at the cuffs of her jumper, waiting for an explanation. She is more curious than impatient. She doesn't have the faintest idea why we've turned up unannounced so obviously the police haven't paid their visit yet.

Anna and I have already discussed what we would say to her. There's no point lying, since she'll find out sooner or later. We tell her the simple facts. Nick is missing, and we think it might have something to do with that awful week. She takes us into the house, through the wide hallway with its grand mahogany staircase, and into the warmth of the kitchen. I can't help staring round me, trying to imagine a younger Nick in this place, stuck here, with no one except a thirteen-year-old girl to talk to. No wonder he gravitated towards Angus. He must have been miserable. It makes me furious with Anna, but I push it down. I'm sure Nick forgave her a long time ago. He's not the type to bear grudges.

'I wasn't there that afternoon,' Mrs Burrows says, setting the kettle on the range to boil. 'But even before the tragedy, that holiday wasn't a success.' She glances at Anna. 'You probably didn't notice – you had the twins to distract you – but those new ones . . . what were their names?'

'Tim and Cora Ritchie,' I supply.

'Yes, them,' she says. 'I had nothing against Nick.' She looks at me. 'He was quiet and polite, but he didn't fit in any more than his parents did. That mother.' She rolls her eyes. 'She was a piece of work. Treating me like I was there for her pleasure. That's why I made myself scarce as much as possible.'

That sounds like Cora. 'So there's nothing you can tell me about Nick specifically?'

'I wish I could help. He was unhappy, but I put it down to his age. My son was the same. There were some days when he barely spoke a word to anyone.'

I'm not sure whether she's referring to her son or Nick.

'You lot,' she adds, looking at Anna. 'You older girls didn't have much time for him, did you? I'd have thought you'd have been delighted to have a good-looking boy around. But perhaps, with three girls, it was tricky. There'd be jealousy.'

I glance at Anna to see how she's taking this. Her mouth is set in a thin line.

We change into our walking boots. Despite the sunshine, there's a nip in the air and I wrap my scarf around my neck, do up the zip on my coat and raise the faux-fur collar. We walk across a wide lawn, and I can't stop looking, taking it all in. There's a huge Victorian greenhouse to the side and barns behind it. Over to my right a swimming pool, still in its blue winter coat, is surrounded by lichen-covered stone. There's a wooden changing room and beyond that, a tennis court. We walk past a shrubbery that obscures a compost heap that fills my nostrils with the smell of rotting vegetation and damp earth, then we veer off down a gravel path that leads to woodland. Anna is walking fast, picking up real momentum, as if she can't slow down because she fears that if she did, she'd turn back. I watch her thick hair bouncing, the sway of her hips.

In the wood the air cools even more and the mud paths, untouched by the sun, are a black and claggy mess of human and dog prints. The air is full of birdsong. We hear a lot in our garden, but nothing like this. It's an orchestra, melodies sung back and forth through the trees.

233

Anna turns her head and says over her shoulder, 'Glad you brought your boots?'

'Absolutely.'

She slows down to let me catch up, even though the path is too narrow for us to walk side by side.

'This must have been heaven for you as children,' I say.

'It was. When it was just us and Pansy and Freya, it was like we were the only people in the world. We made up such great games. Everyone got along, even Rory. We looked after each other. It was short-sighted of Mum and Dad to invite the Ritchies. It changed the dynamic.'

'They had never met Lorna and Angus?'

'No. It was Dad's idea. Tim had got him interested in his restaurant. He was going to make Dad's fortune – ha ha. Dad thought Angus would like him, but it was obvious from the moment they met that Angus thought Tim was an idiot. Of course he was friendly and polite, but the atmosphere was all wrong. Mum and Dad were being snarky with each other. Cora Ritchie sulked because she felt left out. Angus was playing the Lord of the Manor card. Tim was doing his best to ingratiate himself with him, but it was a losing battle.' She stops to take a breath.

By this time, we are deep in the woods and the path is beginning to slope. To my surprise Anna takes my arm and pulls me into step beside her. We are crammed together, our feet churning up the damp earth. Perhaps I should have brought Toffee. He would have loved it. He would also have been a distraction.

'I've thought about this so often; I've wondered whether Izzy would be alive if I hadn't behaved so badly.

234

I was only angry with everyone because I knew that what I was doing was wrong, that my friends were getting pissed off with me. Even the twins. They had nothing against Nick – they barely knew him. He was male, our age and they were at a girls' school, so obviously they found him interesting. I was jealous and unhappy, and I didn't know how to handle the situation.'

'Did the adults not notice?'

She flushes. 'Possibly. Probably. I'm not sure. I caught Lorna looking at me in a funny way sometimes. Nick rather attached himself to Angus – they liked having long discussions about history – and that probably happened because he was trying to protect himself. He was as confused as I was. Shit. I was a crap friend. I did apologize.'

'At the time?'

'No.' She adds, ruefully, 'Last week. I was eighteen years too late. I should have managed it better, so that I wasn't such a shock to him.' She stops suddenly.

I turn and look at her, as she puts her hand against the bark of a tree and drops her head.

'Are you OK? Do you feel faint?'

She looks up, her eyes sparkling with tears. 'I can hear the river.'

Through the rustle of the leaves and the call of the birds I hear running water. I feel warmth on my neck as the sun finds its way through the foliage. The water is hypnotic once I start listening.

'You can stay here if you don't want to come any further. This must be so hard for you.'

She takes a deep breath and holds out her hand. I pull

her up and she brushes the leaves off the seat of her jeans.

'Come on,' she says. 'I need to do this.'

I stand at the edge of the river and peer across it, while Anna stays a few feet back, her hands in her pockets, her chin dipped. She is tense and watchful. Unsurprising, I suppose.

She joins me and points to a shallow inlet. Grasses and leaves wave languorously, caught at the edge. The water ripples but it isn't flowing particularly fast. Last night, after Anna gave me the address, I looked the house up on Google Earth and zoomed in on its surroundings. The river meanders through miles of farmland, then broadens, winding snakelike until it reaches Dartmouth where it spreads and empties into the sea. It's a long way for a body to travel. Surely if Nick had decided to drown himself his body wouldn't have made it far? Someone, a rambler perhaps, would have found him.

Anna looks around and seems confused, as if she's expecting to see something that isn't there. Is Izzy so vivid in her mind that her subconscious is looking out for her? She strides forward, then stops. I follow her to a muddy spot where the ground drops into the brown water less abruptly.

'This is where Izzy went in, where her shoes were found,' Anna says. 'We swam here. Izzy wasn't allowed unless there was an adult with her because she wasn't a strong enough swimmer. She had weak lungs and her heart had been operated on when she was a baby, so she wasn't supposed to over-exert herself. The problem was, she was determined to do everything we did, not to be the wimp.'

'She sounds like a feisty little thing.'

'She was. The current can be strong when the tide changes and the Dart gets sucked towards the estuary. It was pouring with rain that day. And after heavy rainfall it can rise suddenly and become much more dangerous.'

'How far downriver was she found?'

'About a mile. She . . . She was caught on a fallen tree.'

The image is so unbearably sad that my throat constricts as I try to hold back the tears. Izzy Wells wasn't much older than Lottie. I wipe my eyes and blow my nose on a tissue I find in my pocket. 'Why do you think she came down here?'

Anna looks away. 'There could be any number of reasons. She was bored. She wanted to prove something. Someone upset her.'

Nick? I wonder about that, but I can't imagine it.

I don't want to leave the spot I'm standing on. There is a strange force keeping me here, weighting my feet to the wet earth. I think about Izzy taking off her shoes and wading in, getting out of her depth, the currents wrapping around her slim child's body and dragging her down and along. It must have been terrifying. Is that what happened to Nick?

I turn and start walking, back into the woods, away from the peaceful sound of rushing water, a beautiful sound that once tempted a thirteen-year-old girl to jump in on a wet summer's day. I stop, and Anna almost collides with me.

'But if it was pouring with rain,' I say, 'why would Izzy go swimming? Why not wait until the sun came out? What was so important?'

'I don't know,' Anna snaps. 'Don't you think I've asked myself that question a thousand times?'

She stomps ahead of me, and I run to catch up as she crosses the lawn back to the house. Then she holds me, pressing her cheek against mine.

'Sorry. I'm sorry. This is so hard for me.'

'I know, Anna. I understand.'

I don't care what she did as a teenager, I'm not going to judge her for that – I can't pretend I was a model citizen myself at that age – I care what happened two weeks ago, when my boyfriend crossed her path for the first time in eighteen years. I care about the earthquake I'm certain she and her brother caused.

GRACE

Thursday, 26 April 2018

'YOU DON'T MIND IF I CARRY ON, DO YOU?' MRS
Burrows says as Anna and I unwrap the lunch we bought
at a service station on the way. 'The family are coming
down for the bank holiday. The place has been locked
up since Easter. I have masses to do.'

'We won't be long. I want Anna to show me the house,
if you don't mind.'

'I don't mind in the slightest. I like to have people
about the place.'

Anna goes first, and I follow her up a narrow flight of
white-painted stairs. The treads are bare and scuffed,
worn down by countless feet. There is a lovely, warm,
lived-in feel about this house. It is entirely without
pretensions. Beautiful objects rub shoulders with bits of
tat, stuff that the children made, stuff that means something, recalls a particular moment in time. What a lovely,
privileged upbringing those children had. A far cry from
mine where nothing of value was bought or kept, where
promises were only made to be neglected and broken. I

shake the past off my shoulders and focus on why I'm here.

'When you told me about Nick and Izzy's relationship, about it becoming a bit blurred around the edges, you meant something, didn't you?'

'It was a throwaway remark.'

'Nothing is throwaway. You implied they were closer than they should have been.'

She turns and looks down at me. 'It was a feeling, you know, that he felt guilty about something.'

'Like what? Is there something you're not telling me? Please, Anna. This could be important.'

'There's nothing. As you say, he's a good man. He wouldn't deliberately hurt anyone.'

'So you think he did hurt her? But that it was accidental?'

'It's a possibility, surely? We don't know what happened. Maybe we never will. All of us feel guilty to some extent. I failed her. I have to live with that.'

'I'm sorry.'

'It doesn't matter,' she says brusquely. 'We all failed her one way or another.'

What do I really feel about this woman? I've only known her a short time, and yet here we are, part of each other's emotional experience, her head full of what happened eighteen years ago, mine full of what's happening now. We've both experienced loss, but she's accustomed to hers, while I wear mine like someone else's clothes.

She takes me into an attic room furnished with twin beds. She sits down on the end of one of them, and I sit on the other. The room is long and narrow and has sky-lights either side of a pitched roof and a small window at each end. The windowsills are scattered with the carcasses of long-dead insects; flies on their backs with their tiny legs in the air. Sun-shredded curtains hang from yellowed curtain wire. There's a camp bed folded up against the wall. It smells strange, not just of dust and damp, but of human occupation. Maybe the twins still use it. Or their kids, if they have them. Whatever, the place needs airing.

Anna sees me wrinkle my nose. 'It's not exactly five-star luxury, but Pansy, Freya and I always had this room; it's the furthest away from the adults.'

'Did Nick ever come up here?'

She looks down at her hands. 'No. He was banned. I'll show you his room. Come on.'

The room where Nick slept was on the first floor, down a corridor and round into the north wing. It's large and chilly, but a lot cleaner and better cared for than the attic room and it doesn't have that musty smell. Anna stands in the doorway while I look around. I inspect the bookshelf, wondering if Nick found solace in books that summer. They are a mixture: crime and young adult, classic and chick lit. Coincidentally, one of them is the thriller Nick was reading when he left. It's still beside our bed in London. I pick it up and run my thumb over the cover. It's dusty.

'Their friends leave books behind when they come to stay,' Anna says. 'That's nice, don't you think?'

I picture Nick finding respite in here during the day

while the others were outside having a jolly time together. He'd have been lonely and angry, wondering what the hell he'd done to offend his friend, why she had set out to humiliate and isolate him. Anna must have been a gorgeous teenager, all pouting lips and batting eyelashes. Even while she hurt him, she would have expected his allegiance, his adoration. Has she changed that much? I'm not sure. No one really changes; we learn to moderate our behaviour, but it's still our behaviour.

She takes the book out of my hand and puts it back where we found it. 'I'll show you where he hid that afternoon.'

I look back once before I leave the room, and I see my love lying on the bed, his hands locked behind his head, staring up at the ceiling. I feel his presence so sharply, I almost gasp.

Why didn't you talk to me about any of this?

The house is a rabbit warren with separate wings and additions built across four centuries. There are three sets of stairs: the grand central staircase, with its deep oak skirting on which are displayed all sorts of odd things – stuffed birds, pieces of sculpture, an ostrich egg, clay objects created by children. Another smaller staircase leads from the linen room up to the attic. The narrow, painted servants' stairs that I'd noticed earlier climb from the snug up to a shadowy corner of the first floor, and this is where Anna leads me. On the bend, there's a door about three feet high. Anna opens it and leans in to flick a switch and a low wattage bulb floods the nook with yellow light. She stands back so that I can see inside.

Planks have been laid loosely over joists and there's a collection of bunched-up carrier bags containing yellowing papers pushed into the corner. Abandoned spiders' webs hang between bare rafters, blanketed in dust.

'It's the first place I'd look for someone,' I say.

'That didn't matter. Nick knew that if anyone found him they'd ignore him. Except Izzy,' she adds. 'My sister was in here with him.'

'With him? How do you know that, if she went missing while the rest of you were hiding?'

Anna scowls and her tone is defensive. 'I found her, OK? She was upset. She told me. Then she said she was going to hide again and ran off. It was the last time I saw her.'

I try to put things together in my head. The bullying of Nick. The child running out into the rain. The motivation she might have had. And what about the other stuff that was going on?

'What about Tim?'

'What about him?' Anna replies. Her fingers move to her hair, combing into it above her right ear and pressing into her scalp.

'Well.' I start again. 'Is this where it happened? Is this where he seduced you?'

'I wish I hadn't told you that.'

'But you did. Was it?'

'No. That was later, when we were back in London.'

'But this is where it started, though, wasn't it? You developed a crush and he noticed you. Consequently, your little sister felt as neglected and left out as Nick did.'

243

Her eyes darken and she stands up slowly.

'I don't want to talk about this.'

'I didn't mean to upset you. I'm just trying to work out what might have been going through Izzy's head.'

'Well, don't. You don't know anything about us.'

'It's what I'm here for, Anna,' I say, exasperated. 'I need to see and feel what Nick was going through and that means understanding Izzy too. Please don't take it personally.'

She screws her face into an expression of scorn. 'How am I meant to take it, then? Am I just supposed to let you play detective? You are so fucking arrogant, it's unbelievable. I wish I hadn't come.'

'Anna, please . . .'

She glares at me, then turns and runs downstairs.

I stand for several seconds, transfixed by the space she's left, then I go after her, skidding on the painted steps and grabbing the banister to stop myself landing on my bottom. I almost catch her in the hall as she throws the door open, but Mrs Burrows appears from one of the rooms and blocks my way.

'Let her go,' she says. 'She was always one for flouncing out. It won't last long.'

Anna's feet pound across the hardstanding, then there's silence as they hit grass. I watch as she marches across the lawn, Mrs Burrows beside me, a restraining hand on my arm.

We all hear the car at the same time. Anna stops in her tracks, as though she's frozen, and my nerves leap as it comes into view. It's the police. At last.

'They'll be here about the robbery,' Mrs Burrows says.

'What robbery?'

'The shed. Garden burglaries are very common round here. The gardener noticed when he came this morning. It's been broken into, and one or two things are missing.'

'But what . . .'

She moves me out of the way impatiently, and strides to meet them. Anna is still standing in the middle of the lawn, looking like she's forgotten where she was going. I walk over, and she turns to me.

'What do they want?'

'They're investigating a shed burglary.' I smile. 'We're not in London any more, Toto.'

'What?'

'Oh, nothing. I'm going to talk to them.'

I walk over purposefully. Mrs Burrows has her hands on her hips and the policeman is nodding sagely. He looks up as I approach.

'Hi,' I say. 'My name is Grace Trelawney. I was wondering whether you were investigating my boyfriend's disappearance.'

He looks at me blankly.

'His name is Nick Ritchie. Detective Inspector Marsh from London CID will have got in touch about it. I came down expecting to find the river being searched, but there's no one there.'

He looks like he's barely out of college and obviously doesn't have a clue, but he obliges me by radioing it in. I

245

wait with Anna and Mrs Burrows. Mrs Burrows makes the occasional remark, but neither of us respond. We're both too tense.

'Right,' he says to us, looking pleased that he has something positive to relay. 'A team is coming. They're starting tomorrow. London will be informed if anything is found.'

'Perhaps we should show you the spot,' Anna says.

But I don't want to go back down there. I've seen the river and the mud, I've trodden the path and smelled the leaf rot. It's too miserable.

'Mrs Burrows can do that. Come on, let's go home.'

Anna gazes at the woods longingly, then back at the house. I can feel how torn she is, how much she wants to stay, to spend more time where she last saw her sister. Her shoulders slump as she trudges towards the car.

Douglas calls when we're about twenty minutes outside London. The Bluetooth picks it up.

'Hey, where are you?' he says.

'On the M4.'

'Really? Where've you been?'

'To Devon.' I glance at Anna, but she's politely looking out of her window. 'I've got a friend with me, Douglas. What do you want?'

'Just catching up. Who's with you?'

'A friend,' I repeat.

'Hello, Grace's friend.'

Anna turns her head with a grimace. 'Hello.'

'I would have come with you, if I'd known that's what you wanted to do, Grace. You should have called.' His voice is pleasant, but I sense a hint of disapproval in his tone.

'We went to a place where Nick spent some time when he was younger. Anna knows the area.'

'Anna?'

'I've told you about her. You've met her, remember?'

'Oh, Kai's mum. That Anna.'

It's a bit like knowing owners by their dogs.

'Douglas, can we not have this conversation here. I'll speak to you later.'

'Wait,' he says. 'Don't hang up. Anna. I understand you used to know Nick.'

Anna glances at me.

Sorry, I mouth. I don't remember telling him but I must have. My mind has been all over the place.

'Yes I did,' she says.

'Well, it's very kind of you to help Grace, but I don't think you should be getting involved. This is a police matter. Grace shouldn't be there, and you definitely shouldn't.'

'I didn't want to come,' she says sharply.

'It's not your fault. I know how manipulative Grace can be.'

'Goodbye, Douglas.' I touch the screen and end the call.

'Why do you let him get away with that?' Anna asks.

'It's the way he is. He seems to still think he owns me, even though we haven't been together for years. He's never really accepted that I can love someone else after him. Big ego.'

'Has he had other girlfriends since you split up?'

'Yes, several, but they never seem to stick. He gets

bored and starts finding fault and then he dumps them. Douglas isn't capable of truly loving a woman. There are always conditions. It's exhausting.'

'Maybe he hasn't found the right person.'

I glance at her and smile. 'That's the kind way of looking at it.'

GRACE

Monday, 30 April 2018

MONDAY. ANOTHER WEEK TO GET THROUGH. MORE questions to ask, more reality to accept. Anna, I think, as I get dressed. Anna, Anna, Anna. If Devon told me anything, it's that she's damaged. But is Nick's disappearance her fault, or merely collateral damage from that summer? And where does Tim feature?

Lottie and I spent a lot of time with Cassie and Evan over the weekend, urged by our friends to treat their home as a sanctuary. The Morgans live in a modest semi-detached 1930s house on a busy road on the less expensive side of the Common. It's light and bright and has an enormous garden and I actually think they have more fun over here, where there's less pressure to conform than in my exclusive enclave. We arrived at twelve o'clock on Saturday for lunch and didn't leave until eight o'clock that evening, and then we went to Richmond Park with them on Sunday. I didn't much like leaving Tim and Cora to their own devices, but I reasoned that if they wanted to pry, they'd had ample opportunity.

After spending Friday with Anna, particularly those eight hours in the car with her, it was such a relief to be amongst people that I trust, and who know me. Lottie was happy too, because she had Hannah all to herself. When the girls were out of the room the only topic of conversation was Nick. I didn't mind; it was good to have friends to chew it over with. When I told them about Anna's connection Evan's eyebrows shot up.

'God, that is weird, isn't it? I mean, there is no way the two things aren't related. I can't believe the police aren't taking it more seriously.'

'It still doesn't explain what happened.'

'Well, obviously, she scared him. For her to come back after so many years, accusing him of doing I don't know what to her sister . . .'

'He didn't do anything. You know he didn't.'

'I never said he did,' Evan said, back-pedalling. 'There's no way he would. I know Nick. He's a good guy.'

'Anna denies that they talked about it. She says it was just a chat about her moving here.'

'Oh, come on, Grace. You don't really believe that, do you?'

'No,' I said quietly.

Evan leaned back in his chair and laced his fingers behind his head. 'But something happened all those years ago. And whatever it is must have gone very deep. Maybe it's PTSD?'

'That's what I've been thinking,' Cassie said. 'You know, what with his nightmares and everything.'

I had a large glass of wine in front of me. I picked it

up and swirled it slowly. 'I know you're right,' I said. 'But I refuse to believe that Nick has done anything wrong. He's honest and gentle and he just wouldn't.'

'Of course he wouldn't.'

Cassie took the glass out of my hand and set it down on the table. I hadn't realized how much I was trembling.

'No way,' Evan said. 'He's a good mate. Don't worry, Grace. I'll bet, once you scratch beneath the surface, you'll find Anna's at the bottom of this. There's something not right about her.'

Cassie laughed. 'Didn't stop you flirting with her at the Filbys' drinks.'

'What do you mean?' His face was all innocence. 'We were discussing Brexit.'

'You were putty in her hands.'

I watched their to-and-froing with amusement, then interrupted, addressing Evan, 'Is she really attractive?'

He stretched a kink in his neck. 'Well, you know.'

'No, I don't know. On a scale of one to ten, where would you put her?'

He widened his eyes. 'You're asking me to tell you that in front of the wife?'

'Don't mind me,' Cassie said. 'Go right ahead. I'm interested.'

'She's striking,' Evan said. He rubbed his jaw, looking from me to Cassie. 'Oh, for Christ's sake. Right, you asked for it. Anna is a nine.'

'Wow,' Cassie said. 'What does that make me?'

'I knew you would take it like that.' He sighed and stretched across the table to take her hand. 'You are gorgeous, darling. Anna is a nine, but she's trouble, so she scares men off.'

'Digging yourself even deeper, dear,' Cassie said.

I remember Evan's words as I make breakfast for Lottie. Anna scares men. Why? What is it about her that provokes that reaction? I wish I had questioned him more closely, but I thought it best to change the subject. What I think is that it's the conflict between the predator in Anna and the needy, vulnerable woman that creates the problematic vibe.

Trouble.

I spend the Monday morning taking an inventory in a swanky apartment round the corner from Harrods, and I'm home and about to turn into my driveway when I stop myself in time. There's a car parked across the entrance to the forecourt, blocking Nick's car in. I stare at it, infuriated. It doesn't belong to Marsh, and it doesn't look like an unmarked police car. Perhaps Cora's invited a friend over. I get off my bike and manoeuvre it through the gap.

I let myself into the house quietly, expecting whoever it is to be in the kitchen. But they're not. I can hear Cora's voice coming from upstairs. She's using the tone she used with Douglas that day she first met him: earnest, interested, verging on flirtatious. There's no welcome from Toffee, and his lead is not on its hook, so I deduce that Tim has made himself scarce. I slip off my leather jacket, unzip and tug off my boots, then follow the voices up to my bedroom.

A man is opening and closing the wardrobe doors, peering in and casually flicking through my clothes. He and Cora sense my presence at the same time. There's a long, uncomfortable silence before Cora bustles forward.

'Grace. I wasn't expecting you back so soon.'

'What's going on?'

Her companion extends a hand. 'George Bonner. From Bonner and Brightman. I was just admiring the quality of the carpentry. You have a beautiful house.'

I stare him out. 'Why are you here?'

'I'm—'

'I asked George to do a valuation,' Cora interrupts, stepping forward, as if to protect him from the volcano bubbling up inside me. 'I thought in the circumstances it would be a good idea to find out where we stood.'

I turn back to George. 'I'd like you to leave.'

He doesn't move, startled into catatonia.

'Now.'

My voice is sharp enough to knock some sense into him. Cora and I listen to his footsteps, and the shamefaced click of the front door.

'Explain,' I say. 'Tell me why you've invited an estate agent into my home behind my back. I'm interested.'

She draws a breath. 'Someone has to be practical if—'

I clench my teeth. 'Don't say it.'

'I have to, Grace. If the worst turns out to be true, can you afford the mortgage on this place?'

'That's my business.'

'Face it,' Cora says. 'You can't. You have a job that

253

pays for your little luxuries, but without Nick's income, you'd be in trouble.'

'I wouldn't be the only one, would I?'

'I was only trying to help,' she sniffs. 'I've got some shopping to do. I'll get out of your hair.'

'That would be nice.'

'Why are you so hostile?'

'Me? You're the one who's here uninvited. You're the one creating a horrible atmosphere.'

Her expression is sour. 'You are not married to my son and he isn't the father of your child. In his absence Tim and I have as much right to be here as you, if not more. We're not going anywhere, so you might as well get used to it.'

'You've got to be ready,' Douglas says. 'If Cora is getting a valuation, it means they're going to make a claim.'

Douglas arrived at two o'clock, fresh from a meeting in town, in a suit and tie. He looks good; elegant and authoritative. I asked him over so that I could discuss Cora's latest outrage with someone who understands the law.

'She wouldn't dare.'

'For God's sake. What do you think this is about? Stop blinding yourself to the truth. You have zero rights in the event of Nick's death. The only thing you can do, if it comes to that, is make a claim on his estate. You have to establish your right to be here. This is nuts. You could lose everything if you're not careful.'

'He's *not* dead.'

'And you have your head in the fucking sand.'

'I don't want to talk about it.'

He throws up his hands. 'What am I here for, then?'

That's a fair point. I stare into my cooling mug of tea, wishing it was a glass of wine. 'Sorry.'

He lets out his breath. His tone becomes gentle. 'You cannot afford to react to the Ritchies by getting hysterical. You need to keep your cool. There's a lot at stake here. This place must be worth two million at least. If it does turn out that Nick is dead . . .'

I scowl, but this time I don't interrupt.

'You'll have a battle on your hands, but your relationship and circumstances will be taken into account and you will probably come away with something. If Nick isn't found, this could drag on for years, but you won't need to leave the property, not until he has a Declaration of Presumed Death. Those two will fight you for everything, they'll make your life uncomfortable, but you mustn't give up, for Lottie's sake.'

'But this house won't be mine, whatever happens?'

I look around and he follows my gaze. This big, light room was my fantasy. I designed it. The floor is stone, the work surfaces glittering granite, the cupboard doors a relaxing shade of grey. The downlights are industrial pewter, sourced from LASSCO in Vauxhall, the stainless-steel fridge-freezer was shipped over from America. My God, the money we spent. And I could lose the lot to Nick's parents.

'Not legally, no,' Douglas says. 'That's why you have to be clever. I'll help you. I'll make sure you're treated fairly.'

This has got to be my darkest moment: when Nick's

absence boils down to nothing more than money; to house prices; to net worth. To a grubby battle over his assets. It makes me feel sick, but so does losing, so does seeing my daughter going without. I glance at Douglas's face. Not long ago he was talking about leverage. What is he prepared to say to get that? What part will I have to play? It doesn't bear thinking about. On the other hand, what Tim did to Anna was appalling, and if it comes to it, I'd rather use that than involve Lottie.

He sees me looking at him and smiles faintly.

'Douglas.' Do I really want to say this? 'Tim seduced a girl when she was fifteen. That's rape, isn't it? Neither of them would want that coming out.'

'*What?* Who?' he asks.

'The daughter of a family friend.' Best not to name Anna yet. Approached carefully, she might be willing to make a complaint of historical rape, but I don't want her scared off by Douglas. 'Don't say anything, all right?'

Before he can respond, the front door opens and Toffee's lead jangles as it's unclipped, keys are dropped on to the dish.

'Oh great,' I say. 'That's all I need.'

'Grace,' Tim calls. 'You in?'

'In here,' I shout back. 'You'd better go,' I tell Douglas.

'I'll stick around. I'd like to see Lottie.'

'No. Just go. You'll see her at the weekend.'

'No?' He looks down at me, his lip curled. 'You don't get to tell me what to do. Back off, Grace.'

I recoil. I hate it when he's in this mood; sneering and cruel.

He plasters an insincere smile on his face and looks past me. 'Cora.'

I didn't know she was there. She's wearing a tailored wool coat that looks expensive. I've never considered or felt irked by the amount Cora spends on her clothes, but in the last few days I've become hyper aware of expenditure, and it annoys me even though it isn't a new purchase. Nick pays for his mother's extravagance.

'What's he doing here?' she says.

Gone are the flirtatious smiles; her eyes are like flint. Her son is missing, and I'm home alone with his rival. She doesn't like it one little bit.

'I invited him in. Cora, honestly, you have to stop this. I'm not being disloyal to Nick. And anyway, how I live my life is really none of your business.'

'I only hope you know what you're doing.' Cora turns on her heel and stalks out of the room.

'Oh dear,' I say.

'She'll get over it.'

Tim is the closest to the door when Lottie bangs the knocker. He sweeps her into his arms and swings her round, even though she's getting too big for such treatment, and frankly our hall isn't wide enough to accommodate her gangly legs any more. She adores the attention but for the first time I feel a twinge of unease. I have to stop myself from ordering him to put her down. There is nothing wrong with their relationship. What happened with Anna was different. If he had malicious intentions, I would have felt it.

The furrows between Douglas's brows deepen. I wish

I hadn't told him now. I can feel his resentment building. I know him well enough to understand something of what he's feeling. He puts up with enough from Nick, but this other man's familiarity with his daughter is rubbing his nose in it, and now he knows what Tim did, he can't bear it.

My ex's mood isn't without justification; Tim is deliberately baiting him. The atmosphere is thick with testosterone and suppressed anger, but Tim ignores the signs, treating Douglas like a rival for Lottie's affections, punishing him for provoking Cora. What angers me is that Lottie is being used as a pawn. I'm about to intervene, but Douglas gets there first, snapping abruptly, his voice like the crack of a whip,

'Lottie. Go up to your room.'

Lottie glances at me. 'What's happening, Mum?'

'Nothing.' I glare at Douglas. 'Sweetie, go upstairs, just for ten minutes. Dad and I need to have a private chat with your grandparents.'

'We're not . . .' Cora starts, but Tim shushes her.

Lottie makes a face. I raise my eyebrows, forcing a smile. She wrinkles her nose and slouches out of the room with a teenage pout.

'You shouldn't have spoken to her like that,' I say. 'None of this is her fault.'

'You should go, Douglas,' Cora says. 'You're making everyone uncomfortable.'

When Douglas speaks his voice is dangerously soft. 'I'm so sorry if my presence is upsetting, but I'm protecting the most important person in my life. I need to know that my daughter is safe in this house.'

'Oh for goodness' sake,' Cora snaps. 'Of course she is. What on earth do you think is going to happen to her?'

He ignores the question and turns his attention to Tim. 'I've been having a look at you. You have quite a history, don't you? Bankruptcy, screwing your friends out of their savings. And the rest.'

Tim's jaw tightens. 'I don't know what you're talking about.'

Even I'm shocked. How the hell does Douglas know this? I didn't tell him. He works in tech security, so I presume he has ways and means; it's the only thing that makes sense.

Douglas says something under his breath. The effect is immediate. Tim pales.

'You arrogant sod.'

Douglas grabs him by his shirt and propels him back on to his chair. He leans over, and I see spittle on Tim's face as Douglas hisses, 'Am I making myself clear?'

'Get off him,' Cora shrieks. 'You leave him alone.'

'Douglas.' I try to pull him away, but his sinews are like iron rope. 'Stop it, for Christ's sake.'

Douglas lets go, turning away and brushing his hands against his black jeans, as if to remove something unpleasant.

'It's nice when your ex-lovers rally round, isn't it?' Cora says sarcastically. 'I'm sure my son would be grateful.'

I glare at her. 'I've put up with your snide comments for long enough. The only reason you're worried is because of Nick's money. You've been sponging off him. You got our house valued.' Years of pent-up resentment come gushing out. 'You're a vulture.'

'I despise you,' Cora says. 'I've despised you since the first time I saw you.'

I look her up and down. 'The feeling is mutual.'

Tim turns with a groan. 'Cora, I think we should leave.'

'Stop being so weak and back me up,' Cora snaps.

Douglas catches my eye and I scowl, but he smiles. He likes what's happening, gets a kick at seeing those two at each other's throats. He picks up his keys and strolls out of the room.

'What did you say to him?' I ask at the door.

'Shh,' he says.

'No, I will not 'shh'. Tell me.'

'I hinted that I knew what he was.'

'Douglas. I told you not to say anything.'

'He was manhandling my daughter. What did you expect me to do?'

Once he's gone, I come back into the room to find Cora sobbing – an ugly, grating noise. Tim has his arms around her and is talking to her gently. I don't know why the sight of Tim demonstrating love to Cora should be such a shock, but it is. I rebuke myself; just because I don't love her, doesn't mean no one else can.

'I'm so sorry about that,' I say.

'I don't think it was a personal best for any of us,' Tim responds with a smile. 'Why don't you go and check Lottie's OK?'

I grimace. 'I hope she didn't hear.'

Toffee follows me upstairs and sits obediently outside her bedroom door while I wait for an answer to my knock. There is none. I call her name, and then knock a second time and tell myself that she has her earphones in. I feel a deep sense of unease as I open the door. Her bed is rumpled, but empty. I try her bathroom, but she's not there either. I lean over the banister and shout her name. No response. I run downstairs and burst into the kitchen.

'I can't find Lottie.'

GRACE

Monday, 30 April 2018

'SHE MUST HAVE HEARD US,' I SAY, SHAKING AS I OPEN my car. I get hold of Douglas. He isn't at the station yet and says he'll do a circuit of the streets.

I ask my mobile to call Cassie as I pull out. A horn blares and I brake hard and jolt forward. I sit, gripping the steering wheel tightly. That was close. Cassie answers and I explain briefly, my voice cracking.

'We're not at home,' she says. 'Hannah? Have you had any messages from Lottie?'

'No,' I hear Hannah reply.

I call Mara, and while she runs upstairs to ask Leila, I turn on to the parade and pull into a parking spot.

'She doesn't know anything about it, I'm afraid,' Mara says. 'Try the others. And call me if you hear anything, I'll be worrying.'

I put my head in my hands, then someone bangs on the window. It's a mother from the school.

'Grace, are you all right?' she asks.

'I'm fine. A headache, that's all. You haven't seen any

kids on the street, have you? Only Lottie is out with her friends, and I need to get her back in for her tea.'

She gives me a disapproving look. 'No, I haven't seen them. But if I do, I'll tell them to go straight home.'

'Thanks.'

She now thinks I'm an appalling mother. She doesn't know what being neglected and left to roam actually means. It's not our carefully brought-up girls, playing out with their friends in a place where they know practically everyone, it's a tired and hungry child kicking her heels on dirty, litter-strewn streets because she can't get into her flat and has no idea where her mother is or what time she'll be back. I feel tears welling up and hurriedly wipe them away, then start the car. I'm sure Lottie is fine, just lying low, making a point. She's a sensible girl. But that woman's disapproval is infectious, and panic begins to creep in, an insidious tide.

There isn't a paedophile behind every tree, I tell myself. Keep things in perspective. And yet the look on that woman's face, and the judgement implied, has spooked me.

Douglas calls to tell me that he hasn't found her and he's going to call the police. I want to be sick. The next time my phone rings it's Anna.

'Grace? Is everything OK? Lottie's come over. I didn't forget a playdate, did I?'

'What!' I hit the brake and earn my second angry blast. I hold my hand up to apologize. 'No. She ran out of the house. I've been looking for her.'

'I had no idea she was here until two minutes ago. Kai must have sneaked her in while I was on the phone.'

'Oh God. Thank you. Thank you so much. I'll come straight over.'

'You're shaking. Sit down and I'll make you a cup of tea. Don't be cross with Lottie.'

The remark jars. It's none of her business, and I haven't settled within myself how to react. Obviously, I don't want to overdo it, but neither do I want to pretend it didn't happen, that I wasn't frightened. Lottie knows the effect it would have had on me, or she wouldn't have come here. It's the last place I'd have looked. That was an act designed to cause maximum distress, without being overtly bad. Shades of her father, I think with a wry grimace.

Anna leans against the kitchen counter and studies my face.

'She's never done anything like this before,' I say. 'I didn't know she and Kai were such good friends.'

'Nor did I. Young love, do you think?'

I smile reluctantly. 'Maybe.'

'I'm sorry you were worried.' She hesitates, her eyes on my face. 'You do know this is about her father, don't you?'

'She's naturally worried about him.'

'No, I meant her real dad. Listen, Grace, do you think you should be spending so much time with him? From what she's told me, it's confusing her that you get on so well.'

I raise my eyebrows. She hasn't seen us fight. 'We get on well because we make the effort, for her sake.'

'I know. Damned if you do, damned if you don't. She

loves him and she obviously adored Nick, and this is a huge blow to her. Massive. She might not show it because she's anxious about worrying you, but I think she's struggling.'

'Adores.'

She frowns. 'What?'

'You said adored. Please don't refer to Nick in the past tense.'

'I'm really sorry, I didn't mean it.'

'And I can't avoid Douglas,' I say tartly. 'I'd better get Lottie and go. But thank you anyway.'

'Wait.' She sighs. 'I've been on my own on and off for five years, so I know what it's like and I know how tempting old loves can be when you're at rock bottom, but going backwards never works.'

I look at her with horror. 'I don't know where you're getting this, but it's rubbish. I'm not going to get sucked back into a relationship with Douglas.'

She narrows her eyes. 'You do mention his name a lot.'

Do I? I hadn't realized.

When I don't reply, she says, 'Don't take this the wrong way, but from what Lottie's told me, it sounds like you're making a play for him.'

'When did she tell you that?'

'Oh, don't worry, we haven't sat down and had an in-depth conversation. It's just from remarks she's made.'

'Well, I've no idea where she's got it from, but it's a million miles from the truth.'

'You're blushing.'

'That's because you're making me feel guilty even though I haven't done anything.'

265

'OK.' She holds up her hands, palms towards me, friendly. 'I didn't mean to offend you; just to warn you. Sometimes children find it hard to talk to their parents but will open up to an aunt or a family friend. Oh, and she told me something else you might be interested in.'

I groan audibly. 'What?'

'When she stayed with him last weekend, she overheard him talking to someone on the phone. She said it sounded like a girlfriend from the way he was speaking. She thinks he's seeing someone. So, if you are thinking along those lines, it's best you don't get your hopes up.'

My muscles tighten, particularly the ones in my face. I pull my mouth into a smile. 'Good. I'm glad. It's about time he had someone in his life.'

I grab my keys and leave the room, calling up to Lottie. She comes out of Kai's bedroom looking shamefaced and defiant. I wait for her at the bottom of the stairs and when she reaches me I pull her into a hug and kiss the top of her head.

'I'm sorry about that, darling. I am truly sorry.'

Her face is blotchy with tears. 'You were all screaming at each other, Mum. It was horrible.'

I stroke back her hair. 'Sometimes adults go a bit mad. It's been a tough couple of weeks.'

'Cora hates me.'

'No, she doesn't, Lottie. She's just scared.'

Kai is sitting on the top step and I smile up at him. 'Thank you for looking after her.'

'Nah,' he mutters back. 'S'all right.'

* * *

At nine Tim and I take Toffee for his last walk of the day. It was my suggestion. I wanted to try to calm things down. I know I've said things I can't take back, but so has Cora. I have apologized but I was glad when she said she didn't feel up to coming with us.

Being out and about with Tim is a bit of an eye opener, even at this time of night. We're stopped twice by locals wanting to chat. People do that when you have a dog, but this is different; he's only been here a couple of weeks, and already everyone seems to know him.

'Can we talk about Devon?' I ask.

'What do you want to know?'

How can I say what I want to say, without betraying Anna's trust? I think for a moment. One little white lie won't hurt. 'Alex Wells told me that Nick was bullied on that holiday. Were you aware that was happening?'

'I knew he wasn't settling in and that the girls weren't being particularly helpful. But I thought they'd sort it out between them eventually. Kids will be kids.'

I look up into his face, surprised. 'You didn't see that your son was deeply unhappy, that he was being ostracized by the others? How could you not have seen that?'

'They were supposed to entertain each other, and we assumed that was what they were doing. However, since you ask, I chose to ignore it because I believed my son had to learn to fight his own battles.'

'You could have given him some fatherly advice.'

'And humiliate him further by letting him know I had noticed? I don't think that would have helped.' Toffee deposits a stick at his feet, and he picks it up and throws it, sending the dog careering after it. 'I was under a lot of pressure at the time.'

'Yes. The restaurant. And your mishandling of Sean Wells' investment?'

He brushes the comment away. 'Nothing was mishandled. Sean knew that restaurants are high risk. Money should never come between friends.'

I try and reel myself in, to not turn my mouth into a weapon, but the words come of their own accord.

'But it does, doesn't it? You convinced him that his money was safe, that your restaurant was a sure thing, and you let him down.'

'I was badly let down myself.'

'Tim, can't you see, it's not so much the loss of the money as your attitude. You might not have meant it to come across that way, you might have been being defensive, but it felt to them as though you shrugged it off. If they hate you for anything, it's your lack of remorse.'

He hunches his shoulders and we walk a few paces. 'You may be right. It was hard, and I was embarrassed. And if they feel like that, then I'm sorry. But it was such a long time ago and it has no relevance to Nick's life now. We've all moved on.'

'You know that's not true.'

He sighs. 'Yup. But we all want the same thing, though, don't we? We want Nick back home. Let's try not to squabble.'

He links his arm through mine, and we walk on. I feel sorry for him, but this is a man who seduced his best friend's fifteen-year-old daughter and was never taken to task for it. Well, he's being punished now.

When we get back, I check my steps, something I haven't done in days. Knowing how far I've walked and how many calories I have burned has slipped way down on my list of priorities. Only just over two thousand, but at least I've been out. Tim glances over my shoulder.

'What's that?' he asks.

I turn the screen towards him, giving him a friendly smile because I know his question is an olive branch and I want Lottie to see us presenting a united front.

'It's to motivate me. Look.' I tap on groups and show him the little cartoons. We both go silent and I know he's looking at Nick's avatar: the cheerful little cartoon bird.

He hands it back to me. 'Can I get that? Cora's always on at me to do more exercise.'

I hesitate, then say, 'Sure. I'll invite you, you accept my invitation. Then you're on.'

'As simple as that, eh?'

'As simple as that.'

The next morning, I'm checking through my handbag to make sure I've got everything I need for an appointment with Rupert's architect, when someone comes up the steps. A shadow appears behind the door, so close to me that I start. My mind immediately goes to Nick, to the police, to Douglas. Toffee comes running out of the kitchen and I grab his collar and tell him to shush. A heavy ache settles into my diaphragm, as if someone's pressing their fist in there. I open the door.

Marsh's expression is grave, and I buckle, the blood draining from my face. He grips my elbow, then puts a fatherly arm around me and leads me into the sitting room.

'Mr and Mrs Ritchie,' he says, spotting them standing together in the kitchen doorway. 'You need to hear this as well.'

Cora is as white as a sheet as she follows us into the sitting room, Tim wooden. They sit down on the sofa and hold hands. I take the armchair.

'We've found something,' Marsh says.

GRACE

Tuesday, 1 May 2018

EVERYTHING DROPS AWAY: THE FLOOR, THE WALLS, the props that held me together; the hope and the belief that things like this happen to other people. The room spins and stars cluster in front of my eyes. I put my hand on Toffee's head, and he rests his chin on my knee and gazes up at me. Beside me Cora subsides, her shoulders curling forwards.

Devon and Cornwall Police have found a carrier bag filled with things that they think might belong to Nick, close to where Izzy allegedly went in.

The WPC accompanying Marsh comes in with cups of tea and sets them down on the coffee table, then stands to one side.

'But I would have seen it,' I say. 'I was right there.'

'If it was Nick, he went to some trouble to hide it. It'd been buried under leaves and dirt in the undergrowth, about twenty feet from where Izzy's shoes were found. You could easily have missed it. Did he really never tell you about that day?'

'No, not a word.'

'Well, obviously, we can't jump to conclusions, but from what we've been able to piece together about Nick's state of mind, it's looking like he took his own life. I think you were right, Grace. I think that being approached by both Alex Wells and Anna Foreman after so many years brought all the guilt back. We're looking at Izzy Wells' case in the light of this.'

'My son,' Cora says, drawing herself up to her full height, 'had nothing whatsoever to do with that child's unfortunate death.'

'Hang on,' Tim says, leaning forward. 'Who is Anna Foreman?'

I shrug. It's out of my hands now. 'Anna Foreman is Taisie Wells,' I say. 'She lives round the corner and her son is in the same class at Cedar Heights as Lottie. She had a conversation with Nick shortly before he disappeared.'

Tim and Cora are both staring at me, like I've just walked off my spaceship.

'Why haven't you shared this with us?' Cora asks.

'She asked me not to.'

'So your loyalties are with her, rather than Nick's family? That's fantastic.'

'Cora,' Tim admonishes her. 'Let's not worry about Taisie now. Let's worry about Nick.' He turns to Marsh. 'Surely if he drowned his body would have been found? It didn't take long to find Izzy.'

'I don't have an answer to that, I'm afraid. With any luck the divers will find him – bodies can get stuck in logjams.'

I flinch.

'How can you be so sure they're Nick's things?' Tim asks. 'They could belong to anybody.'

'That's true, of course, and I'll need Grace to have a look, but we found his wallet too.'

'Perhaps he's faked his death,' Cora suggests, looking pointedly at me.

'Why would he do that?' Marsh asks. 'Is he involved in anything illegal?'

'No.' I glare at Cora. 'Nick is not a coward. Whatever it was, he would have faced it.'

Marsh glances from me to Cora with interest, before speaking. 'The other reason we know they belong to Nick is because he left a note tucked into his wallet. It's addressed to you, Grace.' He hands me a pair of latex gloves. 'Sorry, but it's evidence.'

I lift my eyes to his face as I pull them on. 'Have you read it?'

'Yes.'

I take it from him and walk away from Tim and Cora.

Darling Grace, I've wanted to talk to you about this for a long time, but haven't been able to pluck up the courage. I love you so much and don't want you to think less of me. I shouldn't have involved you in my life, not until I'd told you everything.

The next line wavers, and my heart breaks for him. What he must have been feeling when he wrote this.

I'm sorry. I am so sorry. Please forgive me. I love you both so much.

'He didn't finish it,' I say when Marsh holds out his hand. I give it back to him reluctantly. 'I don't believe it's a suicide note. He wanted to tell me something.'

'He's asking you to forgive him,' Marsh points out. 'Perhaps he's expecting it to become public knowledge, and he couldn't handle it. He took the only way out.'

'No. That letter has been crumpled up at some stage, so that implies he threw it away, doesn't it?'

Marsh sighs. 'We'll show it to a psychologist. See what they say. But at the very least, this proves that Nick was in torment.'

I put my hand in front of my mouth to stop the moan of despair. Marsh holds the door open and settles me in the police car.

An officer lays the bag on the table and opens it with latex-gloved hands, and an odour of damp leaves and dirt fills the room. There are the blue deck shoes Nick had been wearing. His wallet. A pen. A blue cotton hanky. The officer opens the wallet so that I can inspect the credit cards. There's a lump in my throat as I shake my head and look down at my hands.

He misinterprets. 'The items don't belong to Mr Ritchie?'

'Yes. Yes, they do. Sorry, I . . . I don't need to see any more,' I say. 'It all belongs to Nick.'

It's midday when I'm delivered home in a police car, drained and emotionally exhausted. I can hardly believe it was only yesterday that I found Cora showing an estate agent round. Too much has happened, and my mind is reeling. I let myself in, and walk straight to the fridge, take out a bottle of white wine even though it's early afternoon. I pour myself a generous measure, wander outside and sit down. Toffee mooches around the flower beds, following the scent of Mrs Jeffers' cats. They treat these gardens as their fiefdom. I stare at the blossom, thinking how much Nick loved this time of year, how much he loved to see things change. I changed when I met him. I blossomed and thrived, but the rot was there all the time, I suppose.

Tim puts a sandwich down in front of me. I pick it up and nibble the edges. After a minute or two Cora comes out and the three of us sit side by side, in an oddly companionable silence. Tim looks older and smaller. Cora is diminished too. All I can think is that now, surely, they will go.

A bag containing items believed to be the property of missing thirty-four-year-old banker Nick Ritchie has been discovered concealed close to the banks of the River Dart in Devon by police sniffer dogs at around 8 a.m. today. A spokesman said that investigations are ongoing and confirmed that while they are keeping an open mind, it is increasingly likely that the inquest will return a verdict of suicide. As a teenager Mr Ritchie was on holiday in the area when a thirteen-year-old girl drowned. The girl was a friend of the family. Sources close to Mr Ritchie have said that he subsequently suffered depression. Mr Ritchie was

*reported missing from his two-million-pound home
by his girlfriend Grace Trelawney on Sunday, 15th
April, after leaving his house the previous evening to
go for a walk. Anyone with information should get in
touch with Greater London Police on the following
number.*

A photograph comes up on the screen. It's me and Nick
at a charity ball, taken at least two years ago. He's in a
dinner jacket and I'm in a slinky blue dress. I remember
that night; we had a good time. Nick drank too much
and bid for a weekend at an expensive country house
hotel. I'm glad they chose that one, rather than his work
portrait, it's truer to how he really is, but I guess they
liked it because of the human interest. A happy young
man with a pretty woman on his arm.

I switch off the television, and five minutes later the tele-
phone starts to ring. That's how long it takes to track
someone these days. Even though Marsh forewarned me
about the statement and its probable result, I answer
that first call.

'Miss Trelawney. James Pickett from the *Mirror*. How
much did you know about your boyfriend? Did he murder that little girl? Is that why he killed himself? Because
he couldn't bear the guilt any more?'

I put the phone down and don't answer it again.
Within the hour, there are several journalists loitering
outside my house, taking pictures. They talk to each
other while they fiddle with their cameras. They don't
ring the doorbell, but I guess that's because they

know at this stage there's no point, but their presence there makes me feel breathless. A feeling of dread descends.

I go upstairs and find an old jumper of Nick's. I press it to my nose and sigh with relief as I breathe in his scent. I take it to bed with me and stare into space, not moving, unable to do anything. I can't accept this. If they had found his body, then of course, but they haven't. As far as I am concerned, Nick is not dead.

Cameras flash with a staccato barrage of clicks, blinding and confusing me as I open the door and find Douglas on my front step. Everyone shouts at once.

'Grace! Fabulous house. Must be worth a couple of million. Who inherits?'

'Did Nick do something to Izzy Wells? Is that why he topped himself?'

'What's your relationship with Grace, mate?'

Douglas moves past me and I fling the door shut. Silence descends like a fisherman's net, trapping us together.

'What're you doing here?' I say. 'You can't just turn up without warning me first.'

'If you don't answer your phone, what do you expect? I've had the police asking me all sorts of questions. If I get dragged into your mess, I've a right to know what's going on.'

'Well, I'm sorry. I'm still getting used to this. They were bound to talk to you; they'll be talking to all my friends, I expect.'

I stand between him and the kitchen door and don't

invite him further into the house. The light is dim, and I hope he can't tell how much I'm shaking.

He sighs. 'Where is everyone?'

'Lottie's at Hannah's. Tim and Cora have gone home. I think they need time alone to process this as well.'

He makes a face. 'Really? For good, I hope.'

'I don't think so.' His face blurs and I turn away, fighting a wave of emotion.

'Grace.' His voice is soft. 'It's going to be OK.'

'What am I going to tell Lottie?' I burst out. 'If his body had been found, it would be easier. At least she could say goodbye. But this way she's always going to hope. *I'm* always going to hope.'

'They still might find him. It's early days. But we need to tell her the truth, because she'll read about it. We can't stop that happening. We'll tell her together.'

I push my fingers through my hair and swear under my breath. 'I think I'm going mad.'

'It's natural to feel that way. This would be a difficult and confusing time for anyone, let alone someone . . .'

He stops, but I'm easily able to fill the gap. 'Someone like me.'

'You've come a long way from that girl,' he says. 'A very long way. Look at you. Look at what you've achieved, what you have.'

He's right. I have solid walls around me and a roof over my head. I have a community and friends who think I'm ordinary; just another mum like them. But all this stuff, all these material belongings, they'll vanish along with Nick. Because without him, I am nothing. I fold my arms and take a deep breath.

'Stuff's going to come out about me, Douglas. About us. Things I really don't want people to know. I don't think I'll be able to cope if the papers get hold of my history.'

He smiles down at me and strokes my hair. 'You're not going to be held accountable for something you did in your teens.'

'Of course I am. That's the way it works. Everyone loves a fall from grace.' I smile. 'No pun intended. What I did to you . . .'

'I forgave you a long time ago.'

'Forgiven but not forgotten,' I retort.

'Absolutely that.'

He untucks his shirt, and I reach to touch the scar, an inch below his ribcage. I run my fingers gently over its puckered surface. The things we do when we're young and desperate. He holds my hand against it, then lets it go. I dry my tears and pull myself up with the banister.

'You'll be a fifteen-minute wonder, that's all,' he says. 'You know what you have to do when the big wave comes at you.'

'Hold my breath and dive under it.'

'That's right. Now, why don't you go and get Lottie. The sooner we tell her, the better.' He takes my jacket from its hook and holds it out for me, and I slip my arms into the sleeves, as obedient as a child.

In the hall I take a deep breath then pull open the door and dive out into the fray. I pretend they aren't there, that their voices are geese clucking, the flashes are lightning. My heart is pounding, my ears ringing with the sound of my own name, with Nick's name. With Izzy's.

We gather round the kitchen table – father, mother, daughter – and I tell her what's happened. There is no way of softening the blow. I watch Lottie's face as it pales, as her eyes redden and her chin trembles. She gets up and buries herself in Douglas's arms. I feel a flash of jealousy, so inappropriate that it shocks me.

'It'll be all right, baby,' Douglas says. 'Everything will be all right.'

He glances at me over her shoulder, his eyes warm. I gaze back, with a dawning sense of shame. I'm letting him in, letting him get under my skin again; and that's what he wants. This situation suits him down to the ground. Anna warned me about this, about the temptation of old loves when you're feeling vulnerable. I insisted she was wrong, but she was right. Douglas knows me, and he's here, flesh and blood, whereas Nick has gone and may very well be dead. I need to be on my guard.

'We'll be fine now, Douglas,' I say, glancing pointedly at the door.

He hesitates, but I stand up and wait until he has no choice but to take the hint.

I fetch his jacket from where he hung it over the banister and hand it to him without saying a word. Lottie and I accompany him to the door. He dips his head to kiss my cheek, but I twist out of reach, leaving him floundering. As if to make up for my coldness, Lottie hugs him hard.

'See you Friday, kiddo,' he says.

He opens the door, hesitating in front of the cameras, before striding down the steps and elbowing his way through the press. He's taller than any of them. When I close the door the house releases its breath. It's been tough since Nick went missing, but I have a feeling that my problems are about to get worse.

GRACE

Friday, 4 May 2018

TIM POURS ME A GLASS OF WINE. I TAKE IT OVER TO the table. Cora darts him a look and purses her mouth. They've been back since two o'clock this afternoon. He takes a seat and folds his hands in front of him. The last three days have passed by in a state of suspended numbness, but now we are gathered at my kitchen table to talk about The Situation, while Lottie is out of the way with her father.

'Nick's body may be found, but equally it may not,' Tim says.

I keep my hands folded over my stomach as I listen, staring at the blank sheet of paper in front of me. Tim put it there, in case I want to make notes.

'If that proves to be the case,' he continues, 'we'll have to accept that we'll be in legal limbo at least until the Guardianship Act becomes law.'

I've looked into this. The Guardianship Law allows relatives to look after the affairs of loved ones with disabilities, but the new Act will cover missing persons as well. At the moment families have to wait seven years; a horrible situation, and one that I'm beginning to feel the effects of already. I can't talk to Nick's bank, I can't close down standing orders; even the utility bills are in his name. Nick set them up when he bought the house; I didn't think to suggest they were put in both our names. I can see how much danger Lottie and I are in; how much we could lose.

Cora is speaking now. 'But the Act has passed three readings, so it's more than likely it'll go through, and when that happens, Grace . . .' She pauses, then says, 'Tim and I will be applying for guardianship of Nick's estate.'

I'm confused at first, then the penny drops. This is exactly what Douglas warned me about. 'You are joking?'

'Certainly not. This is extremely serious. As Nick hasn't made a will, there's going to be a complicated process which I hardly think you have the education to follow.'

'Douglas will help me.'

'Give me strength.'

'Cora,' Tim says, quelling her.

She folds her arms and sits back. 'You forget; we are his next of kin.'

'I haven't forgotten that. You won't let me.'

Tim cuts in. 'Cora and I appreciate that Nick wouldn't have wanted to leave you and Lottie high and dry . . .'

'High and dry?' I echo. 'I can't afford to walk away from this. How are we expected to live?'

Cora's gaze moves swiftly over my face. 'You have a job.'

'What's that got to do with anything? I don't make nearly enough money to cover our outgoings.'

'That's my point. None of us do, so the sooner we can work something out the better.'

'Yes, but—'

'Just to clarify one or two things,' Cora says. 'Could we—'

'Remember what we talked about, darling.'

I look from one to the other. 'What did *we* talk about?'

Cora puts her hand on Tim's arm, as if to silence him. 'We need to make sure everyone's on the same page.'

'And what page would that be?'

'Perhaps later,' Tim says. His protest is feeble, and Cora loses patience.

'It's best to be prepared. We know you wouldn't want to take anything that isn't rightfully yours, so I was going to suggest that you have a look round the house and place Post-it notes on the items that you paid for.'

I look at Tim, but he averts his gaze. The silence is treacly.

'We are prepared to be reasonable when it comes to your settlement,' Cora goes on. 'Which you have no legal right to demand, of course. When this house is sold, we'll use part of the proceeds to set up a trust that will pay for Lottie's university education. I think that's very generous, considering she isn't a blood relation.'

My jaw has dropped so far, it's practically scraping the floor.

'We're prepared to give you and Lottie one month's

notice, but after that I'm afraid you'll have to make other arrangements.'

'This is my house.'

'No, it isn't. The deeds are in Nick's name. You weren't married. Everything that belonged to him, will belong to us. I'm sure there are one or two articles of furniture we can let you have, to help you set up, but otherwise, I'm afraid, this house and its contents are ours. I refuse to believe my son saw you as a permanent fixture in his life. He expected it to end at some point and, when it did, he would have fallen in love with . . .' She pauses meaningfully. 'With a more suitable girl and married her. He would have given us grandchildren.'

We sit in silence. Tim fiddles with his phone. Cora looks down at her clasped hands. My mouth is dry.

I drink some water, then say quietly, 'Nick loved both of us very much. We were his family. More than you've ever been.'

'I beg your pardon?' Her voice is full of bile.

'Maybe we should leave it here,' Tim says. 'Before someone says something they regret. We'll give you a chance to get your head round what we've said. It's a lot to take in.'

'You take over my home, with no regard to my feelings, and stake your claim at the first possible moment. For God's sake, there's no real proof your son is dead. You are unbelievable.'

'Nick is dead,' Cora says, folding her arms. 'That will be proved sooner or later. I've accepted it and you need to accept it as well, for your own sake and your daughter's.'

'You can't do this.'

'Yes, we can. And yes, we will. I've never liked you, Grace.'

'You could have fooled me.'

She tuts. 'Nick was such a happy little boy and he would have been a happy man if he hadn't met you.'

'He was happy,' I say through gritted teeth. 'We loved each other.'

'So why, when Douglas Parr clicks his fingers, do you come running? Nick hated that man.'

The word hate jolts me. Nick wasn't Douglas's biggest fan, but he respected what he meant to Lottie. 'They were fine. Don't exaggerate.'

'I'm only repeating what he said to me.'

'I don't believe you.'

'Be that as it may. The fact remains that you are now here on sufferance. You'd better start looking for something more modest. I hear there are some perfectly decent ex-council properties in the same catchment as Lottie's school, so at least she can keep up her friendships.'

I say, very slowly, 'This is my home, my house. The things in it, Nick and I chose together, bought together.'

She shrugs. 'That won't make any difference, I'm afraid. If he had loved you that much, he would have married you.'

'We were engaged. We were committed to each other.'

She laughs. 'You're not wearing an engagement ring.'

'That's because he had only just asked me.'

She raises her eyebrows slowly. 'Grace. He didn't. You're clutching at straws, and it's pathetic. Now, I don't know where you came from, but quite frankly, you're not one of us. You're still young, and you're an attractive woman; I'm sure you'll find another wealthy man to leech off.'

'How dare you? I have never leeched off anyone in my life. And I don't have to go anywhere.'

Cora smirks. 'Neither do we. We're putting our house on the market and moving in here permanently. Now, I have things to do, so if you wouldn't mind . . .'

'I do mind, actually. You don't get to dismiss me, Cora. This conversation isn't over.'

She looks down her nose. 'I'm afraid it is. Without my son you are nothing.'

I race upstairs to the spare bedroom where I begin tearing clothes off hangers and throwing them into their suitcases. Cora pounds up after me, bursts in and pulls one of Tim's sweaters out of my hands.

'Get out of here! Don't touch our things, you little bitch.' She starts clawing at me, grabbing at my hands, her manicured fingernails gouging at my wrist. It hurts so much that I elbow her hard. She falls against a chair, rights herself and comes for me. I duck out of her way, pull open the chest of drawers and scoop armfuls of underwear on to the bed. Bras and knickers, tights, Tim's socks and boxers. Cora keeps shoving them back in, but I pick up a bundle of clothes, take them out of the room and throw them over the stairs. Some of them get caught on the banisters on their way down, giving the stairwell a chaotically festive look.

Cora comes storming out of the bedroom, her hand raised. I step to one side to avoid a slap and she trips over Toffee, who has sprung forward to protect me. Tim catches her, and they struggle, almost falling downstairs. Cora, normally so coolly elegant, lands heavily on her husband in an ungainly sprawl.

I come to my senses. Horrified, I try to help her up, but she shoves my hand away.

'That's assault. I'll be reporting you to the police.'

'But I didn't,' I splutter. Then I look at the three of us and feel sick. I shouldn't have lost my temper. The last time I lost control this badly was with Douglas. He still bears the scar to prove it, and I have a criminal record. 'I'm sorry,' I say. 'I shouldn't have done that.'

Tim rubs the back of his head. 'Oh Lord,' he says. 'That was a bit . . . uh . . . unexpected.'

'I'm not sure I can stand,' Cora says.

I wince. 'Shall I call an ambulance?'

'No. Just get out of my sight.'

I hesitate, thrown by the vitriol in her voice. 'I'll get some ice.'

I run downstairs and into the kitchen. Cora's mobile starts ringing. Ignoring it, I get a packet of frozen peas out of the freezer and wrap it in a clean dishcloth. Then I pick up the phone and go back up.

'Your phone rang,' I say, handing it to her. I kneel down next to Tim and press the improvised ice pack against his bump.

Cora taps her phone, checks the display. 'It's my mother's nursing home.' She swipes the screen, puts it to her ear and stands up, surprisingly lithe considering her injuries. We listen to her side of the call. It's obvious things aren't good.

'Something up?' Tim grunts, when she finishes.

'Mum's worse. The manager thinks it's pneumonia, but whatever it is, they don't think she'll last. I'll have to go tonight.'

'I'm so sorry,' I say.

She doesn't reply.

Once Cora has left, the house feels different; not better or worse, but weirdly expectant, as if it's holding its breath, as if it knows something will happen. I'm on my own with Tim and despite his easy charm, I'm on high alert. I like him; I've always felt that he's on my side, but now I'm not so sure. Nick made excuses for his father, but the very fact that he did told its own story. Tim is a coward; the kind of man who says one thing to one person, the opposite to another, because he's scared of not being liked. What would he do to prevent anyone finding out how morally bankrupt he really is?

I wonder if, in actual fact, he hates me, wants me out of his life as much as his wife does; and the sooner the better. I've rocked the boat.

'We're not going anywhere, are we, darling?' I whisper to Toffee, who pricks his ears, looks up at me from under his old man's eyebrows, then sighs and sinks back into his dreams.

PART 3

PART 3

ANNA

March 2017 ◆ One Year Earlier

IN A MOMENT OF WEAKNESS, ANNA CONTACTED ANGUS
Moody and met him for lunch. She chose Angus because
once upon a time the Moodys might as well have been
family. She and her siblings had treated him and Lorna
like uncle and aunt, Pansy and Freya like cousins. She
had thought about calling Lorna, but she had been her
mother's great friend and ally. She would be judgemental
in a way that Angus wouldn't.

Time had been kind to her parents' old friend: his
hair was silver grey, his figure trim, his posture still
upright; a testament to his early years in the army. He
took her to an expensive restaurant and in the spotlight
of his gaze, the words spilled out. They talked for over
an hour, mainly about her, but also about Izzy and the
effect her death had on them all. If asked, she wouldn't
have been able to say what she had been eating or which
wine he had ordered. It was so all-absorbing, so intense.
She told him about Ben's suicide, and about Kai. And
later, when her pudding had been set down in front of

her, he said, quite casually, 'Of course, Nick's working for me these days.'

Her breath caught. 'I didn't know that. That was good of you.'

'I didn't do it out of the kindness of my heart. I did it because he merits it. He's turned into an exceptionally fine young man.'

She felt unaccountably irritated. 'Maybe you'll give Kai a job too one day.'

He nodded. 'Of course. If he shows an aptitude for business. I'll be happy to talk to him.'

She smiled. 'I'll send him over in five years' time, shall I? So, how is Nick these days?' She couldn't help dripping vinegar into the way she said his name.

His eyes narrowed. 'Jealous?'

'No.'

He continued looking at her until she blushed. 'Yes, OK. A little.'

She felt a frisson and it crossed her mind that they could start an affair, that despite, or because of, the age gap, she wouldn't be averse. He was so charismatic. She silently chided herself. She would have to be nuts to go there. This was Tim all over again: her falling for a father figure. Ben had been much older too. Seventeen years her senior. She should stop looking for a daddy and find someone her own age.

He was talking to her, telling her about an author whose work he enjoyed, and she was mesmerized, though not by what he was saying, but by his mouth. It was the combination of relaxed self-confidence and the dizzying sense of ruthless power that provoked the fantasy.

'It's been good to see you again,' Angus said, smiling as she put on her coat. 'I hope I've helped.'

'You have.'

'Speak to your mother. It would do you both so much good.'

She shrugged, a lump forming in her throat. 'She never loved me as much as the others.'

'You mustn't think that, Taisie. Parents are always harder on the oldest. It's just the way things are.' He smiled. 'Not a problem Lorna and I had, of course.'

'My name is Anna now. I'm not that little girl any more.'

He looked directly into her eyes. 'No, you're certainly not.'

They stood in the street, and it was as if the world fell away. The silence between them was almost a living thing, surrounding them with its tentacles, drawing them together.

'Can I take you to bed?' he asked.

'Yes,' she replied.

He strode past her, lifted his hand in the air and a taxi pulled into the kerb. The next thing she knew they were kissing, and the smell of his shaving lotion was in her nostrils, their mouths were locked, their hands roving under their coats. She barely had time to notice the wide avenue, the stucco facade of the house they drew up in front of, or the stone steps up to the pillared portico, before he swept her inside and upstairs, where he undressed her slowly. He didn't appear concerned about Lorna suddenly turning up, so Anna assumed she was away. She wasn't going to be crass enough to ask. The sex was utterly fantastic. The chest hair, which had fascinated her as a child, was grey now, but just as abundant. She ran her fingers through it and tugged playfully. He grasped her wrist and dragged her against him.

He was getting dressed in the en suite bathroom when the doorbell rang. He told her to stay put, closed the bedroom door and ran downstairs. Hearing raised voices she came out on to the landing to listen. Whoever it was, was male and Angus was trying to calm him down. What she heard was enlightening.

'It's against the law, Angus. I can't believe you're justifying it.'

'You've got it wrong.'

The man laughed. 'I don't have to be particularly intelligent to know dodgy when I see it.'

'No one's been hurt. I smoothed profits, that's all. It's technical.' His voice was calm and assured, but there was an edge to it.

'You paid millions under bogus re-insurance contracts so that you could bring the money back onshore in fallow years. All perfectly legit, if ethically unsound. Then you realized that no one had missed the money paid offshore, and you couldn't resist the temptation to trouser it. I've found it, Angus, including the captive insurance company. Christ, you even made sure it was associated with a Swiss bank. All above board? I don't think so. It's sleight of hand.'

Then the door closed, and she didn't hear any more until the front door thudded shut. She sat on the bed, thinking. It was impossible to know, but that could have been Nick Ritchie. Would he have been either courageous or foolish enough to confront Angus in his own home? Possibly.

Five minutes later, when Angus came back upstairs, he was keen for her to leave. It was a little humiliating, but she understood that he had a problem. She tucked the information away in the back of her mind.

You never know, she thought, as she got into the cab, it might come in useful one day.

They only slept together that one time, and that seemed right. He was a wealthy, successful older man; she was a young woman with a tragic past. What they gave each other was balanced, was perfect.

What remained with her was the image of an adult Nick Ritchie at his side, like some kind of dynasty. She couldn't imagine what Nick looked like now, so she googled him and found a photograph on the Financial Logistics website. He had broadened out; he looked confident and muscular, pleasant. Angus had talked about him a lot and she didn't like it. The Moodys had been her family friends, not Nick's. He had insinuated himself in there, and now he was taking what should have been hers and her brothers'. Angus hadn't offered jobs or mentoring to Rory or Alex, she noticed. He had shown no interest at all in them.

Angus had let fall enough to allow her to stalk Nick online and off and build a picture of his life. It was so much better than hers. He was more than financially secure, he had a beautiful house, a pretty woman at his side, and the look of someone for whom success has come easily.

It was simple enough to find herself a snug little house close to where Nick lived when she sold the flat she and Ben had bought together. It was a probate sale and unmodernized, so she could afford to buy it outright.

There was no problem getting Kai into Cedar Heights either. It was oversubscribed at the bottom, but by Year 6 the classes had thinned out, with families moving out of London. Yes, she had to congratulate herself. She had been stuck in a rut for years, but now she was being proactive; creating an opportunity to have the life she wanted and deserved. If that meant Nick Ritchie suffered, she could live with that.

GRACE

Friday, 4 May 2018

'I'M SORRY,' TIM SAYS. 'REALLY, I AM. WE COULD HAVE handled that better.'

'Understatement of the year.'

I could tell him he's weak. I could tell him I can't stand to even look at him, but I really don't have the energy. With Cora out of the house, the fight has gone out of me.

'I'm cooking supper.' His hangdog expression almost makes me smile, but not quite. I'm still in shock.

'Thank you.'

I switch the television on and search for something to take my mind off all this, but my heart is racing and I can't settle. I throw the controls to one side. Tim is conciliatory, but I'm tired of their good-cop-bad-cop nonsense. I sit hugging my knees, focusing on the middle distance, trying to work out what to do. With Cora out of the way, it should be possible to have a sensible conversation with Tim. Maybe. I drag myself off the sofa and open the door. In the kitchen, Tim has put on my Jack Johnson CD. The one that I play when I need to unwind, when I don't want a random stream from Spotify to ambush me with something inappropriate to my mood. And, true to his word, he's cooking. Tim does charm well, but two can play at that game. I nip upstairs, put make-up on and run a brush through my hair.

His smile, when I appear looking normal and cheerful, is genial. He pours me a large glass of Nick's favourite wine. We maintain a flow of chatter, mostly about Lottie and her school, and the locals who he's fast getting to know. I laugh too much but he doesn't seem to notice that. I steer the conversation round to him and he becomes expansive. In a small corner of my mind, I'm thinking, what would Anna do if she wanted to wrap a man around her little finger? I run my fingers through my hair and flick it back.

Tim serves up a grilled-chicken risotto and baby new potatoes roasted in garlic, rosemary from the garden and olive oil. On the side we have French beans, steamed to perfection, with a melting knob of butter drizzling over them.

'Smells delicious.'

'Oh, I make it all the time,' Tim says. 'It's my stress-free supper. Bon appétit.'

Tim is comfortable at my table, with me, the woman he's just told he's intending to kick out of her own house. He's comfortable because he only ever looks for the easy option, and right now, the easiest option is to go with the flow. I am being friendly, so he's happy to be friendly too. It's the way he's built. I've been blind, deliberately so, because he's so much easier to like than Cora. As I watch him eat, I wonder if Cora knows this, whether she married him to disguise her own deficiencies. If I was being really bitchy, I'd suggest that people put up with her because Tim is such good company. Without him, I reckon half her friends would fall away.

I rest my knife and fork on the plate and sit back. 'Can I ask you a question?'

His eyes widen. He looks like Nick when he does that, and my heart contracts.

'Do you think Nick's dead?'

To his credit, he doesn't hesitate. 'I don't want to, but I do. You should try and accept it too.'

'You know I can't, Tim.'

He nods, understanding. 'You must do your best, though. It'll eat you up otherwise. You've got so much going for you.'

I smile at that. 'So my friends keep telling me. Are you happy with what Cora's doing?'

Because it is mostly Cora. On his own, Tim wouldn't have the energy.

He sighs. 'My darling girl. Of course not. I'm extremely fond of you. You know that. But you can't expect Cora to hand everything to you on a plate.'

'I would honour Nick's wish to help you,' I say. 'You'd lose nothing.' Inside I grimace. I'm not at all sure this will be possible. I think Tim knows that too, but he's kind enough not to point it out.

'I don't need much. But Cora, well, she's used to better. She doesn't like Leicestershire, to tell you the truth.

She wants to be in London again. It's where most of our friends are. She gets bored.'

'She could get a dog.'

He laughs. 'Grace. I wish none of this had happened, with all my heart. I miss my son. But he's gone, and things are changing. Cora and I are in our sixties, we don't have opportunities any more. You have years ahead of you. You can pull yourself out of this, start again. And like we said, we'll set up a trust for Lottie. Nick would have wanted that.'

I look at him. 'Was that your idea, or Cora's?'

'We came up with it together.'

'Uh huh.'

'Well, maybe I suggested we do something for her, and Cora thought of that. We adore Lottie. As far as Cora and I are concerned, she is our granddaughter.'

'I don't think Cora thinks that way.'

'Of course she does. What she said . . . Well, she was only trying to needle you. You have to forgive her.'

'Why?' I'm really interested.

'Because she's lost so much.'

'She's gaining a house. I hate to sound heartless, but won't her mother leave her anything?'

'Well, no. The house had to go when she went into care. It wasn't worth much anyway. Most of it has gone.'

He starts clearing the plates, scraping the food into the recycling and rinsing them, while I polish off a glass of wine.

'Please try and change her mind,' I say.

'I can't. I'm sorry.'

I hand him my empty glass and leave the room

without a word. I'm so angry, I don't trust myself to speak.

'Grace,' Tim says, coming after me. 'Whatever Cora says, I know how much Nick loved you. No one can take that away from you.'

'Much good it did me.' I hit the wall with the side of my fist, choking on a sob. 'You should be ashamed of yourself.'

Tim's phone beeps. He pulls it out of his back pocket, reads a text, and his eyes shutter. I take the opportunity to escape, running up to my bathroom to rub at my cheeks and eyes with cotton-wool balls soaked in make-up remover. I stare at my blotched face. What the hell was I expecting?

He's coming up, as I come down. He's in his coat; a Barbour. Another expensive purchase.

'I'm going to the pub,' he says.

'Right.'

We look at each other, then we both speak at once.

'Tim . . .'

'Do you want to come?'

His expression tells me he's only asking out of courtesy. I could go. That would throw him. We could sit in the Queen's Arms and discuss the past. I pretend to think about it – for long enough for worry to start rucking his brow. Finally, I let him off the hook.

'I'm tired. You'll be OK on your own?' Of course he will.

'Toffee and I will keep each other company.'

'I thought dogs weren't allowed in there.'

'He's invisible to this particular landlady.' Tim winks.

'You're quite a hit round here, aren't you?' I say.

He catches my tone, tilts his head and looks at me. There's a nervous energy about him that turns the charm into something else, something with a fizz of threat. 'Grace . . .'

'Got your key? I'm going to have an early night.'

He nods, chucking it up in the air and catching it. 'I'll see you in the morning.'

While I wait for my bath to run, I go on to In-Step and my group. There are only two people on the move, which is normal, because most of us are home right now, except Nick, of course, who isn't moving for other reasons. I should take him off, but I can't bear to. No, the two who are moving are Anna and Tim. I feel a quiver in my belly. How long ago was it that I sat watching Nick's and Anna's steps? I test the water, turn off the cold tap and look again. They're still moving. Tim is walking Toffee and then going to the pub; Anna, frankly, could be anywhere. I try not to look but I can't help it. It feels like my life is on repeat. Tim stops. Anna keeps moving. So it's nothing.

I light candles and turn off the spotlights, shake a few drops of essential oil into the bathwater, then slip out of my robe. Before I get in, I can't resist one last peek at my screen. Neither Anna nor Tim is moving. This is paranoia, I think. To stop myself looking again, I put the phone out of reach and get into the bath. The water is the way I like it, hot enough that it takes a second or two to get used to, stinging my skin. I sink down with a sigh. A weight has been temporarily lifted. I am on my own; or as good as. Cocooned like this, I can imagine

304

that Nick is downstairs scrolling through our TV recordings to see if we have an episode of some engrossing drama to catch up on. I feel a lump rise in my throat. There are several things on there that we had been enjoying together, that now he won't see the final episodes of.

In the privacy of my bathroom, with the steam rising round me, I allow myself the luxury of crying.

When I come out, warm in my dressing gown, the house is silent. I've never felt nervous on my own here before, but something raises the hairs on the back of my neck. I move aside the curtains and look up and down Burnside Road, but even its respectable serenity unnerves me. A car turns the corner from the direction of the Common and I'm sure it slows as it passes this house. My heart hammering, I open Nick's wardrobe, push his clothes aside and lean into the corner where he keeps his old school cricket bat. I lay it on the carpet beside the bed and it makes me feel better.

I read for half an hour, then switch off my bedside light and fall asleep. Some time later I'm woken by a sound and sit bolt upright. I bend slowly and reach for the bat, curling my fingers around the handle. Then I hear the distinctive jangle of keys and breathe a long sigh of relief, but I still creep out on to the landing holding the bat, in case I'm wrong.

Downstairs Tim tells Toffee to sit. He says, 'Good boy.' He takes off Toffee's lead, and the dog's toenails skitter on the floor as he runs into the kitchen to look for me, then runs out again.

There's a moment of silence, then Tim calls my name softly.

I don't answer. He goes back into the kitchen and I close my bedroom door. It's eleven thirty. I read a new chapter, to settle myself, then switch off the light and watch the numbers on the digital clock slowly change. Somewhere in the house running water burbles from a tap.

My mobile vibrating against the painted wooden surface of my bedside cabinet wakes me up. I fumble to twist the clock round and stare bleary-eyed at the time. Almost one in the morning. I check the caller display, recognize Anna's home number and very nearly don't pick up. Then I reason that for her to be ringing at such a late hour, it can't be for anything trivial.

'Anna?'

'It's Kai,' a small voice responds.

I'm immediately alert. 'Kai? What are you doing up this late?'

'Mum's not come home.'

ANNA

March 2018 ❧ Two Months Earlier

'YOU'RE A STAR,' GRACE SAID. 'I AM SO GRATEFUL.'

Anna had her mobile trapped between her shoulder and ear while she rinsed her paintbrushes under the tap in the kitchen. Creamy-white swirls spiralled around the stainless-steel sink and disappeared down the drain.

'No problem. What time will your ex pick her up? Will she want dinner, or does he like to do that himself?'

'Oh. Gosh, I don't know. I'll text him if you like.'

'No, don't worry. I'll give her a snack when we get in, that way she won't be starving, but she won't have spoilt her appetite either.'

Anna was gushing, trying too hard to please Grace Trelawney. Grace's ex, Douglas Parr, was supposed to be collecting Lottie from school, but he'd been delayed, and Grace was in town, picking out soft furnishings for some swanky house she was getting ready for tenants and meeting Nick for supper and the theatre. Anna wasn't sure why she had been chosen to help her out instead of one of Grace's small coterie of close friends, but maybe none of them were available. She didn't mind that she was way down the list if it meant she got her foot through the door.

She wanted to meet Nick Ritchie again casually, to be introduced to him at a dinner party or something like that. She wanted to see his face as he tried to work out where he knew her from. To be honest, she was getting a little impatient. It was very cliquey round here, though they were friendly enough. Perhaps it was because she was on her own. Maybe they were the sort of women who had the vapours at the very idea of uneven numbers. She had only moved here six weeks ago, but she was beginning to get a sense that this was the case. It wasn't easy to break into established circles. Everyone had been welcoming, but there'd been a point where she had felt encouraged to stop and come no further. Like a line drawn in front of a cash machine or a dartboard. It was early days, though. Things would change. Grace asking for her help was proof if she needed it.

It had nothing to do with money – Cassie Morgan, for instance, was as poor as a church mouse – it was all to do with bonding at a certain time of life, and that time was when the mother still had the power to dictate her children's friendships and develop her own off the back of them. Kai was perfectly capable of finding his feet at school. He didn't need her help with that.

Grace had called the school office in advance, so Kai and Lottie knew about the arrangement. They ran over when they saw Anna. She felt a surge of pride and made a great to-do about checking they had everything, then strolled to the gate with the two of them at her side.

Soon enough, she thought, these women would come round. She had made a mistake at the first evening event she'd been invited to, flirting with the husbands. But she had been expecting Grace and Nick to be there, and when they hadn't showed up and she heard someone bemoaning the fact that they had gone away for the weekend, she had been so disappointed, she had drunk too much.

Lottie was fascinated by what Anna did. She stood in the conservatory taking it in, inspecting the rustic wooden signs hanging on hooks waiting for the next craft fair. They said things like *Home Sweet Home*, *Eat Laugh Love*, and *Love Me Love My Mess*. She had sold thirty of the things at the Christmas Fair at Kai's old school last year.

'It's cold in here,' Lottie said.

It was true. The conservatory was distinctly chilly. Anna was used to it, but she had to wear fingerless gloves when she was working. She couldn't afford to have the heating on all day, so it went off as soon as Kai left for school. Embarrassed, she spun the thermostat until it clicked, then jacked it right up to 21 degrees. No half measures.

'Can I make one?' Lottie said, indicating the signs.

'Sure,' Anna said, even though the bits of naturally sanded and weather-bleached driftwood that she and Kai scavenged from the Dorset beach close to where Ben's parents lived, were sacrosanct. Apart from being integral to her work, they also gave her a reason to be out of the house and away from her in-laws. They'd been hinting lately that Kai was old enough to stay with them on his own. She was beginning to think it might not be such a bad idea.

Anna picked out a small one. 'Paint the background first, then do the writing in pencil.'

'I know,' Lottie said, as though it was obvious.

Anna and Kai watched her, Kai eating a piece of toast and strawberry jam. Lottie was painstaking, anxious to get it right, her tongue caught between her teeth, her blonde hair tucked behind her ears. It had gone dark outside and Lottie was reflected in the curtain-less window, a skinny child with her mother's delicate bone structure. When she'd finished the background she left it to dry while the two of them played a computer game. Anna expected her to forget all about it, but far from it; she went back to her artwork, picking it up and turning it both ways before setting it down and picking up the stencils.

'What do you want to write?' Anna asked.

'I'm thinking about it.'

Lottie chewed her bottom lip and sat back, contemplating the space before making her first mark. She worked slowly, carefully lining up each letter, spacing them out. Once that was done she dipped her brush into a pot of grey-green paint and began to fill them in. *I Love My Dad.*

'That's sweet,' Anna said. 'You've got two dads, haven't you? Is that for your real one?'

Lottie turned her china-blue eyes on her. 'They're both real. They're just different sorts of dads.'

'That's a lovely way of putting it.'

She shrugged. 'It's for my birth dad. For his birthday.' Then she wrinkled her nose. 'I don't really think Nick would appreciate this sort of thing.'

She was an oddity, Anna decided. A typical only child, like Kai, precocious in a way that manifests in a greater articulacy than their peers. Thoughtful, too. She had a pensive face.

When Lottie had finished, Anna picked the piece of wood up and laid it carefully with the others on the shelf against the painted brick wall to dry.

'Can you turn it round so Dad doesn't see it?' Lottie said, suddenly anxious.

'Of course. You wouldn't want to spoil the surprise.'

She wondered what time Lottie's father was intending to pick her up. It was gone six thirty, and she wanted to kick back with a glass of wine.

'Mum!'

The shout startled them. Kai was standing by the kitchen sink, looking down at his feet where water was pooling under the units. Anna rushed over and pulled open the cupboards, but the pipes under the sink seemed fine. Something must have happened when she turned up the heating. The plumbing was at least fifty years old and she couldn't afford to get it overhauled. When she moved there had been no one to ask about things like stopcocks and boilers because the previous owner had died. Unfortunately, because Ben had killed himself, his life insurance didn't pay out.

She turned the heating off, but the puddle kept spreading. She ran upstairs to the bathroom, but there was nothing visibly wrong there either. Back downstairs she opened the cellar door and flicked the light switch. Water was dripping through the ceiling on to the washing machine. Within seconds the bulb popped, plunging her into darkness.

'Mum,' Kai shouted. 'The lights have gone out!'

'Shit,' she muttered. 'Shit, shit, shit.'

Back in the kitchen Anna lit candles, to Kai and Lottie's delight. It was pretty, but she didn't find it delightful at all. No electricity and no water. She thought about Grace Trelawney, living with Nick, cushioned by money – it was a safe bet her pipes never burst – and felt a deep, deep well of bitter loneliness. Anna had been a beautiful girl, and she was a beautiful woman. She should have had a handsome and wealthy husband. She should not have been living in a poky worker's cottage eking out a living painting clichés on driftwood and bringing up a child on her own. Nick's success galled her.

And Tim. She found it hard to think about him without becoming furious. She had been so young, so naive and so deeply unhappy. What kind of man takes advantage of that? Only creeps. Looking back, she can't believe it happened. A fifteen-year-old and a forty-five-year-old man she had known since she was two. She would bet her last penny that Tim and Nick would do anything to keep that particular scandal from being made public.

'Pick up your shoes and rucksacks and take them upstairs,' she yelled as she whisked up her own shoes, handbag and anything else she could manage. She heard them laughing and stopped panicking for a moment to listen. Ice broken, she thought with a smile. Something good had come out of this at least.

The water had spread across half the kitchen floor and was running between the painted floorboards. If it got into the front room the carpet would be ruined. She needed to turn the water off; something she had never attempted before.

There was a torch, thank God. It was in the drawer in the dresser, where she kept odds and ends, and it worked. A miracle. She went back down to the narrow, brick-built space with the ceiling that skimmed her head and searched, not sure what she was looking for, but following pipes to their source, and finally, to the right of the washing machine in the space between it and the dusty wall, she found what she hoped was the stopcock. She felt rather proud of herself.

The gap was too narrow, and her elbow became wedged as she reached in, straining her shoulder. A drip of cold water caught the nape of her neck and trickled under her top, making her shudder. She raised the torch to the dark patch spreading across the dirty plaster then contemplated the bulk of the washing machine. With a huge effort, she managed to shift it an inch, enough to get her arm all the way in and to grip the handle, but it refused to budge, and she was jammed at too awkward an angle to put any welly into it.

Anna straightened up and cast around for something to help crank the washing machine further away from the wall, but there was nothing. Her cellar was full of stuff that she hadn't got round to unpacking and probably never would. Her mistake had been to allow Ben's brother and parents to choose what they wanted, but at the time she had been too dazed by events to stop them. They left her to cope alone, and when she finally managed to sell the flat and moved here none of them offered to come and help fix it up. Selfish bastards; they never liked her. If it hadn't been for Kai, they would have dropped her entirely.

The doorbell rang. She quickly wiped her face on her sleeve and noticed a rip in the underarm of her shirt, where it had been stretched against the corner of the washing machine. This was not the impression she had hoped to make on Grace's ex-boyfriend.

Upstairs, Lottie was hanging off a tall, thin bloke. Anna deflected the torch beam to the floor so as not to blind him and distinguished short salt-and-pepper hair, prominent cheekbones, grey eyes, hard mouth. In the shadowy light, the effect was magnetic and disorientating.

'Douglas Parr.' He raised his eyebrows in a friendly way and held out his hand. 'I appear to have come at a good time.'

There was humour in his voice, but also a certain authority that immediately reassured her. Help had arrived.

Douglas took charge, first switching off the electricity, then addressing himself to the washing-machine problem. He squatted, pressed his shoulder against the wall and shoved. It resisted, then gave. Anna shone the torch into the space. Douglas reached in, twisted the stopcock, then straightened with a grunt, brushing a spider's web from his sleeve. He grinned, his head cocked to one side, his hand pressed against the ceiling, as if he was hoping to create more space.

'There you go.'

'Thank you so much.'

He switched the electricity back on and, from upstairs, Lottie and Kai shouted, 'Hey! Switch it off.' There was a peal of laughter.

Douglas grinned and Anna's whole body responded. 'At least someone's happy.'

'I know. I think they've bonded.'

'Do you have a plumber you can call?'

'No, but I can ask Grace. She must know loads in her line of work.'

He took out his mobile, scrolled through his contacts and asked her for her phone number so that he could send her Grace's plumber's details. Anna hesitated then thought, *what the hell*? And gave it to him.

The plumber promised to come by eight o'clock the next morning. They could cope till then. While she mopped the kitchen floor, Douglas stayed out of the way, in the conservatory. He had broad shoulders and a rangy, loose-limbed elegance. She found his bandy legs both funny and sexy.

'Cottage industry?' he said.

'It puts food on the table.'

'You're very talented.'

She wrung the mop out, twisting it hard, and started again. 'I make a lot of that stuff. You get better with practice.'

He picked up one of the larger pieces and read it out

315

loud. '*Did I say I wanted children? I meant to say choc-olate!*' He laughed. 'Where do you sell?'

'Craft fairs mainly, but I'm negotiating with Not On The High Street. If they agree to take me on, my orders should increase. Can I get you a drink? I feel I owe you. I've got wine. No beer, though, I'm afraid.'

He hesitated and in doing so acknowledged that she had signalled that there wasn't a man in the house, pos-sibly in her life. She had only met him twenty minutes ago, but the effect he was having on her was unsettling. For the first time in ages she felt her sexual power; it crept through her, filling her veins, tweaking her body language, bringing a smile to her lips.

'A glass of wine, if I'm not putting you out.'

'Putting me out? You've saved me.'

She raised her eyes to his face. He was looking intently at her, as though he was examining her for flaws. Heat rose into her cheeks.

'You're divorced?' he asked.

'Widowed.'

'I'm sorry.'

'It's fine. It's been five years now.'

I'm moving on, open to offers.

I find you extraordinarily attractive.

What do you see when you look at me, Douglas Parr?

She swept her fingers through her hair, smoothing it out, a gesture that wasn't lost on him. They eyed each other like two animals, circling, wondering if what they felt was worth pursuing. Anna felt light-headed, ready to say something idiotic if only to release the tension,

316

then Lottie came in, skirted the wet section of floor and put her arms around his waist.

'Can we go now, Dad?'

'Sure. Get your coat on. Sorry, we'll have to take a rain check,' he muttered to Anna. 'Are you going to be OK?'

'I'll be fine.' She hid her disappointment. 'The insurance should cover the damage, and it's not as if I have expensive flooring or anything.'

She didn't tell him that stripping the varnish and painting the old boards took her the best part of two weeks, that it gave her splinters in her hands, that her knees had felt bruised for ages, but she sensed that he'd guessed at least some of that. He understood.

Anna closed the door and hugged herself, euphoria spiralling through her. She hadn't felt like this for a very long time.

Not since she was fifteen. Her happiness curdled.

Look where that had ended.

GRACE

Saturday, 5 May 2018

KAI'S VOICE BREAKS. I JUMP OUT OF BED, TUCKING THE phone between my shoulder and my ear as I pull on my jeans.

'I'm on my way. I'll be with you in five minutes. Don't worry. Stay in your room and don't answer the door without checking it's me first.'

I scribble a message on the back of an envelope and place it against the kettle where Tim can't fail to see it, then I hurry out.

Kai is wearing his pyjamas with an over-sized green hoodie, his hair spiked in opposing directions. I get him to tell me what he knows, but it isn't much. He'd woken in the middle of the night because he'd had a bad dream. He got up and went to the loo, and peeked in on his mum, but she wasn't there. He phoned her mobile number, but she didn't pick up. He kept trying, leaving messages every few minutes, then found the class address list and called me.

'I'm sure she's fine.' It's difficult to think of anything to say that will reassure him. 'Does Mum have a boyfriend?'

'I don't know,' Kai says. 'But I think there might be someone, because she's sometimes whispering on the phone.'

'That's probably what's happened,' I say brightly. 'She's out on a date, but she decided not to tell you in case it didn't work out. She'll be back soon.'

He doesn't look convinced.

'Kai, why did you call me instead of one of the other mums?'

His lip quivers.

'It's all right. It doesn't matter.'

He wipes his nose on the sleeve of his hoodie. He's trying so hard not to cry, it makes me want to. 'I thought she might have gone where Lottie's stepdad went.'

'Oh, Kai.'

His reaction is entirely understandable. Lottie's step-dad vanished, and the police have been here asking questions. And now his mum has gone. I'm not sure whether to hug him or not, but when I put a tentative arm around his shoulder he leans into me. 'Of course she hasn't. I expect she's lost track of time. Please don't worry.' I feel his skinny body shaking with tears and draw him closer to me. 'Everything's going to be fine.'

'I don't want to be on my own.'

'You won't be. I'll stay and look after you till she comes back. Do you think you can go back to bed now? Mum will be here when you wake up. I promise.'

I feel a trickle of cold slither through my veins. I made that promise to Lottie not so long ago. I should learn from my mistakes.

Once Kai has plodded back upstairs, I go into the kitchen and put the kettle on. Anna hasn't tidied away her supper things. There's a glass on the side, its bowl stained with the evaporated residue of red wine, and her supper plate is still on the table. I almost tidy them away but change my mind and leave them where I find them, in case she thinks I'm making some kind of point. The sort of thing Cora does. I touch the In-Step app on my phone and open groups. Anna's done two thousand three hundred and sixty-seven steps today. That's about one and a half kilometres in In-Step-speak. She's not walking now. Maybe her phone is lying switched off beside someone else's bed, or in her bag, slung over a chair in someone else's kitchen. As distressed as I am at the neglect this implies, I hope this is the case.

I have a look round. She's finished Thomas's chair and started on the next one, lightly pencilling in the name 'William' with a stencil. I chew my lip. I have an opportunity here. I need evidence that Anna was expecting to see Nick that Saturday night, that she lay in wait for him, and that Nick is the reason she moved here. If someone comes to the door and I'm downstairs I can hit the sofa; if I'm upstairs, I can get into her bed and pretend to be asleep. Anna will be bewildered, possibly cross, but she won't be able to say anything. She's the one who's left her ten-year-old alone because she doesn't want to pay a babysitter while she's on a date; I'm almost certain that's what it is. I expect it's unusual for Kai to

320

wake up in the night and she thought she could get away with it.

I start in the kitchen, working my way through the cabinets. I move into the dining area where there's an old dresser. The drawers contain paper, sketchbooks, crayons and felt-tip pens. Kai likes to draw seascapes full of weird and wonderful creatures.

The tiny front sitting room is equally fruitless. The shelves are loaded with books and DVDs. It's an inviting room, mellow and cosy. Upstairs there are two bedrooms and a bathroom, and above the landing a hatch in the ceiling; a pole with a hook on the end leans into the corner. I creep past Kai's bedroom door and enter Anna's room, close the curtains and switch on the light, then tackle her bedside table before moving to the wardrobe. A moth flies out as I open the door, and another as I flick through her clothes.

There's a painted chair in front of her dressing table; I drag it over, climb up and check the top shelves. All I find are bags of jumpers, vacuum-packed presumably to protect them from the moths, and baby things neatly folded that give me a pang of want. Nick and I would have had a child together. Does Anna yearn for another one? Is that what she's looking for in a man? Someone to help complete her family? To complete her?

I get down off the chair and sit on the bed, tired and fed up, the adrenaline all but gone. I check underneath it and find a folded carrier bag. I pull it out and open it. Inside is a cheap mobile. I sit with it in my palm, then press one of the keys. It lights up, but it needs a passcode, so I put it back where I found it. Why would Anna

321

have a second mobile hidden under her bed? Maybe it's an old one she couldn't bring herself to discard. She's the thrifty type. I don't have an answer. I find myself yearning to sink into the pillows and close my eyes, so I force myself up, switch off the light and part the curtains. Street lights bathe the road in their yellow glow. The night sky is scattered with stars. It's a quarter to two in the morning and a mother has left her son. What Kai said about worrying that she had gone where Nick went, like the children following the Pied Piper, blindsided me. The poor boy must be terrified.

Come back, Anna. I press my palm against the glass. I should call the police, I think. And I will. But there's one more place to look.

In the loft, itchy from the fibreglass insulation wedged between the joists, I sit back on my heels, my prize in my hand. The date stamp on the photos I'm holding under the single bare bulb is July 2000. From a quick shuffle through the pile, it quickly becomes clear they were taken during that holiday. I recognize a young Alex Wells, slouching against a wall, frowning at the photographer. He's a cool kid. There's another one of him, his arms and legs dangling over the edges of a wheelbarrow while his little brother pushes, running barefoot and bare-chested across the lawn. There are slim pickings of Nick. The photographer has caught him looking up from his book in one, his shoulder and part of his profile in another. In neither does he look happy. I run my finger over it, a lump catching in my throat. What happened to you, my love? If you aren't dead, then it's time to come home. It's not too late.

I discovered, spending time with Nick, that relationships don't have to be abusive, that you can love without an agenda, that it isn't a matter of keeping one step ahead of the enemy, of watching what you say and what you do every moment you're with them. I discovered give and take, tolerance, humour and warmth. I saw that what I'd had with Douglas was unhealthy, and that this had been bad for me and worse for my daughter. I discovered that I had a mind of my own, and that I wasn't unintelligent, just poorly educated. I should have found some backbone, told Nick what I had done, and taken the consequences. He might have understood. Now, I'll never know. The past attaches itself to me like cobwebs.

I go through the pictures again. I assume Anna got hold of the film in the aftermath, when the last thing anyone wanted was a visual reminder of that summer. Anna's mother might be glad to have the pictures of Izzy. She's a smiley little thing, less robust than the other children whose rude good health appears vulgar beside her translucent pallor, but her face is open, and you can tell she has a good nature. Although that might just be my interpretation, because I know that she was kind to Nick when he needed a friend.

I put it to one side, because I may take it away and see if Alex Wells wants to take it. Anna will never know; I doubt she's looked at them in years.

I pull a few more items out and find a letter in an envelope addressed by hand. That's unusual enough to merit inspection. I put it to one side to take downstairs and dig around some more. My fingers touch something thin and rubbery. It turns out to be a small, clear-white plastic strip with a sticker attached. Lottie had one of these around her wrist after she was born. This must be Kai's. I lift it closer to the light so that I can read it properly. And then I read it again, because it isn't what I expected at all.

There's a metallic clank, the unmistakable sound of someone putting their weight on the ladder. Shit. I stuff the bracelet into my back pocket and slide the letter under my top, pulling the waist of my jeans over it, then I turn as a tousle-haired Kai puts his head through the hatch.

'Oh, sorry, Kai. Did I wake you?'

'I woke up anyway.' He looks round, his eyes large. 'What are you doing?'

My mouth is as dry as the wood in the rafters above me. I think fast. 'Your mum told me she had some old junk for the school fair up here, and as I couldn't sleep I thought I'd take a look.'

'Can I come up?' he asks.

'No,' I say quickly. 'It's filthy. I'm coming down.'

The school summer fete has a bric-a-brac stall, and we've all had a letter asking for donations, so as excuses go, it's not a disaster. Kai looks sceptical but evidently decides not to press the point. I climb down after him and close the hatch, then put the hook back where it came from.

ANNA

April 2018 ~ One Month Earlier

SITTING ON THE VICTORIA LINE, ANNA TRIED HARD TO concentrate on her book. It was Saturday and Kai had gone to Ben's parents for the entire weekend, she was all dolled up and on her way to meet Douglas. It was a real date. She gave up on the novel, and discreetly studied the other passengers. A man, younger than her, caught her eye and she sensed a spark of interest, but he got off at the next stop. Even so, that tiny connection made her bloom. Anna wondered what Grace would think if she knew who she was meeting. She had given Anna a bunch of yellow tulips to thank her for helping her out that time. It was a sweet gesture, but it didn't give Anna any pleasure. If they had been true friends, gifts wouldn't change hands; it would be assumed that they were there for each other. But it was a beginning, and she mustn't get neurotic. It would happen. She would get to Nick, and through Nick to Tim. Those two owed her. Between them, they had stolen the last precious years of her childhood. They had betrayed her.

Thirty-three years old. She felt a thrum of panic. What if?

What if she falls for Douglas and he doesn't fall for her?

What if he has someone? No one's told her he doesn't. She's brought up the subject of Lottie's situation a couple of times with Cassie and the others, in a kind of round-about way, but no one's mentioned Douglas's domestic arrangement. Why would they discuss Grace's business with her? They barely know her.

What if Kai doesn't like him?

She didn't mention the date to her son, but if it did come to something, she'd have to tread that line between needing his approval and not wanting him to get too attached in case it fizzled out. The last real relationship she had was three years ago, and that had been a disaster. She had thought two years was long enough, that Kai would understand, even expect her to start dating again. But no. He had a meltdown. Since then, it had been Tinder hook-ups if she could work up the energy.

This tiny bud of a thing with Grace Trelawney's ex-boyfriend was different. She could feel it in the way her hands were shaking, her palms damp with sweat. She had to wash and dry them before doing up the mother-of-pearl buttons on her shirt. This meant something.

He had asked her not to tell Grace.

Did that mean something too?

Douglas was waiting for her. She reached up to kiss him on the cheek and his long fingers curled around her shoulder. They crossed the road and made their way towards Knightsbridge and the Italian restaurant he'd booked.

They talked about this and that, Anna telling him about her day, trying to be witty and self-deprecating, and Douglas telling her about his. He wasn't self-deprecating at all. From what he said, Anna gleaned that he was self-employed, worked in tech in some mysterious capacity, having decided that law didn't suit him. The conversation as they walked along the busy Brompton Road didn't exactly flow, but the traffic was noisy, there were a lot of people around, considering most of the shops were closed, and it was icy, so they were muffled in scarves. She had noticed that he was freshly shaved though, and she was encouraged by that.

She drank too fast. He didn't. He was disconcertingly in control. She could appreciate him properly now; the fact of it being a date giving her permission to study his face, to appreciate its attractive asymmetry, to lose herself in his eyes. His mouth fascinated her. Between their main course and pudding, she felt emboldened to touch on more personal subjects, particularly the one that interested her most: the triangular relationship between him, Nick Ritchie and Grace Trelawney.

'So, you seem to have a very civilized relationship with Grace.'

His fingers stroked the stem of his glass. 'You gotta do it for the kids,' he joked, then looked serious. 'Lottie is the most important thing to both of us.'

'What does Nick think about that?'

His eyes narrowed. 'I'd say he takes it in good part. He knows I'm not walking away from my child to convenience him.'

'Can I ask you a personal question?' she said.

'I think you just did.'

She held his gaze steadily. 'Another one, then. Which one of you is the cuckoo in the nest?'

Douglas laughed out loud, and she was pleased that she amused him. He reached over and touched her cheek, and she felt joy blossom inside her.

'I'm not trying to get in the way of Grace's relationship. I don't want her back.' He paused and scrutinized her. 'Are you jealous?'

'No. Not at all.' Angus had asked her that. She would have to watch herself, if that was the vibe she was giving out.

'But you rightly want to know how things stand before you decide whether to let me into your life. I understand that, Anna. And I'll tell you. I was very much in love with Grace, and she with me, but it didn't work. She needed my help, but she found it hard to accept. She thought I was trying to control her; but I wasn't, I was trying to ensure she didn't fall back down the hole I pulled her out of.'

'What kind of hole?'

'If she wants you to know, then I'm sure she'll tell you. You can ask me anything about myself, but I can't share her secrets. It wouldn't be fair.'

So Grace had secrets. The waiter offered them the dessert menu, and Anna ran her eyes over it while she took stock. She fancied Douglas, but there was danger there. With Ben she had been in control; was loved more than she loved. She had been cherished. Something told her that it would be different with Douglas; that she would be the one who clung. On the other hand, just being aware of that made her stronger. She could easily hide her insecurities, couldn't she? Self-knowledge is power. He evidently still cared about Grace, but Anna could handle that. Grace was attractive enough, but she was hardly going to stop traffic. She was your typical girl next door. Some men liked that sort of thing, obviously, or there would be a sharp decline in population, but Anna knew her own power.

Bring it on.

She was drunk, on him as much as the wine. His glance made her giddy, his touch turned her insides to butter, his voice wrapped her in static anticipation. She didn't want the night to end. She had an enormous urge to offload everything, to tell him about Izzy, about Nick and Tim Ritchie and Ben, but she had the sense to pull back from the brink. He was still too close to Grace, and she didn't know yet whether she could trust him. She would wait until she had him at her feet.

She contented herself with telling him about her very brief liaison with an older man. Douglas looked Angus Moody up on his smartphone and raised his eyebrows.

'He's seriously loaded,' he commented. 'Shame you didn't stick around a little longer. You might have got a pay-off. A bit of Cartier, perhaps.'

'I'm not that sort of girl.'

She laughed, because he was only joking, but she found herself telling him what she had overheard at Angus's house that afternoon, about the dubious nature of his business dealings, flattered by the way Douglas seemed so absorbed in her tale. It was only later that she discovered his interest was a little more than superficial.

GRACE

Saturday, 5 May 2018

ONCE I'VE SETTLED KAI BACK IN BED, I TAKE THE LETTER out from under my top and unfold it.

22 March 2017

Dearest Taisie,

Anna! (I'm finding it impossible to think of you as anything other than Taisie I'm afraid.) Thank you from the bottom of my heart for this afternoon. I will treasure the memory. You are a precious, special young woman and I hope you will always know this.

I have such fond memories of those summers watching you and your siblings growing up. I'm just so terribly sorry it all ended like it did. It was an idyllic time. I sense that you don't think as well of yourself as I do, so do something for me. Try not to allow past hurts and grudges to fester. Take my advice and talk to your family. They miss you very much. You've made the first step now. It'll be easier to make contact with the others.

I get the feeling I may have put my foot in it, as regards Nick Ritchie. I want you to know that I certainly don't favour him over you. I would have encouraged any young person who showed a genuine interest and followed it up with such persistence. Send Kai my way when the time comes. I'll be happy to help in any way I can. He sounds like a wonderful young man.

Yours
Angus

The notepaper is expensive and has Angus's Kensington address embossed in a black font. He used a fountain pen, and his signature is restrained but confident. I lay the letter on my knees, feeling a little ashamed of myself for prying.

I've never been good at thinking things through. My brain can't always work its way round a maze of information, like some people's do with such ease, as if they were floating above it. But I try now. Were they lovers? There's a hint of that, but nothing specific. Maybe he didn't trust her. I don't, and I don't know her as well as he appears to. The letter doesn't prove that she came after Nick, meaning to disrupt his life, but it's surely enough to make the police accept that Anna may well be the key to all this.

What else does it tell me?

Anna made that first move towards reconciliation by getting in touch with a close family friend the year before she moved into this area. She didn't take Angus's advice and speak to her family, but she did make contact with Nick. She denies being in touch with Alex, but she could

331

have lied. I can imagine a scenario where Alex got in touch with her as part of his recovery, and she spotted an opportunity and persuaded him to put pressure on Nick, having already started the process the evening before.

Why did Anna go to see Angus in the first place? Because she was lonely? I remember my own first impression of Nick's boss: utterly in control, courteous and charming. I'd guess she contacted him and not his wife because she's more comfortable with men than she is with women. And the Moodys rather than the Ritchies because of what Tim did to her. He had betrayed her parents' friendship and made a mockery of her childhood.

As for the women, if Cora and Jess Wells were anything like Cassie and me, they would have been in and out of each other's houses when the children were tiny. I sigh inwardly. Is any of this even relevant? I should call the police.

This house is so cold. I pull a soft woollen throw from the back of the armchair and wrap it round my shoulders, then go to the door, open it and wander out into the street. I breathe in the heady scent of the wisteria that covers the house next door, its flowers dripping shades of purple. It's such a tranquil road, but who knows what goes on behind the prettily painted walls?

A siren wails in the distance, and I look up, my stomach flipping. Above the roofs, over in the direction of the Common, a halo of blue lights pulses a grim rhythm. I go back inside, quietly close the door, pick up the phone and take it back upstairs to Anna's bedroom. From her window, I can see the lights better. It's definitely the

Common. There are problems there from time to time, especially with underage drinkers – groups of teenagers buying booze from the minimart and gathering in the gloom. I tend not to walk Toffee there at night if Nick isn't around. Once someone was stabbed in the playground. It could be anything. I'm sure this has nothing to do with Anna.

'I want to report someone missing,' I say into the phone, my eyes fixed on the lights, and it all starts again.

'What is your relationship?'

'She's a friend.'

'Does she have health issues?'

The voice could belong to the same female operator. I wait for her to comment on this, to mention the remarkable coincidence of me calling to report a missing person twice in three weeks, to make some light remark about lightning not striking the same place twice, but she doesn't, and maybe she's not the same person anyway.

I know what the routine is, that she's about to tell me to wait until tomorrow. I turn away, and sit down on the end of Anna's bed, exhausted.

'I'm really concerned about her,' I say. 'She's left her child—'

There's a noise, a quiet shuffle, and I turn to find Kai standing in the doorway, his eyes huge. I go to him, put my hand on his shoulder and lead him gently back to his bedroom. He climbs obediently back into bed, but I can tell he's hyper alert.

'How old is the child?' the woman is asking.

The doorbell rings and I sag with relief. Anna must have forgotten her keys. Maybe she's drunk.

'It's OK,' I say. 'She's back. Sorry to waste your time.'

Kai springs up, but I block him. I want to check what kind of state his mother is in before he sees her. He struggles in my arms.

'I want to see Mummy.'

The doorbell rings again, more insistently this time. I'm torn, but in the end I insist. It's the right thing to do.

'She'll be cross if she finds you up,' I say urgently. 'And I'll get into trouble.' He looks at me and I can feel him wavering. He's utterly exhausted, poor child. 'Shut your eyes and count backwards from a hundred.' It sometimes works with Lottie.

I close his door behind me and run downstairs, ready with my excuse for being here, my unjudgemental smile firmly in place, but it isn't Anna standing on her doorstep, looking sheepish. It's Detective Inspector Marsh. If he's surprised to find me here, he doesn't show it. I look behind him, but I only see his car, double-parked. No Anna getting out of it.

'I've just been on the phone to the police,' I say. 'Has something happened to Anna?'

He follows me into the kitchen, and I shut the door so that Kai can't hear. I fill the kettle, but he doesn't want anything. I want to do something with my hands, but I don't want to appear nervous, so I lean against the counter and hook my thumbs into my jeans pockets.

'Why are you here, Ms Trelawney?' he asks.

'Her son called me. He was worried because she hasn't come home.'

'Why didn't you alert the police immediately?'

I frown. His question feels like an accusation. 'I assumed

she would be back. I didn't want to get her into trouble for leaving Kai on his own if she was going to reappear at any moment.'

'What time did he call you?'

'Around one o'clock.'

'So you waited for, what, two hours?'

'I didn't want to turn this into something it wasn't.'

He peers through the glass screen door into the small garden. 'Where did she tell Kai she was going?'

'She didn't. He got up in the night to go to the loo and noticed that she wasn't in bed. That's when he called me.'

I'm starting to tremble inside. Of course I should have called. What stopped me? Was it because I'm suspicious of Anna and wanted to spend some time snooping round her house? I glance at Marsh's face, but it's impossible to read. He looks tired too.

'You didn't think it was odd?' he says. 'After going through the same thing yourself so recently?'

'I didn't relate the two events. I don't know why not. I assumed Anna had told him a white lie; that she was meeting someone – a date. She does use online dating sites.'

'Is she the type to go out without arranging child-care?'

'I don't know. I haven't known her very long. Will you please tell me what's going on?'

He picks up a sheaf of papers from the table and looks through them. It's mostly stuff from school: newsletters, sports slips for her to sign. He puts it down.

'When did you last see Anna Foreman?'

335

I try and remember but my brain is all over the place. Since Nick left, time has stretched, occasionally snapping back and catapulting me forward, but mostly the days have felt like weeks.

'I think it was last Monday. Yes, it was. Definitely last Monday.' That was the afternoon Lottie sneaked out and came round here. 'Shouldn't you be looking for her?'

'We don't need to.' He traps me in his gaze. 'There's been an incident.'

NICK

Thursday, 12 April 2018 ❧ Three Weeks Earlier

NICK TAKES OFF HIS SUIT JACKET AND ARRANGES IT carefully over the back of a chair, twitching the corners into place. He loosens his tie and undoes the top button of his shirt. It's good to be home, to breathe the same air as Grace and Lottie, to feel the warmth of their welcome after a long day, his mind dizzy with figures and conference calls, meetings and briefings. Even after the walk from the station he can feel the tension. But he can't keep blaming the work itself. It's more than that; something more insidious, potentially more damaging.

He's beginning to think, rather late in the day, that the world he's chosen isn't for him. It's not the stress – he's never minded that – it's the growing realization that he doesn't want to be like the people at the top of the business. In particular, he doesn't want to be like Angus. This is a conversation he will need to have with Grace. Not yet, but soon.

'God damn it. We're out of milk,' Grace says. She closes the fridge door and looks around for her keys.

'Don't worry, I'll go,' he says.

Grace protests that he's only just got in, but a walk across the Common with the dog is exactly what he needs. He'll be less of a bear when he gets back. Toffee leaps up, tail wagging as he trots into the hall, beating him to the coat hooks, where he sits, eyes glued to his lead, tail thumping.

As Nick leaves, a picture lingers in his head: Grace with a loose strand of hair falling across her cheek. She curls it behind her ear. He strolls along their street, enjoying the sinking sun and the pink cherry blossom, then turns left in the direction of the shops. It's only a ten-minute walk, but he gives in to temptation and the balmy spring evening to cross over on to the Common and allow Toffee a run. The little dog is delightfully grateful, springing up and resting his paws on Nick's knees, and licking his hand.

He passes a man with his son, on their way back from a school event, the boy in the uniform of the local secondary. He is looking up at his father, describing something, his eyes aglow, his hands animated. It makes Nick think of his relationship with his own father. He knew from a young age, possibly as early as his midteens, that he couldn't and shouldn't trust him, that as a role model he lacked the necessary qualities. He remembers being glad his parents didn't have more children, because he would have felt responsible for their happiness.

On the other hand, had there been siblings, his parents' focus wouldn't have been entirely on him, especially now that they were getting older. They live on the edge of their overdraft limit, with several over-burdened credit cards between them. Every month, he hands over a chunk of money. He could be petty and cut them off, but he's determined to be a good son, to be the bigger person. He is exasperated by them, but he loves them too. What makes him cross is the way his mother constantly undermines Grace. What hurts Grace, hurts him. If only they would treat her with more respect.

They do a quick circuit, nodding at canine acquaintances and their owners, then cross back over, and that's when he sees her: a woman coming towards him, a look of intent in her eyes. He glances round to see if there's someone else, a friend perhaps lurking behind him, but there's no one there, so he smiles and waits.

'Nick,' she says. 'I thought it was you.'

Toffee strains at his lead, gives a friendly bark and lets her pat him. Nick frowns, puzzled. It doesn't take long to work out that he knows her, especially when she straightens up and runs her fingers through her hair, the gesture so familiar, it wakes a dormant horror. His heart slams against his chest.

'Taisie,' he says.

'Anna. I call myself Anna now.'

'Oh. Right.' The happiness and sense of contentment he had been feeling has vaporized, replaced by the chill of despair. 'What are you doing here?'

She smiles, despite his lack of civility. 'I live here. But only since January. My son's in the same class as Lottie. I know Grace.'

Her voice is friendly, like she's just one of the other mums Grace talks to; perky and bright. He looks into her eyes, tries to see beyond them, but they give nothing away.

'She might have mentioned you,' he murmurs, checking his watch to give the impression he has somewhere to be. 'But I wouldn't have put two and two together.'

'No, of course not. That's why, when I spotted you, I thought I'd say hello. But don't worry,' she laughs. 'I'm not going to tell her your secrets.'

There it is, then. His stomach clenches. She's here for a reason. She may even have lain in wait, or spotted him and followed him, taking her chance while there was no one else to witness their encounter. How many years has it been? Nearly eighteen. Over half his life.

He swallows hard. 'What secrets?'

'Oh come on, Nick. You know what I'm talking about.'

He pulls himself together. She's caught him on the back foot, and he needs to regain control. 'Actually, I don't. Perhaps you'd better spell it out for me.'

'If that's what you want. Once upon a time there was a girl. Let's call her Isabel. She was a sweet child, but fragile. One day, she found herself shut in a cupboard with a boy she trusted, an older boy.'

He laughs. 'Not that again. We were kids. We were playing Sardines. It was nothing. I wouldn't have told you if there had been anything wrong with it.'

'You told me yourself that you kissed her.'

'That's not true, Taisie. What I said was that she was kissing me when I woke up.'

'She also said you groped her breast. Why would she lie?'

Why would Izzy have said that? He can't believe it.

340

Taisie was the manipulative one, not her little sister. Izzy was always so honest. 'I don't understand. When did she tell you that?'

She shrugs. 'Right afterwards. She was as white as a sheet.'

He stares at her, bewildered. 'You spoke to her? You never told me; you never told anyone.'

'I was protecting you.'

She put her hand on his arm and he recoiled. 'Protecting me? Why the hell would you do that? You hated me.'

'I didn't hate you. I was hurting, but you were still my friend. It was chaos. Don't you remember? I wasn't thinking straight.'

He backs away from her, his mind churning, trying to make sense of this new information. 'If you thought I'd had anything to do with Izzy's death, you would have told your parents, or the police.'

'I was messed up. And the Ritchies and the Wellses, we were like family, weren't we? I'd have been pulling down the whole edifice of my childhood, and I didn't have the courage. It was too late anyway.'

'Why didn't you try to stop her?'

'I couldn't. I got distracted by one of the others; and how was I supposed to know she'd go outside? It was pouring with rain.'

His eyes bore straight into hers. 'Which others?'

'Pansy or Freya; I don't remember which now. But they caught me. I tried to tell them I wasn't playing any more but they wouldn't let go of me.'

'OK. Stop. I'm not listening to this crap.' He tugs on Toffee's lead. 'I'm going.'

'I'm not finished.'

'Well, I am.'

She sighs. 'Then I'll just have to offload my traumatic memories on someone else. I'm sure Grace would love to know more about your past.'

'Leave her out of this.'

'I can't, can I? She has a young daughter.'

His eyes bulge; he thinks he's about to have a stroke. He realizes he's stopped breathing and drags oxygen into his strained lungs. 'Taisie, you know me. You know I wouldn't do a thing like that. I told you the truth. I had a nightmare, I thought I was being attacked and I lashed out. I scared her, and she ran away. If she deliberately went into the river, then it wasn't because of something I did. And if you think that I could molest a child, then all I can say is you have a warped mind.'

Toffee whines and circles, getting tangled in his lead. Nick sorts him out, using the time to gather his thoughts. When he unbends, she is still looking at him, a small smile on that near-perfect face. What else did she see? Did she see him run after Izzy? Did she see him cross the lawn to the woods? Did she see him come back alone?

'Why would you do this?' he asks.

'Because your family took everything from me.'

'Oh Christ,' he says. 'It was a bad business deal. It happens.'

'Oh right. Great. A bad business deal,' she mimics. 'Get over it, Anna. Wow. You arrogant prick.'

'I'm not arrogant, I'm practical. I apologize for the way my father behaved, and I'm sorry that Sean trusted

342

him. Angus warned him not to and he . . .' He hesitates. 'Well, I know that it devastated you. That you lost so much.'

'You have no idea what I lost.' Her face reddens. 'You have not got a fucking clue what your father did to me. What he took from me.'

Nick rubs his head with the tips of his fingers. This is something he wasn't aware of. Should he have been? Perhaps she doesn't mean what he thinks she means. He sincerely hopes so.

'You've lost me now. What did Dad take from you?'

Her mouth is pinched, her whole body language folded in and withdrawn.

'Everything.'

He sighs and holds out his hand, trying to placate her, to make her feel that old connection, but she shrinks away from him. He has a sudden vision of his father, rising godlike from the river, water running down his torso in rivulets; three teenage girls cavorting round him, vying for his attention. He looks closer at Anna, right into her eyes, and sees the hurt in there, the broken girl.

'My father seduced you.' It isn't a question. His heart sinks. 'You have every right to be angry with him, even with my family,' he says. 'But don't destroy me because of who I am.'

The tears have gone, and she's looking at him as though he's something she found under a rock.

'Tim wrecked everything for me, so I want compensation. I know Tim can't afford it, but you can.'

'For Christ's sake. I've done nothing wrong.'

She cocks her head to one side and smiles. 'Nick,' she

says with mock sympathy, 'I only have to tell the police what Izzy told me.'

'No one will believe you.'

'It doesn't matter if they do or not, does it? You'll still lose everything. You and your father are going to pay for what you did to my family.'

He was already paying, wasn't he? The guilt eating away at him. Spoiling his life. 'You're deluded. It's blackmail.'

'No, Nick. It's revenge. But go to the police if you like; draw attention to yourself. How would you like to be told you're not allowed in the room with Lottie without another adult present? How would you like Grace to start wondering if her daughter is safe with you? No smoke without a fire. What about Lottie's real dad? I don't suppose he'd be too happy.'

He's appalled by the picture she paints, and for the first time he feels real fear. What she's suggesting is outrageous, but entirely possible in these suspicious times. Toffee tugs on his lead.

'What is it you want?'

'Twenty thousand pounds immediately, and a standing order of a thousand pounds a month paid into my bank account.'

He listens to all this with his mouth gaping. 'I don't know how you can live with yourself, Taisie.'

'Anna. And I could say the same for you.' She stalks off.

When she's gone, he breathes out and walks in the opposite direction fast. Then he remembers the milk and hurries back for it, scooping the dog into his arms instead of tying him up because Toffee is trembling, alarmed by his master's anxiety, his rescue-dog insecurities resurfacing.

It's dark now, and cold. He wants Grace; he wants her so badly his throat aches. It's not the money, although frankly he has more than enough strains on his wallet, so much as the memory of that summer that kills him. Izzy's tragedy and his own nightmare. It crippled him emotionally, sucked all the confidence out of him, brought him to his knees, so that when the black clouds descended he had no defence, was unable to control what happened. He lived in darkness, breathing in the fuggy smell of his own unwashed body for months. Only when her family left London did he emerge, blinking, into the light.

He goes home, feeling wrung out, and walks into a house full of light and laughter. It's almost too much, but he puts a smile on his face and joins in, using the banter with Lottie to cover up the fact that's he's been knocked for six.

After Lottie has gone up to bed, he tries to chat. Usually they have no problem, but this time Grace is doing all the work, telling him about her day, about the latest house her boss has bought, about how much potential it has. He's so glad she's found this career, that it gives her so much pleasure. He loves to watch her while she speaks, especially when she's animated.

The problem is Taisie, or Anna as he should learn to think of her. He won't be able to relax until he's at least tried to make her see sense. He would do it tonight – the class address list is stuck to the fridge – but he can't leave Grace again, not now that she's had a glass of wine, she's happy, and giving off clear signals. He'd be rejecting her, and he won't do that. And frankly, today has been bad enough; he just wants to feel her arms around him.

After they've made love, Nick leans on his elbow and runs his hand along the undulating curve of Grace's ribcage, waist and hip. He wants to remember her for ever like this. She's more beautiful tonight than she's ever been; her skin glowing, her eyes darkened, her cheeks pink, and he's overwhelmed by love for her. She holds his gaze for so long that he laughs.

She smiles back, a twitching, ironic smile. 'What is it? What are you laughing about?'

'Nothing. You just make me so happy.'

That night the creatures come at him with such a surge of energy and violence that he throws himself out of bed, and crouches pressed up against the wall, his arms covering his face. When Grace rushes to his side, he throws his arm out, catching her on the shoulder.

'Ow. Nick, wake up. You're having a nightmare.' She takes him in her arms and rocks him as he shudders. 'It's OK. Everything's OK.'

GRACE

Saturday, 5 May 2018

MY STOMACH DROPS. 'WHAT DO YOU MEAN BY 'INCIDENT'?'

'Mrs Foreman has been violently assaulted,' Marsh says.

'Jesus. How awful. What am I going to tell Kai?'

'Say she's been in an accident, and she's in hospital. You're going to have to make a statement . . .'

There's a noise and we both turn. Kai is standing in the doorway staring at us.

'Where's Mum?'

I go to him, but Marsh gives me a warning look. We don't know for sure yet, his eyes say. Do not throw this at the child.

'She's not home yet, sweetie.'

Kai looks from me to the inspector. 'Why is he here?'

'I called him because I was getting a little bit worried. Are you hungry, sweetheart?' It's barely four o'clock, but I don't think there's any point forcing him back to bed when he'll just lie awake worrying.

Kai nods.

'What do you usually eat for breakfast?'

'Porridge. But Mum makes it.'

'I can make it for you.'

'S'all right.'

He goes to the cupboard and pulls out a box of cereal, the fruit and fibre kind, finds a clean bowl and brings them to the table. Marsh signals me to follow him out of the room and closes the door.

'We'll be in touch as soon as we know anything. Can you look after Kai until her family comes to get him?'

'He's never met them.'

Marsh raises his eyebrows.

'It's his dad's parents he's close to. I'm sure Kai will have their number on his phone. I'll call them for you if you like.'

Oh shit, I think as I see the two of them out. I've been through this with Lottie, so I know what will happen. No answer will satisfy Kai's craving. He wants his mum like Lottie wanted Nick, and when he twigs she's not coming home he's going to want to know why.

By this time a faint milky dawn is filtering into the house. I go back into the kitchen where Kai is sitting with his bowl of cereal untouched. I persuade him to brush his teeth and pack a few things, then I take him home. I let Toffee out into the garden and Kai goes out after him, but instead of throwing the chewed-up ball that Toffee offers him, his tail wagging, he stands there, staring at the houses behind, his shoulders slumped and his hands stuffed into his pockets. He comes back inside, I put the television on in the front room and he's asleep on the sofa within seconds. At six, I phone his grand-parents and speak to a sleepy Paula Foreman, Anna's mother-in-law. She immediately says they'll get a train to London and meet me and Kai at the hospital later today. She sounds a practical sort of person.

At nine Tim comes downstairs, freshly shaved, dressed in chinos and a pale-pink shirt. 'I thought I'd go to the RA,' he says. 'Get some culture.' He spots Kai and raises his eyebrows. 'I got your note. What happened?'

'This is Kai, Tim. Anna's son.' Kai is petting Toffee now, so I lead Tim out of earshot. 'Anna was attacked last night.'

I watch him closely, but nothing in his reaction is abnormal, just surprise, shock, compassion.

'Oh. I am sorry. That's terrible. Poor Anna.'

'Who was your text from?'

He looks at me innocently. 'What text?'

'The one you got before you went out last night.'

'Oh, that. That was Cora giving me an update about her mother. She's still with us, bless her.'

Some time later the police come to my house. Two of them, not Marsh, standing on my doorstep, asking to see Tim. I back into the hall as they advance.

'Tim,' I say, keeping my eyes on them. 'You have visitors.'

'On my way.'

He comes out of the kitchen holding a mug, a puzzled smile on his face that disappears when he sees the uni-formed officers. I show them into the front room and close the door, listening for long enough to hear one of the officers ask why he'd met Anna last night. Apparently, they were seen by a barmaid outside the Queen's Arms. Tim responded that it hadn't been a pre-arranged meeting, he'd just happened to bump into her. Then I move away. Tim met Anna? Why didn't he say so earlier? What is he hiding?

Five minutes later the three of them appear. Tim is pale.

'What's happening?' I ask.

'It's nothing to worry about. I'm helping these fellows with their inquiries. Now don't worry, Grace. I'll be fine. I'll come straight home.'

'Shall I phone Cora?' I wince as I say it, imagining her reaction.

Tim looks at me in horror. 'No. It's lovely of you to offer, but Cora has enough to worry about with her mother. It's a mistake. It'll be cleared up in a trice.'

I follow them outside, watch Tim being escorted to the car, the door being opened. He looks straight ahead as they drive off. I feel a presence at my side and turn to find Kai standing next to me.

'Why've they taken Lottie's grandad?' he asks.

'I don't know.'

'Is he under arrest?' His tone is more interested than dismayed.

'No, he's not. They just need some information from him.'

'But they did that thing ... when the policeman pushes the criminal's head down to make him go in the car.'

'I think that was to make sure he didn't hit his head on the door frame.'

I chivvy Kai inside and settle him down with his book then open my laptop and try to work, but I can't focus. I'm not sure I believe Tim about the text. It could have been Anna asking him to meet her, wanting to confront him about the past the police will check. The idea of Tim using violence on a woman is hard to accept, but who knows what people are capable of, if pushed too far.

I drum my fingers on the table top until Kai looks up and frowns. I've been awake most of the night and the morning feels endless, the minutes ticking away. I keep the landline and my mobile close to hand.

We take Toffee for a quick walk round the Common. In the distance I spot the telltale police ribbon cordoning off an area close to the pond. I steer Kai in the opposite direction. I wish Lottie was here. It would be so much easier with Kai if she was around. As it is, he walks along beside me, his shoulders slumped, his hands deep in his pockets, responding politely to my attempts at conversation before lapsing back into silence.

We get home and I check the landline for messages. Nothing from Tim. After lunch it's time to go to the hospital.

Kai and I follow the signs to ICU and wait in Reception. Down the corridor a police officer stands guard outside one of the rooms. Kai can't take his eyes off him. After a few minutes we're collected by a nurse, told that we can see Anna and are given five minutes. The nurse holds the door open for us and points to a bed at the end. Anna is lying there, her head swathed in bandages, attached to a drip, a heart monitor tracking her pulse, oxygen whooshing in and out. Kai's hand tenses in mine and I give it a squeeze. Harry and Paula Foreman rise to greet us. Harry is dressed in dark-brown trousers, green shirt and mustard V-neck, Paula in dark jeans and a navy-blue-and-white striped top. They are a lot older than I expected, closer to eighty than seventy. I wonder how they are going to cope.

'Come here, darling,' Paula says.

Kai walks straight up to her, wraps his arms around her and allows himself to be tightly hugged. Harry ruffles his hair with the intimacy of a long-standing fondness, and I feel relieved of a burden. Kai will be safe with them. Paula leads him to his mother's side and rests her hand on his shoulder. He looks up at her for reassurance and she nods. He takes Anna's hand, lacing his fingers through hers.

'Mum,' he says, his voice wobbling. 'Please wake up.'

'How well do you know Anna?' I ask, when we've left ICU.

Harry flicks a look at his wife. She nods, understanding.

'Shall we go and get you a comic?' she says to Kai.

'We made a decision,' Harry says, once they're out of earshot, 'after our son's death, that we would maintain a civil relationship with Anna, for Kai's sake. We don't like her and, quite frankly, we blame her for what happened to Ben, but both of us love that boy dearly. We don't want to lose him.'

'Your son killed himself?'

'Yes. She made his life a misery.'

I feel defensive on Anna's behalf. 'Nothing is that simple. You can't know for sure what went on between them.'

Harry shrugs. 'All I know is that he changed when she came along.'

'Didn't you change when you met Paula?'

He smiles reluctantly. 'For the better, I hope.'

'You want someone to blame. That's only natural. Look,' I say, to forestall an argument. 'All I want to know is what you can tell me about her personality. Why it is that when Anna meets a man, it tends to end in disaster for him, whether she's to blame or not?'

He nods. 'You've hit the nail on the head there. Anna is the type of woman who is so convinced that she can wrap men around her little finger that when something happens to contradict her view of herself, it comes as an almighty shock. She doesn't much like women. She makes bad decisions under stress. But she's a good mum,' he adds, glancing at Grace. 'She loves that little boy to bits.'

Later that evening, Tim comes home. He looks worn out.

'What happened?' I ask.

'Nothing. I gave my statement, then hung around while they corroborated it. Then they let me go. Friendly bunch. Marsh, especially. Charming chap.'

'Well, good.'

I pause, wondering whether to ask him to elaborate, then decide not to. I'm existing on two hours' sleep and I'm bone weary. He's here, isn't he? Proof that he's done nothing wrong. But still, there's a lingering niggle. He's suspiciously unperturbed by his experience. And he hasn't asked me questions about Anna. Surely, if he had seduced her, he would be curious, or even worried that his past misdemeanours were catching up with him. He'd ask me leading questions.

'Everything OK?' he asks.

I shake myself. 'Yes. Fine. Are you hungry?'

'Famished. Why don't we order something in?' He pulls a bottle of wine out of the fridge and gets down two glasses. 'What do you fancy?'

Over supper, he tells me all I need to know without me having to ask. There was a text from Cora. And none from Anna, but he could easily have deleted that. Even so, the man had several witnesses, people who had seen him and Toffee after he had parted company with Anna.

It's an anti-climax. I had convinced myself that he had gone to meet Anna. It all fitted so conveniently. She confronted him about what he did to her, maybe threatened to accuse him retrospectively of rape, and he flipped. Only that's not what happened.

I fall into bed at nine o'clock and for the first time since Nick went, I drop off immediately. In the morning, I stare at my clock, astonished to see that it's past eight. I put on my dressing gown and come downstairs to find Tim's suitcase in the hall. He's dressed and ready to go. Cora needs to be close to her mother, and he's going back to Leicestershire to support her. I allow myself one mean thought. Thank God for Granny.

NICK

AT WORK THE NEXT DAY NICK CAN BARELY CONCENTRATE. Between phone calls and meetings, he searches online, looking for information on Izzy, typing in *Isabel Wells drowning 2000* and finding himself down a rabbit hole, reading articles with a greed and masochism that shock him.

Is Taisie justified in saying he owes her? More than she thinks. He could have ignored Izzy's furious outburst and stayed with her. It's the biggest regret of his life that he didn't. Maybe he should give Taisie the money to get rid of her. It's worth some thought, but he doubts it would stop there. He has to try again.

His mobile rings and he glances at the display. He doesn't recognize the number. The voice on the other end is unfamiliar and over-friendly.

'It's Alex. Alex Wells.'

'Alex,' Nick says, pushing himself away from his desk and standing up. After being confronted by Taisie last night, he's not as surprised as he might have been. 'How are you?'

What else do you say after almost eighteen years? He hasn't seen Alex since Izzy's funeral. He must be, what, twenty-nine now. If this is a coincidence, it's a massive one. Maybe Taisie phoned her brother. Maybe they are both in on it. Alex had been firmly under her thumb as a child.

'I found you through LinkedIn.'

'Oh. OK.'

He waits for more, wandering over to the window and looking down into the narrow street where two office workers are smoking, their smoke reaching the windows above them before finally dissipating.

'Is it a bad time?' Alex says.

'No. No, I'm just surprised to hear from you. What're you up to nowadays?'

'Nothing very exciting. I played it safe and got a law degree. No, the reason I'm calling . . . This is going to sound a bit random, but I've been thinking about that summer a lot recently.' His voice thrums with embarrassment. 'To tell you the truth, I've had some difficulties and I've been seeing a psychiatrist. This is about Izzy.'

Nick's voice is icy. 'I thought it might be. I suppose you've been talking to Taisie.'

'No.' Alex sounds genuinely baffled. 'I haven't seen her in years.'

'You want me to believe that it's a coincidence that you've got in touch the day after she did?'

'Did she? Wow. No, sorry, Nick. I had no idea. I hope she calls me. Did she give you a number?'

'No.' Nick sighs. 'All right. What do you want?'

'To talk about my little sister. You two were like

356

partners in crime that summer. Great big Nick and shrimpy little Izzy. She idolized you, you know. Followed you around like a puppy.'

'I don't know about that,' he says.

'The thing is, Nick, I think, if you want to move on, it's important to face up to your own mistakes.'

'I'll bear it in mind.' He frowns and taps his pen on the side of his desk. He has no idea what Alex is getting at and is not sure he wants to know. 'Are you calling everyone?' he asks, thinking of Rory and the Moody twins. All the adults. Since half of them weren't speaking to each other, it wouldn't be an easy task.

'Pretty much, but I particularly wanted to speak to you, because I reckon you might have said something to Izzy. Maybe rejected her?'

'Rejected her? What the hell are you talking about?'

'Oh come on, Nick. She was besotted with you. Think about it.'

'Well, I . . .'

'I'm to blame too. I played Taisie's game. We bullied you. You wouldn't have had to rely on Izzy for company otherwise. My psychiatrist suggested that I apologize. So, here it is. I am sincerely sorry. I was too young to realize how much damage we were doing.'

Nick doesn't want to talk about this. It was humiliating enough at the time. 'Apology accepted,' he says, in a bid to close the conversation. 'I appreciate it.'

But Alex isn't listening; he has to have his moment. 'All this time, I've blamed Taisie, but I now realize that I need to take responsibility. I should have stood up to her.'

357

'Is that it?'

'Yeah. Well, not quite. I just wanted to say that your dad was not entirely to blame for his restaurant going under.'

Nick flinches. For Christ's sake. 'I don't want to be rude, Alex, but would you mind if we don't rehash all this? I've moved on. Nobody cares any more.'

'OK. Sorry. I just thought you should know; it was Angus Moody who persuaded your dad's investor to pull out. I mean, I kind of wish he had persuaded my dad as well.' He laughs nervously. 'But that's another thing altogether. I've forgiven Tim for that, even if Dad and Mum haven't. It was Pansy who told me. She feels bad about it. She said she'd like to see you.' Alex's speech fizzles out, as he becomes aware that Nick is no longer responding. 'Well,' he says awkwardly. 'I'm sure you're very busy. I'll let you get on. Perhaps we could meet for a coffee some time.'

Nick holds the phone away from him. He taps the disconnect icon and places it screen-down on his desk. Angus's office is three doors down from his. In between them is Phillipa Travers, the gatekeeper. He buzzes her and asks if Angus is free, and on being told that he is, puts his jacket back on.

Angus Moody. This is a man Nick looks up to, a man he thinks of as a mentor, someone who once saw a desperate and miserable sixteen-year-old boy and helped him without embarrassing him, who held out a hand of friendship without implying that he thought Nick needed a friend.

In return, not only has Nick worked hard, but he's lied for him about those non-existent insurance contracts. He did it because Angus meant something to him, and he couldn't stand by and see him fall. And for what? The friendship means nothing. Angus Moody is just another entitled, arrogant arse. If he has no integrity, then what is the point? He feels anger building in his veins, throbbing at his temples, and knows that he should wait until he's calmed down. But he can't. He has Anna Foreman on his shoulders, and the stress of that, the threat she's holding over him, means that his mind isn't doing its habitual Connect-4 kind of rationalization. The discs are all over the place.

Angus half stands, his expression welcoming. Nick closes the door behind him. His face feels tight, his hands twitch.

'Everything all right?' Angus says, gazing at Nick through his bifocals.

Nick doesn't say anything. He stares at his CEO.

'Trouble?' Angus prompts.

'You could say that. I've just had an interesting conversation with Alex Wells.'

'Alex? I haven't heard from him in ages. How is he?'

'Never mind how he is. He told me something.'

Angus raises his eyebrows. 'It's obviously serious. Perhaps you'd better tell me what it's about.'

'He said that you persuaded my father's investor to pull out of Ritchie's.'

There's a short silence, then Angus shrugs. 'I was doing a friend a favour, that place was never going to succeed.'

'How the fuck did you know whether it was going to succeed or not?' Nick explodes. 'You pulled the plug on it. My dad threw his heart and soul into that place.'

The door opens and Phillipa comes in, looks from one to the other, apologizes for interrupting and backs out. There's a long silence before Angus speaks.

'Your father never threw his heart and soul into anything. He's lazy and he's a bad bet.'

'Maybe he is, but what the fuck's that got to do with you? Why did you interfere?'

'Because Peter Mayhew is a friend of mine, and I didn't want to see him lose money. I tried to persuade Sean out of it as well, but he wouldn't listen. More fool him.'

Nick bristles. He leans against the desk, his hands fisted. 'It was none of your damn business. It wasn't your money. You've got a lot to answer for.'

'I'm a businessman and I can smell potential failure a mile off. I could smell it on your father. I've done you a lot of favours—'

'You can stuff your favours.'

Angus's benign expression hardens. 'Keep your voice down. Listen to me, Nick. You've worked hard and you're a real asset to this firm, but that doesn't give you leave to throw your weight around. Don't make it personal.'

'It *is* personal. Dad made a hash of it, but to go behind his back, to go behind my back . . . But I might have known.'

'What do you mean by that?'

'I covered for you. I shredded papers and deleted files. I thought you had put things right, but now I can see I was mistaken. You're ruthless.'

'Let's not get into that,' Angus says.

'No, let's get into it. You acted illegally. You put this entire company and its employees' jobs in jeopardy. I got my hands dirty for you, and you did *that* to my father. Well, I'm not going to put up with it any more.'

'For God's sake, shut up. Phillipa will hear you.' Angus picks up a pen, twiddles it, then puts it down and moves it so that it lies parallel to his keyboard. Nick recognizes the signs of anxiety. Angus tries to hide it, but his eyes give him away; they looked startled.

'I didn't delete everything,' Nick says.

Angus goes preternaturally still, and Nick asks himself if he's gone too far.

'Now why would that be?'

'To be honest,' Nick responds, 'I have no idea. A sense of self-preservation, I suppose. At any rate, since you're not the man I thought you were, since you've turned out to be a devious bastard, I see no reason why I should be mixed up in this any more.'

Angus shoves his chair back, stands up and walks right up to him. He prods him in the chest. 'You'd better be extremely careful. You don't know who you're dealing with.'

Nick moves Angus's hand away. 'I think I do.'

'What I did, didn't hurt anyone.'

'When you facilitate a crime, someone always suffers.'

'What are we talking about here, Nick? Are you asking for a pay-off?'

Nick grimaces. 'I've only just found out what you did to my father, I haven't had time to process it. But I think I need to do the right thing. You do too.'

There's a flash of genuine fear in Angus's eyes, but it's gone so quickly that Nick wonders if he imagined it.

'You'd shaft me because I prevented a friend from losing money? You would give up everything you have here, out of spite? You need to think about this. There are implications. I don't want to scare you, but I'm not the only one involved, and the others aren't as nice as me.'

'You're not scaring me.'

'No? Come on, Nick.' His demeanour changes, he clamps his hand on to Nick's shoulder. 'Let's not argue. When you've slept on it you'll appreciate that I behaved perfectly reasonably. You would have done the same in my shoes.'

Nick glances pointedly at Angus's hand. 'You've got until Monday to put it right, or I'm going to the Serious Fraud Office.'

Angus frowns and says curtly, 'I thought better of you. Go home, Nick. Take the rest of the day off. We'll talk next week when you've had a chance to calm down.'

To his relief the house is empty when he gets back. Even though it's only three o'clock he grabs a beer from the fridge and pops the lid. The hour it's taken to get home has given him time to cool off. What has he done? Maybe he shouldn't have lost his temper. He knows Angus well enough to understand his behaviour. He knows his father well enough as well. Wouldn't he have done the same in Angus's shoes? He reaches for his phone, finds Angus's number, then puts it down. Not yet. He's not grovelling. Monday will be soon enough.

He hears the girls come in and wanders into the hall to meet them. Grace raises her eyebrows.

'This is a surprise! What are you doing home so early?'

'I missed you,' he says.

'Yeah, right.'

'Have you been fired?' Lottie asks.

'No. Just fancied an early one.'

'Well, it's lovely for us,' Grace says, looking puzzled.

Later that evening, he pokes his head round Lottie's door to say goodnight. She's awake and holds out her arms to him. He sits down on the edge of her bed, leans over and kisses her cheek.

'Sleep well, Shrimpy.'

'Shrimpy?' She wrinkles her nose. 'I'm not Shrimpy.'

In the darkness he flushes. 'Damn, I'll have to make up a new name for you,' he says, adjusting quickly. 'What about Octopus?'

'No.'

'Heffalump?'

Lottie giggles and thumps him.

'Go to sleep, then. You can tell me who you are in the morning. Love you.'

He should tell Grace what's happened, but he can't. It's too soon and he's too wound up, and anyway, it might all be straightened out by Monday with no one any the wiser. He knows how much she worries, understands that her upbringing has made her unduly anxious about money and stability. He has to know the answers to the questions she's going to ask, before she asks them.

GRACE

Monday, 7 May 2018

I WANDER AROUND THE HOUSE, CARRYING A CUP OF coffee, alone except for Toffee who refuses to let me out of his sight, even scratching at the bathroom door when I have a shower. I have an appointment later, but not until eleven thirty, so I'm rattling around, unable to settle to anything, feeling listless and drained of energy. The spare bedroom is neat and tidy, divested of most, but not all, of Tim and Cora's belongings, as if they're telling me not to get too comfortable. In fact, I heard from Cora an hour ago; she sent a text saying that her mother had died in the early hours. They'd be staying for a couple of weeks to have the funeral and deal with everything, but they would be back as soon as possible. I messaged back with my commiserations and urged her to take as long as she needed.

In Lottie's room, I empty the contents of her rucksack on to the bed and sort out the clothes that need washing from those that just need folding back into her chest of drawers, then I go downstairs to the utility room. My clothes are in the basket. I take each item out and throw it in, checking pockets for stray handkerchiefs or, better still, loose change; and that's when I find it. The baby wristband. I lay it on my palm and smooth it out. With all that's been happening, I had forgotten all about it. It has *Daughter of WELLS, Anastasia* written on it in biro, and the date: *30.07.2001*.

Anna had a baby before Kai. That child would be sixteen by now, around the age Anna would have been when she had her. She hasn't mentioned her, and, apart from this souvenir, I found no clue to her existence in the house. Alex had said Taisie went off the rails, so it could have been some random boy, but I can't help wondering if Tim is the father. She leaned on him because he was very attractive, he was in control and he made her feel better. He took advantage of an unhappy girl, a girl whose family was reeling from the loss of her sister. He messed Taisie up while his son was steeped in his own personal hell, retreating to his bedroom and locked in depression. What a total and utter bastard.

I find a scrap of paper and write out the months, counting back. The baby would have been conceived in the autumn of 2000, so it fits. The family would still have been living in London then, the restaurant about to open, Tim stressing about investors, trying to keep up a confident front, realizing that this was his last chance of success, feeling vulnerable about middle age, looking for something, or someone, to make him feel young again. Anna would have felt so alone; her parents drowning in grief for Izzy, her brothers too young to be of any help, her friends unable to understand, Nick as good as gone, and anyway she had thoroughly alienated him on that holiday.

Did she come to this part of London to settle old scores? Did she threaten to expose Tim, encouraged by women coming forward in the media with tales of historic rape and assault by seemingly respectable men? Or did she come to find the Ritchies because she hadn't got either of them out of her system? Whatever the truth, Nick vanished on Saturday, 14 April, forty-eight hours after Anna confronted him. *Day Zero*.

I pick Toffee up and hug him, pressing my cheek into his soft fur. He twists his head round and licks me.

I smarten myself up for my appointment, take Toffee and let myself out into a blessedly quiet street. One knock-on effect of Anna's attack is that the press have lost interest in me, a young mother being left for dead on the Common weighing more in the balance than a thirty-four-year-old missing man. That may change of course, when they spot the connection, but for the moment I'm just grateful to be left alone.

I didn't think I was up to it, but in fact getting away from the area is exactly what I need. I feel a burst of energy as I put the Common behind me and ride towards Chelsea. The house I visit isn't Rupert's yet, but he's interested. He wants to know what I think, whether it has potential.

Rupert is standing outside the property, looking up at the facade with the agent, a pretty blonde woman in a bright pink jacket. I park my bike between a Porsche Cayenne and an Audi, remove my helmet and quickly run my fingers through my hair.

'You look shattered,' Rupert tells me, as he kisses my cheek. 'Are you OK?'

My boss is in his mid-forties, tall and broad, with a florid complexion and sandy hair. I've never seen him out of a suit.

'I'm fine.' I shake hands with the agent, taking pride in my professionalism. No one would have a clue about the turmoil I'm going through. She walks up the steps, holds open the door and we go in.

'No word then?' Rupert murmurs as we inspect the front room.

'No.'

The house has belonged to the same family for seventy years, and the last resident, a ninety-seven-year-old man, died a month ago. I look up, and take note of the large brown stain, roughly the shape of Australia, and the damaged but beautiful cornicing. The house will be worth a fortune once it's done up, but it'll cost a lot to restore and the executors are asking an eye-watering price. I'm not sure it's worth it.

We spend three-quarters of an hour exploring the house and grilling the agent, then I make my way home. Away from Rupert, and the buzz of a potential new restoration, I start to think about Anna again. The wristband is in my bag. The fact that she had, and presumably gave away, a baby daughter, is heart-breaking. She was so young; several years younger than I was when I got pregnant with Lottie. I find it all too easy to empathize. We were both a mess, both torn about what to do, both with the wrong man. Douglas at least faced up to his responsibilities and fell in love with his daughter. If the baby was Tim's, then he walked away and lived his life without a second thought.

I slow at the corner to my street, then keep going without turning. I can't go home now. Instead I ride to the hospital and find my way back to ICU. The nurse on duty tells me that Anna's parents are with her but that I can poke my head round the door and say hello if I want.

Jess and Sean Wells look up when I walk in. I compose myself and come forward. They both stand. Jess is petite and plump, with dyed brown hair. She wears clothes that fit snugly over her curves, a woollen dress over woollen tights worn with flat brown boots. Sean is wearing a lumberjack-style flannel shirt over blue jeans. He is almost entirely bald.

'How long have you known our daughter?' Jess asks after I've introduced myself and explained my presence here.

'Not long. Only since the start of the year.' I hesitate. 'I understand you were estranged?'

'It wasn't our choice.'

She gazes down at Anna then smiles, and her smile reminds me of Kai.

'Did you want to talk to her? Sean and I need a break anyway. Why don't you stay a minute? I'm sure she'd love to hear your voice.'

I look at Anna, at the tubes keeping her alive and the monitors charting her vital signs. 'Yes,' I say. 'If you don't mind.'

When they've left, I sit down and rest my bag on my knee. I open my mouth a couple of times, but nothing comes out. I hadn't realized how hard it would be to even begin to unblock the lines of communication when someone is in an unresponsive state.

'Anna,' I say experimentally. 'Anna, it's Grace. I'm so sorry about what happened to you.' I pause, my mouth bone dry. I open the zipped section in my bag and take out the wristband, put it in her hand and fold her fingers around it.

'I'm on your side, Anna. I want you to know that whatever has happened to Nick, I understand that you have been through a lot. If you said something to him to make him leave, please tell me. I won't hold it against you. I know you've suffered terribly. I wish you had told me about the baby when you told me about Tim.'

I listen to the sound of her breathing, until its rhythmic pulse begins to make me zone out. She is so still, so defenceless. In that moment I feel nothing but sympathy. I don't like her, but the things I don't like about her are the same things I dislike about myself. The lying, the insecurity, the distrust of others. We are not so different, when it comes down to it.

I stand up and hook the strap of my bag over my shoulder. I consider leaving the wristband in her hand, but I don't do it. It wouldn't be fair.

On my way out, I pass Sean and Jess. They look at me eagerly, hoping, I imagine, that I will give them some insight into their daughter. I want to give them something so badly, but I can't think what.

'Kai is a super little boy,' I say. 'You'll love him. Anna's done a fantastic job. She's a wonderful mum.'

It was both the right and the wrong thing to say. Jess starts to cry, and Sean puts his arm around her.

'Thank you, Grace. That means so much. We're meeting our grandson tomorrow. We can't wait.'

I watch as they walk back along the corridor. I feel so lonely I could cry.

I haven't been in my house for five minutes before the doorbell rings. As usual my heart does a flip. As usual I force myself to control my expectations, to quash the spark of hope. It won't be Nick. It's probably Mrs Jeffers wanting me to change a light bulb for her, or something like that. Even my fretful neighbour's company would be welcome right now. I see the two shadowy figures through the opaque panes and my heart drops to my stomach. Toffee barks, and I grab him before opening the door. He raises his front paws, straining at his collar, when he sees the two police officers.

'Grace Trelawney,' the WPC says. At her tone, flat and heavy, I step back instinctively. Toffee growls. 'I have a warrant to search the premises.'

ANNA

Saturday, 14 April 2018 ❧ Day Zero

THERE WERE TWO EMPTY WINE GLASSES, EITHER SIDE of her bed. Kai was at Hannah's birthday sleepover, Anna had just had the shag of her life, and she was happy.

Douglas's ribcage rose and fell under her head. She could feel his heartbeat. Every so often his stomach gurgled. He played with her hair, smoothing it through his hand. He stroked her back too, in an absent way, but his hands were so warm and firm that it felt akin to a massage. The smell of his skin was seductive, a cocktail of male musk and soap. When they made love she had pressed her nose into his neck, breathing him in. She ran her fingertips over his stomach muscles, then slid them up to his scar. He had told her he'd got it in a brawl when he was younger. She loved all his imperfections.

Anna was overwhelmed by emotion. She had known when she met him that there was something there, but this had taken her by surprise. She thought about what she had lost over the years: the betrayal by the first man she loved, the baby she'd had adopted, the family who turned cold, the husband who took himself from her. Tears started to run, trickling from the corners of her eyes, down her cheekbones to her ears. Douglas touched her face.

'Was it something I said?'

She laughed and wiped the tears away. 'No. Just feeling shaky.'

'Come here.' He pulled her up, and she curled against his chest. He held her like a child. 'Tell me.'

'It's nothing.'

'It's evidently something. Vain as I am, I'm not deluding myself that my superior sexual performance has left you an emotional wreck.'

She chuckled. 'Well,' she said, tipping her head up and letting him drop a kiss on her lips. 'There is that, of course. Obviously, it was the best sex I've ever had.' Another tear fell, and her laugh must have sounded forced, because he held her closer.

'It's a pathetic story.'

'I'll be the judge of that.'

She went silent, thinking. Where should she start, and how much should she tell him? She didn't want to sound like she was whinging, but then again, this was part of her and if Douglas loved her he would understand. Her mouth was dry, but they hadn't brought any water upstairs with them. She reached for the wine bottle and drank straight from it.

'Easy there.'

She put the bottle down with a grimace. She already knew that Douglas found excess unattractive. 'When I was fifteen years old I was seduced by Nick Ritchie's father.'

She had already told Douglas about Izzy's death, but not about the part Tim and Nick played in her life. Now she was ready to talk, wrapped in her lover's arms, his scent in her nose, his hand tracing the curves of her body. She told him about Tim, how he had encouraged her to turn to him in the aftermath of Izzy's death. How the secret affair had allowed her to occasionally forget what had happened.

Her heart was racing. She had kept Tim's secret for so long that it felt monstrous to betray it, but Tim had betrayed her first.

She leaned back with a sigh. 'But then everything changed. Ritchie's collapsed and my parents were left with a huge hole in their finances. There was nothing we could do but sell up and leave London. I was still in love with Tim, I thought he loved me. I was young, and it was a fairy tale. Then I found out I was pregnant.' She swallowed hard, that old humiliation still raw. 'I was so happy. I called him, and we arranged to meet. He sounded on edge. Christ, that should have given me a clue.'

'Go on.'

'I naively thought he would leave Cora and we'd set up home together, but it turned out it was a kiss goodbye, not hello. He told me that it was wonderful to see me, that I was adorable and would always have a place in his heart, but that I had my whole life ahead of me and it couldn't include him. He said he loved me, but he didn't want to ruin my life; or his. When I explained about the baby . . .' She took a deep breath and closed her eyes. 'I thought he would be pleased. I had this fantasy . . . but he told me none of it could happen, that it would destroy him, and he could end up in prison. I loved him, so I agreed to keep quiet.' A tear makes its way down her face. 'I managed to convince Mum and Dad that it was some random guy I'd met at a party, and since I was a total nightmare at the time, drinking and staying out all night, they believed me.'

'Did you have an abortion?' Douglas asked, wiping her tears for her.

'No. Tim wanted me to, and offered to pay for it, but I couldn't so I had her adopted.' She sniffs. 'It was hard, but it was the right thing to do. After that I moved back to London and sofa-surfed with friends for a while, but usually their parents got fed up with me pretty quickly. I was a mess.'

'Poor Anna.' His arms tightened round her. 'Poor baby.'

She snuggled into him. 'You won't hurt me, will you? You wouldn't treat me like Tim did?'

'Of course not.'

'Only I don't think I could bear it if it happened again.'

She only worried because her attraction to him felt similar to the way she had felt with Tim – insecure; scared that this all-consuming love might not be reciprocated, that she was being toyed with again. She felt him withdrawing and decided to reveal more, to pique his interest.

'I have a few mementos.' She sat up and pulled the covers over her, hunching over her knees. 'I wanted

374

proof of where she came from, so I pulled out some of her baby hairs.' She smiled, remembering. 'She screamed like crazy, but I have her DNA.'

The revelation has the desired effect. 'Clever girl.'

'I didn't feel particularly clever,' she grumbled. 'I felt like an idiot. I'll never forgive either of them.'

'Either of them?'

'Nick too. But that's another story.'

'I'm not going anywhere.'

'Are you interrogating me?'

She hopped out of bed and went into the bathroom, turned on the tap and angled her mouth beneath it. Her face was still flushed and her eyes bright. She splashed her cheeks with cold water and dried them with a towel.

'I want to know everything about you,' Douglas said.

How far could she trust him? She barely knew him. But Douglas wasn't Tim and she had to talk to someone about what happened. It had been poisoning her for so long. She crawled back under the blankets and snuggled up to him, closing her eyes tight.

'Talk to me, Anna. I don't want there to be any secrets between us.'

She hugged her arms around her knees above the duvet. 'The reason Izzy ran down to the river was because something had upset her, had scared and shaken her so much that she wasn't in her right mind. Before she went, she told me she had been hiding with Nick. She was trembling from head to toe, and she looked like a ghost.'

She felt Douglas's body tense.

'What are you saying?' His voice had bite in it. The loving quality had gone.

'We'd been playing this silly game, pretending Nick didn't exist. Izzy didn't like it and would sneak off and spend time with him when she thought no one was watching. But I knew. I suppose they got close and Nick misinterpreted the signals and took things too far. He was a very troubled teenager.'

Why did she add that last lie? He wasn't troubled, at least not before that summer. Had she really been that powerful? It seemed extraordinary now.

'He changed after she died; became withdrawn and depressed, everyone knows that. It wasn't as if he had lost a sibling, so it must have been a guilty conscience. He did something to her, then made sure she couldn't tell. He knew she was a weak swimmer. I think he may have followed her down to the river that day.' She takes a deep breath. 'And something happened. Obviously, I can't prove that.'

'For Christ's sake, Anna. Get to the point. What did he actually do?'

'She said he had his hand on her breast.'

'Fuck.' He raked his hand through his hair. 'Why the hell didn't you tell the police?'

Because in her heart she knew it wasn't the whole truth. In her heart, she knew it was her fault.

'Because I had no proof. Also, he might have only meant to scare her, but lost control of the situation, or misjudged the river, and she was swept away. I'd known Nick all my life and I didn't think he could do anything like that, and it was all so fragmented: the storm, the game we were playing, Tim kissing me. It was this weird kaleidoscope. It was only years later that my memories started to resolve themselves into something coherent. It seems so obvious now, but it wasn't then.'

Douglas is grinding his teeth. It was the first time she'd seen him do that.

'I shouldn't have told you.'

'Don't be stupid, Anna.'

The words stripped the warmth from the room. 'I'm not . . .'

'He's parenting my daughter, for fuck's sake. Jesus.' He thumped his fist down on the mattress. 'I don't believe it. If you knew that about him, why didn't you say something to Grace?'

Had she gone too far? Nick had come close to the bone when he asked her why she was so keen to lay the blame at his door, but she refused to feel guilty. He was his father's son. She waited, then said quietly, 'Because I wanted to use the information and I was waiting for the right time.'

'What do you mean? Use it for what?'

'For money.'

There was a long, long silence. A door closed with a bang somewhere down the street. Anna imagined she could hear the fridge humming. Douglas got out of bed and pulled on his boxers, then went to the window, opened the curtains and looked out, his hands pressed against the frame, his shoulder blades jutting like fins. When he turned he was backlit by the street lights. The headlights of a passing car lit the room. She drew her knees up to her chest and covered her face with her hands.

'How much money?' he asked softly, coming to sit beside her.

'Twenty thousand pounds down, plus a thousand a month,' she mumbled into her palms.

'And that's what you think my daughter's safety is worth?'

She dropped her hands. 'No! Of course I don't think that.' That was not what she meant at all, but why hadn't it occurred to her that this would be his reaction? She back-pedalled quickly. 'She isn't in any danger. I could be wrong about Nick. That's only my theory. Douglas, don't you see—'

But he's already out of the bed and pulling on his trousers. He does up his shirt before looking at her again. 'You've done a lot of damage, haven't you, Anna? You're going to have to put this right.'

GRACE

Monday, 7 May 2018

'AM I A SUSPECT?' I ASK DETECTIVE INSPECTOR MARSH.

I've been brought to the police station to help with their inquiries. Like Tim, I was taken in a police car. I thank God Lottie didn't see it. I had to tell Cassie, though, in case I'm not home in time to pick her up. If necessary, she'll look after Toffee for me as well. The energy I had earlier, that little reserve, has entirely gone.

'Why would you think that, if Nick killed himself?'

I support my head with the palm of my hand. A stone-faced WPC called Venetia Grant is sitting next to the detective. Her cool blue eyes don't leave my face. It's disconcerting. Occasionally I stare back, but she doesn't blink.

'But I don't think he did,' I say. 'I don't think he's dead.'

'It seems odd that Nick never told you about that summer. If you were so important to him, surely he would have confided in you.'

I shrug.

'Why do you think he didn't tell you?'

'I don't know.'

He smiles. 'But you can guess, surely? We don't tell the people we love everything. We gloss over the stuff we're ashamed of, the guilty secrets, or we miss out certain events because we're scared of getting found out.'

I clasp my hands together and press my knuckles against my teeth. My skin feels dry.

'I don't know,' I repeat. 'I have a lot of questions. I wish he was here to answer them.'

'So do I.' Marsh picks up his mug, peers into it and puts it down, disappointed. He taps his pen against his palm and flicks through the brown manila folder to a page with handwritten notes.

'Did you suspect Nick was having an affair with Anna Foreman?' Grant says. It's the first time she's spoken.

I don't miss a beat. 'No, I didn't.'

'Did you add the pair of them to the app because you thought something was going on?'

I shake my head. 'No. And it was Cassie who added Anna, not me. I only added Nick.'

'But you were watching Nick's and Anna's progress that evening? Why was that?'

'Idle curiosity – it's what the app's about. There's a competitive element.'

'And a nosy element.' She smiles like we're in this together.

'Well, yes. It's supposed to be fun.'

'Until your partner stops to talk to the woman you suspect him of having an affair with.'

'I did not suspect them. I didn't think they'd even

met.' My palms have started to sweat. I wipe them surreptitiously on my jeans.

'Your kids go to the same school. You share a friendship group. Are you asking us to believe that Nick and Anna never ran into each other?'

'She only moved round here in January. And it's not as if we socialized together. We probably would have done eventually, but these things take time.'

'You were jealous of Anna, weren't you? When you started to suspect that Nick was involved with her. How did that make you feel?'

I frown. Why is she pushing this so hard? 'It didn't make me feel anything, because I am not jealous of her.'

That isn't entirely true. I remember how I felt on seeing Anna's and Nick's footsteps stop climbing; the sharp ache under my ribcage, the feeling of nausea and the surge of adrenaline.

'Did you follow Nick that night? It would have been understandable in the circumstances. You were already suspicious about his relationship with Anna. He made yet another excuse to go out on his own. Weren't you curious to see where he went the second time?'

'None of that even occurred to me.'

'When you went looking for him, did you walk or go by car?'

'I walked.'

'Where did you go?'

'Around the local area.'

'Did you go straight home?'

'Yes, I did.'

'You didn't take a detour down Camomile Avenue, out of curiosity?'

'No.' A little worm wriggles in my tummy. I've told a lie.

'I'm surmising,' Grant says. 'If it crossed your mind that he might be with Anna Foreman, the obvious thing would have been to have a look at her house.'

'But it didn't cross my mind,' I insist. 'I trusted him.'

'Are you sure about that? You tracked Nick on the app.'

'I didn't track him,' I say impatiently. 'As I've explained, In-Step tells you how many steps your friends are doing. There's no map; it's just numbers.'

'Fine, but you were curious about where he'd been and upset enough about your suspicions to mention them when you reported him missing. It would have been natural for you to wait and see if he came out.'

I sigh. 'But I didn't. I went home, and I went to bed. I finally fell asleep about an hour later. When I woke, he hadn't come home.'

Grant leans back, and Marsh lifts his gaze from the files.

'Did you put Nick's body into his car?' he asks. 'Did you drive him down to Devon?'

'No, I did not.' I laugh, because the idea is so far-fetched. Marsh doesn't crack a smile. 'Look, what is this about? I don't understand what I'm doing here.'

He nods, then leans back. 'You're here because I think you're right, Ms Trelawney. I think it's very likely that Nick did not kill himself, that he was murdered.'

* * *

382

'What can you tell me about your relationship with Douglas Parr?' Marsh asks.

The questions have been going on for over an hour now, and I'm feeling ill with exhaustion. Marsh and Grant look as fresh as they did when we began.

'Civil.'

'No conflict at all?'

'Some, but it's minor irritations. More like an annoying itch than pistols at dawn. Douglas has Lottie every other weekend. He adores her. It works because we both want it to, for her sake.'

'I only ask because Cora Ritchie mentioned that he had some influence over you. She said that when he found out that her son was missing, he was straight in, telling you what to do, behaving in a hostile and threatening manner towards her and Tim.'

'Cora is prone to exaggeration. Douglas has no influence over me. He has a strong personality, and she probably assumed I was affected by that. It isn't true. I don't care what he thinks any more. What has it got to do with Nick, anyway?'

Marsh raises his arms up and back and locks his hands behind his head, has a good stretch. He glances at Grant, who takes up the baton.

'Grace,' Grant says. 'The police were called to the address you shared with Douglas on more than one occasion, when neighbours became concerned that a row had become violent. Once because they thought someone was going to get killed.'

She contemplates me, then sits forward, pushes the folder towards me. Paper-clipped to the top sheet is a

383

picture of me, my mugshot in fact, taken that night in the police station. I look dull-eyed and very young. My hair is tied back and I'm wearing a white T-shirt. I remember that it had a slogan on the front, in sloping bright pink letters, that read, *I'm Trouble*. A WPC had commented, not unsympathetically, that it should have said *I'm In Trouble*.

I flip the folder shut and push it back with the tips of my fingers. 'How long have you known?'

Grant ignores my question. I glance at Marsh, but his face is stony.

'You tried to kill your boyfriend,' he says. 'You stuck a knife in him, rupturing his diaphragm. He lost four pints of blood and needed a transfusion and narrowly escaped death. That's bound to make us wonder, don't you think?'

I'm trembling like a leaf, like Toffee when he's scared. 'I didn't try to kill him; I lost control. Douglas will tell you. He was happy to take the blame, and say he provoked me. I didn't go to prison. I got a suspended sentence on condition I saw a psychiatrist. I did all that. Where did you get this information?'

'A witness came forward when she saw the photograph of you and Nick on the news. She recognized you.'

'A witness?' I say. 'Do you mean the woman he was sleeping with?'

I hadn't even known what her name was. Douglas had persuaded her to keep quiet about the incident. He probably paid her. No doubt this is going to end up on the front pages.

'Why don't you explain what happened.'

'All right. It was before I had Lottie. I don't think it would have happened if I'd been a mother. Douglas brought the woman to the flat while I was out. I walked in on them. At that time I was completely under his control, utterly infatuated . . .'

'And psychotically jealous?'

'I'd had a tough upbringing. I'd been in care. I was heavily dependent on Douglas, and his betrayal tipped me over. We were bad for each other. The relationship was toxic. He drove me crazy. When I caught him with that woman, he was so cold about it, treating me like I was being hysterical. I got frustrated and lashed out.' I remember it as if it was yesterday. The amusement in his eyes. The cold smile. Brushing me off. I went into the kitchen and grabbed a knife. I wasn't thinking, I was reacting. I remember the blood. Her screams. His surprise. 'I was very young. I'm a different person now.'

'But the fact remains, your partner is missing, presumed dead, and you have a history of violence.'

'It was one time,' I protest. I sit back in my chair and fold my arms. 'I want a lawyer.'

He closes the file and switches off the recorder. 'Fine. But we'll need you to come back in as soon as you've found one. Tomorrow at the latest.'

I walk out of the police station, shaken to the core, and breathe in deeply. I tell myself it will be all right. I had nothing to do with what happened to Nick or Anna.

NICK

Saturday, 14 April 2018 ⤳ Day Zero

HE SITS IN HIS STUDY, STARING AT THE BLANK SCREEN. Grace is upstairs, running a bath. He's moved the keyboard out of the way and has a sheet of paper in front of him. It won't do. He can't hide behind a letter, he needs to tell her to her face and be man enough to take the consequences. He trails his pen across the next line, then sighs, and writes, *I'm sorry. I am so sorry. Please forgive me.* Then he crumples it up and throws it in the bin. Why did he ask her to marry him? He should have waited until all this was sorted out. It had been an impulse, and it came from the wrong place, a place of loneliness and fear. He had wanted to tie her to him. Stupid.

He stretches his legs out, folds his arms across his chest and leans his head back. He stares at the ceiling until it blurs, then groans and takes the screwed-up sheet out of the dustbin, smooths it out, folds it and shoves it into his back pocket. He can't risk it being found.

He goes out on to the landing and calls her name. She comes out of the bedroom, wrapped in a towel, her hair bunched up.

'I'm just nipping out,' he says.

'But it's almost nine o'clock. Why do you need to go now?'

'Tension headache. I need air.'

'OK, darling.' She pauses, and he winces inwardly. She's not happy about it. 'Don't be long.'

Downstairs, with uncanny perspicacity, Toffee is waiting underneath his leash.

'Not this time, boy.'

Nick leads him back into the kitchen where he checks the class address list that Grace keeps stuck to the fridge, then slips out and closes the door on Toffee's reproachful whine.

He hesitates before he leaves the pub, the taste of whisky still in his mouth, questioning what exactly it is he wants to say to her. Perhaps it was a mistake to come here first, another mistake to have ordered a double. But he needed it and it's done now anyway.

His phone vibrates in his pocket as he's turning the corner. He takes it out and glances at the message. It's an unknown number. The message makes his blood run cold.

Be very careful, Nick. If you take a wrong step now, there will be consequences. You won't be able to protect Grace or Lottie.

He reads it again. Who is this and how do they know

387

their names? It must be about his conversation with Angus on Friday. Angus had mentioned others, hadn't he? He had warned Nick that he didn't know who he was dealing with.

He's almost ready to forget about Anna and walk away, but that isn't the way he's built. One problem at a time. Solve the threat from Anna. It won't take long. Then he'll go home and call Angus. He will tell him that he's changed his mind; that he'll keep his secret. He won't do anything that might put Grace and Lottie in danger. The idea makes him feel physically sick, but there's no alternative. It will be the last time he ever speaks to Angus Moody. He'll write his letter of resignation tomorrow and think up a convincing story for Grace. He switches his phone off and hurries to Camomile Avenue.

Nick wants Anna to explain and, for Christ's sake, to see reason. They are not teenagers any more; they are adults with dependants and responsibilities who should be capable of behaving in a considerate and rational manner. Taisie – Anna – has obviously been brewing this for a long time.

He rings the bell, then bangs on the door for good measure. The lights are off, but he has a feeling she's in, and that she knows it's him. When no one comes he steps back and looks up. He can see nothing, but he senses energy, movement behind the dark window. He's woken her, maybe her son as well. Finally, he hears heavy footsteps descending the stairs. The door is pulled open abruptly and he comes face to face with Douglas Parr.

Nick stares at him, open-mouthed, trying to make sense of this entirely unexpected development; then Douglas grabs him by the collar of his shirt, drags him in and rams him up against the wall. It happens so quickly that it feels surreal, like a dream; a man's face in his, contorted with fury, spitting words, propelling him through the house to the kitchen at the back and pushing him down into a chair. He tries to stand up, but Douglas thrusts him down again.

'Have you touched my daughter?' Douglas spits. 'If you have I'll fucking kill you.'

Nick looks beyond him, to Anna in a white towelling robe, hair loose and make-up smudged.

'What is he talking about?'

She doesn't respond, so he repeats the question, shouting it this time.

Galvanized, she launches into an explanation. 'I told him about Izzy; what you did. That you sexually assaulted her.'

'What? No. That's a lie,' he says, horrified. 'I didn't touch her. You've twisted what I told you. Christ, what have I ever done to you?'

'You're a creep,' Anna says. 'Like your father.'

'I know he treated you badly, but that was nothing to do with me.'

'You're just like him though, aren't you?' Douglas snarls. 'You like underage girls.'

Nick scrambles up and barges into Douglas, locking arms with him, but Douglas, although leaner, is muscular, and he pushes Nick into the conservatory, where they crash against the table. It scrapes along the quarry-tiled

389

floor and a jam jar of paintbrushes falls and smashes. Anna screams as Douglas picks up a child's wooden chair and sends it flying at Nick's head. Nick raises his arm to deflect it, and Douglas charges him, crushing his fist into Nick's diaphragm. Winded, Nick drops to the floor and rolls on to his hands and knees, sucking in desperate breaths. Douglas grabs him by the shoulders and pulls him up, then pushes him into the wall. The room is so small, they knock into furniture and pieces of painted driftwood fly from the dresser. One lands between them.

I Love My Dad.

Douglas kicks it out of the way, then picks it up and looks at Nick. 'I'm applying for custody of my daughter. You can't be trusted. Grace will leave you when she finds out what kind of man you really are.'

'She won't believe you,' Nick gasps. 'She loves me. We're getting married.'

Douglas hesitates a second and then he laughs. 'You poor bastard.'

Nick hadn't realized until now how much he hates Douglas Parr, how visceral his loathing is, how much he wishes he would sod off out of Grace's life. If it wasn't for Lottie, he would have told him to get lost ages ago. As it is, he has to grit his teeth every time Douglas enters his house. He hates his arrogance, his smugness, his ego; but most of all he hates the effect he has on Grace. She tries to hide it, but he knows that she's scared of his dark side, wary of annoying him.

This is all going wrong. He needs to talk to Anna on her own, to make her understand about the dreams, about the kiss coming from Izzy. He wants to explain that he does feel guilty; not about what happened in the cubbyhole, but about what happened beside the river; about Izzy screaming at him to go away, to leave her alone; about the way he shook his head, then turned his back on her, shoving his hands into his pockets and sloping off, back through the woods to the house. That was his guilt; not what she thought, or wanted to think, he had done. But he can't explain all this while that man is here, maybe he can't say it at all. Maybe he'll never get to say it, because people will take it the wrong way. He needs to get out, go home, get to Grace before Douglas does.

'I don't know why you'd want Grace anyway,' Douglas says. 'She's violent.' When Nick doesn't respond, he shrugs. 'I gather she's been economical with her past. Well, let me fill you in. Grace stabbed me with a kitchen knife. I rescued that woman from the streets, cleaned her up and sorted her life out and she repaid me by trying to kill me.'

He raises his shirt and Nick blinks when he sees the puckered scar, about two inches wide, halfway between Douglas's hip and his navel. It's shocking, but he stands by Grace.

'She must have had good reason.'

'Is there ever a good reason to attempt murder? I didn't press charges, but she was charged anyway. Suspended sentence. So do yourself a favour and get out of my daughter's life. I don't want you or your father anywhere near her.'

Despite the pain he's in, Nick draws himself up to his full height. 'I'll do no such thing. I'm marrying Grace,

391

and Lottie will be part of our family. I've done nothing wrong. My father acted reprehensibly—'

'Reprehensibly?' Douglas sneers. 'He got Anna pregnant.'

Nick feels his colour drain. He turns to Anna, a question in his eyes.

She doesn't say a word, but her eyes fill and overflow. Her tears fall silently.

'Oh, you didn't know about the baby?' Douglas says. 'Your half-sister was adopted. Tim wouldn't face up to his responsibilities. Fortunately for him, Anna kept his name out of it. She doesn't need to do that any more though, does she? Tim should pay. If you don't pack your bags and leave immediately, the newspapers are going to hear all about that, and all about how you molested poor little Izzy Wells and drove her to her death. I'll destroy your family before I let you near Lottie again.'

Enraged, Nick launches himself at Douglas, hatred convulsing his features. Douglas is caught off guard, surprised that a man like Nick, normally gentle and measured, is capable of such violence. Before he can react, Nick has him down on the floor and is kneeling on his chest, his hands wrapped round his throat. Anna grabs at his shoulders, shouting at him to let go, but Nick ignores her. As he squeezes, he can feel the hard nub of Douglas's Adam's apple against the base of his palm, and the hot, panicky beat of the man's pulse.

Douglas's eyes bulge, but Nick can't stop. A red mist has descended, obliterating reason. Then something moves behind him, something dark and swift that descends on the back of his head with a sickening crack.

Someone is sobbing; the sound goes on and on.

Someone is panting, out of breath, like they've been running.

'Grace,' Nick breathes, before the room shrinks to a tiny dot and is finally extinguished in the blink of an eye.

GRACE

Tuesday, 8 May 2018

HARRIET GAYLE IS A COOL BLONDE, HER HAIR TIED tightly back, a pair of understated silver knots in her earlobes. She's wearing a trouser suit with heels. She is quite perfect, from her plucked eyebrows to her exquisitely painted fingernails. She is also tough, no nonsense. Cassie gave me her number. She's an old friend of Evan's. After a shaky start, I ended up telling her everything about the various strands of our lives that knitted together at the point where Nick disappeared. I admitted I had been suspicious about Anna and Nick and had gone out searching for him, my heart racing, half expecting to see them together. I told her I'd stood at the corner of Anna's street, waiting for him to come out of her house. All the things I should have confessed to Marsh. No WPC Grant this time.

She advises me to deny watching the house, because it only complicates things. I have denied it, but Marsh evidently doesn't believe me and thinks it's the key to unlocking what happened.

'Have you any idea why Anna Foreman would have walked across the Common on her own in the dark?' Marsh asks.

'None at all. It's not something any of us would do.'

'Then she must have been meeting someone. Was it you, Grace?'

'No. Absolutely not.'

He steeples his fingers and looks at me over them. 'You had the opportunity, with Lottie not being at home. We all know you're prone to flashes of violent temper. Stop lying, Grace, and tell me what really happened.'

Harriet turns to me. 'You don't have to answer that.'

'No comment,' I say.

'You have no evidence that my client has either committed or colluded in a crime,' she tells Marsh. 'No evidence either that Nick didn't kill himself. You might have had a motive if Nick and Grace had been married, but as it is, you have nothing.'

He leans back, stretches out a crick in his neck. 'I would call jealousy a motive, wouldn't you?'

'I'm not like that,' I protest, even though I know it's not entirely true. 'I don't get jealous.'

Harriet puts a hand on my wrist and applies gentle pressure. I take the hint and clamp my mouth shut.

'What about your attack on Douglas Parr? That was provoked by jealousy, wasn't it?'

'That was years ago. Douglas and I have a good relationship these days.'

'Are you still as volatile?'

'No.'

'That's not what Cora says.'

'That woman hates me.'

'You pushed her over,' Marsh says.

'I didn't push her. She tripped over the dog. She told me that they wanted me out of the house, and I admit I lost it, but I didn't physically attack her.'

'Fine. How did it feel when you thought Nick and Anna Foreman were having an affair?'

Harriet cuts in. 'Don't answer that, Grace.'

I'd felt hot and bothered when we first came in and I had taken my jacket off, but now I'm chilly, goose pimples on my arms. The milky coffee in the plastic beaker in front of me has gone cold.

'Were you angry, Grace?'

I don't answer.

'Did you use a knife again?'

'That's enough,' Harriet says.

I lean forward, my hands clasped on the table. 'I didn't hurt Nick. I loved . . . love him very much. We were planning to get married. We had just got engaged.'

'All the more reason to lash out when you discovered his betrayal.'

'Which I didn't.'

'Did you or Nick mention your engagement to anyone? Maybe he called his parents to tell them the good news. Did you tell Lottie?'

I have a sinking feeling. 'We didn't have a chance to tell anyone.'

'So, none of it might have happened. You might have made up the conversation to deflect suspicion about the state of your relationship.'

'I'm telling you the truth.'

396

He flicks through his notes, then smiles to himself. 'If Nick was intending to kill himself at the site of Izzy Wells' death, the most obvious thing would have been for him to drive himself to Devon. But the car was back in its space on your forecourt the next morning.'

'His car was there when I went looking for him. It hadn't moved.'

An officer puts his head round the door and signals to Marsh, who pauses the tape and leaves the room. Harriet and I sit in silence. I wonder what's happened, what new piece of evidence has come to light. Something that exonerates me, I hope. Why do I feel so guilty about Anna when I haven't done anything wrong?

Marsh comes back in. He sits down. We wait.

'You'll be pleased to hear Anna has regained consciousness,' he says, his eyes on my face.

I breathe a sigh of relief. 'Thank goodness.'

'Are you relieved for yourself, or for her?'

'For her, of course. But she'll tell you I had nothing to do with the attack.'

He smiles and switches on the recorder. 'Let's go back to the question of why Nick's car didn't leave the forecourt on the night he ended up in Devon. We only have your word that it was there all night. None of your neighbours can remember. You could have driven him, dumped his body in the river, hidden the bag and been back by dawn. Then when you subsequently visited the place with Anna Foreman, she pointed out where her sister had left her shoes at the water's edge, and you realized you'd left the bag in the wrong place.'

I'm so incredulous, I laugh. 'Even if that were the

case, which it's not, there's no way of getting to that stretch of the river in a car. I'd have had to have carried him a quarter of a mile down a rough footpath.'

'But, if Nick knew where Izzy went in, if that place meant so much to him that he chose to die where she did, then why did he leave the bag fifteen yards down-river? It doesn't feel right.'

'No,' I agree. 'It doesn't.'

'If he didn't drive himself there, then someone else did. You didn't know exactly where Izzy went into the water, did you?'

'No, but I didn't know Izzy Wells existed until a couple of weeks ago.'

'So you say. You agree that, in the dark, it would be easy to mistake the footpath and leave the bag in the wrong place.'

'I think we've heard enough of this,' Harriet says impatiently. 'My client maintains that she did not drive her partner's body to the river. Once you've had Forensics examine the car I'm sure you'll be able to prove either case to everyone's satisfaction. But until then, per-haps we can move on?'

'One moment.' He holds his hand up. 'There is the small matter of the missing wheelbarrow.'

I lean back in my chair and wait.

'It was found in the woods. It's being tested for traces of your and Nick's DNA. If we find it, we will take that as confirmation that Nick was murdered. And don't worry, we will find his body, Grace. It's only a matter of time. Devon and Cornwall have a team working on it right now.'

I remember something. I see Anna striding away from me, and Mrs Burrows preventing me from following her. 'Anna took off in a huff in the direction of the river. If she had expected to see the bag, and hadn't, perhaps she'd been waiting for an opportunity to check without me there. Her temper tantrum did seem a little contrived. But she didn't make it further than the lawn because a police car turned up.'

Marsh looks at me through narrowed eyes. 'Why wouldn't she have put it in the right place at the time?'

I lean on my elbows and press my fingers into my head. 'God knows. She was in a hurry? She made a mistake? It's been eighteen years since her sister's death, and it was pitch dark. She could have taken the wrong path. She would have been exhausted, and maybe the environment had changed, and she didn't recognize the spot. Or maybe it wasn't her at all. Maybe she had an accomplice.'

I realize as I'm saying all this how desperate I sound.

'You really hate her, don't you, Grace?'

'No,' I protest. 'That is not what this is about. She has an agenda. She's the one who was stalking Nick, not me.'

'Right. I think that's quite enough,' Harriet interrupts. 'It's patently obvious that this is a fishing trip. Without a body, you can't prove definitively that my client's partner was murdered. If you have no evidence with which to charge Ms Trelawney, we'll be going.'

She drops her pad into her briefcase and slides her pen into the inside pocket of her jacket, then stands up.

Marsh sighs and pushes his chair back.

* * *

I lean against the wall of the police station while Harriet sends a text. Then she drops her phone in her bag and smiles.

'Don't worry, Grace,' she says. 'They're clutching at straws. There is very little they can achieve without a body, frankly, and bar finding Nick's blood in the boot of the car and a blunt object with your fingerprints on it, I can't see what this achieves, apart from demonstrating to the taxpayers that they are actually doing something.'

'They have to look closer at Anna.'

'They will. They should be able to question her soon. If there is a link between the attack on her and Nick's disappearance, they'll find it.'

'Let's hope so,' I say, sincerely. 'I don't know how much more of this I can take.'

She pats my arm lightly. 'You'll be OK. You're tougher than you think.'

ANNA

Tuesday, 15 May 2018

ANNA CLIMBED OUT OF THE UBER AND CROSSED THE pavement to her front door, grabbing at the wall to steady herself. She half expected to find the police waiting for her, but there was no one there. She wobbled as she struggled to find her keys.

The policeman who had stood guard outside her ward had left his post, so she had quietly dressed amid the snores and rustlings of her fellow patients and left too. At four o'clock it had been quiet. The nurse on Reception had looked up from her phone and questioned her, but Anna kept walking, shoving through the swing doors and running down the stairs. At one point a wave of dizziness left her slumped against the wall, but she made herself keep going, listening for steps ringing out behind her, doors slamming, alarms sounding. But there was nothing. It was a hospital, not a prison. What could anyone do? She was a free agent.

Douglas was waiting for her as he'd promised to be when she'd texted him earlier, but she still got a fright when she opened her door and found him standing in the dark. He must have been listening for the car. She fell into his arms. He pushed the door shut with his free hand and took her bag from her.

'Have you said anything to the police yet?' he asked.

'They questioned me yesterday. I said I couldn't remember anything. They said they'd be back this morning.'

She caught him looking at her critically and touched her shaved head. The stubble pricked her fingertips. She winced, realizing how awful she must look. The wound was covered by a dressing, but at least the cartoonish bandage had been removed.

Douglas led her into the kitchen, where there were signs that he'd been tidying up. She looked around the makeshift room. After the stark whiteness of the hospital it seemed chaotic, over-colourful. The house smelled different too: musty and deserted, like someone had moved out in a hurry. The post was on the table, most of it junk. She barely glanced at it, her eyes following Douglas greedily as he made a cafetière of coffee and warmed milk in the microwave.

'OK. Let's talk.' He glanced outside, where the dawn had touched the windows of the house behind with a pink glow. 'I need to be out of here in an hour if I'm not going to be seen.'

'Red sky in the morning,' she said inconsequentially. 'It's going to rain.'

He poured steaming coffee into her mug and set it down on the kitchen table. The fragrance lifted her spirits.

'It's very tidy in here,' she commented.

Douglas ignored her. 'Tell me what went wrong.'

It was because of Douglas that she had phoned Angus and arranged to meet him on the Common that night. Douglas had said that they were going to have to start new lives somewhere else, and to do that properly they needed more money than either of them had. She wished now that she'd never told him, but at the time she had been trying to make him jealous, bragging about her wealthy ex-lover, hinting that he hadn't always behaved himself, that he was at heart a crook.

It had been Douglas's idea to wheedle money out of him and she had gone along with it because she could see no other way out of this horrible situation. Living round here, in the house where Nick had died, was killing her. She heard the crack of his skull a hundred times a day, saw his body fall to one side, heard the sick thud as he rolled off Douglas. The image would play through her consciousness while she was painting, making her hand pause mid-brushstroke. His knock on the door still rang out, his shout of anger hadn't lost its power to make her cringe in horror. She'll never get over it, just like she'll never get over Izzy, because, no matter what Tim or Nick did that day, her own actions, her own selfishness, jealousy and desperation to be loved were at the root of it.

'I arranged to meet Angus at eleven.' She closed her eyes. She felt so guilty about Kai. He'd never been alone in the house before. She couldn't imagine what he had felt when he woke up and found her gone.

'Go on,' Douglas said brusquely.

What she hadn't bargained for, when she set off for her assignation, was that she would bump into Tim. She decided not to tell Douglas about that, it would only complicate things, but Nick's father had left the Queen's Arms at the exact moment she was walking past. They had seen each other at the same time, and both had looked ready to bolt, but she had steeled herself to confront him. It had been a long time coming.

Tim had looked dismayed, before his customary bravado reasserted itself and he greeted her warmly. She hadn't meant to say anything, but it flooded out of her. She laid into him, accusing him of rape, of child molestation, of walking away from his responsibilities. She threatened him, told him that, unless he paid up, she would go to the police with her accusations. When he said she couldn't prove it, she had reminded him about the baby. She wouldn't even have to find her – something died inside her when she said that – she had her DNA.

'I don't have anything to pay you,' he had said, holding out empty hands. 'I'm flat broke.'

The barmaid came out to fetch the ashtrays in, and they went silent until the door had closed again behind her.

'You won't be broke for ever, though. Not once you inherit Nick's estate.'

He stared at her then, and suddenly he looked terribly old. She almost felt sorry for him.

After dwelling on their affair for so many years, fantasizing about what she could have done or said at the time, to come out of it with her dignity intact, she found that she felt nothing for him. She even wondered how she could ever have slept with him, let alone thought she was in love. Compared to Douglas, and Angus for that matter, he was insubstantial. The only thing she felt was a searing guilt over the fate of his son. His shoulders were hunched as he walked away.

She waited until he was out of sight, then made her way towards the spot where she had agreed to meet Angus, close to the playground, out of sight of the parade.

He had been waiting for her, she told Douglas. Tall and elegant, leaning nonchalantly against a tree. The plan had been for her to weave her spell, wrapping him around her little finger, reminding him of the afternoon they had spent in each other's arms. If necessary she would gently hint that she knew his secrets. He didn't bite at all, to all intents and purposes immune to her charms, so it was necessary.

'Is that why I'm here?' he had asked, his voice dripping with scornful disbelief. 'You want money? Have some self-respect, Anna.'

'I lost my temper. I told him that I knew what he had done and that if he didn't give me the money, I knew an investigative journalist. He called me deluded, but Douglas, there was a moment – so quick that I could have been mistaken, but I'm sure I wasn't – when he looked frightened. That should have rung alarm bells; men like Angus don't scare easily. He must have had a lot to lose.'

She has a memory. She had been pulling at a leaf on an overhanging tree. It came off its twig, and she crunched it up in her hand. She had felt a twinge of fear herself then and had wondered whether to leave or press on. She had pressed on. She had talked about his wife.

'I asked him what Lorna would think, and I mentioned that she might be interested in the fact that her husband not only defrauded his company of millions of pounds but shagged her oldest friend's daughter. I threatened to say that he had shown an interest in me early on and that I would tell the police that the reason I had been acting up that summer was because I was being interfered with. Then he punched me.'

'You underestimated him.'

'I know I did.'

Her head had snapped sideways. She reeled, holding her hand to her face, fell against a tree and slid to the ground. They were deep in the shadows, well away from the main path and there was no one out walking their dogs; no one she could see, at least. She pushed herself up, steadying herself against the tree trunk, and staggered away from him. She thought he was letting her go, and started heading in the direction of the parade, her eyes glued to the faraway lights in the shop windows and the flats above, but Angus caught up with her. Before she could scream his hand was over her mouth. He swung her off the path and into the bushes, then threw her down. Her head had hit something hard, a stone or a discarded brick. She remembered the pungent smell of fox. Then the sound of footsteps hurrying away. After that, nothing.

'What do I say when they question me?' she asked.

'You can't tell anyone it was Angus. He was Nick's boss. Nick disappeared. If the police find out it was

Angus who assaulted you, they're going to make some unwelcome connections. We have to shut this down now.'

'But I've got to have a reason for being there. I left Kai alone. Either way it's going to look bad.'

'An online date?'

Anna laughed and it hurt her head. 'No sane woman would go to meet a stranger in the middle of the night, on an unlit path.'

'Perhaps you met a guy, you hit it off, you had a romantic walk and were so caught up in the moment that you didn't realize you'd wandered off the beaten track.'

'It's all checkable,' she said, dropping her head into her hands. 'I'm sorry, I've ruined everything, haven't I?'

Douglas went and leaned against the door, his arms crossed, his head dipped, deep in thought. To Anna it felt as though he was deliberately blocking her exit. Eventually he spoke. His voice was soft.

'You're going to have to admit to meeting a lover but refuse to tell them who it was. There's no other way.'

'So Angus gets off scot-free. He tried to kill me.'

'It's the lesser of two evils.' He stepped forward and dragged out a chair, sat down and leaned towards her. 'Look at me.'

She looked into his face and her breath quickened. Even now, she wanted him.

'Do you love me?'

She nodded.

'What did you do with the mobile?'

After Nick's death Douglas had erased all their text

407

messages and had bought them both pay-as-you-go phones. She had used that to contact Angus.

'It's in a bag under my bed.'

He went upstairs to get it and she moved into the sitting room and lay down on the sofa, pillowing her head on a cushion, because she felt so weak. She could hear him above her. She and Kai were in his hands, but at least she wasn't alone any more; she was speaking to her parents again. When she woke up, her mother and father had been at her bedside. She had felt the enormity of what she had done by cutting her and their grandchild out of their lives. Last week they had finally met Kai and they already loved him. It was time to let bygones be bygones. She thought about water under bridges. It was an idiotic saying because the water kept coming. Nothing ever really goes away.

Kai was a worry. The Foremans wouldn't be able to keep him for long. He either had to come home or spend a week or so with her parents, just until she was capable of looking after him again. She couldn't imagine looking after herself, let alone her energetic son.

She sighed and glanced up, half expecting to see him, and found Douglas watching her. She must have dozed off. It was a relief to know that after everything that'd happened, after her failure, he was still here. But then Nick's death was as much down to him as it was to her. If he hadn't flown off the handle like that it might not have been a civilized encounter, but it wouldn't have ended in a fatality. And Douglas had implicated himself by disposing of Nick's body, so he must truly love her. They had rolled him up in an old blanket. Douglas had driven off with Nick in the boot of his car at two in the morning. The shock of it had nearly tipped her over the edge, but he had steadied her, drummed into her what they needed to do. Anna had spent the next two days scrubbing the house and had almost been caught by Grace when she turned up on her doorstep on the Monday wanting a cuppa and a sympathetic ear. Jesus. She had scared the life out of her.

'I have to go,' Douglas said.

'When will I see you again?'

'Soon. Who the hell's that?'

Someone had knocked on the door. Not the tentative knock of a concerned neighbour, but a firm, double rap that smacked of authority.

Douglas ducked out of sight of the window, then motioned her to follow him and keep down. She slid off the sofa and crawled out into the hall. They hunkered at the bottom of the stairs, Douglas with his finger pressed against her lips. The house seemed to pulse with an unfamiliar energy.

'Anna Foreman, can you open up, please? It's the police.'

She froze, her heart crashing.

'Shit,' Douglas muttered.

'Mrs Foreman? The hospital says you walked out. We just want to check you're OK. There's nothing to worry about.'

Anna waited, pressed into Douglas's frame, his body heating her, their heartbeats in sync. The crackle of a police radio was audible.

'She's not here,' the officer said. 'Waste of time. We'll come back in an hour.'

Another ten seconds and a car door clunked shut. As the car drove away, Anna released her breath.

Douglas unfolded his body and patted her on the shoulder. 'This is not going to work. I shouldn't have come here. I'm finishing this, Anna.'

Her blood stopped moving. 'What do you mean, finishing?'

'It's too dangerous for us to be together. You can see that, can't you?'

'But you can't walk away from me.'

'Of course I can.'

'I won't let you.' Her voice was urgent, frightened. Her head ached so much.

He looked down at her and frowned. 'Don't be silly. There's nothing you can do.'

Anna burst into tears and took hold of his wrist, pulling his hand to her lips and kissing his knuckles. 'I can do better, Douglas. I love you. I promise I won't get you into any trouble. But if you leave me, I might not have the strength to keep lying. There'll be a lot of pressure.'

Douglas sighed, then his expression altered, his eyes softening. He touched her head briefly. 'I didn't mean it.'

She let go of the breath she was holding. 'I knew you didn't.'

'Listen, get yourself better and then we'll speak. Is there anyone you can stay with? You shouldn't be here on your own.'

'I'm all right. I won't say anything to anyone. I promise. Please, Douglas.'

He shook his head impatiently. 'One of us has to be sensible and make the difficult decisions. I've done little else but think since you've been in hospital and, believe me, it's the only way. We can't see each other until all this blows over.'

Her throat threatened to close up, to choke her. Her mind was fogged with misery.

His eyes narrowed. 'Your pupils are different sizes.'

She stiffens, blindsided by the change of subject. 'It's the injury.'

'And what else did the injury cause? Can I trust you?'

'Of course you can.' She snaked her body closer to his. 'I'll be fine here. We can meet secretly, like we used to.'

He moved her to one side and sat down on the stairs. 'Anna. Anna. What am I going to do with you?'

She rested her hands on his knees. 'We have each other. That's all that matters.'

'Don't you understand anything? You're going to need help and it can't come from me. The best thing you can do is stay with your family. It's what a normal person would do.'

'But why? I can't leave London. My friends will rally round. Grace has offered to help. She sent me a really lovely text.'

'Jesus. You killed her bloody boyfriend. What's wrong with you?'

She gasped, and he stood up abruptly, so that she had to grab hold of the banister to stop herself falling backwards.

'How can I put it so that you understand? You have to take yourself right away. I don't want to see or hear from you until all this blows over. It's too dangerous.'

He put his hands on her shoulders where they rested, heavy and cold as chains. 'When you're back to your old self, we can meet properly, through Grace or the school or whatever, and start something then.' He wiped a tear away from her cheek with the pad of his thumb. 'Give it a year.'

'A year!'

His fingers tightened, pressing into her muscles. 'For us, Anna. Because we love each other, and we want a future together. You, me. Lottie and Kai. We could even have a baby. We'll be a family. I promise. The time will pass quickly, you'll see. Ring your mum.'

'But she hates me,' she wailed, tears coursing down her cheek.

He wrapped his arms tightly around her trembling body and kissed her forehead, a cool, passionless kiss that scared her more than anything else.

'No she doesn't,' he murmured. 'No one hates you. We all love you.'

She sniffed, not reassured. 'Am I repulsive?'

'The bruises will go. You won't look like this for ever. I'm going to take care of you, Anna. I'll wait for you. Can you hold on to that?'

'Promise you won't leave me.'

'I promise. And you know what the most important thing is, don't you?'

She gazed up at him. 'That we love each other.'

The corners of his lips twitched. 'That you think before you speak.'

412

GRACE

Friday, 15 June 2018

I WAKE FROM A DREAM ABOUT IZZY WELLS, A DREAM IN which sadness seems to mist from my breath. I pull on my dressing gown and go downstairs. Two months have passed since Nick vanished and the house is eerily quiet. Lottie has been away all week, on a residential trip to Dorset, an event I would have been delighted to make the most of in happier times. Now I just feel lonely. One day, when she leaves home, I'll truly be on my own. I wipe away a tear and tell myself off for being mawkish.

My situation has improved in one respect at least; I'm in the clear. Marsh's hope that he'd find my DNA all over the wheelbarrow hasn't proved as daft as it sounded when he first mooted it. Nick's DNA is present. Unfortunately, the identity of the person who lifted him in and wheeled him to the river remains a mystery.

If Marsh has his theories, which I assume he does, he hasn't shared them with me, and I don't want to think about it. I want to preserve my memories of Nick as a living man, not a corpse in a wheelbarrow.

Marsh has gone quiet since my interview. I've called him for updates, but all I'm told is that the investigation is ongoing but there is nothing he is able to disclose at the moment. I find that puzzling. To me it feels as though he's lost interest in Nick and moved on. Harriet says he may be embarrassed about his treatment of me. But I don't know, something feels fishy. On the other hand, it's a great relief not to be his focus.

Each morning, when I come downstairs to make my first coffee of the day, when Toffee yawns, stretches and pads over to greet me, I have to remind myself that Nick is not coming back. Sometimes I find it unbearable, sometimes it feels as though life is moving on. Sometimes I stand in the middle of my kitchen and wonder who I am and what I'm doing here. Sometimes I feel nothing at all.

Work-wise, I'm on a mission to persuade Rupert that instead of buying the Chelsea house with its narrow profit margin, he should invest in property south of the river, aimed at professional families rather than the uber-wealthy. Not to neglect those, of course, but to create another arm to his empire which I would run and from which I would take a share of the profits, rather than a salary. I had the idea driving back from Chelsea after that first viewing. I don't care what it takes; I'll work hard. I am determined never to be financially dependent on a man again. Which takes me to this house, my house, in Burnside Road. And to Nick's parents.

Tim and Cora have backed off, for the time being at least, although the legal situation with Nick's estate is going to have to be addressed at some point. They will probably win, but at least if we do have to wait seven years, as Harriet Gayle advised could be the case, Lottie will still be able to grow up here. I won't have to leave until she's preparing to go to university.

I get a text and slide my phone across the table. It's Douglas, wanting to know about arrangements. He's keen to be waiting in the playground when Lottie's coach arrives. It's the first time she's been away from both of us for more than a night. I text back that I'll meet him at the school. I don't want us to go together, it sends out the wrong message.

I settle down to work, the radio playing in the background. I'm surfing the internet for suitable properties when a name catches my attention. I dash across the room to turn the sound up, but I've missed the section. Frustrated, I go back to my laptop and search for the news. And there it is. Angus Moody, CEO of Financial Logistics, is under arrest following a covert investigation by New Scotland Yard Serious Fraud Office.

I read every word, looking for a mention of Nick. I find it eventually, at the end of the article, the investigative journalist pointing to the interesting coincidence that one of Angus Moody's employees disappeared in April. Police sources deny that there is any connection between the two events, but I don't believe it for one minute. Even writing that paragraph connects them. I call Detective Inspector Marsh, go through to his voicemail and leave a message asking him to get in touch with me urgently. I explain it's about Nick's boss. There must be something in this. There has to be.

415

I glance at the clock. The day is getting away from me. I've got a viewing in half an hour and I haven't walked Toffee yet. I decide to combine the two, quick-marching my patient little dog along the paths that criss-cross the Common. At the parade, I tie him up outside the estate agent's – not Bonner and Brightman, George Bonner still scuttles off if he sees me coming – and glance at the photograph of Anna's house that appeared in the window last week. It's available to rent, and this morning there's a red Let sticker across the price. Someone has snapped it up. I'm glad because it means she can't change her mind now. She won't be back for at least a year, maybe even three if it's a long let.

The agent I'm dealing with, Eva, a Polish woman with a bouncy ponytail and large hoop earrings, rises from her chair to greet me. She's wearing heels and they click on the pavement as we make our way to the house. The quickest way to get there is down Camomile Avenue.

There's a van parked outside Anna's house, its back doors open. I twitch my collar up and walk faster, praying that Anna doesn't come out. Eva is making small talk beside me, but I stop listening because Alex Wells comes out carrying a box. He puts it in the back of the van and goes back for more. He hasn't seen me. Eva and I reach the end of the street and I finally tune in to her voice.

'So, my sister is coming to stay,' Eva says. 'She'll be sleeping on my sofa, but that's OK. It's a big flat.'

'How lovely,' I respond. 'I see Camomile Avenue is let.'

'Thank goodness.'

'Why? Were you worried it was going to be hard to shift?'

'No, not at all. It was her. Nightmare client. She's the lady who was attacked on the Common last month.'

'Oh really?' I say innocently, my eyebrows shooting up. 'Yes, I do remember that. Poor thing.'

'I think that bang on the head did something to her. She's not right. Always on the phone, always complaining, demanding. Do this, do that. And so picky about tenants. My God, you'd think it was a ten-thousand-a-month property.'

'I expect she's anxious. Being assaulted does that to you.'

Eva flushes. 'Well, I know. But she's always talking like this is a short-term thing, like she's coming back. There's some man. But I think he's messing her around.'

'You know a lot about her.' More than me, it would seem. Didn't Kai mention something? Well, good luck to her. I hope she finds happiness.

Eva smirks. 'People talk to me. In this job it is like being a hairdresser. A friendly face, someone who does not judge. She says this man loves her, but she has to wait for everything to be right.' She shrugs and laughs. 'Sounds to me like he's trying to get off the hook. Maybe he has a wife.'

The house is at the end of an attractive Victorian terrace, safely within the catchment for Cedar Heights school. It's unmodernized and brimming with potential. I push all my worries aside and get stuck in, enjoying myself immensely. My experience means that I have a

417

nose for problems and an instinctive feel for which of them are deal-breakers and which can be used as leverage for a price reduction. I make notes and I ask questions; I tease up corners of carpets and peel back wallpaper; I check the state of the neighbouring gardens from an upstairs window. Bar one or two letting the side down with clapped-out barbecues and overgrown lawns, they are well kept and most show signs that there's a family in occupation; a small goalpost here, a slide or Wendy house there. It's perfect.

I finish my viewing and arrange to come back with Voytek, the builder Nick and I used on Burnside Road, at eight o'clock tomorrow morning. Eva has another appointment at the house, so I walk back alone. At Camomile Avenue it looks like Alex and Anna have gone, their rented van replaced by one for a cleaning service. So that's it, for the time being at least. I stroll home, wondering about the boyfriend. She's kept him close to her chest; but then she's good at that. Even the arrest of Angus Moody hasn't shaken my conviction that she's involved in Nick's disappearance. Marsh's lack of interest in pursuing that line of inquiry infuriates me. What on earth would it take to make him sit up and pay attention? Nothing short of a full confession, I suspect.

After lunch, I do my chores; shopping for the weekend and a quick once-over for the kitchen and bathrooms, while I figure out how I'm going to sell Rupert on that house. When I'm ready, I sit down at the kitchen table and call him, my fingers crossed.

'It's perfect,' I gush. 'It still has all its original features, and a decent garden. It's belonged to the same couple for forty years. It has a really lovely atmosphere. You can tell they were happy there.'

'Is there enough money in it, though?' Rupert asks.

It's not what he's used to. This is a great location for families, but it doesn't attract the kind of client Rupert normally deals with.

'I know the people who live here, and I know what they want. We can definitely make money out of it.'

I tap my fingers on the table, hoping desperately that he'll go for it. He's having to weigh up his desire to help me get a foothold in the industry against his instinct to go for the megabucks. I'll understand if he pulls back, but if he agrees, it'll be life-changing for me.

'I won't let you down,' I blurt out, when his silence gets too much.

Rupert sighs. 'I'm only concerned you might neglect my clients.'

'Of course I won't. I just want . . .' I stop.

'What is it you want, Grace?'

'To deal with normal people.'

That makes him laugh. 'This is your thing, but ultimately it's my risk.'

I can feel him wavering. 'I know what I'm doing. And I'm going to have more time anyway, with Lottie going to secondary school in September. What I do for you takes me maximum three days a week; not even that sometimes.'

'Send me some figures.'

Someone's at the door. I tell Rupert I'll call him back and shake the tension out of my shoulders. I know I can

419

persuade him but it's a good thing we stopped there. I was beginning to get emotional.

'Anna.' I step back in surprise.

'You don't mind, do you? I've been clearing out my house. I thought I'd come and say goodbye.'

She looks frail. With her face free of make-up, her cropped hair and the jeans hanging off her hips, she bears a disturbing resemblance to the young people I used to help when I worked at the charity all those years ago. Empty eyes, lost soul.

'Of course I don't mind. Come in. I was just cleaning up.'

I peel off my rubber gloves and look past her, to see if Alex is there, waiting in the van, but there's no sign of him. I close the door and usher her into the kitchen.

'You look so much better,' I say over my shoulder as I reach automatically for the kettle.

'No I don't.' She touches her hair and grimaces. 'I look like shit.'

'Don't be so hard on yourself.' I take two mugs out of the dishwasher and drop in teabags. 'I saw your house was let. Have you given up on London?'

When I turn round, she's studying the photos and calendar stuck to the fridge. 'Not entirely. I haven't made my mind up yet.'

There's something absent about her, but I put it down to the injury and I'm prepared to be kind. All the same, she's making me uneasy. She's twitchy in her movements, and she won't settle. Her eyes are everywhere, scanning the room, watching me, zooming in on family photographs.

'How's Kai?' I ask to distract her and calm my own nerves. 'Lottie misses him.'

Her face brightens. 'He's doing well. He's got into a good secondary school.'

'Are you still with your parents?'

'Yes. No. Well, I won't be for long. I'm working things out. So how are things with you two?'

For a moment I think she means me and Nick; but then I realize she's talking about me and Lottie.

'Oh, we're doing OK. Trundling along as usual. Lottie's been on the Dorset trip all week.'

'I feel so bad that Kai's missed out. He would have loved to have gone.'

The kettle boils and I pour water on to the teabags, add milk and stir them. There's no answer to that. As I pick up the mugs and set them down on the table, I check the kitchen clock, then catch Anna watching me.

'Are you in a hurry?' she asks.

'No, it's fine. The coach is expected back at four. That's all. We want to be there to meet her.'

'We?'

'Her father wants to be there too.'

Anna moves away from the fridge and sits down. I'm over-aware of her movements. It's as if she's a ticking bomb. I try and second-guess why she's here, what it is she really wants.

'Oh, right.' She blows on her tea before sipping it. 'Is he around as much?'

I'm not sure why she might think he wouldn't be, but I let it pass. 'Yes. No change there.'

She nods, her bottom lip caught between her teeth.

'Why do you ask?'

She shrugs. 'Oh, no reason.'

There's a pause and I cast around for something else to talk about. Suddenly, four o'clock feels a long way away. I wish I'd told her I had to be somewhere earlier.

'So, are you in London to hand over the keys to your place?'

'Something like that. Just tying up loose ends.'

She sits forward suddenly, and the air goes still. She pushes her chair back, gets up and walks over to the sofa. Over the back, neatly folded, is a black fine-wool sweater. She picks it up, opens it out and turns to me.

'Are you seeing someone?'

The idea is so outlandish that I laugh. 'No, of course not. That belongs to Douglas. He must have left it behind last time he was here.'

But she's not listening to me. She runs her fingers over the soft wool, then puts it back, and it's the care with which she does it, stroking it smooth, and the sensuality of the gesture, that sends the tension inside me sky-rocketing. Something has gone on between Anna and my ex. The thought leaps into my mind and once it's there, I can't dislodge it.

ANNA

Friday, 15 June 2018

GRACE WAS FROWNING. 'ARE YOU ... UM,' SHE SAID slowly. 'Are you and Douglas ... Did you?'

Anna didn't speak and Grace's face fell.

'Oh, Anna. You poor thing.'

'What do you mean?' The sympathy was false; Grace was jealous. 'We're lovers. He loves me.'

'I'm sorry, but the only person Douglas Parr loves, other than himself, is Lottie.'

'You don't know anything about it.'

She felt threatened by Grace, by her assurance, by her grand house and expensive furnishings. She thought she knew it all, but she didn't. She knew nothing. It was clear to Anna that Grace had never really got over Douglas. Anna should be the one feeling sorry for her.

'When did it start?' Grace asked. She was trying to sound casually interested. It wasn't working.

'That evening he came to pick up Lottie.'

'Of course. I forgot about that. He fixed your plumbing.'

423

Anna smiled, remembering. 'We just clicked.'

She was proud of this, proud to have fooled everyone, but it was such a relief to be able to tell, to say, *you never guessed! Ha ha. Aren't I clever?* Childish, but immensely satisfying.

The moment was short-lived, spoilt by Grace's look of pity. 'You must have something he wants. He isn't in love with you.'

'Why the hell shouldn't he love me?'

'Sorry, that came out wrong. Why did neither of you say? It wouldn't have bothered me.'

Anna paced over to the sink and bent to drink from the tap, raising her right arm automatically and crooking it over the back of her neck to scoop away hair that wasn't there. She dropped her hand, embarrassed.

'He didn't want people to know.'

'Didn't you question why? You had nothing to be ashamed of.'

'Unlike you.'

'What are you talking about?'

'Douglas told me you stabbed him.' She had actually found out when Douglas had taunted Nick with it. She had asked him later on why he had lied, and he had shrugged and said it was none of her business.

Grace opened her mouth, grappling for words, her eyes full of hurt. 'He told you that?'

'He tells me everything. I know all about you attacking Cora. You're still capable of violence, aren't you? And look at poor Nick.'

'What about Nick? He never knew what happened

with Douglas. Did you say something when you met him?'

She wrinkled her nose. 'No, it's none of my business. But perhaps you should have come clean. Secrets have a habit of coming out.'

The doorbell rang, long and loud, and they both went still.

'Are you expecting someone?' Anna asked.

'No.' Grace grabbed Toffee's collar and pressed her fingers on his muzzle, silencing him. 'It'll be a delivery.'

'Wait. Don't answer it until we know who it is.' Anna ran into the front room and peeked between the slats of the wooden shutters.

'Anna?' Grace stood in the doorway, looking uncertain.

'It's the police,' she whispered.

'It'll be about Angus Moody. I'm letting them in.'

'Angus?' Anna frowned. What the hell had Angus got to do with any of this? 'No, don't. Leave it.' The sound of her blood ringing in her ears was deafening. 'Why would they want to talk to you about Angus?'

'Haven't you seen the papers today?'

'No, I've been too busy clearing the house.'

'He's been arrested for fraud. I think it might be connected with what happened to Nick. Let me open the door.'

'No. Not yet. We need to talk first.'

'For God's sake.' But she didn't move.

Grace's mobile phone started to ring, and Anna shook her head. They waited for it to stop, then Grace listened to Marsh's voicemail. Afterwards, she put it on speaker and played it again, the phone on her knee between them. She held Anna's gaze.

'Grace. It's DI Marsh. Call me back soon as you get this. Just one thing, if Anna Foreman comes round don't let her in. Call me immediately.'

Grace's expression became wary. 'I want you to leave.'

GRACE

Friday, 15 June 2018

I EXPECT ANNA TO GO ON THE OFFENSIVE, BUT INSTEAD she crumples. Toffee watches us, perfectly still, his ears pricked, as if he senses an impending catastrophe.

'It wasn't my fault,' Anna says, her eyes filling with tears.

'What wasn't your fault?'

She sways, and I'm so worried that she's about to either faint or have a panic attack that I pull her down on to the sofa. She doesn't seem dangerous. The opposite, in fact. She seems fragile; as if she'll break into a thousand pieces if I don't hold her together.

'Nick came round. Douglas let him in, and they got into a fight.'

As she tells me the story, I grow cold. I listen, my hand over my mouth, tears filling my eyes. I can't believe what I'm hearing. Any last vestige of hope I might have had is gone. Anna is sobbing wildly. I suppose she wants my pity, but this is a mess of her own making, because of her vanity, her grudge-bearing, her own guilt.

'Did he suffer?' It sounds such a pointless thing to ask, because what's she going to say? Yes, it hurt like hell, of course he bloody suffered, you idiot.

'I don't know,' she sobs. 'He just slumped. I think it was instant.'

I bite my bottom lip to keep from crying. 'So it was Douglas who got rid of his body?' My ribcage feels so tight I can barely breathe.

Anna tugs her cuff over the ball of her palm then uses it to dry her tears and wipe her nose. 'Yes. I drew him a map of the grounds and woods. I thought I knew that place like the back of my hand. I must have made a mistake because the bag wasn't where I expected it to be.' She frowns, as if she still can't believe this to be true. 'I was agitated and panicking, and it'd been so long since I'd been there.'

I let her cry while I fetch a box of tissues. 'We're going to the police station.'

She blows her nose. 'But what about Lottie?'

That pulls me up short. After what I've just heard, I'm not sure I want Douglas in sole charge. 'No, you're right. You'll have to go on your own. Promise me you will.'

She nods, but she looks bereft, like I've abandoned her. She needs ordering around like a child, guiding to where she's left her bag hanging over the back of a kitchen chair. She's fighting with the zipper of her coat and I'm about to lose patience and help her, when the doorbell rings again.

'Jesus,' I say, grabbing Toffee and lifting him into my arms. 'This place is like Clapham Junction.'

Anna's eyes are huge. 'Don't answer it.'

428

'Don't be ridiculous.' I leave her in the kitchen and go to the door, hoping it's Marsh saving us a trip, but it turns out to be Douglas.

'I thought we were meeting at the school,' I say. Fear tightens my ribcage. I'm sure my voice will give me away. This is the man who colluded with Anna in the killing and disposal of my boyfriend.

Toffee whines and scrabbles at me so I let him go and he scampers back into the kitchen.

Douglas walks past me, without waiting for an invitation, saying over his shoulder, 'I was early. We can walk there together.'

Anna is standing in front of the wall of windows, the sun creating a halo around her. Her face is a picture of guilt.

He raises his eyebrows. 'Sorry. If I'd known you had company . . .'

'You could have rung, Douglas,' I point out. 'Anna dropped in to say goodbye. We've been catching up.'

'How cosy.'

'We haven't spoken for ages, have we, Anna? So it was a lovely surprise.'

'What have you been talking about?' Douglas addresses both of us, his smile fixed.

'Oh, you know,' I say. 'The usual. Kids, schools and house prices.'

I turn my gaze to Anna, silently pleading with her to back me up. She swallows and forces a smile. 'I've let my house,' she says. 'It's time for a change.'

There's a long silence. Douglas's jaw works. 'You always were a bad liar, Grace. And what about you,

Anna?' He walks over to her and cups her face in his hands. 'What's going on?'

I remember he used to do that to me if I was being stubborn. I can still feel the warmth of his palms, the pressure of his fingertips against my cheekbones, his thumbs firm against the corners of my mouth. I would try not to blink first but I always did, just as I know Anna will blink first now. I can feel the horror starting in my gut and spreading.

'You don't have to tell him anything.'

'Mind your own business, Grace,' Douglas says.

'I . . .' Anna falters.

'Go on.'

'I promise I didn't tell her. She guessed. She knows we're together.'

'What exactly have you said?'

Anna dissolves and he lets her go with a sigh of scorn. She can't speak and tears are rolling down her cheeks.

'For God's sake,' I say. 'It's over, Douglas. I know what part you played in Nick's death. I will never, ever forgive you for what you've done, and I'll make sure you never see Lottie again.'

Before I can take evasive action, Douglas pushes me against the countertop and clamps his hand over my mouth. Anna edges slowly towards the table where I've left the phone, stretching out her hand until her fingers touch it. Toffee snarls.

'Anna,' Douglas says. His voice is steady. 'If you call the police then it's over. Do you understand? You have to make a choice now, and it's important you make the right one. If you follow my instructions, then we can be together. Remember; this is your mess. I've only tried to help you.'

'I don't know,' Anna says. 'I'm not sure I can do this any more.'

'Do you love me?'

My eyes widen as she nods, tears falling down her cheeks.

'Then work with me. There's no alternative, OK? She knows too much.'

My screams are muffled by his hand as he drags me across the kitchen, Toffee leaping and barking beside him. Douglas gives him a kick that sends him squealing back to his bed. I grab the door frame, my fingernails breaking against the wood.

'Anna,' he says sharply.

After hesitating she comes running, forces my fingers free, then grips my wrists as he pulls me backwards and up the stairs. Toffee comes back, yapping at Douglas, trembling like he did the day Lottie and I adopted him. Anna won't look me in the eye, she just keeps moving, restraining me, until we're in my bathroom. Shut out of the room, Toffee barks and barks.

Douglas tells Anna to run a bath, while he holds me pinned against him. His heart is racing as fast as mine. I struggle, but the arm he has round me is like iron and the hand across my mouth and nose makes it hard to breathe. The taps run, steam rising, and I panic like a bird caught in the jaws of a cat.

At a command from Douglas, Anna leaves the room and comes back with a sharp knife. She presses herself against the door, watching the water gush. She's pale, wraithlike as her figure melts into the steam.

'Don't just stand there, get her boots off.' Douglas's voice cuts through the warm mist.

She drops to her knees and takes hold of my foot. I kick her in the shoulder; she springs back and tries again, tugging at my heel while I contort my body. Once both boots are off, thrown into a corner of the room, the two of them hold me down, my back pressed into the tiled floor, Douglas at my head, Anna at my feet, until he motions her to turn off the taps. Between the two of them, they get me into the bath and duck me underwater. I close my eyes, screaming and choking each time I manage to surface.

'Jesus,' Douglas snaps. 'Keep her still.'

It turns out it's not that easy to kill someone, especially if you want to make it look self-inflicted. It means he has to be careful not to slash me anywhere but on my wrists. I keep moving, fighting them for every scratch, every cut, making myself picture Nick and Lottie. I imagine their arms around me, their lips pressed against my cheeks. I remind myself of the wonder I felt when Lottie was born, of the long lashes draped against the translucent skin beneath her eyes, her little mouth pursing, tiny fingers gripped around mine. I raise my chest, rocking from side to side, until Douglas finally loses patience and plunges my head under the water.

His hand is splayed across my face and my lungs are bursting. Through the noise of my breath bubbling to the surface, I hear a dulled, drawn-out ring. Douglas's grip loosens, and I rise up with a yell. He shoves a wet flannel in my mouth to gag me. Water dribbles down the back of my throat, making me choke. Downstairs, Toffee is going crazy.

The bell rings again and again and, after it stops, all I can hear is the sound of my heart pounding. Toffee goes silent and despair sweeps through me, leaving me as weak as a baby. There's a few seconds of blessed stillness, before Douglas jams the point of the knife clumsily against my wrist. For him, and for Anna, there is no going back. I briefly register the door opening before the sharp pain at my wrist takes over everything, making my vision blur.

ANNA

Friday, 15 June 2018

A BEARDED MAN WAS FRAMED IN THE DOORWAY, backlit by the light streaming through Grace's bedroom windows. He lingered in that brief moment, as if someone had pressed the pause button. But maybe there was no moment. Maybe it was just in her mind that time stood still, because there was noise all around her: swirling, splashing, barking. And then everything started to move again – arms and legs flailing, water dyed pink with blood sloshing up the sides of the bath.

The stranger, who Anna had concluded was a plainclothes police officer, grabbed Douglas by the collar and wrenched him away from Grace. Douglas lurched up, holding the knife in front of him, tripped over Toffee, who yelped, and landed on his knees beside the basin, his elegant limbs as graceless and awkward as those of a newborn calf.

Grace pulled the flannel out of her mouth and yelled, scrambling out of the bath and throwing herself at the stranger, her fists connecting with his shoulders as he

434

reached for her. It was the mix of fury and relief that finally made the correct connection in Anna's mind. This was no stranger, this was Nick. She ought to have recognized him.

'You died,' she whispered. 'I saw you dead.'

She caught his expression when he glanced at her. Disbelief. Dislike. But all she felt was a relief so huge she almost burst out laughing. It was over and whatever happened to her now, whatever people were going to say about her, they wouldn't be able to call her a killer. It wasn't too late.

Douglas pulled himself up, roughly elbowing her out of the way to get to Nick. Anna dropped to a crouch, instinctively shrinking down into the gap between the loo and the bath, covering her head with her arms. In the confined space, hampered by tiles that were wet and slick, her lover and her childhood friend wrestled. She couldn't bear to look, so she didn't see when one of them hit the floor, but she felt a hand land against her foot. She opened her eyes a crack. The fingers were broad, not long and fine; Nick's. Douglas was kneeling on Nick's chest, his hands in his hair, pulling his head up, then whacking it down on the tiles. Grace hooked her arms around Douglas's neck, but he rammed his elbow into her chest, sending her flying against the radiator. She slid down and started to crawl towards the door.

'For fuck's sake, Anna,' Douglas yelled. 'Don't let her get away.'

Anna didn't move, she couldn't. She just wanted it all to stop. There was blood everywhere, great gobs of it, droplets and smears, some bright red, some diluted; the walls, the floor, the side of the bath, the basin pedestal; nothing had escaped. She closed her eyes, ducked her head and covered her ears with her hands, but she still heard what Douglas said. What he called her.

'Move, you stupid cunt!'

She flinched. Pressed against the door, Grace looked ready to collapse, her face drained of colour, her hair bedraggled, dripping wet, blood all over her. Why hadn't she left when she had the chance? The entreaty in her eyes was impossible to misinterpret.

Change sides.

Anna stood up and edged unsteadily past the two men. Nick made a grab for her ankle, but she kicked his hand away. His eyes rolled up as he lost consciousness. Douglas dropped him and tried to get up, but Grace draped herself over his back and clung on.

Reaching across the bath Anna picked up a bottle of shampoo and squirted some of its contents into her palms, then edged to the side and got down on her knees. She leaned in front of Grace, clamped her hands across Douglas's eyes and rubbed cruelly, getting her soapy fingers right into the corners. He bellowed, and Grace twisted the knife out of his hand. The two women grasped his arms and hauled him out of the bathroom. Grace slammed the door, threw herself against it and shut the bolt.

'Jesus!'

'What do we do now?' Anna said, panting. 'We're trapped.'

'Oh fuck, I don't know,' Grace gasped, dropping to her knees beside Nick.

He was covered in blood, but it wasn't his; it belonged to Grace. Anna glanced down at the smears on her own clothes. She could smell the iron tang of it. Beside her, Grace was beginning a slow slump to the right. Anna reached for the hand towel that hung beside the basin and wound it round Grace's wrist, then leaned her against the side of the bath. The blood soon spread like a rose through the fabric.

'Anna.' Douglas banged his fist against the wooden panels. The door shuddered but held strong. 'If you stay with them you'll be sent to prison for attempted murder. You'll lose Kai. You'll lose everything.'

Anna snivelled, wiping her eyes on the back of her sleeve. 'Go away.'

'For Christ's sake.' He smashed at the door and one of the panels started to give, splintering. 'Fuck you,' he said. 'You've screwed me over. You're going to regret it. If I go down, so do you. And as for you, Grace; you always were a grasping little bitch; always on the look-out for a man to take care of you. The moment you saw Nick's wallet, you were in there. Poor fucker.' He shouted louder. 'You didn't stand a chance, mate.'

'Stop it,' Grace cried. 'Shut up, Douglas. Leave us alone.'

'Ignore him,' Nick muttered, struggling on to his knees. He swayed, and Grace reached him, but he was too heavy for her and she collapsed under his weight.

Anna surveyed the scene: the floor flooded with blood and water; the petrified dog; the blood-soaked towel and the two people she had all but destroyed, lying entwined in the mess. She stood in front of the

437

door with her feet apart, her arms heavy at her sides, took a deep breath and spoke.

'It was me who persuaded Izzy to go into the river.'

Grace pushed herself up on her elbow. The banging on the door stopped, as if Douglas had heard.

'I wanted Mum to be pleased with me for once. It was always Izzy and my brothers, never me. I wanted her to see me. Izzy was going to pretend to get into trouble in the water and I was supposed to save her. I told her not to get out of her depth, but she must have, or she lost her footing and got caught in the current. And I wasn't there in time . . . I didn't . . .' Tears spilled from her eyes. 'Your father was there, Nick. He kissed me. I was so staggered, I . . .' She swallowed to get rid of the hard lump in her throat. 'I thought I was in love with him.'

'You let me believe it was my fault,' Nick said.

'You still frightened her.' Her voice rose. 'That was true. I just let you believe that was the only reason. You must have known deep down that you hadn't done anything bad. But you still could have stopped her, you could have explained it was a nightmare, calmed her down.'

'You could have taken responsibility.'

Grace lifted her head. 'Stop it. Izzy is dead and nothing either of you say is going to bring her back.'

'Anna.' It was Douglas, calmer now, his tone placating.

At the sound of her name, Anna turned and put her cheek to the door.

'Anna, I'm sorry. Let me in, and we'll talk about this.'

'Leave me alone.'

438

'Baby.' His voice was low, almost a caress. 'Don't you trust me?'

'I can't.'

'Yes, you can. Unlock the door. I won't hurt any of you. I just want to talk. Please, Anna. Before it's too late.'

'Go away, Douglas,' Grace shouted. 'We don't want you here.'

His fist crashed against the wood and Anna leapt backwards, frightened out of her skin. And then it wasn't his fist. The edge of a cricket bat broke through the panel, splintering it. Douglas's hand reached through as he felt for the bolt. Nick pulled himself up off the floor, grasped it and bent it back and Douglas screamed in pain. Nick signalled both women to be quiet. Anna held her breath and Grace did the same. They stared at each other, neither of them moving a muscle.

There. Anna heard it again. A siren.

'It's the police,' Nick grunted, his shoulders relaxing. 'I asked Mrs Jeffers to call them when I went for the spare key.'

The last thing Anna saw before she was led out of the room was Grace folding Nick into her arms, squeezing him hard, her face pressed into the crook of his neck. He wove his fingers into her hair and held her like his life depended on it. Anna dropped her gaze and turned away.

She and Douglas were put in separate cars. He refused to look at her and she assumed he thought she had done this on purpose, sabotaged his life, but she hadn't. There was no real reason for any of it: that was the tragedy.

She glanced through the window as the car carrying Douglas pulled out first, overtaking hers. He was staring straight ahead. She tried not to look at him; he had used her, betrayed her and broken her heart, but she couldn't help herself. She drank in his profile, memorizing it, imprinting it on her brain.

Where would she be if she had never met him? Would she and Nick have had a long conversation that night, putting both their worlds to rights? She imagined she was running downstairs to open the door to him, not Douglas. She would have offered him a glass of wine. He might have agreed to help, to undo the damage his father had done. Somewhere out there, there was a teenaged girl who connected them by blood. With Tim and Nick's help they might have found her. She might look like Izzy.

This was not her fault. She was as much of a victim as Nick.

Finally her car pulled out and moved down Burnside Road. She touched her short hair, felt the still sensitive ridge of scar tissue. By the time her case came to trial, she would be pretty again.

GRACE

July 2018

IT'S AMAZING HOW QUICKLY WE RETURN TO AN OUTWARD normality. We kiss as we pass in the corridor, he touches my shoulder, moving me out of the way to get to the mug cupboard, I glance at his size-twelve shoes, kicked off in front of the sofa. Toffee stretches, yawns widely and mooches over to be stroked. The smell of coffee. A sleepy Lottie appearing in the doorway, her hair all mussed, wanting food.

Wanting to check he's still there.

We keep checking, keep pinching ourselves. But that's the surface. Underneath it's different; there are currents that are impossible to control with smiles and kisses and reassuring words.

I glance at my daughter, watching her move between the fridge and the larder cupboard. This is hardest for her. She's lost the father she adored. Douglas was part of her. I've tried to talk to her about it, but she's rebuffed my efforts. I don't know if she blames me, or if she blames anyone, all I know is that she's wounded. She trusted him completely.

It was the cleaning company who found the vital evidence: Nick's credit card under the space between the skirting and an uneven bit of wood flooring in Anna's kitchen. They recognized Nick's name from the news and contacted the police, who moved with surprising speed, considering their sluggishness up until that moment. It was enough to secure a warrant for Anna's arrest that afternoon, and a search warrant that eventually placed both Douglas and Nick in the house. Traces of blood spatter were found in Anna's kitchen. Nick's blood.

But that wasn't what Marsh had called round to discuss that morning. He had come to talk about Angus Moody. He had known nothing about the find at that point. If Anna had allowed me to let him in, he could have told me that Nick was alive, that Nick was coming home. He had known since the end of May but had had to keep it secret because it was imperative that the men involved in Angus's fraud weren't alerted to Scotland Yard closing in on them. Marsh had been in danger of unintentionally wrecking everything with his investigation into Nick's disappearance, hence the reason for its abrupt loss of momentum. He'd had to keep things ticking over, without actually doing anything.

Nick had regained consciousness in rushing water, caught between the branches of a fallen tree. Somehow, he found the strength to drag himself out. He lay on the bank floating in and out of consciousness, listening to

442

the birds and the river, the rustle of leaves in the breeze. He had staggered through the woods, eventually finding himself behind the Moodys' swimming pool changing room.

'It was so strange,' he told me. 'Because I thought I was sixteen, that somewhere around, the other children were together, hiding from me.'

He went to the house and knocked on the door, but there was no answer. He remembered where they used to hide a key and let himself in. He was concussed, in shock and delirious and convinced that it was 2000 and he was there with his parents. He had hallucination after hallucination, until it got to the point where he was too scared to sleep.

'It was like the day Izzy drowned was on repeat. Everything I did. Every conversation I had. That moment I woke and she was kissing me, and I reacted like a lunatic. It was torture.'

He's not sure how many days passed before things improved. Maybe three. Possibly as many as five.

'I suddenly knew how old I was. I remembered what had happened, the sequence of events, everything.'

He told me about the menacing text he'd received, only minutes before he went to Anna's house to confront her.

'They threatened to hurt you and Lottie. I realized that Douglas and Anna had given me an opportunity. For as long as Angus and his associates thought I was dead, you and Lottie would be safe. So I called Scotland Yard and told them everything. They moved me to a safe house, and that's where I've been for the last two months. I was prepared to play dead for as long as it took. I am so sorry to have put you through it. I wanted to contact you so badly, but I couldn't. Not until now. Then they told me they were planning a dawn raid on Angus's house, and once I heard that it had been successful, I came straight away. I couldn't wait another hour.'

'Are you sure we're safe now?' I asked.

'Grace, they've been named and they're in custody. Angus knows there's nothing more I can tell the police. He's not a killer, he's just another greedy egotist who thought he was too big to go down.'

'What about Anna?'

His face clouded. 'Anna was trying to protect Douglas from me. I can't blame her for that. I was choking the life out of him. It wasn't self-defence at that point, it was rage. I honestly believe I would have killed him.'

I picked at a loose thread in my jeans. 'Was it because of what he told you about me?'

'No. Grace, I know you. You're not that woman any more.' His eyes darkened. 'Anna accused me of molesting Izzy and Douglas believed her. He said he couldn't trust me with . . . That I would lose . . .' He squeezed the bridge of his nose. 'Sorry.'

'It's all right. I understand. You don't have to say anything else.'

'Izzy's death wasn't entirely Anna's fault; I played my part too. I want you to know what really happened.'

He steepled his fingers and pressed them to his forehead.

'I'm listening.'

'I was watching from an upstairs window and I saw Izzy run down to the end of the gardens and vanish behind the changing rooms, so I went after her and caught up with her at the river. She stood on the bank and screamed at me to get lost. She wasn't wearing a coat, and she looked like she'd had a bucket of water thrown over her, her hair dripping, her shirt soaked through. We had been mates, but she was yelling these horrible things. I told her to come back to the house, not to be stupid, but she told me to fuck off. It sounded awful coming from her. I turned round, and I walked away, and she went quiet instantly, as if she hadn't expected that, as if she had wanted me to keep on pleading with her. It was the loneliest silence. That's what I can't forgive myself for. I left a child on her own. I should have stayed until she calmed down or someone else came.' He leaned back with a groan and swept his fingers through his hair. His eyes were hollowed out, blue-shadowed. 'I can't get it out of my mind. I wish I could turn the clock back, start again, stay with her.'

'We all have things we can't escape, things we regret, things we can't undo. You have to learn to live with it, Nick.'

'I don't think I ever will, not fully at least.'

I looked at him closely. He'd been through so much and kept it locked up inside him for so many years. How do you walk away from those thoughts, that kind of torment? I felt inadequate and ill-equipped to help, but I had to, otherwise we would flounder on the irrefutable truths, because, whatever part Anna played, nothing will change the fact that Nick turned his back on Izzy

Wells and walked away, any more than I can walk away from the fact that I stabbed Douglas in a jealous rage. There's something faulty in me too.

'We are what we want to be,' I murmured.

'What did you say?'

'Nick, you have to do something. Something you don't think you have time or headroom for. Something that makes you feel better and squeezes your nightmares into a smaller space.'

'I have both of you.'

'Of course you do, but we're not enough. There has to be something else. You have to make time to do the things you know you need to do. Listen to your gut.'

His eyes burn into mine. 'I wish you'd told me what happened to you.'

'I wish I had, too.'

'I wouldn't have let that man in the house if I'd known how much he'd hurt you.'

'My scars are emotional, his are physical. I think I'd rather have the physical ones.'

'Does he still have a hold over you?'

'No. I have no feelings for Douglas. None at all.'

Nick sighed with relief. 'Can we get over this? Because I don't want to lose you.'

I smiled and touched his cheek. 'There's never been any danger of that.'

Douglas and Anna are on remand, pending their hearings in January. Both are accused of attempted murder, perverting the course of justice and aiding and abetting. Tim is facing a charge of unlawful sexual activity with a child under the age of sixteen. Anna's first child is proof of that, but Tim isn't denying it. He's seeking to justify it.

Cora and Tim have been to see us. It took a great deal of tolerance on my part. I had to bite my tongue on numerous occasions. I didn't tell Nick about their attempts to take the house from me, and nor will I unless they give me a reason to; his father's treatment of Anna is enough for him to process. Cora was humble when she arrived, although her visceral dislike of me did occasionally peep through the facade. Tim was characteristically unbowed, cheerful and friendly, but refused point blank to discuss that summer. The one thing he did, and for which I'm grudgingly grateful, was persuade Lottie to open up. I don't know what he said to her, because he won't tell me, but she now talks about her father and writes to him. I don't think Douglas will have a long sentence. I certainly don't think he's gone for good. The same applies to Tim, if he does any time at all. Anna has the most to atone for, but I expect, after a while, she will begin to see herself as the victim again.

I look up. Nick is watching me from the door, a half smile on his face.

'What?' I ask.

'You look pretty.'

I grin. The thumb of my right hand automatically goes to the solitaire diamond on my ring finger. It still feels unfamiliar, still gives me a happy shock.

'I've decided not to go back into banking, Grace.'

The sense of relief is overwhelming. 'Good.'

'We'll have to downsize.'

'I'll get on to it straight away.'

He grins. 'You seem to be taking it well. Are you sure?'

I look round at my swanky kitchen, at the gleaming units, the wall of glass, the expensive American fridge-freezer and feel no sense of impending loss, just excitement at the prospect of a new adventure.

'I'm happy wherever you are. I'll find us somewhere, don't worry. It's what I do. It's my idea of fun.'

'I'm applying to train for a Doctorate in Child Psychology.'

I go to him and plant a kiss on his lips. 'That's fantastic. You'll be brilliant. Are you all set?'

He looks taken aback, then realizes I'm not expecting him to dash off to his first lecture right now. He puts the folder he's holding down on the table, opens it and checks the printouts – eTickets, car hire confirmation, hotel confirmation.

'Yep. All set.'

We're packed and waiting for our cab. Toffee has gone to Cassie's, where he'll be spoilt rotten. Lottie is sitting on the floor at the bottom of the stairs cramming last-minute necessities into her carry-on luggage. It's time to draw some kind of line. It won't be perfect, it will have gaps in it, but it'll exist, nonetheless.

Even before Nick told me what he was planning, I had already decided that Burnside Road had to go; I was already building up to suggesting he didn't re-enter the world of banking. He's not hungry enough and I am not banker's wife material, and nor will I ever be. This gorgeous house, with its prestigious address and conservation status, has always felt like someone else's clothes. That woman isn't me and, above all else, I want to be me; I owe it to the people I love.

I would like a modest thirties semi like Cassie and Evan have; a bright, laughter-filled home with room enough for one more child, the kind of house my grandmother aspired to; a house that will suit Toffee, my scar-faced mongrel, down to the ground. Nothing is going to take away Nick's pain, but we'll do this together. We will move forward and make a good life. It's my mission.

THE END

THE END

Acknowledgements

This is my third novel and I'm still pinching myself. So the first thank you goes to Transworld Publishers for continuing to believe in me. I am so grateful.

I would like to thank my brilliant agent, Becky Ritchie, for her support and enthusiasm, and my fantastic editor, Tash Barsby, who has done an amazing job with a complicated plot structure – the next one will be simpler, I promise! Thank you to Tash's colleagues for reading and picking up on things I missed, and to Hannah Bright for the hard work she's put into publicizing my books. To Vivien Thompson and the eagle-eyed proofreading team. To the staff at Richmond Waterstones, you have been amazing from the start. Thanks also to Monica Byles for her advice on my chapter plan, to Bella Bosworth, my first reader, and to Oliver Day, whose graphic descriptions of the hypnagogic hallucinations that he's suffered from since childhood inspired me to write this book. Thanks to the memory of Biff, the extraordinary little rescue dog who Toffee is drawn from; to the PrimeWriters – we go from strength to strength – and the newly inaugurated Psychological Suspense Authors'

Association. Thank you to Dead Good Books and to the book bloggers, reviewers and my friends on Twitter for your continued goodwill. To Steve, Max and Lulu and all my friends and family, I couldn't do this without you. And last but not least, thank you for those chance conversations that spark ideas. They do say, be careful what you tell an author.

Emma Curtis was born in Brighton and now lives in London with her husband. After raising two children and working various jobs, her fascination with the darker side of domestic life inspired her to write her acclaimed psychological suspense thrillers *One Little Mistake*, *When I Find You* and *The Night You Left*.

Find her on 🐦Twitter: @emmacurtisbooks

Vicky Seagrave is blessed: three beautiful children,
a successful, doting husband, great friends and a
job she loves. She should be perfectly happy.

When she makes a split-second decision that risks
everything she holds dear, there's only one person
she trusts enough to turn to.

But Vicky is about to learn that one mistake is all it
takes; that if you're careless with those you love,
you don't deserve to keep them . . .

'A compelling page-turner which kept me
reading well into the night'
Jane Corry

AVAILABLE NOW IN PAPERBACK AND EBOOK

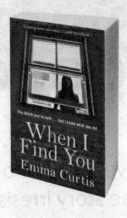

**What do you do when someone takes advantage
of your greatest weakness?**

When Laura wakes up the morning after her office
Christmas party and sees a man's shirt on the floor, she is
horrified. But this is no ordinary one-night-stand regret.

Laura suffers from severe face-blindness, a condition that
means she is completely unable to identify and remember
faces. So the man she spent all night dancing with
and kissing – the man she thought she'd brought
home – was 'Pink Shirt'.

But the shirt on her floor is blue.

And now Laura must go to work every day, and face
the man who took advantage of her condition.
The man she has no way of recognizing.

She doesn't know who he is . . . but she'll make him pay.

'Gripping, tense and twisty'
Claire Douglas

AVAILABLE NOW IN PAPERBACK AND EBOOK

dead good

For everyone who finds a crime story irresistible.

Find out more about criminally good reads at Dead Good – the home of killer crime books, drama and film.

We'll introduce you to our favourite authors and the brightest new talent. Discover exclusive extracts, features by bestselling writers, discounted books, reviews of top crime dramas and exciting film news – and don't forget to enter our competitions for the chance to win some cracking prizes too.

Sign up:
www.deadgoodbooks.co.uk/signup

Join the conversation on: